FIRING PIN

7+1 Stories About a Gun That Don't Fire

Yankee Grawlix

ISBN-13: 979-8-9864881-0-3

Cover design by: Yankee Grawlix
Library of Congress Control Number: pending
Printed in the United States of America

SPECIAL THANKS TO

My missus: The best woman I ever knew.

My readers: V, Brenda, Marge, and my folks

SPECIAL NO THANKS TO

You know who you are.

CONTENTS

CHAPTER 0: DEVIL IN DISGUISE

Conjuring the Devil is an easy thing. Pay no mind to those fellas with their black robes and candles, picking through books, saying old dead words, fornicating, and drawing scribbles in circles. That's all hooey. Those silly cult people, they got this false idea about what the Devil really is. Over and over again, I hear it and it just burns my ears every time. They all say the Devil is a tyrant. The Devil is the king of Hell. That's as far from true as anything ever has been. You don't worship the Devil. No sir. The Devil, he worships you.

The truth of it is that the Devil is an employee. No. That understates it. The Devil is a servant. And he's the best damn servant you could ever ask for. He is there at your beck and call anytime you need him. No one's as diligent and faithful as he is. You put your thumb and middle finger together and he's there even before you can snap. He's only got one job. Just one. And he's the best at it. The absolute best. He'll be there anytime you need him, day or night, to tell you what you want to hear. He's so fast and so close that he's already in your head hearing your thoughts. He'll oblige you in your own voice, in your own mind. The Devil is the ultimate yes-man. He will kiss every inch of your ass. And he says yes to every fucking awful thing you dream up. You don't conjure the Devil. He's right here with you already.

What about the bill? You don't even pay that bill to the Devil!

He won't take it! He is so generous and so loyal, he will refuse anything you could offer him. Don't impugn his honor by palming him a tip. It's not about that for the Devil. The Devil just wants you to have whatever it is you want, so long as what you want is something you shouldn't get.

Make no mistake, though. You'll pay that bill. You pay that bill to no one, but it gets paid alright.

This book you're holding here... if it is a book, I mean. Maybe it's a computer tablet or maybe it's an actor reading these lines to you. Maybe this book is so old there's some other contraption or method of telling stories that no person today would ever even comprehend.

This book is the story of a gun. Actually, it's a story about people who got hold of this gun. They didn't have much in common with each other except they all crossed paths with it. People say that gun's got a curse on it. That's what they say, but they're wrong. The gun ain't cursed. A thing can't have a curse. People, though? People can be cursed. You know cursed people. I know you know a couple. We all do. People who can't do nothin but the wrong thing. This gun has a knack—a talent —for finding cursed people. Good folks who don't listen to the Devil never find no cause to hold on to it. They pass it along and forget about it. But sooner—not later—one of those cursed people always gets their hands on it.

Where'd the gun come from? If you believe what the serial number says, the Colt made it in 1957 in Connecticut. Hard to believe that a gun like that has a history so humble. Maybe it was made by some avenging angel tasked to punish the wicked, but the angel got lazy and made a magical gun so the sinners could punish themselves. Maybe the gun is inhabited by the spirit of a woman who was murdered with it and she haunts any person who holds it, so long as they got a head full of ill designs. Or maybe it's just a damn gun, and that's all it is. That gun's been sold at countless police auctions, and year after year it always finds its way back into circulation.

As for why someone put an image of Elvis Presley on the grip… well… that's a story in itself.

Who am I? One literary type once called me an "omniscient unreliable narrator." I wonder if she even considered the profound and terrifying cosmic implications of that. I hope she didn't. It's best not to ruminate on it too much.

Be careful out there. The Devil is a liar and takes many forms, but his favorite form looks a whole lot like you. Should you ever find this gun in your possession, just take the occasion to make an inventory of yourself, because whatever happens next is entirely your fault.

Oh, and one last thing. The gun don't fire.

CHAPTER 4: MY WAY

Flint, MI

6/30/2005

02:01:04

Flint is a ghost town that's still two-thirds full of people, an orphanage of 360,000 abandoned by Father Buick and Mama Chevrolet. Some are still waiting to be adopted by someone new. Others are still waiting for Mom and Dad to come home from their quick trip to the gas station for a pack of cigarettes that happened 20 years ago. From the outside looking in, the people of Flint are pessimistic. The truth is, they give that city more credit than it deserves, just like kids who lie to social workers about where they got their bruises.

Inside a black and white CrownVic that was barely held together by positive attitude and luck, two officers ate their meals while they looked out their windows at the desiccated suburb they patrolled. Old homes built cheap in the 40s and 50s to accommodate the post-bellum refugee crisis from the South. On one side of the street, things were lit up so you could see what giving up looks like. On the other side of the street, the electric grid was completely shut down. The houses were long abandoned, swallowed up by a darkness so deep even God couldn't see the things people did and inflict his judgment on them.

"The job's just gotten boring, you know?" said officer White.

He took a big bite into his grease-soggy cheeseburger. "I don't know. I've been thinking about maybe doing some contracting work. Back in Afghanistan. They pay pretty good, I hear."

"No way your wife is gonna be cool with that," said officer Black as he stabbed the iceberg lettuce in his salad that was half-balanced on the steering wheel.

"Yeah. You're right. This job is just burning me out. Tiffany thinks I'm mad at her all the time. I'm not. I don't understand why she keeps saying that."

"It's a job. Work isn't fun. If it was fun, they'd make us pay them."

"I just thought…. It's crazy at first. You see a lot of shit that you didn't think you'd see. Then even that just becomes routine."

"You know what your problem is?"

"What's my problem?"

"You're the kind of guy who carries a Beretta 92."

"What's that supposed to mean? What's wrong with my Beretta?" White moved his hand near his sidearm reflexively, like he was shielding it from his partner's insults.

"Nothing's wrong with the Beretta."

"Damn straight, nothing's wrong with it. This model's seen a lot of service."

"The gun's fine. It's you."

"What's wrong with me, huh? I'm using a gun you said was a good gun."

"Okay, John McClane."

"What?"

"Don't go taking it all personal, Martin Riggs."

"Okay, okay," White nodded, "I get it. Cute."

"Do you, though, Johnny Utah?"

"You're way off base."

"It seems like you're packing the same gun that all those action movie heroes in the 80s were packing. Am I right?"

"It's not like that." White set down his burger.

"How old are you? Trying to calculate in my head how old you'd be when *Die Hard* came out... and *Beverly Hills Cop*." Black started using his finger to poke the buttons of an imaginary calculator.

"I didn't become a cop because I wanted to be an action movie star. That's so bogus. I did it because I wanted to help the community."

"The community?" Black snorted and went back to his food.

"Yeah, the fucking community! Look at you! What do you got?"

"You know what I got."

"Sig P226 with a—what is that—an $800 reflex sight? You fucking kidding me?"

"It's a good gun. Good enough for the Armed Forces."

"Good enough for Navy Seals, you mean, right? And you got it custom colored in coyote. Glass houses, my friend! You paid how much extra just to make it invulnerable to salt water? Like that musta added a good 400 bucks, right?"

"It's a tough gun. Buy it for life." He kept crunching away at his iceberg lettuce, impervious to White's criticism.

"You see any fucking salt water around here? This is Michigan! Anyone doing any surfing?" He used his hand as a visor over his eyes, looking around for an imaginary ocean.

"Yeah, yeah, yeah," Black said dismissively.

"You gonna fucking disrespect my Beretta. You better fucking watch yourself. Italians make good guns. Germans get all the attention, but Italians make good guns. Beretta, Benelli..."

"I got it, I got it. Don't be so damn defensive. You're missing my point."

"What's your point?"

"You became a cop so you could be a hero. That's all I'm saying."

"I guess that means you wanted to be a cop so you could, what? Be some badass green beret special operator or something? Huh, Freud?"

"You're making this into more of a thing than you need to. Just chill, okay?"

"I'm chill."

"You don't seem chill."

"You're a poor judge of chillness."

"I just mean," Black sighed, "I think when you signed up at the academy you had some unrealistic expectations about what it is the police do."

White paused for a moment and then said, "I want to call bullshit. But you might be right."

"Damn right I'm right."

"I'm just bored, I guess."

"Yeah. Cus we're not heroes. We're more like... garbage men. But the trash is people."

White turned his head to look right at his partner and said, "That's a fucked up attitude."

"Maybe. Or maybe you're just not ready to hear it yet. We're garbage men with guns. Except people don't hate garbage men. People hate cops until they need us. Then when we do what they asked us to do, they hate us even more."

"That's so negative." White looked forward again.

"How many calls for bodies do we respond to that didn't deserve it? How many bodies we deal with that aren't every bit as dirty as the guy who dropped them?"

"There was that kid on Mansfield. The triggermen were gunning for his uncle."

"Sure, there's collateral damage. And as far as I'm concerned, those collateral victims are the reason we do this job, right? But how many calls are like that kid on Mansfield?"

"A few."

"A few. But most of the time we find a DB, they were a piece of shit with a record and no fucking hope of ever de-fucking their lives. Tell me I'm lying."

"You're right, you're right."

Black set the salad in his lap and said, "I swear to God, dude. The dirtbags in this city got a more efficient criminal justice system than we do. They give each other the death penalty every day for minor infractions. What do we do? We show up, clear the scene, let our people take photos, and remove the bloody trash. We don't do shit. Them though? Fast. Efficient. Brutal." Black snapped his finger to punctuate every word. "An accusation is a conviction, and a conviction is a death sentence. Their system works. We just clean up after."

"See, and that's the problem with you P226 guys."

"What's that?"

"You just want to kick some ass."

"Fuckin' A right we do."

"I think you're bored too."

"Like I said. It's a job, man."

White crumpled up the wrapper of his burger and tossed it into the paper bag it came in. "You know what? I think you're a little jealous."

"Of who? Look at this handsome face. Look at these biceps. Jealous. Yeah right. Who am I jealous of?" Black gave a cocky smile.

"Of them. Of the criminal criminal justice system."

"Criminal criminal justice system. Hm. I like that. I'm gonna start using that."

"Yeah, you wish we could just do what they do."

"Well," Black thought about it, then put the plastic salad container into the garbage bag with the burger wrapper and said, "Like you said, I am a 226 guy."

A call came in over the radio about a guy sitting in a car outside some woman's house acting "menacingly."

Black picked it up. "This is 209. We'll take that."

"I'm not done eating!" White had just started on his fries.

"Finish 'em later."

"Fries suck if you don't eat 'em right away."

Black put the car into drive and said, "It's garbage day, baby."

They rolled up slowly and parked right behind the brown Ford Tempo with expired tags. The car was still running, spitting out a lot of exhaust, sputtering and coughing like it had emphysema. White ran the plates on the console and read the sheet that came up on Spillman. He had a good idea what they were dealing with.

White was about to reach to flash the car when Black said, "Nah. Chill. I wanna see what they do."

The two officers sat in silence and watched the silhouette inside. It didn't move.

"Alright," said Black. White flashed the lights. Nothing.

They both got out. Blacked approached the driver's side, one hand resting on his holstered P226, the other hand pointing his flashlight. White skulked around the other side, leaning in, using his Maglite to light up the inside and peaking through the windows, one hand on the Beretta 92 on his hip.

Black knocked on the window. The man inside didn't move. Mouth open, head back. Black knocked again, louder. "Sir?" He still didn't move.

White yelled, "Free crack! Get your free crack right here!"

The driver woke up, startled, and shaded his face from the flashlight, squinting until his eyes adjusted.

"Good morning, sir. This is the police. Please turn off your engine and roll down your window."

He blinked through the dope-sleep fog and wasn't sure yet what was going on. "What?"

"Kill the engine," demanded White. The driver complied.

"And roll down your window," Black repeated.

"I can't," said the man.

"Sir, I need to speak with you and I can't do that with your window closed."

"The window's busted."

"Okay, that's fine then. Please step out of the car."

"Why?"

"I need to talk to you, sir. Please step out of the car."

"But why, though?"

Black and White looked at each other over the roof of the car. They both reached into their kits and retrieved blue surgical gloves and put them on while the man continued to ask *why*.

White smashed the passenger side window with his light, spider webbing it. He hit it over and over.

"The fuck!" His arms went up to shield himself and he cowered.

White pushed the floppy window into the car and reached in and unlocked the door. He opened it and yelled, "Get out of the car! Now!"

The man reached for the keys in the ignition. That was a mistake. White climbed halfway into the car and punched him in the face, then pressed the button on the driver's side to unlock the door. Black opened the driver's side door and grabbed the man's shirt with both hands and pulled him out of the car, over the curb, and onto the yard grass.

White came around and helped Black cuff the man. He didn't make it easy, yelling, "What did I do? What did I even do?"

Once he was laid out, White started searching the car, looking in every place that years of policing told him people hide their shit. He found a fanny pack, unzipped it, looked in, zipped it back, and tossed it onto the car roof.

"Having a nod, sleeping beauty?" asked White.

"I don't fucking know what you're talking about."

"You wanna tell me the powder and needle in your fanny pack are insulin?"

"That's not mine, man! You planted that!"

White placed a TracFone he found on top next to the drug kit. White kept digging around in the car. "Bingo." He set a 1911 pistol on the roof. "Look at this fucking thing! Holeeeeee shit." White ejected the magazine and cleared it.

"What's that?" asked Black.

"Check this. Chrome plated. Pearl grip with Elvis Presley painted on it. Where the fuck did you even find this thing, Larry?"

"That's not mine neither!"

Black kneeled so he could look the guy in the face. "Let me ask you something, alright?"

"Okay?"

"I've seen your jacket, my man. It all comes up when we scan your plates. You've been arrested nine times since last year. Nine. Did you do any of that shit, either?"

"No!"

"That what you told them when they arrested you all nine times?"

"Yeah!"

"Oh, so this will be the tenth time the police have framed you for something? Holy shit, you hear that?"

White chuckled, "Man, we really enjoy framing this guy, huh?"

Black added, "FPD must have some kind of fucking obsession with you, my guy!"

"I guess so!" said Larry.

Black continued, "In fact, we have a special task force that does nothing but fucking frame you!"

White laughed.

"Yeah, we're the Fuck With Larry For No Reason Taskforce. The Mayor specially created our squad to do nothing but fuck with you! We have 14 cops working just on your case, cool breeze."

Larry relaxed. "Whatever, man. Fuck y'all."

"No, I want to know. I want to know if this shit has ever worked once?"

"No."

"So why the fuck you keep doing it, man? Why the fuck you keep doing the same fucking thing that's never gotten you anywhere?"

He shrugged.

"Answer him," said White.

"Cus. Cus, maybe this time it'll work."

Black looked up at White, who shook his head.

"You're gonna keep doing the same stupid thing every time, that never ever works, cus maybe this time it'll work. That's gotta be the story of your fuckin' life. Are you seeing a bigger pattern?"

"Whatever, man. Fuck y'all."

"Chill right there, a sec, big man," said Black.

He walked a couple of yards away and gestured to White, who met him out of earshot of Larry.

"I got an idea. You gonna back my play?"

"What are you talking about?"

Black kept his voice low enough. "I think we just got us some PC for that Howard Boys' house. The one on Munster."

"I don't know, man," he looked over back at Larry Hendricks. He lay there on his belly, no fight left in him, no arguments, finally accepting his fate in silence.

"We know something's up at that house. How many briefings we hear about that place? People coming in and out all the time. Remember, we had to pull surveillance because they couldn't find shit in a week. Just one week they gave them. You've seen the incident reports by that house. Two girls in that park. Not much older than Laura."

"Hey. Don't do that. My girl's ten. Those girls were fifteen."

"I'm just saying. Laura was five like yesterday, and now she's already ten."

White took a deep sigh, looked down, and put his hands on his hips.

Black pressed him, "Listen, man. You're right about me. I am jealous. And I wanna kick ass. Imagine what this police department could do in just one weekend if we got to play by the same rules they do."

White didn't say no and didn't say yes.

Black said, "They're doing the dirt in there. You know they are. I promise it won't be boring."

White sighed.

Black said, "Two girls, man. That we even know of."

White nodded. "What's the plan?"

Black told him. White nodded and said, "That's not bad."

Black smiled and slapped him on the arm, and pointed at his temple. "That's why we roll together so well. We think alike." Black raised his voice and addressed Larry. "Mr. Hendricks. I have some good news for you."

Larry mumbled some cuss words.

"We're letting you off the hook tonight."

"Man, whatever."

White added, "He's not fucking with you, Larry."

Black helped Larry up and stood behind him, putting his hands on the cuffs, whispering over his shoulder by his ear, "But you just gotta do us a little favor."

"Yo, I ain't suckin' your dick. I don't do that shit no more."

White lost it and laughed so hard he had to lean over.

Black scowled. "I'm not asking for that! I just need you to make a phone call."

"That's it?"

"That's it."

"For real?"

Black uncuffed him. "Officer White will ride shotgun with you in your car. I'll be following in the cruiser."

"I don't think it's good I get seen with a cop riding along."

When White stopped laughing, he promised, hand on his heart, "I'll be discreet." He pushed Larry towards the car.

Larry got in his car and started it up. White removed the window, tossed it onto the curb and wiped some broken glass off the seat, then got in the passenger seat and slunk down out of view. Black got back in the cruiser.

Larry asked, "Where we going?"

"Take Fenton south and then I'll let you know."

They stopped at a 4-way light at a corner with a gas station and a fried pork sandwich restaurant in one. You could smell it from the street. On the opposite corner was a treatment clinic, one of three within a quarter mile. A skinny woman was crossing the street wearing sweatpants and an oversized sweatshirt with the image of a kitten with angel wings. She was stumbling, head lolling about, hair tangled, skin ashy. She stopped in the middle of the crosswalk and she looked over at the car.

"Larry?"

"Fuck," said Larry.

"Fuck," said Black, who was right behind them.

She walked up to the driver's side and said, "Larry! Where you been, man?" She cupped her hands next to her eyes and leaned in so she could see inside without the glare. "Yo, I got this guy, he's got some shit like—" She saw White. "Yo, yo, what the fuck?"

"Roll down the window. Now," said White. Larry did. The woman was already taking some steps back. White said, just barely loud enough to hear, "Bitch, we got a good thing going with the fake police outfits, alright? Don't you fucking blow this for us! There's a real cop right fucking behind us! Don't you fucking give us away or I will smoke you right where you stand. You got me?"

She nodded, "Aight, aight." Her eyes darted back and forth between Officer Black in the cruiser. "It's all good, man. Larry, why didn't you include me, too? I can be useful."

The light turned green. Larry said, "See you later, Tanya." They drove off.

White directed Larry down a residential street. Half the houses were boarded up or had no lights on. "Right here." They stopped. Black stopped right behind them. White gave Larry back his flip phone.

"Okay. See right up there at the end of the block? That big green house with the Chevy on the lawn. All you gotta do is dial 911. You're gonna tell them that some guy is out in that yard, waving around a big, silver pistol."

"That's it?"

"I'm going to get back in the squad car. You'll be on your own. Here. Wait 15 minutes. Make the call. Don't fucking say who you are. Just say the address and that they're waving around a big, shiny, silver pistol. Then hang up. That's all. You got all that?"

"Yeah."

"Then after that, you leave."

"Okay. What about my heater and gear?"

"The gun's mine now. You can keep your fucking kit." White handed him the fanny pack with his drugs. White got out, looked around to make sure no one saw him, and climbed back into the cruiser with Black.

"He knows the plan?" asked Black.

"He knows the plan," said White.

Black took a sidestreet, and they drove slowly around the neighborhood. Quiet night.

White looked at the clock. "I said 15 minutes. That was 25 minutes ago."

"He better not fuck this up."

The radio piped up. "Standby for talk. 3-1 shots fired at 2-4-4-3 Munster. Caller said a man was shooting in random directions."

White responded, "209 responding. We're close."

They gunned it towards the street they left Larry on.

Another car called in, "040. We're at Crenshaw and Hayward."

"I didn't hear any shots," said White.

"Me neither. You think Larry called in shots?"

"Fucking Larry better not have fucked this up."

They pulled up to the Howard Boys' house and parked. The address was 2449 Munster. The next-door neighbor was 2443.

"That junkie motherfucker!" Black slammed his fist down on the steering wheel. They got out. White took the Benelli from the trunk and racked one and turned on the under-barrel flashlight. Black unholstered his Sig. They approached the house. There wasn't a door. A fire had gutted the place before last winter and poison ivy was creeping up through the melted carpet and linoleum.

"No one here. What's the play, boss? We gonna keep doing this or just call in an abandoned traphouse?" White asked.

"We heard gunshots next door. We responded, assuming the caller had the wrong address."

White nodded. "But there weren't any."

"Shots already got called in. What's one more?"

White nodded. They turned off their radios, and White killed the light on his shotgun.

They snuck out the rear of the burned-out house, onto the back lawn. They hopped over the low fence separating the yards between the burned house and the Howard Boys' place. No motion lights. They snuck up on the back porch of the Howard Boys' house and peeked inside the kitchen through the window. The lights were on. No one was there. Some movement down the hall, though. Black tested the doorknob. It was unlocked. He opened it slowly, gun ready. White was close behind. The kitchen was barren except for some Lebanese takeout boxes on a counter. Black took a corner and covered the hallway. White took point and creeped down the short hall to the living room, peering down the iron sights of his shotgun. Creak. Old floors. They didn't build these houses to last. White stopped. Some shadows moved around the corner in the living room. A toilet flushed behind them. He looked over his shoulder back at his partner, with his gun still covering the hall. Black pointed towards the bathroom adjoining the kitchen. The sound of sink water running. White nodded. Black moved next to the bathroom door, ready to ambush whoever came out. White hesitated to move and make another creak. He kept looking back and forth, trying not to miss anything. The sink water stopped. The bathroom door opened.

Black whispered, "FPD. Don't move. Don't make a fucking sound."

The guy put his damp hands up.

"Shit!" The voice came from the living room. White whipped his head back. A guy in his boxers and socks was looking right at him.

"Police! Freeze!"

The boxers guy darted out of sight into the living room. White followed him in and turned left. A man on the couch was looking around, confused. The guy in boxers was digging through a backpack. A flatscreen TV was running a DVD with some ninjas on a jungle gym.

White repeated his command, "Stop!"

Boxers didn't. He turned with something in his hand.

White opened up with his Benelli, tearing the guy's lead hand and face into ground beef and throwing him against the wall. The guy on the couch clenched up, bent down, elbows and knees close together, like a dead bug.

Back in the kitchen, the bathroom man flinched at the sound, and when Black turned his head away for a second, he reached for Black's gun. Black was quick, though. He put a palm into the young man's face, pulled his shooting hand back to his ribs, and fired into the guy's torso. The guy collapsed into a pile of himself. He groaned. Black took a couple of steps back as the pool of blood started creeping towards his boots.

Black called back to White. "What's going on in there?"

"We're good in here. You?"

"We good." Black rolled the limp man over and cuffed him.

White asked the man on the couch, "Anyone upstairs?"

The single survivor said, "No. No one."

Black walked in and joined his partner in the living room. White checked what the boxers guy pulled on him. "A flashlight? Why'd your man pull a flashlight on me?"

The guy on the couch shook his head. "I don't know, man. I don't know."

White handed Black his cuffs. White kept the shotgun on the guy while Black locked his wrists up behind his back.

White told the guy, "If you lied to us and something happens to my partner, I'm shooting you first before going up there after him. You got that? So you're sure no one's up there?"

"I'm sure. I'm sure."

Black took the upstairs, cleared it, then he came down and said, "I'm gonna need to go get the medical kit to make it look like I rendered aid. You good in here?"

"Yeah, we're good."

Black left. White asked the guy, "What guns you have in here?"

"No guns."

"Bullshit. What's stashed in this house?"

"Fucking nothing, man. This is Omar's cousin's place. He lets us hang here."

"Who's Omar?"

The guy pointed with his head at the mess of tangled human anatomy on the floor.

"Fine, we'll find it ourselves."

Black returned.

White pointed at his own face. "You gotta little."

Black wiped his face with the back of his hand and smeared some blood. He uncuffed the guy.

"What're you doing?" asked White.

Black removed Larry's 1911 from his belt. He removed the magazine and showed it to the couch guy so he could see it was loaded. He put the mag back in and racked it, then tossed it into the couch guy's lap. "Catch."

White asked again, "What the fuck?"

The couch guy froze up. He looked at White, with eyes moving so fast they were almost vibrating, looking to the saner cop for some answers to questions he hadn't even been able to think of yet.

"Shoot my partner," said Black.

"What?" both of the other men asked.

Black leveled the gun at the couch man. "Shoot him, or I shoot you."

"I don't want to."

"Okay then," and Black looked down his reflex sight.

The couch man raised up on White and the officer put two shotgun blasts into his chest. He slumped over.

"What the fuck!" White yelled. He pointed the Benelli at his partner.

Black casually pushed the barrel out of his face. "Bitch, please. You weren't gonna do it unless I made you."

"Why the fuck did you do that? He was cooperating!"

"Cus two girls. That's why. What'd we say? The criminal criminal justice system is more efficient. I was in the other room when you were in here. Doesn't make sense if I shot him."

White turned on his radio. There was a lot of traffic. Someone else called in their shots. Dispatch was trying to reach them. White answered, "Shots fired! Shots fired!"

White said to Black, "040 said they're at Hayward and Crenshaw. That's about nine minutes."

Black said, "Start the clock."

White looked at his watch. "Nine minutes starting now."

Black handled the dead man's hand, putting it into his hand and pointing it and the gun to where White entered the room. He forced the trigger. *Click.*

He tried again. And again. White insisted on trying and reached the same conclusion. "Fuck! This gun is totally fucked!"

"Find a gun. Fucking any gun."

White searched upstairs. Black searched downstairs. They tore the place apart, looking. Not a single gun in the house. The place looked more like a college frat at a technical college than a stash house. No drugs. No alcohol. Barely furnished, overdue for a cleaning, with not much besides beds, a chemistry set, a couple movie posters, some engineering illustrations, and a nest of carpenter bees chewing through the walls. Four minutes left.

White was sweating. "I think we fucked up, dude. I don't see any guns or drugs. These guys aren't even wearing colors."

"Doesn't matter. It doesn't matter," said Black.

"The fuck it doesn't! There's no fucking gun in this house. All we got is the Elvis gun, and it doesn't fucking fire. Fuck!"

"We didn't know. He raised up, and we had no way of knowing the gun was fucked."

"No, man! We're here on a gunshot call! Not a fucking guy with a broke gun that doesn't work call! Fuck!"

Black said, "So the shots came from somewhere else. We rolled in here, they attacked us, and we had to use terminal force to protect ourselves."

"No, dude, no! We weren't called to this house! We were called next door! Why the fuck did we come into this house if there weren't any fucking gunshots coming from it? Fuck!"

Black didn't have an answer. He just said, "Fuck. Fuck!"

White had his hands on his head and he was pacing back and forth, "Oh my God. Oh my God! We are going to fucking prison!"

Black said, "What if there was a fourth guy? He ran off!"

"No shell casings, no bullet holes? That won't fly."

"Okay. The fourth guy smoked these other guys."

"Maybe… No. Fuck! They'll run ballistics and compare them. They could tie the guy in the kitchen to your Sig."

Black's veins in his temple and neck were popping out. Then his eyes got big. "I got it. I fucking got it." He smiled. "We need a nail or something like that. And a hammer. Or a rock."

"My kit in the car. Find a nail. I'll be right back." White ran out the front, reached in the car, popped the trunk, and got a hammer.

Meanwhile, Black looked around and found a Phillip's head screwdriver. They met back in the living room. Black directed White to hold the man's hand and gun. Black locked the slide open, placed the screwdriver tip against the round's primer. He counted down. "Three, two, one." He smacked it with the hammer.

The bullet blew out the television across from the couch. The TV kept playing, but the sound came out strange and the image was twisted with distorted colors.

"Shit!" White stepped back and flopped his hand. "Fucking thing burned me."

"You good?"

"Yeah. I'm good."

"See? A negligent discharge while he was showing off his gun to his friends," said Black.

"What if they actually test ballistics on it?"

"Why the fuck would they? I have a 9. You have a 12-gauge. This poor fuck's got a 45. This one's fucking easy."

"Right. Right. That makes sense. But what about against another crime?"

They could hear the sirens now.

"Relax, sweetheart! We did it! We're good! Backlog is weeks on that. We got plenty of time to vanish that shit from evidence before it goes out." Black gave White a big back-slapping hug.

Black opened up the curtains on the side and looked through. A perfect view of the burnt-out house. "See? The window was open. We saw a guy with a gun. Easy."

Backup arrived. They cleared the scene. Their captain told them to keep their mouths shut, and they did. The two officers were checked for injuries, had their weapons confiscated, and they were taken back to the station where their clothes were taken and logged. Black and White were given an interview room to talk to their union rep and lawyer. They went over their story, made sure they had it tight. The men wrote their statements, and they were nearly identical; a job perk that the people they busted didn't enjoy.

Someone from IA came down to talk to Black and White. The partners were separated and interviewed about the evening. They knew exactly what to do. They kept to their stories. They didn't add details. If they didn't know what to say, they said, "I don't remember," or their lawyer would interrupt. The investigators seemed like they were speeding through the interview, checking off boxes, going through the motions to absolve the department of any wrongdoing.

It was easy peasy until Detective Pursh arrived and took over. Pursh was a woman who kept her hair short and never smiled. Nobody liked her, but it wasn't because she was IA. Pursh thought she was better than everyone else. She never said she was, but everyone felt it. But she was good at her job, so maybe she earned the right to be a bitch. Black and White noticed how good she was early into their interviews when she asked good questions the other detectives should've asked.

"Did you two toss the house after the shooting? Because it looked tore up."

"No."

"Why do you think he was reaching for a flashlight?"

"I don't know."

"What happened with the stop on Lawrence Hendricks?"

"Routine. We let him go with a warning."

"How'd you burn your hand, Officer White?"

"Cooking bacon this morning."

When the interviews were over, the captain gave them a week's paid leave pending the investigation. The men found each other in the hall and compared notes, quietly making sure neither of them slipped up. It all looked clear. They shook hands. It was already 5am and White had to call his wife and let her know what was going on.

Black went into the locker room and changed out of his gear, back into his civilian clothes. A sudden burst of clapping, whistling and cheering, someone yelling, "Yeah! Yeah!," like Black was on a gameshow. He turned to see that damn near every cop in the building was walking into the men's dressing room, including the women.

"What's this?"

Lawrence grabbed the back of his head and forced their foreheads together. "You son of a bitch!" with a big grin on his face. Black pushed him off.

"Seriously, y'all, that the fuck is this?"

"That flashlight, man!"

"What?"

Pearson spoke up with her high-pitched voice, "That flashlight was a pipe bomb. That guy was about to blow you all away."

"No shit?"

"That wasn't a fucking dope house, man. They weren't Howard

Boys. They were a terror cell!"

"Whoa, whoa. What the fuck? You serious?"

"You and White took down a fucking Al-Qaeda affiliate! You're goddamn heroes!" They started clapping again.

"Hey, you... you shut the fuck up... that's not..."

"Buddy, no one is shitting you! They tossed the house. They had fucking bomb making equipment everywhere. No guns besides that Elvis pistol and no drugs. They were planning on blowing up the Art Fair in Ann Arbor. You guys stopped a fucking terror plot."

"Ho-lee-shit." Now the ninja jungle gym on the TV and the engineering blueprints made a lot more sense.

White had to get back home to his family, but the others who were getting off shift insisted on taking Black out for drinks at 7am. The bar was open 24 hours, which wasn't entirely legal, but they got away with it on account of it being the favorite spot of the police department. The others paid for Black's drinks and they told every civilian woman they saw that Black just smoked three mujahideen and that he was single. Even the captain made a personal appearance. He abstained from drinking and stuck around just long enough to commend Black in person. He shook Black's hand and let him know that the department made a deal with the news media to keep his and his partner's names out of the press for their own safety.

The morning was going great until Pearson mentioned Homeland Security.

The bar was loud with drunk cops. "Yo, Pearson. What'd you say?"

"Huh? What?"

Black got close and yelled, "What'd you say about DHS?"

"Oh! I was saying they're involved now because of the terrorists. It's out of our hands, thank fucking God. Let the feds handle it."

Black felt his heart stop.

He snuck out of his own party through the back door and into the alley and called his partner.

White picked up. "I just fell asleep, man. What is it? Hold on." White addressed his wife, "Yeah, it's Jacob. I don't know what he wants, I haven't talked to him yet. Well, it probably is important if he's calling this early, you think? Yeah, just go back to sleep. I'll only be a minute." He went back to Black. "Yeah. I'm here. Is this important?"

"Bro, you heard that was a terror cell we shot up?"

White yawned, "Uh. Yeah. Lawrence texted me. Crazy."

"So?"

"So what?"

"So now it's a fucking federal investigation."

"Yeah. And?"

"So it ain't Flint anymore. Flint can't even process most of the rape kits we get. Ballistics only get sent to a lab if it's totally necessary. This is DHS! They got more money than God and they have a fucking mandate to leave no fucking stone unturned."

It started dawning on White. "Um. Oh. Oh fuck."

"Oh fuck is right! What are the odds that they don't fucking open that gun up and figure out what happened?"

"Fucking zero. Fuck. I didn't think of it before, but they'll probably dust prints on every fucking cartridge."

Black yelled, "Fuck!" so loud he woke up the man sleeping in a camping tent in the alley. "There's no way in hell Larry wore gloves when he put those in, if it even was him who loaded it. No fucking way."

White thought out loud, "The busted gun story should be fine. If they could find the screwdriver and hammer, they'll think those punks made a mistake trying to fix it. But Larry, man. They can't question him. That piece of shit will fold the second his high runs out and he needs another hit."

"They were asking a lot about him in the interview."

"Yeah. That's right. Fuck. I don't like how close that connection is."

"We gotta meet up. I'll come get you."

They ended the call. Black was drunk enough that things were swimmy but not too drunk to use the correct key for his car door on the first try.

He drove out to White's place in the suburbs. His head was hurting as the beer wore off. White was already outside in the driveway of his two-story home, yawning. He climbed in.

"So where is Larry?" asked White.

"His sheet said he lives on Hines. I don't remember the address, but I remember the street because it was close to where my sister used to live."

They headed out that way. The sun was still turning the sky from black to blue, and the mostly empty roads were populating with cars. They drove down Hines, looking for Larry's car. No luck.

"This stress has my stomach upset. I need to eat something," said White.

They found a fast-food joint around the corner and got some

drive-thru breakfast, then found a parking spot to eat in the car. They were going over every detail, every loose-end they could think of, every alternative story they could imagine, when they saw a man come out from behind the dumpster, tightening the belt on his pants, pulling up his fly, looking around. White tapped Black on the chest with the back of his hand and pointed. Then another guy came out. Black and White laughed. Then a familiar woman in a butterfly winged cat sweater came out after them, wiping her mouth.

"Shit. Is that Tanya?" White asked.

Black hopped out of the car and walked up to her. White stayed in and watched. He couldn't see what they were saying. Then Tanya moved in close and gave White's partner a flirty, brown-toothed smile. Black pushed her off and started giving her some harsh words and pointing a finger at her like he was a middle school principal. She played her part, rolling her eyes and putting her hands on her hips like a middle school delinquent. Black came back into the car.

"So what's up?"

"She said Larry usually hangs at a shooting gallery on Yearling. You know that old closed-down karate school? *Cheeto Rye You* or something. But he hasn't been there much lately. She thinks he's been buying from this guy called Prince, who sells out of a corner store over by the Art Institute, trading dope for bogus bridge card charges."

"Is Prince his name or his nickname?"

"Fuck if I know." Black fired up the ignition, and they headed out.

They found the store easily enough. A corner shop with big bright neon sign advertising state minimum beers and in-house-made jerky. One security camera was out front and one was by the side door in the alley. They parked the car and waited. And waited.

White fell asleep. Black was so tired that his energy came all the way back around and was alert, running on adrenaline. He saw Larry coming down the sidewalk, scratching his scalp on his way to get his hot breakfast. Black woke White up and pointed to the shop as Larry went in.

"What's the play?" asked White as he rubbed his eyes and stretched.

"Like we did at the head shop on Delphi?"

"Yeah, but do we know this Prince guy is dangerous?"

"I looked him up on FLEX while you were napping..."

"Bro, you can't—"

"Relax, I used Dabrowski's credentials."

"He ain't been with the department for, like, two years."

"I know. IT forgot to delete his account. And I know he uses 'password' as his password for everything. I've been using it since before he left."

"You sneaky bastard."

"Anyway, I found six guys in the area with the alias Prince. One died last year, two are in prison. Of the surviving, unincarcerated Princes, one is black, one's Arab, and one's Armenian."

"Okay, so?"

"Black Prince doesn't have any violent priors. Arab and Armenian Prince both do. So, I'm going in and if Prince ain't black, then we know he's dangerous."

White said, "Alright. I like this plan. Glad you're on my team. Let's do it, man."

They both got out. White stayed back at the car in jeans, a USMC fade, and a UFC 33 t-shirt. Black was wearing khaki shorts and Ray Bans, looking like a grill dad. He adjusted his concealed Sig so he would print. A cop who looked like a cop trying not to look like a cop. He walked across the street and into the bodega with a jingle from the door. Larry was at the counter, talking through the plexiglass to a not-black man in a hideous, colorful silk shirt, with chest hair exposed. As soon as Black walked in, Larry and Prince stopped talking and looked at the new customer. Black wasn't sure if Larry recognized him. The cop breezed by and towards the back of the shop. He made a show of pretending to be shopping and always looking up at the men at the counter, and looking down when they noticed him. He pretended to read the labels of energy drinks and when he caught Prince looking at him, he put his hand to his ear to look like he had an earpiece that wasn't there. Eventually Prince told Larry under his breath to come back later. Larry made a fuss, but left. Black walked up and bought whatever was in his hand at the time and then left.

He stepped out and looked across the street at his partner. White pointed back towards Black's left. He looked around the corner into the alley and Larry was pacing by the side door, dope-sick pacing and jitters. Black walked up to him and grabbed him by the shirt, and pushed him against the wall.

"Hey, slick. Remember me?" He put his sunglasses on top of his head.

"You that cop!"

"Yeah, buddy, from the Fuck With Larry Squad. Gimme your phone."

"What? Why?"

Black punched him in the stomach. Larry crumpled up and slid down the wall onto his ass. Black frisked him down and found his phone. He threw it against a wall, smashing it to bits of cheap Korean plastic, then stomped on it a few times. Black pulled him back up and marched him out of the alley, across the street, and forced him into the back seat of his car. Black sat down next to him and put an arm around him. White got back into the driver's seat and turned around to face the others.

White said, "We told you to say that there was a guy waving a pistol. Not firing a pistol."

Black added, "You know the difference, right, player?"

Larry nodded.

White said, "And we told you the green house with the Chevy. Not the burnt out trap house next door to the green house with the Chevy."

Black asked, "You fucking colorblind, my man?"

Larry shook his head.

White asked, "So how the fuck did you fuck up some simple ass instructions like that?"

Larry shrugged.

Black reached into his pocket. Larry went for the door. Black was quick and grabbed him. White punched him in the face, opening up the cut on his lip White gave him the night before. Larry relaxed and lowered his eyes in surrender. Black reached into his pocket again and pulled out a nice, crisp $100 bill and waved it just under his nose. Black pushed Larry's face against the window facing Prince's shop and pressed the bill next to it.

"Take that money, Larry. Buy yourself something nice. And keep your fucking mouth shut."

"You got that?" asked White.

Larry nodded, but Black kept pressing his face. White stepped out, opened the passenger door, and Larry fell out, face first. He got up, stuffed the money in his pocket, then skittered off back into the alley.

Inside the corner store, a not-black Prince watched the whole thing in black and white, without sound, on the surveillance camera monitors.

That night, White was on the couch at home, watching a movie with his wife, when he got a call from Black. He stood up and told her to keep watching without him, and he stepped into the kitchen to answer.

"Yeah."

"Just got word. Larry turned up dead by the railroad bridge over the river."

"Damn! Already? How'd they do it?"

"I don't know for sure. The ME hasn't looked at him yet, but it looks like Prince saw the little show we put on. Probably gave Larry a heavy dose. The needle was still in his arm where they found him."

"At least he went out doing what he loved, right? That's kinda far out of the way, though. How'd they find him so fast?"

"Okay, so that's the thing. Larry was a CI."

"What? For who?"

"Jarvis."

"That fucking figures."

"When Larry didn't answer his phone, Jarvis went out looking for him and asked a couple questions and it took him there."

White sighed, "Better off this way. It's all done and done."

"Jarvis needed him for a case. He's pretty pissed. He might dig around."

"Fuck. Well. At least Jarvis is semi-retarded. Hold up. Honey? You got that?"

"What's up?"

"Someone's at the door. What? Hold on." There was a pause then, "Yo, what's up? We're in the middle of a movie here..."

Black could hear a woman's voice. "Sorry to come by so late." It was Pursh. That IA detective who interviewed them after the house shooting. Black could spot that woman's voice easily.

White said, "Hey, yeah, I gotta call you back."

"What's up?"

"Nothing. My wife's sister."

"Let's meet up tomorrow."

"I gotta go take the car in. They did a recall on the airbags and I need to get them traded out."

"Alright, well, see you when I see you, hombre."

"Later." He hung up.

Black gritted his teeth. Jarvis was half a retard. But Pursh was smart. Black went into his closet and looked around for his slim jim.

"I really wish you hadn't lied, hombre."

The next morning, White kissed his wife goodbye for the last time. He got into his Toyota Highlander and he backed out of his driveway. A box truck doing 45 in a residential t-boned White's car on the driver's side. White's airbags didn't deploy. The truck fled the scene. White's missus called 911. Her husband died on the way to the hospital. She and her daughter learned that when they arrived at the ER to meet him.

Police found the offending truck dumped a mile away, torched, plates and VIN stripped. The owner reported it stolen a half hour after police recovered and ID'd it. No leads. Just shit luck.

The next day, Black got official word that he and his partner were cleared for the shooting and he was good to come back to work.

The funeral was big. His wife and daughter really loved him. Everyone did. Tiffany played it brave. Laura hid in her room and wouldn't come out. White had a big Catholic family and damn near every cop that knew him by name was in attendance. The wake was rough. People were drinking more than they should have. There was an argument about not giving him a military funeral. Tiffany said he hated the Army and the 32nd Cavalry and that she wouldn't put him anywhere she couldn't be buried, too. A couple of cops asked about the cut just above Black's left eye, which he said was from boxing.

Black was having a beer alone on White's widow's back porch, thinking about all the times he'd eaten dinner with the family. Detective Pursh approached him without sitting down. She gave her condolences and asked to speak with him in private later. He reminded her that the investigation was over. She said it wasn't about that, so he agreed to meet her at a Coney Island a half mile away.

Three hours later, Black gave White's widow a hug and said if she needed anything, to call him. He excused himself and drove to the diner. The IA detective already had a booth seat. He sat across from her. She was already halfway through a Caesar salad.

She said, "Thanks for meeting with me."

"What can I do for you, detective?"

"So formal."

"How about, *What do you want, lady?* That better?"

"That's more you. That's definitely more you."

"Well? What do you want, lady?"

She set down her fork and paused like she didn't know what she was going to say. Then she started. "The thing about Homicide is, they only spend as much time on a case as they can until the next case. They've got a couple days—tops—to have a really solid lead before the next body drops. If they don't know who did it and can prove it, they move on. They can't spend all their time on cases that might never get solved. They work the easy ones. They get the ones they know will stick. Civilians aren't ready to hear that shit. They don't want to hear that hard cases get dumped. Families don't want to hear that Homicide talked to three people and put the evidence on a six-week waiting list for forensics, and the detectives moved the fuck on. By the time they get the DNA and ballistics reports, whoever did it probably got smoked by someone else as payback for the murder Homicide just got inconclusive results on. This broken system relies entirely on the stupidity of perpetrators. Luckily for us, about half of them are really, really stupid."

Black nodded.

"We're eye to eye on that. I'm glad. I don't have time for romantics. I can't waste a second of my precious time explaining to every one of them that things aren't what they ought to be. Pretending things are how they ought to be only makes it worse. You get that."

"Yeah. I get that." He relaxed a bit by her forthrightness and unpleasant honesty.

"But back to the point. You were right to think you were safe. No one was too interested in the details of some shitheads with violent priors getting killed at a known drug house. The only way we would've run that gun is if we had a backlog with an unsolved .45 ACP within the last year. No reason to go back and solve cases older than that. There's no reason to change the clearance numbers for a case older than the current mayor's administration, right? No one gives a fuck. We had two murders with 45s this year. Not a popular caliber as far as murders go, and we already have that guy and we have that gun. No way we would've run that weird fucking Elvis gun. We probably wouldn't have spent more than two hours on it before we moved on. But you fucked up in one way. There's no way you could've known. Stupidity gets most people caught. It wasn't stupidity that got you caught. You aren't stupid."

"Caught? The case is clear, Pursh. I didn't do anything wrong and your department agrees."

She pointed a finger like a bookmark popping out of the top of a book. "That's not entirely true. But I'll get to that later. You know Larry was a snitch, right? I don't know if you knew that. I think you do, but I'm not 100% on that. I just learned that myself. When I started your case, I ran the number that called in the shooting and what do you know? One of Jarvis's CIs. No way you would've known that, but that's the thing about bad luck. It doesn't give a single fuck about how much thought and effort you put in. Am I right?"

"I wouldn't know anything about that."

"It struck me as odd when I saw two officers responding to a call from a guy who just had an interaction with them not even 20 minutes earlier, only now a few miles away, on the other side of the freeway. Shit. I believe in coincidences, but that there is one big fucking coincidence. Right?"

Black answered by folding his arms.

"You got that stone-face, Officer Black. You don't show a thing. You play cards? Maybe you should. A face like that is great for cards. Or maybe not, seeing as how bad luck has a big fucking hard-on and you're wearing the prom dress right now. Being smart's great, but being lucky's better, you know?"

That made Black laugh a little, even though he didn't want to.

"So that coincidence got me looking a little closer. I found blood in the palm of Israel Abdallah, formerly known as Tyreese Nolan. Not his blood. From the guy in the kitchen you killed. That tells me that someone placed the gun in his hand after that same somebody shot his homie in the kitchen. Didn't notice that, did ya? Yeah, a little drop got on the handle when you killed Rahmatullah Yusuf, formerly Nicolas Green. Second hand transfer from a man who died in another room."

Black didn't flinch.

Pursh went on, "Then there was the delay to call it in. Maybe you got caught up in a gunfight and forgot your training. That happens. But I don't buy it. In my experience, cops are quicker to pick up their radios than they are to pick up their guns. You want me to keep going?"

"Not really."

"Okay, that's fine. You get the idea. I got evidence that all stacked up looks more than circumstantial. I've seen DA take a lot less to court. FPD was done with you. FBI and DHS, though? Whoo-boy. They don't leave any stones unturned, especially when a guy who changed his name to 'slave of Allah' was making pipe bombs right under their noses. The feds figured it out. They got you dead to fucking rights."

Black swallowed.

"And they don't care. They know what you and White did, and they don't care. They don't want any noise about it. They're happy to claim that their coordination with local police led to the takedown of a terror cell blah blah blah... some bullshit. The department and city hall won't do fuck all because they're just happy as pigs in shit that the news will talk about defeating terrorism for a few weeks and not day-to-day street violence. They get to look like they actually did something for a change. They know you and White are dirty—were dirty in White's case—but they're not doing shit because there ain't no way they're punishing two hero cops who saved Flint and Ann

Arbor from terrorists. No fucking way."

Black leaned back and cockiness came back to him. "We good then."

"Slow down there, cowboy. You're good with IA, DHS, the FBI, the mayor, the chief of police, your captain, and the people of the city of Flint. They all good with you. If you asked Jesus for forgiveness, he's good with you, too. You and me, though? We ain't good. I know you killed Larry. That's damn obvious. I think you killed your partner, too. Can't prove that, but it seems pretty damn likely. So I'd say you and I are a long way off from good."

"Alright. What now, then?"

"I'd like you to resign from the police force. And I don't want you moving to Kalamazoo or Detroit and trying to be police there, neither. I don't want to find out you're police at all. Anywhere. Ever."

"Why should I do that? Seems like everyone's giving me a pass or doesn't want to know what happened. I'm a hero cop in the department. I'm a pillar of the community. What're you gonna do to me? You're some Ann Arbor dyke trying to slum it in Flint to, what? Prove you're a good person? Why are we even here except for you hoping I'll say something to incriminate myself?"

"You got me pegged, Black. You do. That's who I am. I'm a UofM crim justice degree with no patience for vigilante cops. I would've let it go. But you killed White, too. That's something I can't let go."

"Fuck. You. Talking to me like this after my partner's fucking wake…"

"I know the police made a deal with the reporters to keep you and White's names out of the news for your own safety in exchange for some juicy details about the raid and the terror cell. That's why I sent all your personal information to

Abduraheem Shalhoub."

"Who's that?"

"He's a fanatical hate preacher in the UK. Terrorism apologist, you might say. He's pretty famous over there. They put him on all the talk shows so they can make a spectacle of the crazy shit he says. He gets on TV just to shit on England and America, explaining why every jihadi bombing is justified and every Western bombing is murder."

"What's some Muslim in merry England got to do with me?"

"He's been under the microscope of British police and the IC for years. He's connected. No doubt about that. He'll be sure to pass your info along to the right people. See, I can't touch you. But I figure maybe with a fatwa on you now, there'll be a lot of young bucks with Persian prayer mats who want to get some brownie points with God by martyring themself on you."

"Whoa, wait. What? You fucking what?"

"I feel like I'm being very clear here. I don't know if you actually don't understand what I'm saying or if you aren't able to grapple with the implications of what your life will be from now on. I'll say it again in case you didn't understand. I told a Wahhabi fruitcake with ties to Al-Qaeda who you are, what you did, and where they can find you. Try to keep up."

"What the fuck! What the fuck!" Black loud enough that the other diners were looking their way.

"Yeah. I figure you better get the hell out of here. Might have to change your name and disappear for a while. You might be on the run for the next few years. Try to stay invisible. Move around. You won't want to leave any trace. Better watch your back anywhere you go. Also, you probably won't want to visit anyone you care about. You don't want your sister and her kids to be in the blast radius when some guy walks up on you with a fishing vest full of nitroglycerine."

"You absolute fucking psycho! What the fuck is wrong with you? You can't do this!"

A waitress approached the table and asked them to be quiet and reminded them this was a family restaurant. Pursh soothed the waitress and told her she was leaving. She stood up and took out her wallet.

She gave Black some parting words as she counted out some bills onto the table. "If I were you, I wouldn't be wasting time yelling at me. I doubt those boys you killed are the only terror cell within 500 miles. I sent that message yesterday, so they could be on their way right now. Like I said, you're a realist, like me, and you aren't stupid, like me. I think you get that you should worry a little less about some Ann Arbor dyke and more about getting the fuck out of my city."

She left the restaurant with Black sitting alone, where he sat in deep contemplation about how the rest of his life was going to fucking suck.

Banana Nut Bread Blfgt

I watched two Cajuns have a knife fight about this recipe back in '88. One said to add cayenne. The other said to add a lot of cayenne. They both died in the hospital. By the rules of trial by combat, cayenne is totally optional for this recipe.

Fair warning: You got a lot of dishes to deal with after this and your arm gets a workout if you don't have a stand mixer.

Time: If the bread is made and the tomatoes are prepped? About 15-20 minutes. If starting from the beginning? We're looking at an hour and a half to two hours.

Bread Ingredients

- ¾ of a cup of peanut butter. Crunchy or creamy. That's your call
- ⅓ a cup of butter
- ⅔ of a cup of white sugar. Brown sugar might work. I never tried it
- 3 very ripe bananas. You want 'em going brown
- 2 eggs
- 1 ¾ cups of all-purpose flour
- 2 teaspoons of baking powder
- ¼ teaspoon of baking soda
- ¼ cup of buttermilk
- salt

Fried Green Tomato Ingredients

- 4 big green tomatoes
- 2 eggs
- ½ a cup of milk
- 1 cup of all-purpose flour
- ½ a cup of cornmeal
- ½ a cup of panko bread crumbs
- salt

- black pepper
- 1 quart vegetable oil for frying

Other Sandwich Ingredients

- Half a pound of bacon
- Lettuce

Gear

- An oven
- A deep skillet that's good for frying. Or a frier, if you got one
- 4"x8" loaf pan
- A rack
- A few mixing bowls and mixing spoons
- Spatula
- 3 bowls for breading

Making the Bread

1. Preheat oven to 350 F
2. Grease down a loaf pan with some butter
3. Put the peanut butter and butter-butter into a bowl and mix them together. Add in the sugar gradually as you go. When it's good and fluffy, it's done
4. Beat the eggs into the mixture until they are blended
5. Lose the peels on the bananas and mash 'em up til theyre baby food. Then add that in and stir some more
6. Your arm might be tired from all this stirring. Well, tough it out, buttercup, cus we got more stirring to do
7. Combine the flour, salt, baking powder and soda soda into another bowl. Mix that up. Then stir that mixture into the peanut butter banana mixture
8. Add the buttermilk, and mix *that* in, too
9. When all that's done, pour the batter into the loaf pan
10. Pop that into the preheated oven when the temperature is right. Should take about an hour to be done

11. Old trick: if you want to test if it's done, stick a toothpick in it and pull it out. If nothing's on the toothpick, it's done

Making the Tomatoes

12. Slice those tomatoes up, about a half inch thick
13. You gotta dry em before you fry em. Put the slices on the rack over a paper towel. Sprinkle them with some salt and leave 'em alone for 15 minutes. The salt will pull out a lot of the water
14. While the tomatoes are drying, get the breading ready. Mix the cornmeal and panko crumbs together in bowl #1. Add like a 1/2 teaspoon of salt and pepper. Whatever amount looks good to you
15. Beat those eggs with milk in bowl #2
16. Put the flour into bowl #3
17. Pat the tomato slices with paper towels until they are dry
18. Bread the tomato slices. One at a time, dunk them in the flour first. Get it good and coated on both sides. Let it hang out in that bowl for a half minute to make sure it sticks. Then dunk them in the egg/milk bowl. Then dunk in the panko/cornmeal. Make sure they are good and covered
19. When a slice is covered, put it back on that rack and let it mellow for 10 or 15 minutes so it can set
20. Oil that skillet and get it heated up at medium. If you want to test if it's hot enough, throw a couple panko crumbs in there. If they sizzle, it's ready to party
21. Fry the tomato slices. Usually it takes about 4 minutes per side. You want 'em crispy on the outside and soft on the inside
22. Put 'em on the rack to cool. They love that rack

Assembly

23. Did you cook the bacon yet? Cook the bacon

24. Make a sandwich. Bread slices, bacon, lettuce, tomatoes. You know how this works

Serve with

- Iced tea or lemonade
- The music of *Junior Kimbrough*
- A warrant

Variations

- Slap some mayo on there
- Just buy the bread at the bakery and make life easier on yourself
- Add cayenne to the fried green tomatoes
- To make a total mockery of Southern cooking, swap the lettuce for collards
- If you cook the bacon first, you can fry the tomatoes in the rendered bacon fat

CHAPTER 3:
LONESOME COWBOY

Española, NM

8/16/1988

21:04:36

Kris Kristofferson t-boned a 1975 Plymouth Fury police car with his 1977 Mack RS786LST, but no one was paying too much attention. The big silver screen was playing *Convoy* in front of an audience of classic cars on the dusty lot of the Good Times Drive-in. Juan walked in between the cars, holding a short stack of small quarter sheets of pink paper advertising *The World Famous Española Elvis Presley Museum*, with a washed-out photocopy image of The King performing in Vegas and the address on the bottom.

He tried to make eye contact, but most of the crowd were there to see cars, not Juan. Most people pretended not to see him. Whenever he met their eyes, he'd always be sure to smile and say, "Come check us out," and they always took the flier. He weaved around, admiring the machines with license plates from all over the country, mostly California, Nevada, and New Mexico, but one from as far as Louisiana. A 1952 Rolls-Royce, black and silver, with art déco curves, white-walled tires, flawless, and probably a reproduction. A '69 Dodge Charger, in that distinct orange, two doors, and a fastback profile so you can tell it's a muscle car just looking at the silhouette. A beautiful, powdered blue '53 Cadillac Eldorado; a goddamn work of drive-by art.

Juan stopped when he saw the '58 Chevy Impala. He swallowed hard like a preteen boy who accidentally looked down the dress of his homeroom teacher. It was a sight. Teal-colored, bearing every signature of the American style of the era, whispering to him about a time when American engineering and art were inseparable, the envy of the world. The ride was a thunderous thing that promised the freedom to go where you want, to pick up a girl and just ride through the desert under the Pollock-splatter cosmos, and end the night at a manufactured steel diner on Route 66 to share a malt shake with sweet Mary Jane. His hand reached out, but he stopped himself to be spared a beat down, like the car was a stripper in his lap.

"It's fine. You can touch it," said a man with a pompadour and a white T under an acid-washed jean vest. He flicked open a lighter with the image of a pinup girl with devil horns and tail and used her to light his cigarette.

"Yeah?"

"Go ahead." He watched Juan run his hand along the curves, hesitant, with admiration and awe, and a sense that he was doing it harm with his touch. The smoking man enjoyed watching the kid enjoy his car, just like a parent enjoys watching their kids enjoy a Mouse-branded theme park in Florida. "She's something, ain't she?" The smoke crawled out his nose and mouth.

"Yeah..."

"Climb in."

"For real?"

"I insist." He reached in and opened the door for him. Juan got in. He ran his fingers along the leather steering wheel. The owner climbed into the passenger's seat next to him and flicked the ash off his cigarette onto the dirt.

The man said, "This here is a special kind of museum. It doesn't stay put for long. And when it shows up again, it's someplace else, and the exhibits are all different. No one knows the names of the artists, but we all know the names of the patrons. And it's the only museum I've ever seen where you can step inside the art."

Juan nodded.

"You like cars, don't ya, kid."

Juan nodded.

"Terrible hobby. It's a thing you love but can't have. Only the fantastically wealthy ever sit inside even half the cars they'd like to. Cars like these are things most people only see in a magazine or a movie, and maybe lucky enough to see one passing down the freeway at 20 over the speed limit. Most of them never get to pop that hood and see what's under it. They don't get to lean back into that seat or feel the hum of the engine. It's just an idea in your mind about a beautiful thing you can't have."

Juan nodded.

"Well, you're in it now, boy. You can feel it, right?"

"Feel what?"

"History."

Juan nodded. That's it. That's exactly it. He was feeling history.

"You ever been to Jerusalem?"

Juan shook his head.

"I went there once in the 60s. You want to feel history? You can feel it there. You feel it coming out of the ancient buildings made of clay and dirt. You can feel it in the language. You can feel it tugging you down a street to the golden-domed mosques. It's in every atom of that place. Other places I've been, too. But America is young and we're always tearing things down and building new trash. You don't feel the history here like you do in England in the places the Germans didn't bomb into dust during the war. But what we have here in the USA is cars. That's our history. Every one of them is a little monument. You can see a science-fiction fantasy at the heart of every one. In every car you can see the engineers imagining the aesthetic of what they think the world will be in 20 years. 50s cars with that feel of an atomic robotic industrial future. 60s cars take on that sporty vibe, chrome pheromones, indictments against the old, that everything that came before was just a waste of time. The 70s with muscle and strength and fuck-it-all cus we're gonna get nuked anyhow, big dick disco energy, minus the naivete of the decade that came before it. And then the 80s. No one will hold a museum for the trash we make now. Angular, dull, functional, artless trash. In 50 years, no one will feel any nostalgia for the machines we drive today."

Juan nodded, but he only understood maybe half of all that.

"Nostalgia is the tug of our ancestors, begging us to never forget them."

Juan smiled sideways. "That sounds like something my grandpa would say."

"Your grandaddy sounds like a wise man."

"He was. I mean, he really was. A wiseman."

"You local? Tewa?"

Juan nodded.

"I been to Española. But that was a long ways back before you were born. Gimme one of them fliers."

Juan gave him one, snapping him out of his hypnosis. "Yeah, come on by. It's really great if you are into Elvis or just rock music, really."

"I might just do that, Juan."

Juan got out of the car and said, "Thanks for letting me sit in your car, mister. I gotta pass out more fliers."

"Good meeting you, young man."

After *Convoy*, they showed *Dirty Mary, Crazy Larry.* After Juan was finished passing fliers, he sat on a lawn chair and shared a beer with Kenny, a guy he played football with at school last year.

"Boys," said a man with a mustache and an authoritative timber.

"Shit," said Kenny.

"Hi, Sheriff," said Juan, "You enjoying the car show?"

Sheriff Pineda was in civilian clothes. He was off duty, but he was never off duty.

His hands were on his hips and he used that dad voice he had absolutely mastered. "I know that's not soda. And I know you boys aren't 21 yet because I saw you two kick Bernarillo high school's ass last year, 31-3."

"Aw, come on!" said Kenny.

"This isn't your first warning, Kenneth Myers. You know the drill."

Kenny grumbled and both the boys poured out their beers into the dust. Pineda opened the cooler and saw two more beers, took them, and handed them to two random adult passersby, who tipped their hats and thanked him for it.

"Have a good night, boys," and the sheriff went back to enjoying the cars.

"God, I hate that guy," said Kenny as soon as Pineda was out of earshot.

"He's alright," said Juan.

"Pff."

"He helped me out when I was a kid. He can be a dick but... he's alright."

The boys hung out and admired the cars and the girls and bought some hotdogs from a guy who brought a grill on his pickup. The crowd thinned over the next hour. The cars started leaving. The movie's credits were rolling. Juan bumped fist with his former teammate and they made promises to see each other again. Juan shouldered his backpack and got on his bike and headed home.

The theater was far enough away from town to avoid the ambient light. It was a quick ride onto the road, cutting through the open desert leading back home. The cold air whipped Juan's long hair around and the only light was a half-moon glow in a cloudless sky. It was late and there were hardly any cars, just the rare 18-wheeler passing by that would shake Juan's bike from the air it pushed. The desert was peaceful, vacant of electric lights and machine chatter. He let the gravity of the gentle slope carry him along the road's shoulder. He closed his eyes and imagined himself behind that Impala, that the wind in his hair was the wind of a 55mph cruise. He snapped out of that fantasy when a car zoomed past and it shook Juan's balance for a moment and he slid into the gravel. The car's rear lights went red, and it skidded and pulled over just 30 yards ahead. One headlight was dimmer than the other. Juan knew it was a 1966 Pontiac GTO by the profile, the lights, the curves of the frame.

The passenger door opened and the cabin lights came on, the only light around. A woman got out. He could tell she was a woman from the shape of her, and there were some words between her and the man driving. All Juan heard for certain was him saying, "Get back in the car," and her saying, "No."

Juan slowed his bike down to a walking pace. The woman slammed the door shut and started walking along the shoulder towards Juan. The driver put the car into reverse and slowly paced her so the man could continue shouting at her through the passenger window. Juan stopped. They didn't see him yet, but if they continued, he'd be swept up into their argument. Juan got off his bike and walked it off the shoulder onto the dust and dirt and scrub grass, to walk around their dispute before it arrived.

"But I fucking love you!"

"I don't care!"

The man in the car opened the passenger door, still in reverse, and the cabin lit up again. He reached behind him and produced a big fucking pistol from his belt and pointed it at her.

"Oh shit," whispered Juan, without meaning to.

The woman reached in and grabbed the gun with both her hands. It went off. A loud flash and an echo of the concussion in the dark. She fell back into the dust. The driver shut the door. The cabin went dark, the rear lights went from red to white, and his tires squealed and engine growled and he took off.

Juan ran up to the girl the moment he thought the guy wouldn't see him. He knelt beside her.

"Hey! Hey!"

"Santa..."

He was close enough to her now that he could see her in the dark as his eyes adjusted. She was young. Maybe just a couple of years older than Juan. Pretty. Long black hair. Big shirt with the logo of the XIV Olympic Winter Games and fake gold chain with an image of the Virgin. She started making a drowning sound.

"No, no. I'm not Santa. My name's Juan. Where did you get hit?" He started looking over her, trying to find a wound, but there was a lot of blood and it was too dark. Her eyes started looking dreamy. "Hey, no, don't do that! Stay awake! Please!" He put a hand behind her head and lifted it a little and started gently slapping her cheek like he'd seen people do in movies.

"Help! Help!" Juan yelled into the empty blackness all around him. He yelled in the great emptiness and he only heard the vaguest echo, the blackness was saying his words back to him like a playground bully. She stopped making noise. He listened to hear if she was breathing, but she was silent. Limp. He laid her head back down gently and something slid and made a sound when it hit the dirt. He reached for it. It was the gun. She'd taken it from that man when she was fighting for it.

He had all the thoughts that people have when they are in these situations. What do I do? How can I call the police? I can't just leave her here. He saw the headlights of a car up ahead. It was so dark, but he stood up and walked into the opposite lane and tried waving for help. But the car had one headlight dimmer than the other.

"Oh, shit." He looked back at the vague figure of the dead girl in the dark. He ran up to her and grabbed the gun and put it in his backpack. He got on his bike and started riding perpendicular to the road, deeper into the desert. The terrain was softer and his quads and calves burned, pedaling through it. Juan looked over his shoulder behind him. When the car reached the girl, Juan stopped and leaned onto one leg, and watched. The driver got out and the cabin lights back lit him. His silhouette kneeled, and he was messing with the girl's body. Juan could just barely hear him say something. "Where is it? Where the fuck did it go? Where the fuck?"

He went back to his car and popped the trunk. He lifted the girl and dropped her in it. The guy slammed the trunk of the car, got back into the driver's seat, and drove off for the second time. Juan waited in the dark for an hour, just in case the man came back a second time. Then he got back on his bike and continued his ride home.

When Juan made it back into town, he was glad to see the electric light of the street lamps. He rode past the tan adobe buildings and the steel and aluminum trailers. The streets were empty and silent. He stopped his bike right in front of the sheriff's department and looked at it. He thought about it, rolled it over in his head. Then he kept riding. A half-mile later, he rolled into the garage next to the two-story house with a big sign out front, *World Famous Española Elvis Presley Museum*. The garage was filled with boxes and junk, and no cars. Juan took the wooden fire escape in the back of the house up to the aluminum door on the second-floor, unlocked it, and walked into the tiny kitchen. He flicked on a light and for the first time realized how much blood was on him. He peeled his clothes off and tossed them in the sink and washed his hands with lemony dish soap. He opened his backpack and removed the gun. It had a picture of Elvis on the grip.

He got a piece of paper and a pen and sat down at the coffee table.

Dear Sheriff,

Last night I saw a lady get murdered on NM30 halfway between here and the drive-in. I think it was her boyfriend who did it. He took the body. He drives a black 66 Pontiac GTO with a silver stripe running down the center. His front driver's side headlight is dim.

Love,

A concerned citizen

He wiped off any fingerprints, folded the sheet, put them in an envelope, sealed it, and added a stamp. He rode back out to the police station and looked at the address. He wrote it on the envelope. For the return address, he wrote a "1" then remembered he was trying to be anonymous, so he scribbled it out. He dropped it in the mailbox in front of the post office, which was directly across the road from the station.

Juan woke up to the sound of the doorbell. He rubbed his eyes and slipped into some clothes—jeans, and a Washington Redskins shirt—and went down the narrow stairs into the messy area used as a supply room, nearly tripping over a bow and vacuum cleaner, then through a bead curtained doorway into the main area. He flicked on the light switch and the whole place came to life.

A cassette deck started playing Hound Dog through speakers in all four corners. Lights in the cabinets and on the walls lit up the exhibits. A white suit with golden trimming, bell bottoms, and a low V-neck. A red suit with sequins and a cape. A wall covered with record cases of every album and single, arranged like a quilt. A TV started playing *Speedway*.

It was a small museum of things that would be ordinary at a garage sale, but these were all special. They held a special magic in them because The King touched them. The magic of celebrity is like that. It rubs off. It gets on things and changes them indelibly.

A photo album full of ticket stubs. A mannequin wearing a Hawaiian shirt. Another wearing a Karate gi. Original posters on the walls from movies: *Wild in the Country, Blue Hawaii, Roustabout, Charro*. A case with eight different combs. Some photos of his shows, signed by Elvis. An ashtray that once carried his ashes during a TV interview in Vegas. A pool cue he used when he played a game with The Beatles. A pair of fade sunglasses. A hubcap from a car he once owned. A pair of Army boots. Some letters written by Priscilla. A television set with a bullet hole in it.

Juan yelled through the door, "We're not open til 10."

"It's 10:30," someone yelled back.

"Shit," Juan muttered under his breath. He opened the door and a young man with mutton chops and a cowboy hat was at his step. Juan said, "Hi, sorry, I musta slept in."

The cowboy was chewing fiercely on some gum, "That's all right."

"Come on in, let me just get everything all ready."

The bubblegum cowboy put his hands into the front pockets of his jeans and strolled in, looking around. Juan went back upstairs, took a powerful piss, and started some coffee in the tiny kitchen. He came back down. The cowboy was peeking around the showroom.

"This real?" Cowboy pointed at a shotgun in a glass case.

"Yes, sir."

The cowboy leaned in and read the card in front of it and looked at the small photocopied photo accompanying it. "It says here, Elvis almost blew Tom Jones's head off with that."

"That's what Tom Jones says."

"And that?" He pointed to a guitar on the wall. "That's Elvis's tiny guitar?"

"Yes, sir. Well. Sort of. It's a ukulele. It was a prop in *Blue Hawaii*. He couldn't play it, really. He couldn't really play guitar much at all."

"No shit?" Cowboy looked back at Juan and stroked his burns, one with his index finger and one with his thumb.

"He was just a singer. And a dancer and actor."

"Where did you get all this stuff?"

"My uncle collects it. He goes all over the country looking for this stuff."

"How do you know it's real?"

Juan shrugged.

"Cus, maybe your uncle is buying a bunch of junk that people say were Elvis's but aren't, really."

"He researches it, I guess. I don't know. I never asked him."

"What about those?" The cowboy pointed at the stuffed cougar in the corner and the bighorn head on the wall. "Did Elvis kill those?"

"No, that's my uncle. He's a bow hunter. Well. Not so much lately."

"Bow hunter, huh? Man of my own heart. He any good?"

"Yessir. Are you an Elvis fan?"

"I enjoy some of his music. The older stuff especially. Me, I'm more of a car guy."

"Are you in town for the drive-in car show?"

"I sure am." He walked up to Juan and pulled out a wrinkled flier and handed it back to him. "You don't remember giving me this last night, do you?"

Juan made an awkward smile. "No, I'm sorry. I saw so many people there yesterday, I can't remember them all."

"Don't sweat it. I wasn't wearing the hat yesterday. You got any other Elvis guns?"

"Just the 12-gauge. And a 1911."

"A 1911? I think I'd like to see that."

Juan walked him over to another glass display with all kinds of items and tokens. A ripped ticket to a concert in Memphis, a whiskey tumbler, a beat-up pack of playing cards, a guitar pick, and a chrome-plated Colt 1911, shiny as a car out of the carwash.

The cowboy crouched to get a good look. "Ain't she pretty. Would you mind taking it out of the case?"

"Um, why?"

"I'd just like to get a real good look at her."

"O-okay." Juan took the keys out of his pocket, unlocked the back of the case, slid it open, and took out the gun, and sat in on the counter.

"You mind if I pick it up?"

"I don't know—"

"I'd just like to hold something that Elvis held, you know?"

"Sure, yeah. That's fine, I guess."

He picked the gun up gingerly and looked at it very closely, examining the screws that held the wooden plates to the grip. Then he pulled back the slide and held it up to his nose and took a sniff of the breach.

Juan asked, "What's it smell like?"

"Nothing." He set the gun back down on the counter. "I appreciate you letting me come and visit. What do I owe you for it, by the way?"

"We are technically a nonprofit museum. We accept donations, though, in the jar."

The cowboy opened up his wallet and took out a fiver and put it in.

Juan said, "Thank you."

"I'll be seeing ya, kid." The cowboy turned around and left the way he came in. Juan was putting the gun back when he heard the engine growl outside. He walked up to the screen door and the first sun he saw that day stung his eyes and he shaded them with his hand to see the cowboy's black GTO with a silver stripe kicking up dust and driving off.

Juan took the Elvis gun back out of the glass display and looked it over. He opened a drawer and took out a screwdriver and went upstairs.

It was about 6:45 and Juan was watching the small TV in the kitchen, sitting at the tiny table, eating a bowl of S'mores Crunch cereal, with a 1911 with an Elvis grip sitting on top of a stack of car magazines. He heard the door ring. He walked downstairs with his bowl into the showroom, but no one was there.

"Hello?"

He turned around, and as soon as he was back in the supply room, he had an arrow pointed at him. The cowboy was back, pointing a loaded bow at him. Juan put his hands up without dropping his dinner.

"Found this in the back. Hope you don't mind if I borrow it."

Juan shook his head.

"This your uncle's?"

Juan nodded.

"The deadbolt on your back door's a little loose. Pretty easy to pry it with a flathead screwdriver. Might wanna get that replaced when you have the chance. A place with all these relics needs quality security."

"Okay."

"I'm here for the gun you stole from me."

"What... do you mean?" Juan did his best impression of a confused person.

"Quit lyin, kid. I know it was you last night. Took a little something for your collection here?"

"No, sir. I didn't. I didn't steal it. I took it."

"What's the difference?"

"I took it, but I didn't mean to. I just kind of put it in my pocket and when I saw you, I ran away. I forgot about it."

"You have it?"

Juan nodded.

"Where?"

"Upstairs."

They both heard the crunch of four tires in the gravel parking area out front.

"Another visitor?"

Juan peeled back the beads and could just barely see through the window. "Police."

Cowboy peeked through the gap Juan made to confirm the kid wasn't bullshitting him. "Always a cop when you don't need one. Be cool and don't say a thing or you're both dead, got it?"

Juan nodded.

"Go." Cowboy turned off the light in the storage room and hid in the darkness behind an old couch tilted on its end, resting against the wall.

The door opened and jingled. Juan stepped out to the showroom to greet him and set the bowl down on the counter. It was Sheriff Pineda. Juan could see Deputy Ruiz outside through the window, writing down the plate number of the GT onto a paper pad.

"Hi, Sheriff. What can I do for you today?"

"Oh, I was just in the area and I thought I'd stop on by. Sorry to interrupt your dinner." He pointed at the bowl.

"That's fine."

"How you been?"

"Fine."

"Business good?"

"It's fine."

"Your uncle? How's he doing?"

"He's fine."

"Bet he's itching for hunting season, huh? So everything's fine, then?"

"Yup."

The Sheriff nodded and strolled over to the guest book and unfolded his reading glasses that hung from a chain around his neck and had a look. Then he looked up at Juan and let his reading glasses hang. He shifted his mouth which moved his big mustache. He took out Juan's letter and flipped it open.

"We got a letter this afternoon from a concerned citizen. They said someone got murdered last night on 30."

Juan shrugged.

"What's that? What're you shrugging at? You don't know if I got a letter?"

"No, I don't know about a murder."

"I didn't say you did. I just learned about it myself, so how could you know?"

Juan shrugged.

The Sheriff continued, "Now, I'm happy when a citizen reaches out when they know about a crime. And I understand they don't always want to get involved. They just want to tell the law about what happened and then they want to go back to their normal lives. It's totally understandable. They don't want to be asked a lot of questions, they don't want to testify, and they definitely don't want the police thinking that it was them who did it."

Juan nodded.

In the dark storage area, the bubblegum cowboy could hear everything. He readjusted his grip and wiped his sweat-slippery hands on his jeans.

The Sheriff took off his hat and set it on the counter. "Me and deputy Ruiz went out this morning and spent a few hours up 30, looking for any evidence of a murder. You know what I found?"

Juan shook his head. He looked at the hat, wondering if Pineda planned on staying a while.

"Not much. A little spot of discolored dirt. We took a sample and some pictures. It might be blood, but it's pretty dry out there. Hard to tell by looking at it. Which is why we collected a sample and sent it to Albuquerque for testing. Hell, if it's blood, it might just be an animal. Maybe someone hit a deer and took it home for supper. What do you think?"

Juan shrugged.

"I don't know if I have a murder here or what. Maybe this letter is just a prank, but I think it isn't. There's not much to go on, but I might have some leads. Can I show you something?"

Juan shrugged.

"You don't know if I can show you something?"

"You can show me."

Sheriff Pineda leaned over the counter and invited Juan to come close and look at the letter with him. Juan got close enough.

"See, the letter is anonymous but there are a lot of things about this that tell me something about who wrote it. Here. Take a look. This is a man's handwriting. For sure. I bet you can tell the difference just by seeing all those signatures in your guest book. The murder witness, the man who wrote this letter, he described the victim as a lady. Not a woman. Not a girl. Makes me think the man who wrote this is very polite. Maybe even old fashioned. What do you think? You think he's polite?"

Juan shrugged.

"Then he says right here: halfway between here and the drive-in. That's an interesting choice of words. He says *here*. Where is *here*? I read that and I have to wonder. It makes me think he means here in town. I think this polite man is a local. You think so?"

Juan shrugged.

"Well, I know he sent the letter locally. The post office stamped the envelope, and it was delivered from right here in town. It would be strange to drop the mail here when he isn't from here. And even if he did, who's got stamps and envelopes in the middle of the night in a strange town?"

Juan nodded and shrugged.

"You don't think so?"

"Maybe he was just in town for the car show. You know. Because the witness mentioned the drive-in."

"You know, it's funny you should mention that. This guy definitely knows his cars. If this happened last night, this guy could identify the make, model, and year of a black car at night. That's a real car nut. And he doesn't know the exact spot or the mile marker. He doesn't mention any other features from the area. He just says between here and the drive-in. Why the drive-in? He could've said halfway between here and the cemetery. Or the diner. But he said drive-in. Not the car show. The drive-in. That makes me think maybe he goes to the drive-in a lot. Maybe he was at the drive-in last night when the murder happened. What do you think?"

The bubblegum cowboy snuck out the back door as quietly as

he came in. Neither of the men in the showroom noticed.

Pineda continued. "And on the envelope—I didn't bring it with me, so I'll just tell you—the polite local male car expert started writing a return address and scratched it out. But I could still make out what it was. It was a one. What's the address here, Juan?"

"1835 Salgado."

"So your address starts with a one also, huh?"

Juan nodded.

"And you're a man, right?"

Juan nodded.

"And you live here, right? In this town?"

Juan nodded.

"And you know your cars."

Juan shrugged.

The Sheriff picked up a copy of *Road & Track* that was sitting next to the cash register and held it up.

"Yeah. I like cars."

The Sheriff set the magazine back down. "And you are a polite guy."

Juan shrugged.

"You are. You're very polite. And you were at the drive-in last night, right?"

Juan hesitated.

"I saw you there, remember? I know you were there."

Juana nodded.

"Sounds like you meet all the characteristics of the guy who wrote this."

Juan shrugged.

"Can you think of anyone else who might be the person who wrote this? Besides you, I mean?"

Juan swallowed and shrugged. He looked over the sheriff's shoulder and out the window, but he didn't see deputy Ruiz out there anymore.

"We gonna keep doing this, Juan? There is a black '66 GT with a silver stripe right out front. The exact car mentioned in the letter. I know you aren't a murderer, Juan, so how about you tell me. What is going on?"

Juan's eyes got big when he saw the bubblegum cowboy was outside by the screen door, not behind him in the storage area. Cowboy notched an arrow on Uncle's bow and raised up. Juan yelled "No!"

The sheriff said, "Well, I know it was you who—" but was cut off when Cowboy fired an arrow through the screen door. The arrow pierced the Sheriff's back but his breast plate's interior side stopped it from passing all the way through. The sheriff fell over face first onto the glass counter and the thing shattered under his weight and the sheriff fell through it. Juan ducked behind the counter by a portion that was backed by composite plywood. The sheriff wasn't moving, but he was making a sound like a gargle and a hum. Juan saw the revolver on his hip. He reached through the busted glass display, slowly so he wouldn't cut his arm on the jagged pieces. He was a couple inches away when he heard the creak and slam and jingle of the screen door. He pulled his arm back too fast and cut himself badly along the underside of his forearm.

The cowboy strolled in. Juan tried to make himself small where he was. He flinched when he heard another of his uncle's arrows penetrating the sheriff.

"Just stand up, Juanito. I saw you duck back there."

Juan stood up with his hands up. A lot of blood was coming out of his arm. Cowboy had the quiver on his back and an arrow notched. He gestured with the tip of the arrow that it was okay if Juan put his arms down. Juan clutched his injury, looked around, and saw a t-shirt advertising the museum. He used it to wrap up his cut, and it quickly went from white to red to brown. He wrapped it up with some duct tape from the same drawer he kept the screwdriver in.

"What were we talking about before the sheriff interrupted?"

Juan looked at the sheriff and didn't say anything.

Cowboy said, "I was Kansas state archery champion in high school. Kind of funny, right?"

Juan snapped out of it, "What? What do you mean?"

"I mean, I'm a cowboy. I should have the gun. But I have the bow and that dead Indian cop has the gun. It's kind of funny when you think about it."

Memories are strange. They can come so fast. A few little details open things up like numbers on a padlock. Juan thought about when he was eight and the Sheriff was still a deputy. He came by one night when Uncle was mescal-angry, beating up on little Juanito. Pineda warned him one time, but Uncle acted like the deputy wasn't a man who kept promises. He was. Pineda fucked Uncle up, and took him to jail that night. Juanito slept at the station. After that, Deputy Pineda drove past the museum every day, once in the morning, once at night, slowly, just so Uncle knew he was watching. When he got angry, Uncle threatened like he might hit Juan again, but he only ever put his hands on Juan one more time. Uncle did a lot of cruel things, but Pineda never let that man forget that the law was close by.

Juan's eyes went soggy. He wasn't crying exactly. "It's not funny," he said.

"I know it's not funny like a joke. It's funny, like... ironic."

"It's not funny!"

Cowboy raised up, "Relax, Tonto. Just lemme know where my gun is and I'll be out of your hair."

Juan wiped the salt from his eyes with his good arm. "Upstairs. In the kitchen."

Cowboy shouldered the bow and took the sheriff's revolver. "Lead the way."

They went up the stairs together and Cowboy asked, "What's that about your uncle? Is he around?"

"No. My uncle's dead."

"But you just said to the cop—"

"I lied. My uncle's been sick for years. He hardly ever came out. He's been dead for two months. I didn't tell anyone, so I can still cash his disability checks from the Army."

Cowboy smiled, "Well, ain't you full of surprises. Now where's that gun?"

Juan showed him upstairs, and he pointed to the 1911 on the kitchen table. Cowboy took the Elvis gun into his fist and stuffed the police revolver into the front of his belt. He looked at Juan and it was easy for Juan to see the cowboy was thinking about what to do with him.

"Sir, I know you can kill me, but maybe we can work something out."

"Mm. I don't know." The cowboy scratched his chin with the barrel of the gun. "I suppose there's no harm in hearing you out."

"You like cars, right?"

"I surely do."

"I have a 1948 Ford Super DeLuxe convertible. I'll show you where it is."

"The car from *Karate Kid*? Bullshit."

"It's the truth."

"Where?"

"I have to show you."

"How about you just tell me?"

"I can't."

"Why not?"

"Because it's in a cave out in the desert. I can't give directions. I have to show you."

"You expect me to believe that? Why would you have the *Karate Kid* car in a cave?"

"Because it's stolen."

"Wait, a minute. Wait. A. Minute. Stolen? You got any other cars in that cave?"

"Yessir. A couple."

"That why you hang out at the car shows, ain't it? To scout out cars to steal?"

"Yessir."

"And then, what, you get their info and follow them home and take them?"

"No, sir. My uncle stole them. I just look at the cars, get the owner's information, and reported back to him. And I mind the shop."

Cowboy laughed, "Goddamn, Tonto. You seem like such a nice kid, too." He sighed, looked at the floor, and put a hand on his hip. "I guess I don't see any harm in looking. Sounds like the cops are already looking for my GT. Wouldn't be a bad idea to switch cars anyhow, and a fancy machine like that is a step up. Alright, kid. You're driving." He reached into his pocket and tossed his keys to Juan. The kid almost smiled when he caught it and felt the keys in his hand. Cowboy force-marched Juan back downstairs. The donation jar caught Cowboy's eye, and he reached in and took the couple bills and loose change from it and he stuffed them into his pocket.

They walked out the front where Deputy Ruiz was lying face down in the gravel and dust in a circle of reddish-brown mud. It only took one arrow. A perfect kill shot through the side, threading the ribs, puncturing both lungs and the heart. The most efficient and humane way for a hunter to kill their prey.

The sun was coming down, just a lens flare at the tip of the tan hills. The scrub brushes cast long shadows and the waning day projected a purple and orange glow on the clouds. Cowboy escorted Juan to the GT at gunpoint. Cowboy tossed the bow and arrows into the back seat and they both climbed into the two-door. Juan took a moment to experience the interior. The seats tilted back like a racecar. Big, thin steering wheel. Wooden console and fuzzy dice hanging from the rearview mirror. He let his hands glide over the wheel a few times. Put his hand on the stick. He put the key in and when he twisted it, cracked a little smile, feeling the growl of eight cylinders, turbocharged, 7.5 liters of petrol-chugging American muscle, spitting black smoke like a steel dragon waking up grumpily from a nap. Juan turned the car around and headed straight into the desert, off-road, chasing that setting sun.

"Everything looks the same out here. How you gonna know how to get there?"

"I've been plenty of times. I know."

"Lemme ask you something. How come you took the gun?"

"Last night? I was trying to help your girlfriend, and it was just lying there and I put it in my bag."

"And you saw me coming back? What, you just ran off into the desert?"

"Yeah. Pretty much. I guess I kinda forgot I had it."

"Is that why you didn't use it on me?"

Juan shrugged.

They were quiet as the sun vanished and the purple and navy sky turned black and the only light at all was a few feet ahead of them, unevenly illuminated by the headlights.

"How much further?"

"Almost there. Can I ask you a question?"

"I don't see why not."

"Why did you shoot your girlfriend?"

"You know how it is."

Juan shook his head. "No, I don't."

Cowboy sighed and lit himself a cigarette, cracked the window, and leaned back. "She wanted kids. I didn't. I'm just not dad material. And she knew that. But she gets these ideas about how the world is and how it ought to be and sometimes... oftentimes... she'd forget that the should ain't hardly ever the ought. She chose to be a real bitch about it. Stopped taking her birth control pills. Without telling me, of course. Anyway, she decided for the both of us I was gonna be a daddy. We had some words in the car. Normal boyfriend-girlfriend shit."

"Doesn't seem normal to me."

"Well, who gives a fuck what you think's normal? And where the fuck is this place? We been drivin' since forever."

"Right here." Juan slowed the car down and they could see the cliff side of a mesa and a big, black mouth in it, sloping down just a little, and Juan drove right inside of it, and it swallowed them up. As soon as they were just 15 feet inside, the headlights lit up the yellow De Luxe. Juan parked the car, killed the engine, and they both got out.

"Can't hardly see shit," said Cowboy a second before he heard Juan tugging on a ripcord and heard the chug of a portable generator fire up and the construction work lights came on. There was a lot more to this cave. The De Luxe had a few friends: 1960 Sunliner, '51 Mercury Coup Lead Sled, and half of a '65 Jaguar E-Type. Some tools on racks stacked along the walls, chains, 2x4s, gas cans, cat litter, and dirty oil filters. A whole chop shop.

"Whoo-boy, Tonto! You got quite the collection here! Keys?"

"Right there in the ignition."

Cowboy peeked at the De Luxe and the keys were there, just like he said they were. "Thanks. Shame I'm gonna have to kill ya, anyway. I mean, I can't have you talking to anybody about what happened with the cops and my girl and all. Deputies are probably all over your little museum right now, taking photos of their dead Sheriff, and poking around the crime scene."

"I know."

"You know? You took me all the way out here, anyway?"

"Yeah. My granddad warned me about cowboys."

"You're a strange one, kid." He leveled the gun at Juan and pressed the trigger. *Click. Click.* "The fuck!"

"That's the Elvis gun."

Cowboy began fighting with the gun, trying to clear a jam that wasn't there. "Yeah, I know it is!"

Juan reached into the back of the *Karate Kid* car and took out his uncle's .30-06 that was hiding under a tarp, and wrapped the sling around his left hand and forearm. He shouldered the wooden stock and leveled the glass onto the cowboy.

Cowboy dove behind the Mercury and kept fighting with his gun.

Juan didn't move. "No, I mean that's not your gun. That's the Elvis gun. From the case. The firing pin is gummed up. It was like that when my uncle bought it. The guy he got it from said that Elvis had a bad habit of popping off his guns in places he shouldn't. He could be very irresponsible. He was high a lot. The guy who sold it said someone who worked for Elvis jammed up his guns' firing pins so he wouldn't accidentally kill somebody. The Elvis gun doesn't fire. I just switched the grip plates. So now the Elvis gun has the Elvis grip plates from your gun."

Cowboy stopped with the gun and dropped it. "What? Why'd you do that?"

Juan shrugged.

"Why?" He asked again and drew the sheriff's revolver from his waistband.

"I just thought it would be cool if the Elvis gun had Elvis on it."

"What? That's just… so… stupid."

Juan shrugged. "You know what tonto means?"

Cowboy looked around for a way out of this. Some junk in a crummy, homemade shop. He saw a fire extinguisher just a couple of feet away. Cowboy kept the chit-chat going. "What tonto means? I don't fucking know, some Indian word?"

"Tonto's Spanish. It means dummy."

Cowboy grabbed the extinguisher, pulled the pin, and started spraying overhead, filling the cave with a white cloud. He darted through the cover, firing at where he heard Juan last, and blindly heading toward the GT, and through two deafening cracks of the rifle's return fire. He couldn't see Juan, but Juan couldn't see him either. The cowboy fired his last two more shots into the white void and one hit a work light, dimming the room by a third of what it was. He threw the gun into the void and reached through the open window of the

GT and grabbed the bow and quiver. He knocked an arrow and crouched behind the hood. He crept around the driver's side, peeking through the windows, hoping for just a moment's glimpse of the kid as the white fog dissipated. He kept his eyes open and his ears sharp for anything. He forced himself to take slow, deep breaths. His pounding heart wanted oxygen, but Cowboy couldn't be huffing and puffing and making noise.

With every passing quarter-second, there was less whiteness, and soon it was gone, but so was Juan. Cowboy stayed put for a while, hoping he would hear or see Juan first, but he didn't. He finally crept back the way he came, crouching always, peeking into and around each vehicle, until finally, he saw where he'd seen Juan last. Juan wasn't there, but his shoes were.

The last thing Cowboy saw before he was crippled was a flicker of light in the darkness outside the cave, maybe 50 yards away, and a whistling noise of 173 grains of lead. The shot nailed him in the ball joint of his femur, breaking his ilium and pubis bones. Everything that held the skeleton together between Cowboy's belly and balls was busted up into pieces, collapsing in on his intestines. He hit the ground and his arrow flew and hit the ceiling of the cave and fell down limply.

Cowboy army-crawled underneath the Sunliner like a wounded coyote, incapable of controlling the grunts he made, dragging his two-piece pelvis and useless legs. Another shot rang out and burst into the front-passenger tire, and the car's weight shifted abruptly over the cowboy. The space closing in on him, the crushing weight of the car just two tires away from flattening him like a grape. He dragged himself across the rocky floor with his elbows to escape. Another shot, another tire. The car shifted to a rightward slant and Cowboy's foot got caught. He got halfway out when the third tire burst and there was hardly any room. He rolled over and grabbed the front fender and strained with everything he had until he ripped his foot out. He rolled back over and kept crawling. The last tire burst and it would've crushed Cowboy if he were any slower.

He dragged himself away from the mouth of the cave, deeper into the darkness where the work lights didn't reach, smearing his blood and last meal across the stone floor.

Cowboy went deep enough he couldn't see the light of the chop shop anymore. So dark that he lost all sense of distance. He found another cave wall with his hands and then felt something. A person. He wasn't alone. He didn't see the man leaning against the wall clearly until Juan and his rifle and flashlight caught up to him. The other man was desiccated, shriveled, near-mummified by the dry New Mexico air. The dead man had a bullet hole in the skull. Cowboy was about to ask who the dead man was, but never got the chance.

Fried Bacon Plantains With Thai Peanut Dipping Sauce

Thailand's got the best pool players and the best kickboxers. But their black market animal breeders? Sloppy and unprofessional, in my experience. Never buy a tiger kitten from a Buddhist abbot in Kanchanaburi.

This recipe is much easier than brokering exotic animal sales for a Russian oligarch. You make the plantains. You make the sauce. You dip the plantains in the sauce. Easy.

Time: 15 mins

Fried Bacon Plantains
Ingredients for the plantains

- Plantains
- Bacon
- Some oil

Gear for the plantains

- Toothpicks
- Skillet

Making the plantains

1. Undress the plantains and chop them up so they are chicken nugget sized
2. Cut the pig ribbons in half
3. Wrap the plantain in the bacon and stab it with the toothpick so it'll hold together
4. Fire up the skillet with some oil. A lot of that pig fat will melt and make it's own oil, so don't go crazy here
5. Fry it til it looks good
6. Let it cool on paper towel or a wire rack. The bacon should stay out now, so you can remove the

toothpicks

Thai Peanut Sauce
Ingredients for the sauce

- 1/2 cup of peanut butter. Get the good stuff, the kind where the oil separates when you leave it a while. Don't be cheap, now
- 2 tablespoons less-sodium soy sauce
- 1 tablespoon rice vinegar
- 2 tablespoons brown sugar
- 2 teaspoons of sriracha or whatever kind of sauce is basically the same kind of spicy garlic ketchup. Sriracha is everywhere now. You can find it. Shit, you could probably make your own in a pinch
- 3 cloves of grated garlic
- 1 tablespoon grated ginger
- 1 tablespoon of lime juice. Get a real lime and squish it. Don't use that stuff in the lime-shaped bottle. That stuff is nasty

Gear for the sauce

- A stove
- saucepan
- spoon or whisk

Making the sauce

1. Put all the ingredients in the pot or pan. Apply some low heat. Stir until mixed
2. Add water if you like it a little thinner. Easy

Serve with

- Kingfisher beer
- A water-damaged pool table that's been in the same Chiang Mai bar since American GIs brought it in '71
- The music of *Buena Vista Social Club*

Variations

- Grill it instead of fry it. It's a sin, but I'm no snitch
- The sauce is great on all kinds of things. Grilled chicken, fried Oreos, or mixed in with a stir fry

CHAPTER 5: IN THE GHETTO

Toledo, OH

4/2/2009

12:22:31

You won't find any reviews for Claudette's restaurant on the internet. There aren't any crowdsourced reviews, IRS forms, or records in any Department of Health database. If you know how to find it, it's because someone told you where it is.

Wolf drove through the neighborhoods on Toledo's North End, across the uneven, cracked, and potholed patchy vitiligo pavement. The leaves weren't on the trees yet, still looking withered and naked. The things Wolf drove past were unremarkable in that part of town. A pile of tattered roof shingles on the curb, old and unloved houses, half of them abandoned and boarded up with particleboard. Trash in the streets, plastic grocery bags, a dozen diapers, a busted clothing drier on a lawn, something white and smashed that was probably porcelain, fast food wrappers and cups and straws blocking a gutter and small pools of dirty melted snow collected in the streets. A few cars on the street had garbage bags for windows and expired tags, rusted and dented. Wobbled and bent chain-link fences separated the houses, threaded with brown, twisted, dry vines. Planks of wood propping up awnings over entryways in stark defiance of city regulation and physics. Yards with still unraked dead leaves from last year, and big trees, older than anyone living here, old enough to see this place when it wasn't like this. The best maintained and most loved thing in this neighborhood was a roadside shrine for a dead little girl. Flowers and stuffed animals stacked high and a sign saying, "We Miss You Angel," and a photo of her glued onto a white-painted wooden cross. Wolf wondered, Was Angel her name or was she an angel to the people who mourned for her?

Wolf slowed to a stop. The Crown Vic in front of him had stopped in the street, the engine still running. A young man leaned into the passenger side window and talked to the driver. On the porch of the nearest house, two men sat on a couch, color-coordinated with the guy on the road. They pointed suspicious eyes at Wolf; that same look the cops give them when they drive down this road. When they finished their business in the street, the car began moving again and Wolf could too.

Two blocks further along and Wolf could see he was close. His car started making a grinding noise, and he could smell something coming out of the heating vents. He pressed on the acceleration, but it wouldn't give any speed. He used the remaining inertia to park it by the curb.

He turned the key and silenced the engine. He leaned forward, head on the steering wheel. "Not today. I don't need this shit today. Fuck."

He rolled down his window and reached for the outside handle to open his door because the inside one didn't work. He rolled his window back up, locked up, and walked towards Claudette's. Two blocks away.

Wolf got out his phone. He pressed PTT on his Nextel. "My car broke down. Can somebody gimme a lift back to work?"

"Where you at?" asked the voice of a co-worker.

"I'm bout to pick up some lunch at Claudette's."

"I can be there in like 15."

"Thanks, man."

"Hook me up with a tamale, aight?"

"I got you."

An old 2-story house with a fenced-in yard, much older than the grotesque geometry and palette of the homes they built in the 70s. There were more cars parked out front here than anywhere else on this street; all Ford F150s and Dodge Rams. A neighbor directly across the street from Claudette's was on her phone, angry about something. "I've called you nine times! Nine times! I'm sick of this! I'm sick of it!"

He walked up to the house over the dry, crunchy, brittle grass of the front lawn. He could just barely smell the allspice and cumin and pork fat on the wind and he heard some music, *Si Tu Vois Ma Mère*, with a disarming clarinet and soothing standup bass, and lyrics lullabied by an angel. He let himself in through the fence gate into the backyard and closed it behind him. The yard was tight with plastic lawn furniture, not one piece of it matching another, arranged in tables like an actual, legal restaurant, a bottle of Frank's on every one. The chairs were filled with men who work outside and dress for the cold; tan overalls and neon yellow vests, eating their lunches on paper plates and smoking a cigarette or a Djarum and enjoying a beer and not talking too much. A bit of peace and dignity, 25x20 feet of it, hidden behind some fence. One of the countless gray market businesses in Toledo, committing crimes too minor to bother the police, but not too minor to conjure the health department if one of Claudette's diners or neighbors snitched.

It would be a chilly day for lunch outside but there was a big grill smoking something good and spitting out charcoal heat and the sliding glass door to the kitchen was open and the steam and warmth of a home kitchen fryer, a deep pot of collards, and smoked trotters, all bled out into the yard. The music was coming from a small CD player on a coffee table in the yard's corner.

Claudette came out with a tray and fed some men. She was headscarved with a red and orange bandana, and when she found Wolf she gave him a surprised smile and said, "Hey, you. I barely recognized you! Haven't seen you in a little while, boubout. Ki jan-w ye?"

"I been alright, marabou."

"Ooh," she smiled big and white, "You been learning to flirt in creole?" her eyes narrowed with a playful suspicion.

Wolf took a seat in a canvas camping chair with drink holders in the armrests, in front of a ping-pong table with two guys already dining at the other end.

Wolf smiled at her. Claudette asked, "You cut the beard off?"

"Yeah. Thought I needed a change." He touched his bare face.

"And I don't think I've seen you in glasses since you in middle school."

"Ran out of contacts. Back to these."

"You lookin' good. We made some changes to the menu, alright? I'mma help these folks and I'll be right back."

The menu was a printout on a piece of paper, smudged and oily in the corners from other diners' hands, and just had printed on it:

Empanada $3

Tamale $3

Riz et Pois Rouges $2

Collards $2

Street corn $1

Cornbread $1

~~Pecan Pie $3~~ Cracklins $1

Beer $5

Kool-aid $1

Claudette came back and asked, "What you need, boubout?"

"What's in the tamales today?"

"We got some goat that was on sale from that halal butcher up there by the free clinic. Tastes just as good as beef. That mixed up with chicken."

"How about the empanadas?"

"We out of empanadas already."

"Alright, I'll have four tamales and collards and a beer."

"You got it, boubout."

"Hey, uh, is D here?"

The light in her smile faded a bit. "I haven't seen him yet today. Probably still in his room."

"Is it alright if I go inside and visit him?"

"Yeah, baby. Of course. I'll bring you your food there."

Wolf stood up and walked through the sliding glass door into the kitchen. The girls were busy making food, and the room was warm and steamy and full of chit-chat and jokes and laughter.

Wolf breezed through the kitchen and found the door to the basement, and walked down the creaky wooden steps. The place was glowing neon pink like a strip club, from the LED strips that wrapped the walls near the floor. D was sitting on a plaid-patterned couch, a controller in his hand, his face lit up by the TV's glow.

"D."

D paused his game. "Aw shit, I didn't recognize you at first. What's up, man? You look weird."

"What's up?" Wolf raised his hands a bit and cocked his head. He let the question hang in the air, but D said nothing. He just gave stupid cow eyes. Wolf answered his own question, "What's up is you said you'd have my money."

"Oh, that? Yeah, yeah." He returned to playing the game.

"D!"

"Yeah?" he said, keeping his attention on the game.

"I'd like my money, please." Wolf spoke a little more loudly than he'd intended.

"Oh. I guess you're here for that? I thought you were here to hang out," he said, as though Wolf's words hurt him.

"I gotta get back to work in a minute. Bro, put that shit down. I bought your car out of the tow yard and I gotta make rent tomorrow. Come the fuck on."

D paused the game, stood up, walked to the bed with a sleeping bag for a blanket, sat on it, and pressed his thumb on the bio-ID lock on a fire-safe next to it. When the light turned green, he opened it and removed a blue plastic grocery bag, closed the safe, then walked up to Wolf and handed it to him.

Wolf took it and it felt heavy. He reached into it. His eyes got big when he felt it.

"What's this?"

"That's your money."

"Does this look like money to you?"

"Yeah."

"This ain't money! Money is made of paper. This is a gun!" He held it up to D's face so he could see it up close.

"That's not a gun. That is a nickel plated 45. Sell that for money."

"I don't want a gun, D! I want money!"

"I owe you a thousand, right? That thing will sell for 2 Gs easy! That's more than I owe."

"Sounds like you're just handing me a job you should be doing. Why don't you go sell it if it's worth so much?"

"I don't know anyone who needs a gun, but you do. You got people who are into that, right? Like those militia guys up in Michigan."

"Militia guys? The fuck are you talking about? That's Romeo's thing."

"That's what I'm saying, though. You know a guy! You got connections. Okay, sure, it's a little extra work for you, but you make double what I owe!"

"Does every fucking thing with you need to be a problem?"

"Psh. What're you even talking about?"

"Every damn thing with you. I bail your car out after you were in jail over the weekend. I come to get what you owe me and you're giving me a fucking gun and an errand to run instead of my money. It's always some shit like this with you, man! Every damn time."

"Hey, I thought this was a good deal for you, okay? I'm sorry."

Wolf rubbed his eyes, then looked around the room for something else worth money that wasn't a gun. A shiny new laptop computer, opened up and sitting on a humming chest freezer. He pointed at it. "That."

"What?"

"That computer. Where did you get that?"

"Um, well..."

"You got money for a fucking laptop but no money for me?" Wolf tossed the gun bag onto D's bed, then walked over to the laptop and folded it shut and unplugged it.

"No, wait, you can't take that! It's not mine."

Wolf stopped. "Whose is it then?"

D didn't want to answer.

"Whose, D?"

"Brittany's."

"Jesus, man. You back with Brittany? What is it with you and that crazy girl?"

"She fucks good, man. I don't know."

"She a fucking nightmare, bro."

"I know."

Wolf set the laptop back down and walked up to the bed, and picked up the blue bag. "Where'd you even get this thing?"

"A guy."

"What guy?"

"Just some guy."

"What fucking guy, D?"

"Chris."

"Which Chris? Chris Babcott or Cocktail Chris?"

D didn't say anything.

Wolf pointed at D accusingly and pursed his lips and breathed out slowly through his nose and chose his next words carefully and spoke them slowly. "Tell me you didn't get this gun from Pretty Chris."

D shrugged.

"Oh my god. You did, didn't you."

"Yeah, so?"

Wolf pressed his palms to his temples and squeezed his eyes shut.

"What?" asked D.

Wolf raised a finger like he was about to lecture the boy, but he stopped himself before saying another word. His hand formed a claw, and he closed it slowly like he was strangling the air until it was a fist. He closed his eyes for a moment and relaxed and said, "This time you have outdone yourself, D." Wolf turned and headed towards the stairs with the bag and gun.

"What's the big deal, man?"

"You know goddamn well. Which is why you didn't want to tell me where you got it."

Wolf started walking up the stairs, and at the top, he bumped into Claudette. She said, "I got your food ready."

They both heard D call up from below, "You gonna hang out and play *Tekken*, though? Wolf?"

"I'm sorry. I gotta go," said Wolf to Claudette, not D.

"Stay and eat."

"No, I'm sorry. I gotta get back to work. Could I get that to go?"

Claudette made an exaggerated pout. "I'll forgive you," she said and smiled. He followed her back into the kitchen. She poured his plate in a styrofoam container and put that into a plastic bag saved from a grocery store. "No one leaves my home hungry."

"Can I go out the front?"

She nodded and her mouth smiled, but not her eyes.

Wolf took the bag and walked to the front of the house towards the big wooden door, and Claudette headed back to the kitchen. When Wolf opened the door, he saw the two police coming up the walkway. He slammed the door shut and locked it.

"Shit!"

He was about to call for Claudette to warn her. Then he looked at the plastic bag in his hand with the gun. "Shit! Shit, shit, shit!" Wolf stuffed the gun and bag into the white styrofoam takeout bag. He headed towards the kitchen as he heard the unmistakable drum of the underside of a cop's fist on the front door.

He said, "The cops are here."

Claudette tsked through her teeth and told the girls to go out the back. They all headed through the sliding glass door and told the guests that the meal was over. The diners were quick to get up and walk out the gate to the front. Wolf walked into the crush of people funneling out. A cop was waiting for them and telling them all to leave in an orderly fashion. Wolf walked across the lawn and looked back to see Claudette arguing with the cops while her neighbor across the street, the one Wolf saw before, yelled at her, "I told you! I told you I'd call the cops! I told you!" Three police cars were outside for this bust.

Romeo arrived just as Wolf was finishing his lunch on the hood of the car. Wolf got his tools and belt out of the trunk and then climbed into Romeo's van.

"What's wrong with your car?"

"Shit, man. I don't know."

"Does it start?"

"Nah."

"Oil okay though?"

"Yeah."

"What kinda tamales she got today?"

"You like goat?"

"For real?"

They drove out of town and back to Perrysburg, a place where people protected their property value even more ferociously than Northenders protected their own lives. Through the suburban roads, winding, with lots of stop signs, designed to discourage anyone from coming in unless they had a good reason to. Romeo parked in front of their job site next to Justin's Harley Dyna Glide. The McMansion was a flawless replica of what the Old West End homes looked like in 1930 before that place went to shit. They got out, and Justin was already walking their way. He asked, "What's wrong with the car, Wolf?"

"Made some noise and started smelling bad then pff."

"How's the oil?"

Every other guy in his work crew asked Wolf the same battery of diagnostic questions over the next two hours, and they all told him that his make and year are known for having problems with the starter when it gets cold.

When Wolf and Romeo were framing a door out of earshot of the other guys, Wolf asked him, "Hey, uh. You're into guns, right?"

"Yup."

"You got people who want to buy one?"

Romeo kept working without skipping a beat. "Maybe. What do you got?"

Wolf shrugged. "Big ass, shiny pistol."

"Well, send me some pictures when you can and I'll look at it."

"I got it now."

"You have it on you?"

"Yeah."

Romeo stopped. "Alright, let's see it."

Wolf opened his toolbox and fished it out and showed him.

"That's a pretty looking 1911, you got. Funny Elvis sweetheart grip."

"What's that mean?"

"It's like, uh… in World War Two, GIs all had a 1911. That's this gun you got. You can take the grip plate off here, and a lot of guys put on a picture of their sweetheart back home. Their wife or girlfriend. So they call it a sweetheart grip. A lot of the narcos put art on their grips, too. Fuckin dope ones, too. Like, uh… Yo, Jesus!" Romero waved at him.

Jesus nodded and shut down the circular saw he was using to trim 2x4s. "Yeah?"

"What's the name of that Saint the cartels worship?"

"Who you mean? Santa Muerte?"

"Yeah, like Saint Death or something, right?"

"Holy Death. Why? You need a priestess? I know one, if you want."

"Naw, man. Thanks, though."

Jesus fired up the saw again and resumed his work.

Romeo said, "So they got these sweetheart grips, but it's this Saint Muerte, Saint Death. And she's been, like, hidden in Mexican Catholic art for years. You can see her hidden in old paintings. She's like a grim reaper Virgin Mary. It's real weird. I guess when the Spanish came to the New World, they told the natives that their pagan gods were all really Catholic saints. That's how they converted them quickly. So this Saint Death is like an Aztec death god pretending to be a Catholic saint. The cartels worship her like they're still pagans. They leave sacrifices and stuff."

"I get that you're into melting steel beams and Egyptian aliens and stuff, but this is Elvis."

"Yeah, I'm just sayin."

"That's interesting and all, but I'm just trying to sell this thing off to fix my car and make rent."

"Why d'you have this, anyway?"

"D owes me money, but he gave me this fucking thing instead."

"That fucking guy. I remember him from high school, man." He shook his head slowly.

"Yeah, well. He doesn't have a lot of people in his corner, you know?"

"There's a reason for that."

"You ever been friends with someone for so long, like, you don't know how to not be friends? You don't even remember why you were friends in the first place, but... Does that make sense?"

"Nope."

"That's just me, I guess."

"Yeah, right. I know the reason."

"Why?"

He grinned. "Alright. Keep pretending."

"Say what you gotta say?"

"She fine, though. I mean, give some respect."

"Psh, whatever. You gonna help me sell this thing or what?"

"Listen, if that thing is real chrome, that piece is worth a lot. Set it down there." Wolf did and Romeo took out his phone and took some photos. "I'll share these around and hit you up if I get any attention."

"How can I tell if it's real chrome?"

"Hold it up against some real chrome."

"Where am I gonna find real chrome?"

"Shit. I don't know."

Wolf put the gun into his coat and looked around at the progress of the job and took a deep sigh. That's when he saw his boss's Harley. "Hey, they use chrome on those, right?" He pointed at Justin's bike. Romeo nodded.

Wolf walked out of the wood-framed house with plastic sheeting walls, across the perfect lawn, and stood next to the bike. He took out the Elvis gun and held it next to it and had a good look. He smiled.

"Oh my god!" a woman called out. "What are you doing?"

Wolf turned around to see the customer was on the lawn. He saw the fear in her eyes. She was looking at the gun. "Hey, no, wait! It's cool."

Justin rushed over. "What's wrong? What's going on?"

The customer said, "That young man is brandishing a gun! I'm calling the police!"

Justin jumped in, "Whoa, whoa, hold up. Ma'am, that's not necessary. I'll deal with this."

Wolf put the gun away and held up both his hands to show they were empty. "No no no no no. I'm not brandishing! It's cool. I just wanted to check the metal on it."

Justin asked him, "Why the fuck are you playing around with a gun at a job, Wolf?"

"I'm not! I just wanted to check if it's chrome. It's not even my gun, really."

The customer was making a lot of threats and Justin was getting sweaty and frustrated, while she made it impossible for him to deal with his employee.

She said a lot of things. When she reached her final words on the issue, she repeated it a few times to draw that line in the sand. "I don't want him working at this house again!"

Justin tried to calm the woman down, but Wolf already saw what was coming. Justin had been good to Wolf. He gave him this job and a dozen before it. Justin helped him out and gave him work before Wolf even knew the difference between a flathead and a crosshead. Fuck it. This day was already off to such a fucked start. Why even fight it? No need to put Justin in a spot.

Wolf said, "Hey, hey! You know what? That's cool. I don't have to work this one, ma'am. It's not Justin's fault, alright, it's mine. I'm just going to go. I'm sorry for frightening you. That wasn't my intention. Justin's a good dude. It's my bad, okay? I'm leaving right now."

He gathered his stuff and Romeo promised to collect the rest of his tools for him. As he left, Wolf overheard the woman trying to leverage this on Justin for a discount on the job.

Wolf's walk back towards home was a long four hours by foot. He walked thought the dirt and grass on the side of a road where a sidewalk would be, back across a bridge over the highway. Cars whizzed by him. A few honked to warn him or mock him, he wasn't sure. It gave him a lot of time to think about how the fuck he was going to pay his bills without a car, money, and the Perrysburg job.

The sun was just coming down and Wolf could see his breath while he ate a chicken nugget dinner in the parking lot of a fast-food place a couple miles from his apartment. His phone dinged. He looked at it.

Romeo: *fucked up what happened at work man*

Wolf: *its whatever*

Romeo: *i got good news tho. this big dude is interested*

Wolf: *wym big dude?*

Romeo: *lol his name is Big. thats what people call him*

Wolf: *Okay. How I talk to him?*

Romeo: *he works at Galaxy Bowl. he there tonight til it closes*

Wolf: *how will i know who he is?*

Romeo: *darkskinned n tall af. He look somalian but he isnt*

Wolf: *thanks bro. Fr u savin my ass rn*

Just a couple more miles. Wolf finished his meal and started walking again. The sun was low enough it stung his eyes. The air was getting colder and his breath was becoming visible. He walked across the sidewalks that stretched on past forever. Past the payday lending shops with bars on the windows, past the windows of shops that were painted white from the inside, past gas stations and corner stores, walking over trash like they were leaves in autumn.

The sun was gone when he got there. The place had Galaxy Bowl written in big neon out front. It was a busy night, too. The parking lot was full of cars and young people, like a tailgate. He walked through some kids standing in the entryway, passing a bottle, and in through a couple of glass doors. Friday. They did the place up like a nightclub every Friday. The lights were off except for the black lights and lasers like a disco, and movie theater projectors showing a music video on a big screen on the wall over the pins. It was too loud to talk. The place was banging trap with jittery high hats and sub-bass 808s you don't hear so much as feel. The place smelled like schwag ditch-weed, flavacol, and cologne, and it was warm and humid with people. People drinking from pitchers, rolling scuffed and chipped balls down the lanes and cracking pins, talking and yelling.

Wolf walked up to the counter. The guy there nodded.

"Is Big here?"

The guy shook his head and pointed at his own ear.

Wolf half-yelled it the second time. "I said, is Big here?"

The guy pointed to the far end of the alley, over by the arcade games. Wolf walked along the smelly, psychedelic casino carpeting past the lanes. A man grabbed his girl's arm and yelled at her about something. An old man sat at the bar trying to drink his gin and tonic, crowded on all sides by youngsters shouting drink orders at the bartender. A girl was squatting over the lap of a guy on one of those plastic molded stools and grinding him with what she had. A young guy was rolling a joint while his friends looked at it impatiently and busted his balls about his technique. Two girls were being cruel and nasty to a third who said nothing back, and they pointed long, colorful fingernails in her face and talked so fast and loud no one could interrupt. Boys trying to look as cool as possible, slouched in seats, with NyQuil eyes. Girls peacocking and pretending like they don't want to be looked at.

"Wolf!"

He looked around to find who said his name. A girl wearing an all pink sweatsuit in the seating area of a lane, sitting in a plastic bucket seat, shoes off, feet up and in the lap of a guy Wolf didn't recognize. He rubbed her toenail painted feet.

He walked up, "Hey, Brittany."

"I said your name like eight times!"

"Loud as fuck in here."

"Damn, boy. You lookin like a respectful member of society, all shaven and wearing glasses and shit."

"You like it or nah?"

"The more I look at ya, the more I like it. This is Bryce, by the way."

The guy stopped massaging to offer a hand to shake. Wolf nodded.

She said, "You not gonna shake my man's hand?"

"He's had his hands all over your feet."

"What's wrong with my feet?"

"Nothing. I just don't like feet."

"You walk on em, don't you? If you hate em so much, why don't you go to the doctor and get em amputated?"

"I don't like other people's feet."

"Whatever. I got the cleanest feet ever. Bryce. Tell this nigga how clean my feet are."

Bryce said, "She's got very clean feet."

Wolf started doing that slow walk away to send the message he was done. "Okay. Well. Good talking to you."

"You not gonna have a beer with us? Chris is coming by."

"Nah, I gotta meet a guy. Wait. Which Chris?"

She said, "Babcott."

Bryce added, "He introduced us."

Brittany blew Bryce a kiss. He pantomimed catching it in midair and then stuffed the imaginary kiss down the front of his shorts.

"You are so bad!" she pointed and smiled with a lot of gums.

Wolf asked, "Hey, Brit. Uh..." He looked at her new guy and chose his next words carefully. "What's up with you and D?"

She tsked, chin down, eyes up, like she was looking at Wolf over nonexistent reading glasses. "What about him?"

"You seen him lately?"

"Uh uh." She removed her feet from Bryce, turned to face Wolf. "Lemme tell you something, I know he your friend an all, but that nigga is a menace..." She had one finger pointed in the air. Wolf could see he'd accidentally pulled the ripcord on

Brittany's shit-talk motor. Easier to start than to stop.

"So you didn't leave your laptop at his place?"

"Hell naw! I haven't seen that boy in four months. Did he tell you he has my laptop?"

Bryce asked, "Who's D?"

Wolf tried excusing himself again. "Alright. Anyway, I gotta go see this guy…"

Bryce asked her again, more loudly, "Who's D and why is your laptop at his house?"

"He's lyin, baby! D's nobody!"

Wolf walked away from the lovers' quarrel he'd started, and they didn't stop him. He kept on until he found the arcade area, full of blinking, flashing cabinets. *Galaga*, *Ms. Pacman*, a *T2* pinball game, and the Aerosmith shooter, all flickering and making noises like slot machines. When he rounded the corner, he got a sight of a very tall, dark-skinned guy playing air hockey. He looked Somalian. Then Wolf saw the back of Big's air hockey partner. Wolf stopped in his tracks. Big saw Wolf and stopped playing. His air hockey opponent looked over his shoulder to see what Big saw. Neon yellow hair. Hologram glasses projecting rainbow 3D images of cherries like the kind on those casino machines. A bad scar on his cheek from getting stabbed by his older brother when he was eight years old. Pretty Chris.

Wolf saw them. They saw Wolf. No one moved for a moment. No one said anything. The trap music buildup swelled. Chris took a step towards Wolf and Wolf took a step back. They both froze. Then Big took a few strides towards Wolf on long legs. The beat dropped. Wolf turned and ran. The walkway was thick with people. He pushed through a group of girls, past some people sitting down at their table to eat their nachos, and leaped over the two steps into someone's game, and onto the slippery bowling lane. Big and Chris were right behind him. Wolf jumped over lane bunkers like track hurdles and he nearly lost his footing a couple of times. People were watching, laughing, pointing and rolling balls, deliberately trying to hit him. He ran and squeaked his sneakers as the trap music thumped and blared in the neon blue darkness, his eyes focused on the bright red emergency exit sign by the pinsetters on the far side. He heard someone cussing behind him and hecklers laughing as Chris got nailed by a 12-pounder that rolled into his ankle.

Wolf made it to the emergency door. His hands hit the push bar when he felt a large pair of hands push him through and out onto his stomach on the pavement in the alley next to the alley. He rolled around and Big was over him, grabbing him by the shirt. Wolf ate a hard one to the face. He tried blocking with one hand, while he drew the Elvis gun from his waistband with the other. Big's huge hand snatched it and yanked it from him without effort. He punched Wolf again and bounced the head off the pavement. Then he backed off. But only because Chris finally caught up and kicked Wolf in the gut. Wolf was bent in half like a jackknife, and struggling to get his wind back through all the blood in his nose and mouth.

"Thought you could steal from me, nigga? Huh?" He kicked him again. "Punk bitch."

"I didn't..."

"Lying ain't gonna save you. Why'd you run if you didn't steal it, huh?"

"I swear... I didn't... steal it." His bruised insides told him to stop talking.

Big handed Chris the gun. Chris took it and kissed it.

Pretty Chris racked the slide and pointed it at Wolf. "Funny story. Big here gets a message from this guy we do business with sometimes. Tells him he knows a nigga trying to sell a very pretty gun. Big say, a'ight, I'm interested. Our man sends a picture. Big takes one look at it and think, ain't no fucking way that someone else is selling the same gun Pretty Chris got. So he calls me and tells me. I look inside my bedside drawer, and you know what? My Elvis gun ain't there no more. I din't even realize it was missin. So my man Big, he offers to buy it up just so we can see who it is took it."

Wolf said, "I thought D bought it off you."

"What's that?"

Wolf cursed himself. He accidentally said D's name. "I said, I got it from someone who said they got it from you. But I didn't know they'd stole it."

"Which D?"

"What?"

"Who. Is. D?"

"I said P."

"No, you didn't. You said D."

"Naw, I got it from a guy named P."

"Nigga, ain't no one named urine. That's stupid. You said D. D who?"

Big said, "I think he means Tyler Lemma." Big has a bad lisp. "I used to know that guy."

"Tyler Lemma. Why they call him D? They should call him T."

Big shrugged.

Chris asked Wolf, "Why they call him D?"

"D Lemma. Dilemma," Wolf leaned onto his elbow and spit out some blood onto the blacktop.

"That's stupid," said Chris.

Big said, "I kinda like it."

Wolf said, "Naw, Chris is right. It's stupid. He came up with that in 6th grade and wouldn't answer anyone who called him Tyler."

"Nobody asked you," said Big.

"So D Lemma stole my gun?"

"I didn't say that."

"Uh, yes, you fuckin' did."

"Naw, I said I got it from D. I don't know anything about stealin."

Chris asked, "Where does D live?"

Wolf kept his mouth shut.

"I'm gonna find out, one way or the other."

Wolf said, "But not cus I told you."

Chris said, "D's getting his, no matter what. You wanna be a loyal nigga and get it, too?"

Big interrupted, "I know where he live."

Chris, "Cool."

"But how bout you do the string thing?"

"Why do the string thing? You know where he live, right?"

"Yeah, but I want him to say it." Big pointed at Wolf. "I wanna hear him say the address. Let's see how loyal he is."

Chris got a Cheshire cat smile on his face. "Yeah. Yeah. We ain't done that one in a minute."

"Where at?"

Chris looked around. He pointed at the fried fish place next door. Big helped Wolf up and the two guys dragged him to the back lot of the restaurant, wooden fencing all around it, with a foul-smelling dumpster, some milk crates stacked, and a standing plastic ashtray.

"Stand over there. Against the wall."

Wolf did as he was told, back to the wall of the building, right next to the door. Big took out a knife and kept his eyes on Wolf.

Chris said, "Take your boots off."

Wolf did.

"Take the laces out and give em to me."

Wolf unlaced his shoes and tossed the laces to Chris.

Big pressed Wolf against the wall and made sure he could feel the tip of the blade on his belly. Chris tied the laces together into one long one. He made a slipknot with the shoestring and looped it around the gun's trigger. Then he jammed the gun into the D-handle of the restaurant's back door, so the gun was pointing right at Wolf, ran the string around the handle and tied the string around Wolf's neck. Tight enough so it was uncomfortable, but he could breathe just fine.

Chris set a crate down against the wall right by Wolf. Big forced him to sit on it, back to the wall, and pressed his head against the wall so Wolf was looking straight at the gun. Chris made sure the string was tight.

The physics of it were plain to see. If someone came out that back door for any reason, the door opening would push the gun, pulling the string, pulling the trigger, and putting 230 grains of full-metal jacketed lead into Wolf's face.

"Next thing you say is the address or Big here guts you like the fishes they fryin in there. Smells good, too, damn."

"They're not that good," said Wolf.

Chris took a plastic crate and sat on it. "No tellin' when someone's gonna come out of that door, my man. It's like there's a bomb tickin, but no one knows how much time left."

Big's smile was a couple of inches from Wolf's cheek.

Chris went on, "Sometimes it's a few seconds. Sometimes it's a few minutes. One time, Big here pinned a nigga for an hour and a half. Member that?"

Big nodded.

"We'll be here when you ready to talk."

Wolf could hear the noise through the door. People cleaning pans, pulling things out of freezers, cussing at each other, normal restaurant noises. At some point, someone was going to want to smoke a cigarette or a joint. Someone would take some trash out. Someone would go on break and go out the back for some air. There was no getting past Big. Wolf could see Chris was loving the anticipation.

"I don't even know his address."

"You know where he live, though."

A voice inside the kitchen yelled out, "¡A la mierda, me voy de descanso! Necesito un cigarrillo, "muffled by the door and the clatter inside.

Wolf had worked in a kitchen before. He understood what cigarrillo meant. He yelled out, "I'll show you! Lemme go!"

Big didn't. Wolf stared at the gun, and the gun stared back at him. Chris stood up and walked up to the door like he wasn't in a hurry before he took the Elvis gun off the door handle. A dishwasher walked out a second later. He froze in the doorway. He looked at the three of them standing there: the face-scarred man with the holographic glasses and a pistol, the tall not-Somalian with a knife, and a dude who looked like he'd just had his ass kicked because he had. The guy went back inside without saying a word.

They took the string off him and marched him, stocking-footed, through the parking lot to the car. Big drove. They put Wolf into the back seat and they gave him back his boots and laces. Chris sat shotgun with the Elvis gun in his lap.

Chris said, "Gimme your phone."

Wolf gave it to him.

"Code."

"I'm not—"

Chris showed him the gun again, just to remind him.

Wolf said, "0816."

Chris found D's number in the contacts list and texted.

Wolf: *where you at?*

D: *home rn playin Madden*

Wolf: *cool imma be by*

D: *fsho*

D: *you sell that gun ok?*

Chris said, "I guess you didn't lie bout that."

Big fired up the engine.

"Where he live?" asked Chris.

Big answered for Wolf "Palmetta, between Chase and Windsor."

"How the fuck you know that?" asked Chris.

"I used to fuck his sister."

"What?" came out of Wolf's mouth without thinking.

Big looked back at Wolf, "What?"

"Which one? There's more than one. What'd she look like?"

"Pretty. I don't fucking know. She had an accent."

"All D's sisters got accents. His dad's Haitian and had another family in Haiti before they came over here."

"Why you so fucking interested in which sister I was fuckin?"

Wolf stopped talking. Big drove them out of the parking lot of

Galaxy Bowl and past a couple of exits on the highway. No one said anything. They got on to Claudette's street and Big pulled off in front of the house and put the car in park. At night, you couldn't see the detritus and desperation so much. It looked peaceful.

"This it?" asked Chris, pointing at the gray market restaurant.

Big looked around. Squinting, bending at the waist to check at all the houses. "It's one of these."

"Which one?" asked Chris.

"Shit. I don't remember. It's definitely one of these, though."

Chris asked Wolf, "Which one?"

Wolf didn't say anything.

Chris grabbed the rearview mirror and adjusted it so he could see Wolf. "Yo, I asked you something. It's you or it's him. Listen… wait. What's your name?"

"Wolf."

"Wolf? What kind of name is that?"

"My mom's a hippie."

"I've been thinking about it on the drive. I think I know what happened. It was at the party we had last weekend. I was pretty fucked up that night, so was Big…"

"Hell yeah, I was," said the driver.

"I was showing it around. I don't remember everyone who came by. You? I never seen your ass before. So I think you bein honest. I think your friend, D, I bet he was there at that party. I bet he ripped me off and sold it to you."

"I didn't buy it. He owed me money, but he gave me the Elvis gun instead."

Big laughed.

Chris said, "See? See? That's my point. He robbed me to pay you, and now look at the situation he brought on you. He ain't your friend. Look at you. Look where you are right now. You already need some money, right? And now you need money and you sittin in Pretty Chris's car. D is a fucking problem for you. You know that. This guy ain't your friend. You his friend, but he ain't your friend. I know I'm right cus you ain't even trying to argue. You won't say one fucking word defendin him. Naw, cus you know I'm right. I'm right, right? Tell me I'm not right."

Wolf sighed, "You right."

"Well alright. Lemme go solve this motherfuckin D Lemma for the both of us. Now, point at the house he live at. This it right here?" He pointed at Claudette's place.

Wolf took a long, deep breath.

Wolf thought about the time D stuck up for him in 8th grade. Some bully was giving Wolf a hard time. D wasn't having it, though. He took a dump into some plastic wrap in the bathroom and when the class vacated for assembly, he snuck back in and smeared it on the underside of the kid's chair. When class started again, the whole room smelled like shit and it was coming from the bully's direction, like he'd shit himself. Kids were mean about it cus that's how kids are. That bully beat the fuck out of Wolf for that, too, thinking he'd done it. It was funny, though. Might've been worth it, too. Rumor was the custodian quit after they found where the smell was coming from.

Wolf said, "No." He pointed to the house across the street from Claudette's. "It's that one." The house with the snitch neighbor who'd been shouting during lunch.

"Well, alright then. Big, you keep the car hot. Wolf's gonna gimme an introduction to D." Chris tied a black bandana over his face and pulled his hood over his head.

Wolf bent over to get his boots back on and started threading the lace.

The car filled with blinding light from all directions like an alien abduction. Voices surrounding them shouted, "Hands up! Don't move! Do not move!"

Wolf stayed slunk down in the backseat, so he almost laid on the floor. They continued their commands. "Hands where I can see them!"

Wolf peeked between the driver and passenger seat and could see Chris's hand on the Elvis gun, his trigger finger nervously tapping the side of the frame.

"No no no no no no! Don't do that Chris! Do not do that!"

Chris did that.

He pulled and raised up. "Gun! Gun! Gun!" the voices shouted. The sound of gunfire cracked in all directions, but not from inside the car. The glass broke and spider-webbed. Wolf felt the car accelerating and heard tires squeal and the thud of something it hit. A second later, the gunshots stopped, and Wolf only heard the yelling of the police as they faded behind them and the scraping of something being dragged under the front bumper. Finally, a pair of big bumps under the passenger side front, then rear, as the cop being dragged became unstuck, and the car rolled over her. Big was cussing, but Chris didn't say anything. Wolf just stayed down, fixated by the bullet holes that went all the way through Chris's seat. Wolf could hear some sirens ringing out nearby. He felt another bump and a crash and then he could feel that they weren't driving on the road anymore, they were on grass, then another thump back onto the road, a turn, a squeal, and then it got weird. They hit something. Or something hit them. The car spun, and a door ripped open. Wolf was launched out of the car. He landed about ten feet away.

Wolf lost himself for a moment. He didn't know how long.

Maybe a second. Maybe a minute. He thought he might throw up. He looked up, and he was lying next to a cheap Swedish office chair, a table lamp, clothes, a television, a vacuum cleaner, and a bunch of cardboard boxes. An entire home of stuff all around him in the street. He leaned up on his elbows. Nothing hurt just yet, but it would. He saw the Uhaul truck that Big had hit. The back half was nearly torn off and all the stuff was scattered in the street. Wolf watched Big get out of the car. He limped—more like hopped—off into someone's yard and disappeared. Chris was still in the passenger's seat. Wolf stood up and looked around. The sirens were close, but he didn't see the lights yet. He looked behind them and Big must've taken a shortcut and driven through some yards. He walked over to check on Chris. Airbags had deployed. Chris was a mess. His shirt was red and wet. His glasses weren't on his face and Wolf could see in his eyes he was scared. He was still holding the gun in his lap, groggy and losing blood pressure. Wolf reached out and gently disarmed him, and put the gun back into his waistband.

Wolf walked away and heard Chris weakly say, "Naw. That's mine."

Wolf walked up to the Uhaul and opened the passenger door to check on the driver. She was slumped forward. Wolf climbed in and said, "Hey, lady? You alright? Hey!" She didn't respond. He checked her pulse, and she was still ticking. Wolf didn't even notice the reds and blues flashing until a cop approached the door. Wolf froze, but the cop didn't tell him to. Instead, he asked, "Are you all right?"

"I'm okay. I think. But she's hurt."

"Okay, stay inside your vehicle, sir. An ambulance is on its way." The cop called back to other officers to render aid to the driver of the Uhaul.

Police checked her vitals, and it was minutes later the EMTs arrived and took her out on a stretcher and finally the police told Wolf to get out of the truck. Instead of arresting him, they asked him what his relationship to the driver was and asked Wolf to recount the events leading up to the collision.

He started making some shit up. "She's a friend of mine. I was helping her move." The officer took scrupulous notes and Wolf watched over his shoulder. Half the damn force was at the scene. The EMTs took the woman in the Uhaul first, then Chris, force-feeding him oxygen with a mask over his nose and mouth.

Over the officer's radio, Wolf heard the fuzzy voice of an officer say, "Suspect spotted, on foot at Banfield... uh... 300 block."

Gunshots cracked and echoed in the distance somewhere.

The radio came on again, "Shots fired! Officer down! Officer down!"

The officer talking to Wolf was already heading back towards his car while he quickly recommended that Wolf go to the ER just to play it safe. The cop also said that the truck would be towed but that Wolf should make arrangements to collect as much of his friend's stuff as possible. He nodded along. The cop jumped back into a car with his partner and took off to give assistance to officers with Big.

Wolf looked around the debris field that was once some poor woman's life. A couple of neighbors were outside now, peeking at the carnage.

Wolf headed back towards D's. A block up, he saw the lawn Big had driven through. An ambulance was flashing out front. A man and woman were on their knees crying and yelling at a small, crushed sleeping tent while a couple of paramedics were rushing onto the lawn through the knocked-down fence. Wolf looked away as quickly as he could. "Don't look at that. Don't think about that." He walked a quarter mile on the sidewalk and some police were still there outside Claudette's. Neighbors were on their porches and peeking through their windows and he saw the snitch looking angry as ever. He walked past all of it and knocked on his friend's door.

"Ti-kem! What're you doing here?"

"Hey, marabou. Is D here?"

"Lord! What happened to you?" She reached for the cut on his head and it stung him when she touched it. She pulled him in and made him lie on the couch, and she left him alone. The other two sisters appeared and asked Wolf if he was involved with what happened outside. Claudette came back with a first aid kit and some water and a cloth and she shooed her sisters away, back upstairs. She turned on a lamp to get a better look at Wolf's injuries and insisted he lie back. She knelt on the floor beside him and started working cuts and bruises, dabbing him with the cloth, and stinging him with alcohol swabs.

"I'm sorry about this morning," said Wolf.

"You're a good man. I know you didn't do no wrong."

"No, I know. It was that woman across the street who called the cops about the restaurant."

"Restaurant? What you mean?"

"The cops busted up lunch. What do you mean?"

"Ha! Uh, no ti-chou, they didn't care about that. They came asking about you. The restaurant is just fine."

"What? They came here asking for me? By name?"

"Yeah, boy. What'd you think? They sent six police just for little me?"

Wolf's head was swimming. He wasn't sure if it was the car crash or the information. "Why would they come for me?"

"I thought you would know."

"Where's D?"

"He just left about a half hour ago. You know anything about that out there?" The flashing reds and blues were just barely visible through the gaps in the blinds.

Wolf stared at the ceiling for a moment. "Hey, can I ask you something stupid?"

"Of course."

"When D had his car towed, was he arrested?"

"Yeah."

"Just for his tags?"

"No. Course not. He didn't tell you?"

"Tell me what?"

"He was driving drunk, and he had bags full of pills in his trunk. Yellow jackets, valium. Some bottles of lean..."

"Oh my God." Wolf's eyes stared off into his own imagination.

"Yeah, he lied to me about it at first, but I got it outta him eventually."

"Fuck. Fuck!" He sat up.

"What is it?"

He picked up a pillow from the couch, pressed his face into it and released a whole day's worth of muffled screams into it. The car. The gun. The job. Chris and Big. He screamed at all of it. He kept it on his face for a minute, catching his breath. Slowly, controlled through the pillow. The caveman was gone, and the thinking man could do what he had to do. He took the pillow off his face. Some of his blood was on it.

"Sorry."

Claudette said, "That's okay. What you need? What can I do?"

"I need..." Wolf paused and thought on it. "I need a pencil, some invisible tape, and a rubber cooking glove."

The next morning, D woke up to the sound of angry feet on the steps down to his room. He sat up and saw the detectives were already there.

"What? What's up?" asked D, his eyes still mostly closed. One of them flipped on the main light switch. He covered his eyes with his forearm. "What the fuck, man?"

"Open the safe."

"What?" D sat up.

"Open the safe."

"Nothing's in the safe."

"We had a deal, D. You said you got a guy who moves a lot of firepower in his neighborhood. But you didn't make good on your end. You didn't get Wolf on the laptop cam or mic accepting the gun."

"He closed it! What was I supposed to do about that?"

"Where is the laptop, by the way?"

"I don't know. It was right there last time I saw it."

"That's police property."

D shrugged.

"You didn't get a recording of him taking the gun. You sold or lost a police laptop. And there wasn't anyone with the blue grocery bag like you said."

"I already explained that! He must've hid it or something."

"He wasn't there, D!"

"Yes, he was! He shaved his beard and was wearing glasses! I told you that!"

"And then last night, you called us to say that he was coming by. But he didn't come by. Pretty Chris and Big Chalmers came by and Wolf wasn't with them. Do you understand the magnitude of what you did? Hm? Big ran over and killed an officer, D. Her husband's on the force, too. He might as well be gone, too. Wouldn't be surprised if he eats a gun after what happened. Then Big shot and wounded another officer while he was running away. We lost three cops last night. I got a special ed teacher in fucking critical condition after getting t-boned in a U-Haul. And worst of all, D, worst of fucking all? Big took a ride over an 8-year-old boy who was having a little backyard camp-out in his tent. Doctors can't say yet if that kid's gonna make it. A needle is too good for that piece of shit Big. And you set that all up for us, D. I'm putting all that shit squarely on you."

The partner nodded.

"Yo, that's Big's thing, man! That guy's a fucking psycho. Everyone knows that! I got a text from Wolf saying he was coming over, okay? I showed you! He sent me the text!"

"We got bupkis on this supposed gun-runner Wolf. My partner thinks you are full of shit, and frankly, I'm coming around to his way of thinking."

"I don't know about any of that, man! I did my part, like I said! I got you a gun dealer, okay? Just like we said, you'd drop the possession-with-intent. That's on y'all."

"Our warrant is still valid, D. So open the safe or we'll get a torch and cut it open."

"Fine! Goddamn. Nothin in there, though."

He rolled over and pressed his thumb on the lock. It clicked. He was about to open it when the quiet cop pushed him back away from the safe and the chatty one opened the door. He put on some blue gloves, reached in, and removed the Elvis gun.

D pointed, "Hey, no, that's not. I didn't."

The police gave the same look a parent gives to a child when they're lying with the hand in the cookie jar. D knew it well.

D kept trying, "I swear to god, Wolf took the gun! He did!"

One cop started reading D his rights, the other said, "How does your friend get into a bio-ID'd safe then, huh, genius?"

"I don't know! There's no way."

The cop standing him up said, "I told you."

"D, you've been jerking us around, playing games. You could've just done the right thing, but you're too damn loyal for your own good."

It was early June, and the trees were green, and the birds were chirping again. Some life poked out of the places where there wasn't a cement sheet. Wolf parked his car at the job in Ottawa Hills. He opened the door from the inside handle and carried out a half cardboard box full of goat meat empanadas individually wrapped in wax paper. He walked up to the hungry contractors, who tossed cash into the box and took the food.

Jesus asked, "These are so damn good. You ever gonna tell me where you get these?"

"Never."

The men sat down where they could and enjoyed their lunch.

Wolf's phone rang. Unknown number. He was about to hang up, but something in his gut told him to answer.

"Hello?"

A recording of a woman's voice came on and said, "This is a call from the Lucas County Department of Corrections with a telephone call from…" D's voice came on and said, "D." The recorded woman continued, "If you would like to accept this call, press 1. If you would not, press 2. If you would like to deny all future calls from this inmate, press 3."

Wolf took the phone off his ear and his pointer finger hovered over the screen for a moment. Then the woman's voice started repeating the message and Wolf hit 1. The woman said, "All calls are recorded."

Wolf stood up and walked away from where the other men were eating.

"Hello?" asked D.

"Hey."

"Hey, man. How ya been?"

"What do you want?"

"I'm good. I'm good."

"I didn't ask if you good. I asked what you want."

"Right. So, um. Funny thing happened today. They got rules for the TV on C-Block. Like, not official rules, but the prisoners all know the rules, right? So between 7 and 9 in the morning, the TV plays the news. From 10 to 1, the Latinos got the TV. From 1 to 4, the brothers choose the channel. And from 4 to 7, the whites choose the channel. They got a few special exceptions for game days, but mostly that's how it works. I was sitting with the Latinos and—"

"You don't speak Spanish."

"Yeah, but it's cool if I sit with them. I just can't fuck with the channel."

"Arright."

"So anyway, I'd watch their shows with them and they were nice enough to put on subtitles for me. Mostly they watch these goofy fucking drama shows. I don't know. They like them. But one channel is all American shows but dubbed in Spanish. And I saw that show we used to watch, that one with the ex-CIA-guy. You remember the one. It was like A-Team plus MacGyver. You remember? We used to smoke bowls and watch that all the time."

"Yeah. Maybe. We watched a lot of shows."

"Anyway, I hang with some of these guys sometimes and I was telling them they should try that show. I was saying how good it was, how you and me watched it. And they were like, okay, and they put it on. So in this episode we were watching, the ex-CIA-guy was helping out this hot mom. Her husband owed the mafia some money, but he died, so they wanted her to pay up, but she didn't even know her husband was in the mafia, so—"

"I don't care about the fucking TV show, man."

"Right. Basically, what happens is he cracks a thumbprint safe by scraping some pencil lead on the thumb reader and then he pulls the prints with tape, just like police do. Then he gets the prints onto a rubber glove and uses that to open the bio-ID safe."

"Mm."

"You remember that episode, right?"

"We smoked a lot of weed when we watched that. Hard to remember."

"Yeah. I know. I know you remembered."

"That it? You called to tell me about watching some stupid show with Mexicans?"

"I know you know, Wolf. I know that's how you got the gun back into the safe."

"I don't know what you're talking about, D."

"No, man, listen. It's cool. I'm not mad."

Wolf raised his voice. "You not mad? You? Motherfucker, you think you got any fucking right to even say that to me?"

"No, no, I get it. I get it! You right! You right! You got every right to hate me. You do. I been thinking about stuff. Hey, do you know why they call it a penitentiary?"

"No, man." Wolf relaxed and sighed. "Why?"

"Cus, you're supposed to be, like, penitent. You're supposed to just sit around and think about the bad shit you did. Think about your sins and repent."

"I'm not sure about all that."

"I'm for real. I just learned that."

"Naw, I mean the repentance part. It's a penitentiary, not a… what would you call it… a repentiary."

"Yeah. I got you. That's funny. Repentiary. I miss this, man. I miss just talking like this. I do."

"Listen, I gotta go."

"C'mon. We got like, 4 more minutes left on this call, man, come on. You my only friend."

"Friend? Wow."

"Yeah!"

"Nigga, you tried to frame me and put me in prison."

"Yeah. I'm sorry about that. To be honest, I'd rather be in here with you than be free out there and not be able to hang out with you and smoke weed and play Madden and shit. Seriously, I miss you, bro."

Wolf didn't say anything.

"Cmon. I know you miss me, too, man. You know I'm sorry. I don't even gotta say it. You know I am. That's what I was trying to say earlier. I been doing the penitence thing."

Wolf didn't say anything.

"Hey, uh, Claudette said things are going good for you, that you got like a promotion or something?"

"Justin took on too many jobs, so he put me in charge of one.

Couldn't have me on the Perrysburg job anymore, but he got me running these guys at Ottawa Hills."

"That's great, man. That's so great. You should be proud. I never had that kind of... what's the word? Discipline?"

"No. You didn't."

"It's for the best. I feel like maybe I held you back. I was always dragging you back into shit with me. And now that I'm not there, it's like shit's just working for you."

"Yeah, well. Not a lot of work since all that bank shit, but... Justin's got a good reputation. He can find jobs, somehow. Work's okay."

"You get paid extra doing that? Like a real promotion?"

"Yeah. Of course."

"That's great, man. That's great. Yeah, that bank shit's fucked up. Been hurtin Claudette. She said you still come by a lot and it means a lot to her. Sometimes she'd put something into my commissary to help, but it's like I gotta buy all my own shit. I gotta buy my own toothpaste, my own cream, my own hot sauce, fucking everything."

"You asking me for some money?"

"What? No, nigga! No! I'm just glad that things are working out for you. That's it."

"Sounds like you're asking for money."

"No! I wouldn't. I'm just telling you about how it is in here. You know? I don't have anyone to talk to. Just, like, they don't give me everything I need to live. Glad it's me in here and not you. That's all I'm saying."

"Yeah, well. Me too.

D laughed. "Hey, did you take the cops' computer and sell it?"

Wolf smiled. "I don't know what you're talking about."

"Yeah." D chuckled a little. "Yeah. That's what I thought. I bet Romeo wiped it for ya, huh? Well. I'm glad you made rent."

The others were almost done with their lunches already. "Alright. Well. I gotta go."

"Oh. Okay. Cool. Cool. Can I call you again sometime?"

"I don't know."

"That's fine. I'll just call and you can take it or not. No pressure. Whatever you want to do."

"Alright. Later."

"Bye."

Grilled Bbq Pork

I got this recipe from a human trafficker in Myanmar named Batuhan. After my ransom was paid, he and I patched things up and have become really good friends to this day. He says this dish is very popular with the Australian syndicate.

Time: 15 minutes to prep in the kitchen. Overnight to marinade. 5 minutes prep the next day and then just 20 minutes on the grill.

Ingredients

- 2 - 2 ½ lbs of pork belly
- 1 tsp of minced garlic
- ½ C soy sauce
- ¼ C calamansi juice, or you can sub with lime or mandarin orange
- ¼ C peanut butter
- Half a banana
- A can of citrus soda, like 7-Up or Sprite or something like that
- ½ C brown sugar
- Salt and pepper as you like it

Gear

- A grill
- Skewers
- A brush
- A blender

Prepping

1. Cut that swine tummy into strips
2. Take all that other stuff that isn't pig and throw it in a blender and fire that badboy until it's all good and liquidy
3. Put half the liquid into a container and add the pig.

Let that marinate overnight. Save the rest in another container

Grilling

1. If you're using bamboo skewers, you gotta let those soak in water for 20 minutes before you start stabbing your meat
2. Stab the meat with skewers, fold - stab - reverse fold - stab - repeat. Like you are sewing meat with a stick
3. Get that grill going at a medium heat. I don't know the exact temperature. This is cooking, not chemistry
4. Cook for about 10 mins on each side. Keep brushing on that reserve marinade every minute or so. We want it to evaporate and then you apply another layer. This is gonna be like a delicious, shiny lacquer
5. It's perfect when you get those little black, crispy edges

Serve with

- A side of rice
- Some grilled veggies
- A six-pack of Singha
- The music of *The Reverend Horton Heat*

Variations

You could probably sub the citrus soda for Dr. Pepper or ginger ale. I haven't tried it, but it might be good.

CHAPTER 2: KU'UIPO

Honolulu, HI

11/3/1979

9:44:04

The thick tropical breeze carried the smell of used diapers and rotting chicken carcasses. The nights were too hot to leave the windows closed, but the trash smelled too foul to leave them open. The sun was on the other side of the world and the good taxpayers of Hawaii were asleep while Donny climbed down the fire escape by his bedroom window and into the alley. He looked up to see if the lights were on in his parents' window and they weren't. He unlocked the door of his dad's '65 Ford pickup with the truck bed extended and the walls raised with spare wood. He put the car into neutral and started pushing it out of the alley and when it was just almost in the street, he looked back and saw his parents' window was still dark. He climbed into the truck and started the engine.

He drove through Chinatown and the streets were wet and shining black under the street lamps, just like the garbage bags that were stacked everywhere they would fit. The heaps were spilling off the sidewalks and curbs and into the edges of the streets, blocking the drains, so the water in the street was a half in deep. The sidewalks were half blocked by them, leaking things that were solid two weeks ago. In the alleys, the bags were stacked chest high, garbage cans and dumpster had already overflowed. Critters came in from the wild to look for an easy meal, mostly the nuclear-proof roaches and rats, who kept to the dark when the sun was up but could be heard skittering through the streets when it wasn't.

Donny found his first spot, and pulled into the alley by Ming's. He climbed out of the cab, checked to see that there were no cops, then knocked on the alley door. A man in a filthy butcher's apron opened it up and smiled at him and said, "晚上好," and held up three fingers.

Donny said, "九."

The butcher nodded and walked back inside the kitchen. Donny leaned against the truck and lit a cigarette. He heard a sneeze. Donny looked around into the bed and saw an eleven-year-old boy hiding.

"Hi, Donny."

"Out."

"Aw come on!"

"I said out!"

Jim climbed out slowly, making a show of it like it was so difficult that he barely had the strength.

"Mom and Dad are gonna…"

Jim interrupted, "You snuck out, too!"

"I'm nineteen. It's not sneaking out when I do it."

"Yeah, well… it is when you take Dad's car without asking."

"Why are you in the back of the truck?"

The butcher came out, smiling, and nodded to the boys and tossed a couple trash bags into the back, and went back inside.

"I wanted to see where you were going."

"Well, now you know. So go home."

"Come on! I can help!"

"Do you even know what I'm doing?"

"Umm."

"How are you gonna help?"

"You'll think of something!"

The butcher came out with one last bag and threw it into the truck. He reached into his apron and counted out nine dollars, gave it to Donny and said, "多謝."

"唔使客氣," and the butcher went back inside.

Jim asked, "Whoa, how much was that?"

"Alright, Jim. Shut up and listen. You can tag along. You just need to do what I say."

Jim nodded. They covered the trash with a drop cloth and tied it down before they left. Jim was quick to reach for the radio controls and he tuned the station to something playing disco.

The two brothers rode together to all the places Donny did business with. A fish market, a free clinic, a hotel, and two other restaurants. They all paid $3 a bag and tossed what they had into the truck.

"We gotta empty the truck already. If customers keep telling others about me, I'm gonna need to make several stops a night."

Donny drove the truck out to the marina, where the wind and water slapped the bows of the ships. He parked right next to their father's tour boat. Big, and flat, with bench seating and a canopy roof. The boys got out and Donny double-checked to see no one was around. He started removing the trash from the truck and tossing it onto the boat.

Donny said, "You can be lookout or you can help me move the trash."

Jim objected. "Hey! What're you doing?"

"You wanted to tag along. This is tagging along. Shut up and help."

The two emptied the truck in a couple minutes and the tour boat was nearly full of black bags. Donny climbed aboard and started the engine. Jim began unwinding the lines from the dock and tossed them into the boat, pushing it from the dock just before jumping on board. Donny took it out slowly, engine low and as quiet as possible, and when they had enough distance, he kicked on the engines a bit and out into the black, open sea.

The ocean winds didn't help to carry the smell away or the flies. The ride was choppy so far out. The boat had a shallow keel designed for slow sight-seeing along the coastline. The boys had to hold on tight not to get bounced right out.

Donny looked behind and could barely see the twinkling of the city. He killed the motor. He listened to the darkness. Just wind, small splashes on the hull, and fly buzzes. He took some old twine and tied it to the knot on a trash bag, and another, and another, like a daisy chain of trash. After all the bags were tied, he finished by tying it off to a cinder block.

"Get out of the way, Jim. Go stand over there." Jim did as his big brother asked.

Donny heaved the cinderblock over the side and it splashed and pulled down the whole chain of trash with it, the bags leaping off the side, one at a time, making a series of splash noises, and in a few seconds, the boat was empty.

"Dang. So you've been sneaking off trash out here like this?"

"It's easy money until the Public Workers Union stops striking."

"Man. I kinda hope they never do."

"Just cus you don't have to go to school. You're lucky the school janitors are in the same union."

"How much have you made so far?"

"Don't worry about that."

"Hey, what's that?" Jim pointed off the port bow away from the island.

Donny looked, but didn't see anything. "What?" Then he saw a light flash three times. "I don't know."

Jim walked to the bow and turned on the spotlight and flashed it back.

"What are you doing?" Donny pulled Jim off of the light by his arm and shut it off. "You don't know who that is! That could be coastguard! This isn't exactly legal, you know."

"Maybe they need help."

"Did they flash SOS?"

"No."

"Then they don't need help."

They could hear another boat's engine getting closer. Then lights came on. Red and blue flickers, and a big spotlight filled up the boat and the boys raised their arms to shield their eyes from the powerful glare. The boat pulled up alongside. The two policemen lashed the boats together and one of them invited himself aboard.

Donny started improvising an excuse to the thick-framed cop on his parent's boat. "Hello, officers. Listen, we were just..."

"You're new."

"Um. This is my first time."

The cop who stayed aboard the police boat said, "You expect us to do it?"

"Um. No?"

"Let's go," said the big cop.

The boys complied and hopped onto the police boat. The other cop led the boys through the open door and down the stairs into the cabin. When they were down there, he handed them two duffle bags each, which they took, and the cop said, "That's it."

The boys stood there with the heavy bags for a moment, not knowing what to say or do. The cop finally said, "I said that's all. Get off my boat."

They walked back up the stairs. Jim really struggled with the weight. They hopped off and back onto their dad's boat. One cop made a remark about the smell while he untied them and jumped back onto the police boat. The boat cops killed their lights and drove off back the way they came, vanishing into the dark.

When the boys couldn't hear the police boat engine, Jim asked, "What was that about?"

"I don't know."

"I thought we were in big trouble."

Donny crouched and unzipped one of the duffle bags. Several butcher paper bricks with something written on them in Pashto. He unwrapped it to find it was full of tan powder sealed in plastic wrap. "Oh fuck. We are in big trouble."

When they got back to the dock, they hosed down the boat and the truck. On the drive home, Jim kept asking what was in the bag but Donny wouldn't say. They parked in the alley. Donny hid the duffel bags underneath some other trash in the alley and the boys climbed up the fire escape, through the window, and into the house and went to bed.

The next day, Donny woke up late to the sound of a game show host saying, "The game is fast! It's never slow! So deal out the cards!" Mom and Dad had already left for work and Jim was in the living room watching Card Sharks and eating colorful cereal. Donny slipped out and went downstairs through the apartment's front exit between the hardware store and laundromat. He walked around into the alley. Dad's truck was gone. Donny used a key to open a fence into a small yard with a storage unit shared by the tenants. He found his dad's hand truck, locked up behind him and loaded up the duffle bags, and pushed his cargo towards Hotel Street.

He wheeled the four bags through the streets crowded with pedestrians and the trash that began cooking again in the late morning sun. The trashmen, the janitors, and cafeteria ladies were all in the same union, so when one didn't go to work, none of them went to work. The government said the schools were unsanitary, and the kids were out on an early Christmas vacation. It was Thursday, but the children were out of school, walking around, playing at the beach, but not in Chinatown. There, parents put their kids to work.

Donny walked into the market, a blocked off section of road with wooden traffic barriers, where people sold their food upwind of the smell. Donny side-stepped past the housewives and their children shopping for ube, taro, and longan. He walked past the tourists from Wisconsin and Japan who were lost. He walked past the vendors and fishermen and farmers, arguing over the price per pound. He walked past the rows of fresh fish with surprised faces, past grills cooking spam, past traditional herbal remedies for kidney stones and infertility.

He made it to Hotel Street, named after the countless two-story hotels that used to be full of prostitutes who serviced the Navy during WWII. There was still some of that, and a couple of dirty movie theaters and bookstores, too. This was a place his mom forbade him from ever going, but in the light of day, it didn't look so sleazy.

He pushed the cart to a pool hall called The Big E. The glass windows were painted black except for the name and the silhouette of a Yorktown-class aircraft carrier. He pulled his cart backwards up the two steps and went inside. It was smokey and softly lit, rows of pool tables two wide and three deep, but only a couple games were going. He walked past the bartender and down a hall, past the bathrooms and into the second half of the place, where the sailors and the tourists never went. He walked into a room full of cigarette smoke and clacking porcelain tiles so loud, they could hardly hear the music of Jenny Tseng singing 再見再見有情人 on a record player. Eight small tables, four seats at each, most of them filled with men drinking bottles of Blue Girl. The mahjong room had its own small bar, attached to the same kitchen as the pool room. The pair of ceiling fans did little to ventilate the room, and the beer glasses and men's foreheads were sweating.

"Excuse me."

The bartender looked up from the beer he was pouring. He saw Donny but didn't say anything.

"I'm, uh, looking for Rooster."

The bartender walked away with a beer, gave it to a man dressed in a velour v-neck shirt, and said something to him. The player looked back at Donny and waved him over, palm down. Donny and his bags walked up.

"Are you Rooster?"

"你想要乜嘢?"

"I think there was a bit of a misunderstanding and I was accidentally given something that I think belongs to you."

"咩話?"

"I'd rather not say, if that's alright."

He stood up, suddenly furious. He grabbed Donny's face, squeezing it in his hand so Donny's mouth puckered, and asked in English, "What are you doing here, wasting my time for?"

"坐低," said another man at the table. The angry man sat. Then, in English, he said to Donny, "Rooster is upstairs." He motioned to the bartender with his chin. "Show him."

The bartender escorted Donny to the freight elevator, went inside with him, and took it up to the second floor. As soon as the door opened, two men grabbed him, pulled him out, and took the bags from him. One of them pushed Donny against a wall, while the other opened up the bags and looked at what was inside. They patted him down, lifted his shirt, and examined the bags, and ran a metal detector wand over it. When they were satisfied, they let Donny go and made him walk in front of them down the hall, pushing him from behind if slowed down. They brought his bags for him.

"This one."

Donny looked left into the room next to him and walked in.

The room was decorated with sunflowers. A vast collection of paintings of sunflowers all over the walls of different sizes and dimensions and styles, and side tables with vases with freshly cut sunflowers. A man in a tank top, built like Liu Faregno, benched several plates and grunted and pushed everything he had into his last rep, while another guy helped him set it on the rack. He sat up, put out a hand, and his spotter gave him a towel and he patted himself down.

The bodybuilder sat with his elbows on his knees, and stared at his guest. He was sweaty, breathing heavy, flush from exercise. He looked like he was seething, but he was just cooling down from his workout. No one said a word. Donny was wondering if he should start, but was afraid to. Eventually, a man came in from behind Donny, carrying two folding chairs. He opened one behind Donny, and pushed him down into it by his shoulders. The other chair he unfolded in the corner of the room. An old lady shuffled in, white hair in a bun, dressed in baggy khakis and a floral shirt and dark sunglasses. She looked like a tourist. One thug held her hand the whole way and guided her to her chair. When she got settled, the weightlifter finally spoke.

"What's this?"

A man tossed a brick to him and he caught it, looked at it, then set it down next to him on the bench.

"Where did you get this?"

Donny swallowed and cleared his throat. "Me and my brother were out on the water last night and these boat police came up to us and made us take them. We didn't know what it was until after they left."

"Do you know what this is?"

"Yes. I think so."

"And why did you bring it here?"

"I just thought it was probably yours. I don't want it. I just thought I should return it."

"Why do you think it belongs to me?"

"Because... you're The Rooster."

A couple guys chuckled. He asked, "What do you think that means?"

"You're... the man. You run Hotel Street and most of Chinatown. That's what people say."

"Would you like a reward for this?"

"No. That's really unnecessary."

The man stood up and walked up to Donny, towering over him. He crossed his huge arms. "Don't be stupid. Ask for a reward."

"Honestly, if we could just all forget about this misunderstanding, that would be plenty of reward for me."

"Do you know what this is worth?"

"I don't know. A lot, probably."

"Sixteen thousand."

"Whoa."

"Per kilo."

Donny couldn't speak.

Then he stepped back and sat on the bench. "That's 60 kilos. Are you good at math?"

"Yes. That's... uh... 960 thousand." His mouth was parched.

The man tilted his head a little and was scrutinizing the young visitor. "You came in here and gave me almost a million dollars."

"Yeah. I guess I did."

"Do you regret doing that now that you know what you had?"

"No."

"Why not?"

"Because you would be very motivated to find it. And because... I'm afraid of you." Donny looked around at the men still in the room.

"Smart boy. Good at math. Respectful. And wise enough to know not to steal from the Rooster." He looked at the old lady. She kept the pair of black, round mirrors on her face pointed right at Donny. He looked back at Donny and asked, "What do you do for money?"

"I throw trash in the ocean."

"What's that pay?"

"Three a bag."

"An entrepreneur, too. I'm glad you came here this morning. I had my boys looking everywhere for you. My guy who was supposed to make the pickup came in with empty hands and mouth full of excuses. We talked to the delivery man. They told us about you and about the boat you were on. Wasn't long before we figured out who owned the boat and where they live. I appreciate you coming to me directly. It's good to do the right thing, and you did, Donny Lao."

Donny swallowed hard. "I just wanted to make things right."

"You have, Donny. But now we're out of balance." He used his hands to pantomime an old scale tilting back and forth when a little weight is added to one side.

"What? I don't—"

"You don't owe me. I owe you. And I prefer paying my debts quickly."

"No, sir, Mr. Rooster. We are in balance. It's no problem."

"I've got a job for you. Pays better than three a bag."

"Oh, no, I don't think that's something I would like."

"The job is very easy and it isn't illegal. And I'll pay you a salary."

"I'm not sure I want to."

"You just saved us a million dollars. You will accept my reward. I will pay you 250 a week."

"T.. two hundred and fifty? A week?"

"Cocoa."

"Yeah, boss?" said the guy who'd manhandled Donny.

"This is our new box boy. Make sure everyone knows." He laid back down and continued his workout.

Cocoa pulled Donny up out of the chair by his arm and led him outside. Donny could feel the eyes of that old lady on him behind her dark glasses. Cocoa took him out of the room and back down the hall towards the elevator, and explained the job along the way.

"It's very simple work. Every day, you come by. You don't come into the back or come upstairs. You come in and ask the bartender in the pool room if we have any work for you today. If he says no, you go home. Your work is done. You get paid anyway. If we do have work for you, he will give you a box and a name and address. You simply take the box to the address and give it to the person. Give it directly to them. Not someone else. Not their wife. Not their employee. Them. Then you stay and watch them open the box. Wait for them to make their decision."

"What decision?" Donny asked.

"You'll know when they have. When it's done, you come back to the bar with the box and the contents of the box, and you give it back to the bartender."

"I don't… I don't want to do drug deliveries for you."

Cocoa pushed him into the elevators. "Like the man said: It's not drugs."

"Please, I don't…"

"You start tomorrow."

Cocoa slammed the metal gate down and sent the elevator downstairs.

When Donny got home, no one said hello, no one asked where he'd been, or what he did that day. His mom was sitting at the tiny table by the kitchen, looking through papers, calculating spending, and occasionally talking back and forth with her husband in Cantonese, and he overheard his mom say that the price of food was up 12% but the boat was only getting 70% of what they made this time last year. Donny waved, but they didn't acknowledge him until he started leaving their sight to go to his room.

"Hold on," said Dad.

Donny stopped.

"Where've you been all day?"

"I had a…" he looked at the bills and the tired look in his mom's eyes. He could smell the trash outside that was still stacking up, every day, and thought about all the tourists, too disgusted to come into Chinatown or go anywhere near his parent's tour boat. He finished his sentence. "I had a job interview."

"Eh?" His mother was suddenly alert.

"Job? You? You must be joking," said Dad.

"You didn't want me to come help out you and Mom with the boat, so I thought I could do something else."

"Something else? How about go to college. How about that? Like we talked about!"

"Dad, I know it's real tough out there right now with the business. It's not your fault. It's the trash. I want to help out."

"Oh! Oh, you want to help? Yes! Yes, it's tough! But I don't need you to help! I am the father!" He smacked his own chest. "You are the son!" He pointed at his boy. "I take care of this family! I'm not too old to! I don't need you to help!"

"I know that! I know you don't need me to. It's just a temporary thing until I figure stuff out."

His mother smiled, but that vanished when her husband started speaking again. "You have an American attitude. Figure things out? What's that mean? Everything's been figured out already! You already know what you should do! Figure out? Huh."

"Yeah, I have an American attitude. I'm an American."

His dad looked pissed, especially since he didn't have an answer for that. He made a noise like "bah!" and turned around and waved him away.

Mom spoke up. "What kind of job?"

"It's like a courier."

"What is that?"

"I deliver things."

"Deliveries? Like food deliveries?"

"Mm no, not exactly. It's, uh, expensive things. Important things that we can't damage."

"Oh! Where's the job?"

He didn't dare say Hotel street, so he said, "The Art Exhibition."

"When do you know if you have the job?"

"I am hired."

Mom smiled and clapped her hands together. "Oh! Good for you!"

Dad still wouldn't look at him.

Donny went to bed. Jim was already in his bed reading Hit Parader. He asked him what Donny did with the bags the police gave him and Donny changed the topic and turned the lights out. He couldn't sleep, though.

When Donny went to the Big E the next day, he was hoping it would be one of those "no work days." No luck. The bartender gave him a box wrapped in newsprint, a piece of paper with a name and address, and an envelope. He opened the envelope and peeked inside and saw twelve twenties and a ten. He didn't know the address, so he walked outside and when he found a cab, he walked up to the window and asked the driver where it was. "Over by Hawaii Baptist. Wanna ride?"

Donny declined, which annoyed the driver. Donny just needed directions. He walked a few blocks to a shop that sold surfboards and bikes and talked to the leather-skinned man who ran the shop. They talked about Donny's needs.

"What you need is the Masi."

"Okay. Why?"

"It's the bike from *Breaking Away*. Did you see it?"

"No."

"It's great."

Donny also bought a rear bike stand and a lock. He tied down a newsprint-wrapped box with a name and address written on it. Bradley Manu.

Donny rode out into the suburbs. He rode on the sidewalk under the shade of the tangled banyan trees, with their hanging roots, growing their children beside them, and contorting into one another inseparably. He rode under the big blue sky and the fat clouds stacked high like cupcake frosting. Hardly a car on the road. A perfect day in it wasn't for the swarms of flies making their families in the garbage.

He found the suburbs. He didn't know the roads well, and got directions from a shirtless man mowing his lawn. He found the place. A modest ranch home with several cars out front, and a red 1960 MG MGA sports car in the driveway, and an unblemished piñata hanging from the tree in the front yard. Donny deployed the kickstand and carried the package and knocked on the door. A little girl answered. She was wearing a paper party hat.

"Um, hi. Does Bradley Manu live here?"

"Daaaaaaaad! Someone's here for yooooooouuuuuu!" She walked back into the house and left the door wide open. Donny stepped in. Happy Birthday banners were hanging from the walls, children were running around the house in party hats. A man walked in from the kitchen and saw Donny and the box.

"Hi, what can I do for..."

They realized who the other was at the same moment.

"You're the kid. From the other night."

"You're the boat cop."

Bradley looked around to see if any of his neighbors were looking his way, then shut the door. He closed in on Donny and pressed him against the door. The man had to be close to three bucks, and judging by the man's forearms and speed, most of it was muscle.

He spoke quietly. "The fuck are you doing coming to my home, huh?"

"I have a package for you."

"What is it?"

"I don't know."

"So who's it from?"

"Rooster."

Bradley untied the twine and peeled back the paper. Inside was a gorgeously carved, red-stained wooden box, with the image of an archer with a bow and 9 notched arrows aiming at the sky, and a rooster at his feet. He lifted the lid and peeked inside.

"No. No. Why?"

"Why what?"

"What did I do wrong?"

"Um. I don't know. Maybe cus you gave me all those bags…"

The cop took Donny by the arm and walked him down a hall.

"Honey?" a woman called from somewhere else in the house.

Bradley kept walking and pulling Donny and called back, "Just a minute, sugar!"

"We need you for the piñata!"

"I said just a minute!"

The cop took Donny into the master bedroom and closed the door.

He kept his voice low. "Yeah, I gave you the bags. That's what I was supposed to do."

"I don't know who you were supposed to give those bags to, but it wasn't me."

"What? What the fuck were you doing out there?"

"Dumping trash. Just wrong time, wrong place."

"Then why the fuck would you take it!"

"Cus, you're a cop. You told us to."

Bradley took the box. His eyes and nose got wet. "I can't. It's my daughter's 9th birthday today. Not today. Not here. Please. Yeah, I fucked up. But I can't do this here."

"I don't know, man. I was just told to bring you this box and not to leave until you're done."

The cop's eyes started leaking, "Can I at least speak to the family first? Just say... something. So it will all make sense?"

Donny struggled to say, "No one said anything about that. I'm supposed to stay with you until you're done. That's what they said." He looked at the box, and held it delicately like it was a bomb. He swallowed nothing with a dry throat.

The cop sat on his bed and put his face in his hands and cried as Donny had never seen a grown man cry before. He opened his mouth to say something but he didn't say anything. He tried to look around the room at anything but the cop. A king-sized bed. A dresser. Ordinary things found in every bedroom, and he looked at them all as if they were interesting. A courtesy he learned from his father. Never shame a man in a weak moment by looking at them.

The man started breathing deep, trying to relax. Big breath in, blow out slowly through a mouth shaped for a kiss. He found a book on the bedside table and ripped out a blank page from the back and wrote something on it with a pencil. He folded it and put it in the front pocket of his polo shirt.

"Okay. Okay. I can do this." He set the box in his lap, opened the lid, and reached inside. His hand came out with a big chrome pistol with an image of Elvis on the grip. Donny stepped back. The cop racked the slide, and put it in his mouth, and made a noise like a whimper and a scream. The cop moved fast so he wouldn't have a fraction of a second to be a coward. Too fast for Donny to even realize what was happening until it was too late.

Click.

Donny jumped. "Oh, fuck!" He nearly fell backwards, but the room was small and the door stopped his stumble.

The cop started laughing or crying, or both. He removed the magazine and checked it. Full. He cleared it and slid the magazine back in, racked the slide, and tried again. *Click.* He was laughing harder now or crying harder, if those were even different things.

"What's that mean? Kid, what's that mean?"

"I don't know."

"Did I do it right? Was this just a message? Or do I have to kill myself some other way?"

"I… uh.. don't know."

"Why don't you know? Why? You're the one who brought it! You should know! If I fuck this up, they'll kill my family! Don't you get that? Was this a warning or a mistake? Tell me!" He grabbed Donny's shirt with one enormous hand. Donny tilted his head and closed his eyes, expecting to get hit. But he didn't get hit. He opened his eyes again. Bradley's eyes were overflowing, and his hands held the kid like he was hanging off a thousand foot cliff.

Donny delicately took the gun from him. He gently removed the cop's hand. He could have held on but he let the kid go. Donny put the gun back in the box, took the box, and left the room, hearing the man crying uncontrollably even through the door after he closed it behind him. He walked past laughing children chasing each other, and outside through the front door where Mrs. Manu was calling, "Bradley!" as the kids gathered around a tree where the piñata hung.

"Hey! Who are you?"

"Oh, uh, hi Mrs. Manu. I work with your husband."

"Oh. Okay. Uh. What are you doing here?"

"Just... work stuff. You'll have to ask him about that. I gotta go. Nice meeting you."

Donny got back on his bike. He didn't even tie the box down, he just kept it under one arm and steered with the other. The boat cop's wife yelled after him, demanding to know who he was and what he was doing in her house. He rode at top speed back to The Big E to give the box back.

The next morning, Donny rode his bike to the Big E, but they didn't have anything for him.

He rode towards the docks as the sun was just coming up, and the ocean sparkled, and the waves gently slapped the hulls of the boats on the dock. He wondered why the sky is more colorful during sunsets than sunrises.

"Morning."

"早晨," said his Mom. His dad said nothing.

"Do you need any help?"

"Nope."

Donny walked onto the boat, and it bent and bobbed when he got on, and he took a couple steps by the wooden tips box right by the steps for the exiting tourists.

"I don't have to deliver for the gallery today. Let me help." He palmed a 10 dollar bill and stood in front of the box.

"You want to help? You can tutor your brother, like I told you to."

Donny slipped the money into the tip box slot behind his back so his folks wouldn't see.

"Okay."

He left the boat, and he said, "He needs help with multiplying exponents. We'll work on that today."

Mom smiled. Dad didn't, but he would have if he believed in encouragement. Donny went home and turned off the TV against Jim's protests, and sat with his brother at the table to teach him what his teacher's should have.

It was like that for a while. Donny came by the pool hall every day and asked about the box, but the bartender didn't have anything for him most days. And every day he would show up to his parents' boat and slip in a tenner. And every day they told him to help his brother study.

Ming came around asking for Donny one day. Donny told him he was retired from the waste management business. Ming raised his voice and demanded to know what he was supposed to do about all his trash now. Donny explained he was a courier now for someone on Hotel Street. Ming forced a polite smile and apologized for his rudeness and left in a hurry.

The second man Donny delivered to didn't say a word. He opened the door and when he saw the box, he pushed Donny onto the floor and jumped over him and ran away. Donny chased after, down the stairs, onto the street, but he was long gone. Donny went back to the bartender and told him what happened and returned the box with trembling hands. Rooster's guys weren't mad at Donny, though. They took the box and he left.

The third person he missed just as he left to work in their powder blue Plymouth. Donny asked a neighbor, and they told him he worked at a social security office. Donny rode out there and had to wait outside the office all day because they wouldn't let him in with that box. When he saw the guy approach the car, Donny leapt off the bench, ran through the parking lot, and stopped him just as he was getting in.

"Hey, mister."

The guy saw the box. He didn't cry. He didn't fight. He just said, "Thank you, but I prefer to do it my way." He climbed into the driver's seat and shut the door.

Donny knocked on the window. "No, mister, you have to use the box!" Donny tried to explain it to him without saying that the gun didn't work, but the guy drove off. Donny got onto his bike and pedaled as fast as he could back to the man's house. When he got there, he knocked on the door. No one answered. He tried peeking in through the blinds. Just between the cracks he saw a pair of dangling legs and a toppled wooden chair.

Donny headed home feeling a tightness in his chest that wouldn't quit. Tighter than Officer Manu's grip.

He found the second guy, the runner, the next day when he visited his parents at the marina. The police were fishing his body out of the water with hooked poles. It bobbed with the waves, floating face down in the rainbow-black motor oil and trash that accumulated along the retaining wall. He was wearing the same clothes as when Donny saw him.

Dad said, "Damn drunks. Out swimming at night." He raised a wagging finger Donny and said, "You don't ever do that!"

"I know. I know better than that, Dad."

When Donny rode through town with that box, he sensed something had changed. People acted differently around him. They acted like Ming did when he came to the apartment. Donny thought it was his imagination at first. He didn't know what to call it. People avoided looking at the young man while he carried the box. People made room for him on the sidewalk. If he got a soda while he carried the box, the cashier insisted it was free of charge. People looked at that box like it carried the Mandate of Heaven.

One morning, after getting the box and an address, he got a seat at an outside table at a diner. Today's delivery would take an hour and a half by bike and he needed fuel. He ordered spam sushi for breakfast. The bike was just a few feet from him, so he didn't bother to lock it. A kid jumped onto the bike and pedaled off at top speed. Donny jumped out of his seat and yelled at the kid and ran after him, but the kid vanished. Huffing and exhausted after chasing for three blocks, Donny sat on the curb and contemplated what the Rooster would do to him for losing the box. He thought about when the police finally pulled that man in the water. Bloated, his face full of holes where the underwater things had burrowed.

"I'm sorry."

Donny looked up. The kid had come back. The paper on the box had been peeled back just a bit, then tied back down. He climbed off the bike and held it up so Donny could take it. The box carrier accepted it.

The kid said, "I'm sorry. I didn't know who you were. Please, can we just keep this between us? Please?"

That's when Donny understood what changed. They were afraid of him. Everyone was. No one had ever been afraid of him.

"What's your name?"

"Stephen."

"Stephen what?"

"Stephen Ito."

Donny got back on the bike without accepting or rejecting the apology and left Stephen to sweat it out in the same spot Stephen had left him to sweat it out.

The bartender at The Big E gave Donny an address to an apartment in Chinatown. He walked two blocks and found a name on a placard by the front door written in Chinese. He pressed the button.

"Yes?"

"Package."

The door buzzed and Donny went in and up the narrow, carpeted stairs to the second apartment. He knocked. It opened. An old, skinny man in a t-shirt and shorts and socks answered, saw the package, and then walked back inside. Donny followed him in and closed the door behind him. The room was dark and stuffy. The blinds were drawn, and the windows were closed and there wasn't any air conditioning running. Little particles floated in the narrow beams of light that snuck between the curtains. The place smelled like cats but there weren't any. The old man led Donny into a living room, where he eased himself back into his armchair in front of the television. Donny looked around for a place to sit, but there was only one chair, so he took a chair from the kitchen and set it close to the man, and sat in it.

The old man continued to watch TV like no one had just entered the room. Donny tried to say something, but the old man shushed him. Donny kept quiet. Eventually, the show cut to a commercial. The old man leaned over to the TV, muted it, and swiveled his chair towards his guest, and reached out for the box, his fingers impatiently beckoning it. Donny handed it to him. The old man took it and sat back in his chair and let it rest on his lap.

"你会说汉语吗?"

"My Cantonese isn't that good. I'm sorry. Do you speak any English?"

"You should keep using your language." His accent was strong, but his grammar was perfect.

"It's not my language."

"Where are you from?"

"America."

The old man made a raspy laugh at that and was interrupted by his own coughing. "You know what is in this box?"

"Yes."

"You know what it is for?"

"I think so."

"Do you know why your boss told you to bring it to me?"

Donny shook his head.

"I will tell you. I asked a boss for a favor once. A boss a lot like yours. In Hong Kong. He gave me the favor. He did what he promised he would do. But he asked me to do something for him in return. This box is here because I couldn't."

"What was it?"

The old man smiled and eased himself into his chair and looked off to someplace far away in days and distance. He sighed and started his story.

"My daughter was spending time with a bad man. No man was good enough for her, but that's not what I mean. He was a bad man. You understand? She wanted to marry him. She wouldn't listen to me. I asked the boss to do something about it. He did.

My daughter was sad for a while but she recovered. The boss asked me for a favor after what he had done for my family. He wanted me to hurt a man who didn't deserve it. He gave me a uh, how do you say it… a meat hammer. The kind with spikes for flattening chicken. You know? He gave it to me and said, *Hurt this man and bring me back a piece of him as a trophy to prove you did it.* I took the hammer, and I went to the place the boss said he would be. A bike shop in Mong Kok. Have you ever been?"

"No."

"Mong Kok is a… how would you say… a place you get lost in?"

"Like a maze?"

"Mong Kok is a maze. The streets are narrow. There's no room. None at all. Cement walls. Cement ground. Cement everywhere. Like a prison without a roof. And everyone is in the streets selling things. All the time. Everything. Shoes. Fortunes. Lunch. Fake jewelry. Tickets to cricket matches. Everything. It was in a narrow street, only as wide as two men standing next to each other. This street was like a hallway but above me was drying laundry on strings and electric cables, all the way up, fifty meters, and only a bit of sky up there. I came to this tiny shop. He sold bikes. I didn't know what the man had done, but I saw him and knew he was a good man. Right away, I knew. I pretended to shop. I talked with the man about bikes a little and I left. And I waited until it was dark, when the sun was gone and the electric lights came on. I went back to the shop. When he was pulling down his metal gates, I hit him. No one was around. I just hit him. It was him or me, you see? I told myself that he would kill me, not the boss. I told myself that if I didn't kill this man, someone else would. It was inevitable. This is how I thought about it to make it seem right."

"Did it work?"

"No. Don't interrupt."

"Sorry."

"The man fell down. Someone else saw but they didn't say or do anything. They didn't care at all. A man as old as I am now. He must be dead now. He must be. He watched me hurt that poor bike shop man, and he felt nothing about it. He looked down at me. He looked out his window and looked down at me and smoked a cigarette. He was bored seeing what I did. Imagine what kind of a person could be bored by that.

"Then I left. I washed my hands and shirt in a dirty puddle. It had just rained that morning. The water was everywhere. Whenever you stepped, it was like stepping on the bottoms of your own feet, a mirror that doesn't show right, like a circus?"

Donny said, "Like a funhouse mirror."

"Yes. Like the mirror that makes you," he stretched himself out, arms up, and made a long face, then scrunched up and made a smooshed face, "like that."

Donny nodded.

"It was like walking on a funhouse mirror. And I went home. And when I realized what I had done, I knew I had to leave. I took my wife and daughters and we got on a boat and came here. I didn't know how to fish, but I learned. And I hoped the boss had forgotten me. But I see now he hasn't. He told the boss here, your boss, the one who lives in the mahjong bar. And now your boss has sent you to me."

"I don't understand. You did what he said."

"No. I didn't. I didn't bring him a trophy. I didn't take a piece of him. I couldn't do it. I didn't think I could murder that man, but I did. But I couldn't cut a part off of him. Desecrating a body seemed worse than desecrating a life. It's stupid, but that is how I felt. And it was too late after I left. The police would already be there. I couldn't change my mind. So I came here to America."

"Maybe he wasn't a good man."

"If he was a bad man, it wouldn't make me a good man. I did what I did without knowing. That makes me a bad man. I had to be a bad man to be a good father. You see? That's what it is to be a father. A good father has one moral: to protect his children. All other morals vanish. You see? Do you know 孔子' five morals?"

Donny shook his head.

The old man made a face like it hurt him to hear that. He counted them and showed a finger each time: "仁, 義, 禮, 智, 信. And what if two don't agree? What if being good morals in one makes bad morals in another? Did I commit murder against a good man? Or did I murder virtue of society? Did I sacrifice one man to save my daughter, or did I sacrifice civilization? 己所不欲、勿施於人. How can I do a thing that I cannot allow all men to do? Would I forgive a man who did that to me? I don't know."

Donny said, "I understand."

"That is good. That is good. Because I don't understand. I still don't understand." He opened the box and took out the Elvis gun and pressed it against his heart. "Thank you for listening to me, young man. Old men can't give anything but stories. It's all we have. We think it is a gift to share them. But it is your listening that is the gift to us. When a young person listens and learns, it tells us old men that all we did really mattered. The wisdom won't be lost with us when we go; that someone younger finds value in that we were here at all. You see?"

Donny nodded.

Click. Click. The old man's face didn't flinch. "I got the good one." He put the gun back in the box. Donny took it.

The old man said, "If you like, you can come back and talk to me. You don't need a box to come visit."

Donny nodded.

The old man leaned forward and turned the volume back up so he could keep watching his program. Donny left with the box, leaving the old man there to anesthetize his guilt with game shows, after the old boss of Mong Kok tracked him across the Pacific, 40 years later, just to remind him of what he had done, and not to kill him, just to let him keep living with it.

"Donny. Come here." Donny's father beckoned him to the door. Donny got off the couch where he and his brother were watching tv. "We have to go for a walk." Donny saw his mom look down at the floor, and then she excused herself to the other room.

"Okay."

"Can I come?" asked Jim.

"No," said Dad.

Donny and his father walked downstairs and out into the evening streets. The sun was almost behind Ka'ala and the sky was purple and black. They walked down the street together until they were almost at the beach. Finally, Dad broke the silence.

"Where is this money coming from?"

"What do you mean?"

"Donny. When I lied to my father, he hit me. When I didn't lie, but he thought I was lying, he hit me more because I sounded too sincere, which he thought was suspicious."

"Oh."

"I will not hit you for lying to me. But I will tell you I know you are lying. It hurt me worse when my father hit me for telling the truth."

Donny looked at the sidewalk.

His dad continued, "Where is this money coming from?"

"Did Jim tell you?"

Dad's eyes got huge. "Jim's involved?"

"No! No, he just. He kind of knows about it."

"I know you've been sneaking money into the tips box. We only had four customers today and I know I didn't see one of them tip. But you came by to say hello. So you put money in the box. So where did it come from?"

"Work."

"Deliveries?"

"Yeah."

"Deliveries don't pay so good. Who pays you so much for deliveries?"

"I told you…"

Dad sighed the powerful sigh of disappointment. The crushing sound of a father surrendering their child to be swallowed up by the world. The sigh of a man resigned to the destruction of his firstborn and the acceptance of his own helplessness to do anything about it. The worst sound in the world.

"The man on Hotel Street. The Rooster."

His dad grabbed him by the shoulders. "What are you talking about? How can you do that? What are you doing for Rooster?"

Donny told the story, the whole story, right up to the part where he made his first delivery.

His dad took a hushed tone and spoke closely to him, "That box could have drugs or guns or something in it!"

"No! It doesn't have drugs. They open the box, but they don't take what's inside."

"What's inside?"

"It's a gun."

"What?"

"But it doesn't work, okay? It's broken."

"Why does he send you around with a broken gun?"

"To scare people. I don't usually know why. But they never get hurt." That lie slipped past his father.

"How could you do this? That's terrible. Is this the boy I raised? You would do this to people?"

"No one gets hurt! And we need the money."

"We don't need the money! Not that way! I'm the father! I worry about money, not you! I'll show you how I don't need the money!"

His dad grabbed him by the arm and marched him to Hotel Street like he was just a child. It was the first time Donny had been there after the sun was down and he could see how it got its reputation. Women in hardly any clothes made lewd gestures at them. It wouldn't be the first time a father had brought his teenage son to Hotel Street. Dad took him in through the front door of the pool hall. It was filled with men carousing and drinking, a third of them were Navy sailors just about the same age as Donny, and plenty of girls trying to get their attention and money. His dad demanded to see Rooster, and the bartender said, "Donny knows where the Rooster is," which pissed Dad off more.

Donny took him to the back, into the mahjong room, and he talked to the man at the elevator who let them up. Cocoa checked Donny's father for weapons and wires and then walked them to a red-painted room where the bodybuilder boss was having dinner at a small table with that old lady in sunglasses.

"Dad. This is the Rooster. Mr. Rooster, this is my dad." He gestured to the man.

The muscular boss and the old lady laughed a little and kept eating like they didn't see them.

Dad said, "Donny. That man is not the Rooster."

"What?"

The strong man laughed and kept stuffing his mouth with fried pig intestines.

"But then. Who are you?"

Donny's father said to the old woman, "雞公. My son did nothing to you. You leave him alone. He doesn't work for you. He is going to college!"

She said, "I've given your son a very good job. He is a man. He can work for me or not. You have no business with me."

"No! You intimidated him!"

"Donny already has two mothers. He doesn't need me to be one, too."

Dad lunged for the old woman. She didn't flinch. Cocoa and another man were quick to grab him and hold him back. The strong man stood up and punched the uninvited guest in the stomach and he collapsed onto the floor.

Donny stood in between his father and the bodybuilder. The gangsters all backed away, not wanting to fight with Donny.

The old woman said, "This man is vulgar."

The man who wasn't Rooster nodded.

The old woman said, "Cocoa?"

"Yes, ma'am?"

"Bring up the box for Mr. Lao."

"No, please," said Donny.

Cocoa left the room.

Dad was just catching his breath and asked, "Why are you making my son deliver for you?"

"I'm not making him do anything, Mr. Lao. You have a good son. He's a good boy. I think you know that. He is smart. Smart enough to know who to be afraid of. And now he knows what it is to be feared. That's how things are understood. You cannot understand heartbreak until you've had yours broken and you've broken someone else's. Donny understands that now, don't you?" It wasn't a question.

Donny looked at the floor, like she would see his thoughts through his eyes. He looked at his dad. Rooster was right. Donny had seen nothing so awful as his own father being scared of him. Donny looked back at the floor again.

Cocoa returned with the box and handed it to the woman. "No. It's not for me. Give it to him."

The man turned and gave it to Donny. He hesitated, but took it.

"Now," said the old woman, "Give the box to your father."

"No. I can't do that."

"Yes, you can. You've done it many times before."

"Please don't. I'm sorry. He made me come here. I didn't want to tell, but he knew I was getting paid and…"

Rooster shushed him silently with a many-ringed finger over her mouth. "The police made you take my heroin. I made you take the job. Your father made you bring him here. Everyone is making you. Very un-American."

Donny begged them to leave his family alone. But they didn't respond. They let him say every word he could and gave him silence in return.

"Give me the box," said Dad, who was back on his feet, trying to stand as proud as his battered gut would allow.

Donny handed his dad the box. His dad took it, walked up to the dining table, and dropped it there, loudly. He opened the lid. A chrome 1911 with a sweetheart grip.

"Why do you do this to people?"

She looked at Donny and let him answer. "It's a message. I'm a messenger. If I bring someone the box, they have to use it on themselves or else they know something awful will happen to their loved ones." Donny's father already knew this, but the gangsters didn't know that he knew.

"You will leave my boy alone if I use it, Rooster?"

The old lady nodded. "If you take the test, I'll leave Donny and Jim and Su Yin alone."

He put it in his own temple. No click. No, nothing.

Donny said, "You have to push back that hammer first. That thing on top."

His dad handed him the gun, and Donny locked the hammer back and returned it to his father. His father put it back to his head and looked directly at Donny. The young man could see his father wasn't afraid anymore. He almost smiled. Almost. He was proud to do this for his son. That's when Donny noticed that the grip had an image of Marilyn Monroe on it.

Pb&B&B Pasty

Not to be confused with the things strippers cover their nipples with. It seems like every culture on earth has stuff you can hold in your hands, filled with stuff you can't.

China's got baozi. England's got meat pie. Jamaica's got the beef patty. South America and the Philippines have the empanada.

Portable. Great for kids' lunchboxes.

Time: 3 hours

Ingredients

- 2 cups of shortening. That's four sticks of butter.
- 2 cups of hot water
- 5-½ of cups all-purpose flour (and a little extra)
- 2 teaspoons salt
- Chopped bananas
- Peanut butter
- A couple pounds of thick-cut bacon
- A couple eggs

Gear

- Big bowl
- Rolling pin
- Oven
- Baking sheet
- Knife
- Fork

Dough

1. Mix up the butter and warm water in a bowl until the butter is melted. If it's not working, melt the butter in a microwave first
2. Gradually add in the flour and salt, stirring as you go, a little bit at a time

3. When you have a soft dough, it's done

4. Cover the bowl with a towel or plastic wrap and throw it in the refrigerator. Leave it there for at least 90 minutes

The Insides

5. Chop up the bacon into any size you like and cook it on a skillet. They're done when they look good to eat. I use scissors

6. Chop the bananas into coins. Remove the skin first, obviously

Making Them

7. Take the dough out of the fridge and divide it into 12 equal balls

8. Pit some flour on a surface to work on

9. Use the rolling pin and smush them so they are roughly 8-inch, flat circles

10. Smear some peanut butter on there and stack banana pieces and the bacon

11. Put a little dab of water on the rims, then fold the dough over. Use a fork to press down and seal the edges. They'll look kinda like potstickers

12. When you got all 12 done, place them on a baking sheet

13. Stab each pasty 3 times with a knife. They need to vent while they're cooking

14. Beat the eggs and brush them over the tops. Just a thin varnish is good

Baking Them

- Preheat the oven 350 F
- When it's hot, put em in on the middle rack. It takes about an hour to bake. When it looks golden and delicious, and you can smell the glory, it is done
- Take em out and let them cool. If you bite into them right

away, you will regret it

Serve with

- A yellow reflector vest
- The music of *Billy Strings*
- A photo of your wife and kids

Variations

- Use fully pre-cooked apples instead of bananas, and add a sprinkle of cinnamon
- Add honey

CHAPTER 6: IF I CAN DREAM

Caruthersville, MO

8/16/2015

23:41:44

There's a bar in Missouri just 10 minutes from Tennessee on the other side of the river, 20 minutes from Arkansas, and an hour from Illinois. A strange place at the intersection of the South, the West, and the Midwest. At night, it would be easy to mistake the Carriage House Bar for a barn except for the neon signs in the windows provided by domestic brewery account reps, and the 18-wheelers in the gravel lot that surrounds it.

Behind that bar, Hannah smoked her cigarette and leaned against the aluminum siding under an insect-swarmed lamp. She watched a man and woman arguing in the lot. She pulled on the straps of her tank top. It felt like it was digging in and her basketball shorts felt like they were riding up and she made a mental note to back off the fried food. She flushed that thought out as easily as it came in by taking a deep sip of some domestic in a clear plastic cup. The music coming out the back of the bar was competing with the frogs and bugs in the woods, but the lovebirds fighting in the parking lot were winning the noise competition.

"Ah ain't did nothin'!"

"Ah know you fucked her! Ah know you did!"

"Well, who cares if ah did? You fucked Travis!"

"Yeah, an' you forgave me for that already! So you can't bring that up anymore!"

Hannah looked to her right. It was dark except for the pairs of distant red lights on the highway. She looked to her left, and it was black except for the gas station. The air was hot and the breeze wouldn't budge and her hair kept sticking to the back of her neck.

She saw a man in her periphery walk up from behind her and stand beside her, but she didn't look to see who it was.

"Ain't love grand?" he said. He lit a cigarette.

"Yup."

"Quite a show."

"Better'n TV."

"Why don't they just break up already?"

"If they broke up, they'd never have a reason to see each other again. Then how would they keep hurting each other?"

He nodded and put his hands on his hips.

She looked at him for the first time. "How do I know you?"

"I don't think you do."

"Did you go to high school here?"

"Nope."

"Where you from?"

"A lot of places."

"Well, I know you ain't no trucker."

"Why do you say that?"

"I've known a lot of truckers. Ain't a trucker on earth that looks like you."

"What about my looks?"

"You too handsome to be a trucker."

"Naw. You just had a few too many, is all."

Hannah nodded, "Yeah, you right. You probably ugly as hell when I'm sober."

He laughed at that.

The angry girl broke off her conversation and long-strode crunchy steps through the gravel parking lot, yelling behind her, "Ah can have any man I want! Why do ah need you?"

"The fuck you can!" he said and started walking after her.

The girl who could have any man put eyes on Hannah's smoking buddy. She walked right up to him, putting her hands on his chest and getting in close enough that her forearms pressed on him. "Hey, sweety. This party's gettin old. Wanna go somewhere?"

Her boyfriend's chest puffed up, pointing at the non-trucker, saying, "Hey! Hey! Buddy, you keep your damn hands off my girl!"

The non-trucker looked at Hannah with a what-the-fuck look. She gave him a mocking smile and said, "Good luck with that," and she snuffed out her smoke, kicking up some sparks, and tossed it into a tin bucket with more butts than sand.

She walked back inside through a swinging aluminum door, into the music and chatter. A man on the speakers was singing, "Daddy never was the Cadillac kind..." She walked past the men in paint-splattered overalls, black t-shirts with skulls and threatening words, guys with hats sporting logos of American companies. She walked past women wearing shirts that hardly covered a thing, cutoff jeans, baseball caps with ponytails threaded through the back, big shirts that barely held from slipping off the shoulder with bands like Motörhead and The

Eagles. The walls were fake wooden slats decorated with neon glass logos of domestic beer companies in all kinds of colors that tinted the room in different hues foot by foot. The carpet was dense, like the kind at church. The crack of a cue ball on a freshly racked triangle. The laughter that comes easy when you're on the best half of the weekend. The rattle and hum of an air conditioner struggling to keep everyone happy.

She took her seat back at the bar where she left her phone on the stool to mark it as taken. She ordered another beer before she sat down. As she planted her rear, her phone buzzed in her hand. A text message from a number she didn't recognize.

(901)332-3322: *Hi Hannah! I'm in town rn and thought we could meet up for drinks and catch up! :D <3 Are you free?*

Hannah: *Who this? I dont have this number saved*

The girl behind the bar handed her another frothy-topped golden drink in a plastic cup.

Laney: *Oops! This is Laney!*

Hannah paused and looked at the text again to make sure she was reading it right.

Hannah: *Laney Jacobson?*

Laney: *Yes! But I'm Laney Birch now!*

Her text included a photo of a very large diamond engagement ring.

Hannah: *Oh wow. It's been a while. Im at carriage house rn off exit 55 if you want to come by*

Laney: *I kno that place! Ill be there in 30! I'm so excited to see you! <3<3<3*

Hannah took a white-capped, translucent orange bottle from her pocket with the name Bonnie VanLier on the label. She rattled it near her ear and it made the sound of seventeen. She popped the cap, took one out, and was about to put it back, then took out another before she put it away. She put the white pills on a coaster, put another coaster on top, and crushed them under her palm. She poured the powder off the coaster into her drink and swirled it to let the dust dissolve and sizzled like a fizzy heartburn tablet. She noticed the eyes of a big-bearded older man glance at her from a couple of stools down.

"What're you lookin at?"

"A pretty young lady hurtin herself."

She saw he was drinking a soda, wearing a cross, and had a yellow rubber wristband from going six months. She said, "How about mind yer own damn business?"

"Yes, ma'am." And he did.

Hannah worked on her scratch offs and wiped away the silver dust. The bartender asked how she did. Twenty bucks. Not bad. Hannah was just about finished with her cocktail when Laney came in looking even better than she did 14 years ago. Her yoga pants and pink sweater signaled that she wasn't a regular.

Laney looked around the room and lit up when she saw Hannah. "Oh my God!" She smiled and stretched her arms out for a hug and clicked across the bar floor on her heels. Hannah got out of her stool and hugged her back. She realized this must be the first time they'd ever hugged.

"Oh, my God! You look great, hun!" said Laney, stepping back to look her up and down.

Hannah didn't know what the fuck Laney was talking about, and said, "So do you."

"It's been so long! How long has it been?"

"Since the summer after high school graduation."

"Wow. Fourteen years. It's crazy, right? Sit, sit! Let me get you a drink, hun!"

Hannah got back onto her stool, and Laney sat next to her.

The bartender came up and asked, "What can I get you?"

"I would love a margarita," said Laney.

Hannah just pointed back at her beer and the bartender nodded and went to go get their drinks. Laney was all smiles. "How have you been? What have you been up to? Tell me everything!"

"Not much, I guess. I, uh, I have a daughter…"

Laney interrupted. "That's so great!"

"…she's eight now."

"That's such a great age."

"Yeah."

Laney kept asking questions and kept buying the drinks. They talked more over those first two drinks than they did in all of high school combined. Laney was so animated. She was intense. She hardly broke eye contact. She had energy. Hannah went to bed tired, woke up tired, and stayed tired all day, every day. She never felt that kind of energy a day in her life. Laney had a kind of enthusiasm that gets beat out of most people long before adulthood. She had the vigor of the newly converted or someone with a winning Powerball jackpot ticket in their pocket.

Laney asked and asked. Hannah told her about finally meeting her dad and how badly that went. Hannah told her about her hours getting cut at work, down to fifteen a week, how management was making the staff play resignation chicken, hoping someone would quit so they wouldn't have to lay anyone off and pay for their unemployment. Hannah told her about moving back in with her mom and how her sister had custody of her daughter because of one little mistake.

Laney nodded and said all the things people say. "That's terrible," "No way," and, "What an asshole!" Most people try to change the subject when the conversation gets dark, especially perky people like Laney, but she kept on nodding and saying the right things and paying for the drinks.

Hannah never talked this much about herself. No one wanted to hear about someone else's problems, and most of what she had to talk about were problems. She apologized.

"No, hun! No, not at all! I want to hear about it!"

"Well, how about you? How are you doing?"

While Hannah's story kept a constant linear trajectory downwards, Laney's story had more twists and turns. Laney told her about college and how she met a guy who she thought was The One, but he cheated. She was in a car accident that nearly killed her. Laney described her endless struggle with anxiety. She said she turned it around when she "spoke to the person she was meant to be," and how she's married now to an orthopedic surgeon in Seattle and how they live in a great big house and have three kids and she owns her own business.

"Wow. That's. A lot."

"Yeah! Between the business and kids, I barely have any time for girls' nights out like this!"

"So, you are visiting your parents?"

"Yup. My Mom's not doing so well."

"Shit. I'm sorry to hear that."

"She is so brave, you know? She could have been so much. She thinks she sacrificed all of that to raise us kids. She did, but she didn't have to. I'm grateful for everything, but she wasn't communicating with the person she was meant to be, you know?"

"You said that before. What is that?"

Laney's eyebrows popped up. "The person she was meant to be?"

"Yeah. Is that like a self-help kind of thing?"

"No! Absolutely not! The person you were meant to be is the manifestation of your self-chosen purpose."

"I got no idea what that means."

"It's the reason you chose to be born."

"Chose… to be born?"

"Okay, I am going to send you this video. Watch it later when you have a chance." She thumbed her phone for a moment and then Hannah's phone dinged and Laney said, "That was me."

They talked a little longer, and the words got slurrier, and the topics changed faster, until Laney ended the night by saying to Hannah, "I wish we had become closer friends in high school. I know we had friends who were friends. We were always around each other, but we didn't really get to know each other. I regret that, y'know? And I feel like we did a lot tonight to remedy it, don't you think? Anyway, I was always so intimidated by you because I knew you were so strong and cool and I knew you were destined for great things. But, seriously, watch that video! It changed my life!"

Hannah thought about everything Laney said as she drove home drunk that night. She had no idea Laney felt that way about her. She didn't know that Laney thought about her at all in high school. It's easy to think with a radio playing and the hypnotic pulse of the lights passing by on the opposite road.

Hannah drove straight, but she had a bad taillight and the cop who pulled her over for it smelled the beer on her. The cop cuffed her, towed her car, and Hannah spent the night in a jail cell. In the morning, the judge bounced her on a PR bond on account that the jail was already over-full, and handed a court date eight weeks out. License suspended and car impounded.

She forced a smile at the corrections officer who was processing her release on the other side of a ½-inch thick plexiglass window. She said, "See. I told you I knew you from somewhere. Guess you ain't too handsome to be a CO, huh?" He didn't smile back.

COs returned her personal items to her through a metal slot: her phone, a pack of cigarettes (with two left), lighter, a lotto ticket worth $20, chain necklace and pendant with an image of Saint Ailbe of Emly, a SNAP EBT card, half a bottle of her mom's oxies, driver's license, and keys on a key-chain shaped like a heart in glittery pink with cursive writing that spelled *bitch.*

They didn't release her until 10:30. Hannah's hearing at family court was at 8:45. Her mom picked her up from jail. She didn't say anything while Hannah sobbed the whole way home. Hannah kept texting Gretchen, but her sister didn't respond.

According to the 34th circuit court and the state of Missouri, Hannah couldn't drive, and she wasn't allowed to repossess her car until she could. Her mom had to drive her to work at the Dollar General the day after. Her eyes were bloodshot and the skin around them and her nose were pink and raw from wiping with tissues for two days. She wasn't altogether there. Her boss tried to send her home, and she said, "Fuck you, I'm staying," and he didn't bother her for the rest of the day.

She got a ride home with a guy from work. Her mom still wasn't talking to her. Her sister wasn't either. Hannah sat on the couch next to her mom, who wouldn't even look at her. She kept her eyes on her talk shows. Hannah leaned back into the afghan. It still smelled like cigarettes, even after Mom quit four years ago. She checked her socials on her phone and then remembered the video that Laney sent her. She opened the link.

The soothing sound of Gregorian chant played over a well-produced video slideshow. The green verdure of a tropical forest. "Who are you?"

"Shh," said her mom without breaking eye contact from her

program. Hannah paused it, got up, and sat in the kitchen where the sound wouldn't bother her mom. She restarted the video.

Gregorian chant and tropical forest. "Who are you?"

Then the yellows and tans of the desert sand. "Why are you this person?"

The sands vanished underneath the perfect teal and flickering white of the ocean. "Why aren't you the person you chose to be?"

Then drone footage over a white and black snowy mountain range, with a pristine river cutting through it. "How did you get lost? When did you forget how to speak with the person you really are?"

Shot of a woman crying over an unconscious man lying in the hospital bed. "You didn't choose this for yourself."

Shot of a man leaning on his elbows over a dining table, palms to his temples, looking at a pile of papers labeled BILLS and FINAL NOTICE in bright red lettering. "But you forgot what it is you chose."

Shot of a woman in the driver's seat of a car, sobbing, as the heavy rain came down on her windows. "Somehow you know this isn't your real life."

Shot of the handsome narrator looking directly at the viewer. His suit was expensive, but he wore it as comfortably as sweatpants. "I didn't have the answers. But that's because I asked the wrong questions. But when I finally asked the right questions, it changed everything for me."

Cutaway back to the same characters before, but now the color palette filter wasn't the somber blues and greens, but a warm orangish morning glow.

The sick man was now healthy and jogging with the woman who was faithfully at his side in the hospital. "I changed the way I think."

The man with money problems was now enjoying the pool deck of a mansion, leaning back in a cabana chair while his children played in the pool and his wife in a sundress brought him a drink. "I changed the way I feel."

The woman in the car was hugging a little boy as she picked him up from soccer practice. "I changed my reality."

Cut to the handsome man again.

"Hi. I'm Nathan Davenport. Eight years ago, I was a mess. I couldn't pay my bills. I wasn't the father I should have been. I wasn't a man that my wife could be proud of. I was going nowhere. I was frustrated. I looked everywhere I could for answers. I went to self-help courses. They were all scams. I went to religions, but they couldn't tell me anything I hadn't heard before. I researched philosophers from all across the world, throughout history: Plato, Lao Tzu, Siddhartha Gautama, Thomas Jefferson. They all had great wisdom to teach me. They had so many insights. But they only knew a portion of the truth. They only had one piece to a much bigger puzzle. In my research, I put many of those pieces together. And I continue to, to this day, to learn more about the true meaning and purpose of this life."

Cut to a montage of Nathan Davenport. Running in a marathon. Carving a Christmas ham with a beautiful, happy family in a fantastically large house. Shaking the hands of celebrities. Speaking in front of an enormous audience. Sitting behind the desk of a corner office with a view over a city. All the while, his overlaid voice said things that contradicted the images he showed.

"I'm not a special person. I'm like you: a searcher. Someone who's just trying to figure this all out. I'm someone who wanted answers and I took a lot of bad turns before I found those answers. I want to give to you what no one gave to me:

answers. This is the time you need it most. I want to share with you the answers to the question that you didn't even know you should ask: Why did you choose to be born?"

Cut to video of people working in dignified, respectable careers, with smiles on their faces. "We are looking for people like you. People with dreams. People with ambitions. People who know that something isn't right, but they don't know what it is. You deserve the truth. You can't be who you chose to be while you cling to fear, anxiety, depression, and anger. You are the leaders, healers, scholars, and artists of the future. For too long, you have withheld the greatness inside you. Why? Doesn't the world deserve to enjoy the gifts you can offer? I want to tell you how to speak with the person you were meant to be."

Back to Davenport. "Right now, I am offering free seminars all over the country. If you want to hear the truth, I invite all of you to come and take what is right there in front of you." He reaches out to the viewer and closes his hand slowly.

A logo appeared. A compass with the letters PM. "Come and see for yourself what the PathMinder educational movement is all about. I'll see you there."

There was a link in the description below the video. She followed it to a professionally made webpage, with great photography of ethnically diverse people smiling with perfect teeth and the glowing lens flare suns behind them as they basked in the greatness of their own lives. The front page was a lot like the video, with simple sentences asking the same odd questions. The only link was at the bottom. *Would You Like To Know More?* Click.

The next page was full of short testimonials about how the training course changed their lives. Each one describing their problems and how Nathan Davenport's training saved their marriage, saved them from bankruptcy, drug addiction, and depression.

One link at the bottom. *Are You Ready To Ask The Right Question?*

The page was a map, showing her location and the nearest meetings. The closest was south across the border in Memphis this weekend. About a 90 minute drive. And Hannah with no car. She texted Laney.

Hannah: *I had a good time the other night. I looked at the video you sent me and went to the website. The meeting is really far tho and I dont have my car right now. Theres no way my mom will let me borrow hers.*

Laney: *Let me see what I can do.*

Laney made good on her promise less than an hour later.

Laney: *I reached out to a friend who is also going this weekend and she said you can carpool with her! I gave her your number i hope thats okay. Im so excited for you! This is going to be great!*

Alexis: *Hi Hannah! My name is Alexis. Laney said you needed a ride? The meeting is from 8AM-8PM so we have to get on the road early. It's going to be a long day lol*

Hannah: *Hi Alexis. Thank you so much. My address is 370 Washington.*

The website said the meetings were free, but they required a credit card number for a deposit to hold her seat, which they would refund when she arrived.

It was 6AM on Saturday morning and Hannah was drinking a coffee when she heard a couple polite honks outside. She grabbed her purse, stepped out, and locked the door. A chubby smiley woman in an SUV was waving at her through the car window.

Hannah climbed in.

"Hannah?"

"Yeah, hi. Nice to meet you, Alexis."

They left the driveway and got onto the highway. It was an hour and a half of small-talk. Alexis had a couple of kids and a husband. She moved here to be closer to a job her husband found. She knew Laney from church when they were kids. Hannah looked out the window with her eyes unfocused and the terrain blurred across her vision. She took a pill.

They knew they were in Memphis when the traffic got a little more aggressive and a flipped Crown Electric truck was jamming up the road. They found an exit and Alexis followed her map to an exit into a suburb just on the outskirts of the city. It looked like every town. The same buildings with the same colors and logos that crowded every highway offramp from sea to shining sea. They pulled into a strip mall and parked near the sign that said PathMinder Learning Center, between a Hispanic grocer and a sandwich chain. The large windows were covered with a foggy overlay so you couldn't see inside, but they could see some lights were on.

They were a little early and a few people were waiting in their cars. The door opened, and a woman came out and kicked down the doorstop, inviting people to come inside. People started leaving their cars and walking in. As soon as they were inside, they were in a line. A cheery older woman sat at a card table and was asking people some information and giving them nametags and some forms to fill out. The forms asked their names, where they were from, how they discovered PathMinder, why they came, some legalese that Hannah didn't read, and a place to sign. Then they handed her a pencil and a workbook, like the national exams they gave kids when she was in elementary school.

The place was one big, mostly empty room. The walls were sponge painted in warm earth tones. Framed posters covered the walls with images of happy, healthy people in scenic natural places, with encouraging words in cursive white text.

Fear is the experience of truth escaping the mind

Intention is the engine of greatness

If you won't be yourself, who should be you for you?

All quotes attributed to Nathan Davenport.

There was a platform for a stage. There were no chairs at first, but as each person got past the smiley woman taking people's information, a man placed exactly one chair for each person. People filed in, and after fifteen minutes there were maybe 30 people. Another man was already at the front, greeting people, smiling, shaking hands, asking everyone what brought them. When Hannah and Alexis sat, he came up to them, too.

"Hello, ladies! I'm Steven."

The ladies shared their names, too.

"I'm so glad to meet you! Is this your first time? At a meeting?"

The ladies said yes.

"Gosh, I'm just so excited for you. In a way, I wish I could do my first meeting again. What brings you in today?"

Alexis said, "Oh, an old church friend reached out to me and said you guys could help me with some stuff."

"What kind of stuff, if you don't mind my asking?"

"Just, you know. Regular stuff. Marriage and kids."

"I have five boys, Alexis, so I know a thing or two about that!"

Hannah was sure Steven was gay and accidentally said, "Five? Goddamn." Alexis fidgeted at the sound of blasphemy, but was too polite to say anything.

Steven laughed. "They can be a handful, but they are worth it. The courses here have given me so much more power to be there for my kids... to really become the father that my boys deserve to have. You know what I mean, Hannah?"

Hannah swallowed and nodded.

"Okay, you guys. It was so great to meet you, Alexis and Hannah. We'll definitely have to talk again during the break." Steven moved on to the next person, and smiled widely, and laughed at things that weren't funny, and found points of contact with the person, always putting a hand on their shoulder or shaking their hand.

Hannah looked inside the workbook. It was full of personal questions with spaces for her to write her answers. *What's the worst thing you've ever done to another human being? Write about someone who died, but you don't miss. Who do you love most in the world and why do you hurt them?*

Eventually, a man came up to the stage. The woman who took their info, the chair man, and Steven, all took chairs and joined the audience. The three started clapping, and it was contagious. Everyone else started clapping, too, because no one wants to be the only person not clapping.

The man was pink-skinned and physically big, not just muscular, but big. He had a well-manicured beard and a shaved head. He wore an earpiece and microphone. He raised a hello hand and smiled and nodded. He spoke with a voice that didn't match his body: soft, higher pitched than you'd expect.

"Hi everyone! So glad to see you all. I'm Richard Stockton. It's great to have this chance to speak with you and share the gift of PathMinder with a new group."

Richard moved back and forth across the stage like an Eddie Murphy stand up special. His facial expressions were big so that people in the back could see. His gestures were sweeping, his hands hardly ever stopped moving.

"Why are you here? Ask yourselves that. I know why I'm here. But do you know why you're here? Every one of you has a question. You do. You have a question. It's almost the right question. But it's not the right question. You, sir. What's your name?" He pointed into the audience.

A man in khakis and a salmon shirt answered, "Me?"

"Yessir."

"I'm Hank. Oberland."

"Hi, Hank. I'm Richard. Don't call me by my nickname, though."

That got some laughs from the group, including Hank, and especially the three staff members in the audience.

"Hank, why are you here?"

"Um, my nephew came here and said he learned some stuff, so I thought I could also."

"I'm sorry, Hank, but that's not the reason. You just told me about the past. Your conversation with your nephew. That's not the reason. What's the reason?"

"Uh, I guess I was curious. I don't know." He looked around the room a little, hoping to get some feedback from the other audience members, maybe some hint about what to say.

"Hank, what is the question?"

"Uh… what, uh… What question?"

"Yes! That is correct! Everyone, please give Hank an applause for being such a good sport." Everyone did, and Hank smiled and looked relieved.

Richard continued, "Hank has astutely identified the question! The question is: What is the question? We live our lives asking questions. What is life's purpose? Why do I keep trying and failing? Do I deserve love? What am I doing wrong? These are common questions, but they are the wrong questions. All of those questions have answers. But you can't find the answer by asking those questions. Are you with me so far, gang?"

About half the group nodded, especially the three staff in the audience, who made audible "Mm hm!" noises like amens in a

Baptist church.

"Questions are important. Questions identify a blank space in our knowledge. I want to know the circumference of the earth, but I don't know it. So I ask: how big is the earth? By simply asking a question, you admit you don't know something. It admits that you have a need that isn't being fulfilled. Who asks more questions than anybody, gang? Parents in the group, you know who I mean, right?"

A few people in the crowd said, "Kids," and "Children," and a few laughed at themselves.

"Bingo! Children ask questions. They don't know anything! A little baby knows nothing! And they have to learn everything! That's a lot to put on a baby, huh, gang? That's a lot of work and responsibility! Children aren't embarrassed to ask questions. They know they don't know anything. They aren't supposed to know anything. They're kids! Right? But when we get older, we are afraid to ask questions. We aren't children anymore. Adults are supposed to know stuff already. Only children don't know things, right? Once you're an adult, you know everything, right, gang? Haha. That's what children think! They think you know everything. But really, what do you know? I don't even know how to file my taxes and I am 48 years old!"

The crowd was warming up to him, and they laughed easier at his jokes.

"When you're a kid, you ask all the right questions. Why does the moon look small in the sky if it's really big? Where do babies come from? Why can't I have a puppy? These are all great questions. Kids ask questions so they know where to go next, what to do next. But once we become adults, all the great questions have been answered. We keep asking questions. That never stops. But the questions don't work like they used to. They don't take us to the next step like they did when we were kids. They don't show us our true path in this life. The only question left is, what is the question? What's the question that leads us to the next step, like the questions we asked when we were kids? That's what we're here to do today. I am so eager to share it with you, but we have a lot of things to cover first. I can't just show you the ending to the movie before showing you the beginning and middle, right? The ending wouldn't make sense. You'd be like, who are these characters and why are they fighting? A great movie needs a great ending. And it needs a great start. So we're going to start where, gang?"

"At the start!" a few people in the audience called out.

"Where do we start?"

"At the start!" twice as many answered the second time.

"Great. I love this group. I can feel the enthusiasm in the room. It's a great feeling. A lot of energy in this group. Can you feel it, too? Okay, gang. Open up your workbooks on the first page. Paul, mind dimming the lights so we can get the visuals going?"

For the first fifteen minutes, Richard spoke about how cellphones can distract us, and become a way to pretend like we aren't living in the present. The woman came around and handed everyone a bag. Richard asked everyone to place their phones inside of the bags. Everyone could keep the bag, but they needed the phones inside of them. Everyone complied, keeping the bag and phone in their laps or in their purses.

Richard then brought up the chair guy to tell his story. Chair guy's name was Kurt. Before finding PathMinder, Kurt used to be addicted to crystal meth and strippers. On the outside, he had a great career as a day trader, making six figures. His life was a mess until he asked The Right Question. It changed everything for him. Now he was better than ever making more money from anywhere in the world, just doing two hours of work on his cellphone a day. Richard thanked him for being so brave and speaking so openly. Richard hugged Kurt. He got a big applause as he sat down.

The second hour was Richard talking about where knowledge comes from. How we know the difference between truth and lies. The gaps between knowledge. A lie is when information contradicts what we already know is true. When we know the truth, we know a lie.

Hour three, he had everyone pair up with someone they didn't know. Richard had the group move the chairs so the partners were facing each other, and so close that the participants' knees almost touched. Everyone had to stare into each other's eyes and take turns saying one thing they know is true. Hannah was paired with a thick-legged woman with a Tennessee accent named Mary, who dressed like a kindergarten teacher.

Mary started, "Um... where do I start?" She looked away to think.

Steven caught her doing it and reminded her, "Maintain eye contact, Mary."

"Yes, sorry." She looked back at Hannah. "One truth. Um, I've never done anything like this before, that's for sure!"

Hannah's turn. "Me neither."

Steven said, "Don't think too much about it, Mary. Just say the first truth that comes to mind."

"Um, well, I know I tend to overthink things," Mary laughed a little, self-consciously.

"Good, Mary! You're getting it."

Hannah said, "The drive here was boring."

They went like that for a long time. Everyone did. And when anyone tried to take a break from the exercise, Steven was on them instantly, encouraging them to keep going, always keep going. He told everyone that they are very close to being done. It was awkward when they started, but after the first half hour, Hannah didn't remember how to look away. Time slipped away without a clock to look at. She looked into this woman's eyes for so long she felt like she'd known Mary her whole life. It went on and on and Hannah had to go to the bathroom and was getting impatient. She would've looked at her phone to see how long this had been going on for but she couldn't open the bag. Steven got her back on track.

Hannah said, "I know my boss is skimming at work."

Mary's turn. "I know Jesus loves me."

Hannah's turn. "I know that I've been fucking up lately. Sorry for the language."

Mary's turn. "No, that's fine, sweetheart. Um. Me, too. I've been making a lot of mistakes too, actually."

"I know that... I know I can do more. Do better."

"I know my son is in Heaven with the angels." Mary's eyes got wet, but she wouldn't break eye contact. Those soggy, sad eyes locked onto Hannah. In any other situation, she'd look away. But Steven would see. Hannah couldn't just say, "I'm sorry for your loss," and look away. She had to confront this woman's grief. Live in it. Sit in it. Live it with her in the moment. She had to see her pain and be powerless to ignore it.

Hannah said, "I miss my daughter, too."

"I think I was a good mother... no. True things only. I was a good mother. I know I was."

"I'm not. I'm not a good mother. I know I'm not." The tears started coming out of both of them.

"I know you could be," said Mary.

Hannah started nodding quickly, mopping up the salt water on her face with her sleeves. "I know I could be, too."

Mary continued, "I know that you have a good heart. I know it. You're a good person."

Hannah broke eye contact and was about to stand up and head

to the bathroom when she felt a large hand on her shoulder. The hand was gentle, but it pinned her. It was Richard.

"Wow, ladies." He started clapping. So did the other three staff members. Everyone around them stopped their exercises and focused on Mary and Hannah.

Richard put his other hand on Mary's shoulder and kneeled to be eye level with them, looking back and forth between the two women.

"That was excellent! You two had a real breakthrough, Mary and Hannah. Do you realize that?"

The women looked at each other and nodded, and then nodded to Richard.

Richard stood up and spoke loudly enough that the whole room could hear, "You can feel that power, can't you?" The ladies nodded. "Can't you, gang?" The whole room nodded.

He spoke to the room. "That's the power of truth. That's the experience of speaking the truth. That's what the right question can do. When we speak the truth, we are speaking the answer before anyone asks the question. That's fantastic. Give each other a hug! Just a great group today!" The ladies hugged and laughed and cried, while the whole room stood up and applauded them.

Hannah used the bathroom finally and popped a couple more pills. When she got out, they moved the chairs back to their original positions and Richard took the stage again.

"There is a power in each and every one of us. It is the power of intention. Each person has the power to bring good things by being receptive to good things. There is a law of nature. This is very important. Like attracts like. That's a fact. Like attracts like. Quantum physics has shown that the power of thought can impact the environment on a vibrational level, where the environment matches the vibrational frequency of our intentions. By putting out the positive thoughts, you change the energy around you to match your own energy. It's science. I'm not making this up. I'm not smart enough to understand it, but the scientists who have observed this effect are very smart people. Try it now. Everyone, just take a moment. Let's do this together. Everyone, just close your eyes." Someone dimmed the light a little, and some tranquil new age music started playing somewhere, softly. Everyone closed their eyes.

"Now everyone, I want you to think about your intention. Think about what you want. Don't think about what you don't want. Think about something positive you want to invite into your life. Try it."

Everyone sat in silence. Hannah thought about her girl. Thought about her as a baby, those tiny shoes and her laughter.

"Think of other things. Think of what you want. Create the power of your intention. Imagine all of those intentions now all together at the same time. Imagine what it would look like if all of your dreams came true."

The MC gave them time enough to marinate in their fantasies a moment before he invited them to open their eyes. The dimmed lights became brighter.

"Sandy," he pointed to a woman in the front row. "What did Lucas create an intention for?"

"Oh, uh, I don't know…" she looked to her left at Lucas, a man sitting next to her she'd only met that day.

"Yes, you do Sandy. Close your eyes. Tell us something that Lucas wants." All the eyes in the room were on Sandy.

She closed her eyes, "Um…"

"Don't think about it. Just experience it and tell us. It doesn't need to be specific."

Sandy said, "Lucas made an intention… for… making more money?"

The MC asked Lucas, "Is that right?"

Lucas nodded and smiled, "Yeah. Yes. Yes."

The room clapped. The MC asked Sandy, "Now, how did you know that?"

She laughed and shrugged. "I just guessed."

"No, Sandra. No. You didn't just guess. Lucas changed the surrounding environment by putting out that intention and you could feel that. We can all feel that."

"Really?"

"Yes, Sandy! Yes! Lucas here manifested the vibration for wealth. Nobody here should sell themselves short. We all have the power, but we can't use it until we realize we do."

The drive home was completely different from the morning drive. The two women's brains were on fire, talking nonstop, spinning on a weird new high. Their brains were running so fast, their mouths could barely keep up. The car was full of energy and possibilities, like a cocaine-induced planning session, sans actual cocaine. They were spun up on promises and hope. Neither of them noticed that they never got the answer to the question: *What is The Question?*

When the car stopped in Hannah's mom's driveway, it was already 11 PM. She thanked Mary, and she almost forgot to take the 30x20 plastic-wrapped vision board (with included instructions) that she bought from the small PathMinder shop for $29.99. She snuck inside and went to bed, but had trouble sleeping. Her mind was loud, like a toddler before bedtime. When she finally fell asleep, she slept well for the first time in a long time.

She woke up feeling refreshed and energetic. She was up when the sun was and had a modestly portioned, nutritious breakfast. She texted Laney to let her know she had a great experience.

Hannah went to the PathMinder website again and looked for upcoming meetings. The next one was a full weekend event, all day Friday, Saturday, and Sunday. The site said it was a $1,500 value for only $750, while a timer started counting down from 23 hours until the discount ended. She checked her bank account. All her bills were just paid, and she had $378.22 to last the next two weeks.

She told Laney she couldn't swing the expense right now. Laney got back right away to tell her that if Hannah joined the partner program for $39.99/month, she would get a big discount on her next course. The discount was close enough to cover it, but not quite.

She took her mom's car to the store and bought some markers and some bottom-shelf vodka. When she came back, she snuck past her mom, who was still sleeping on the couch in front of the TV. Hannah went into the kitchen and sat at the table and got out her card-stock vision board, which had VISION BOARD printed on the top. She read the instructions. It started with a brief history of the Shoshone people and their ancient tradition of vision boards. *To help manifest, write words, draw pictures, or paste cutouts from magazines.* She poured herself a cocktail of diet neon-green soda and vodka.

She drew a messy scribble that was meant to be a picture of her with Jenna, sitting together under a blanket fort, eating popcorn, and watching a movie together. She realized she hadn't tried drawing a picture since Jenna was about four years old.

Hannah drew a picture of her with her daughter. Then another of her walking with a man, holding hands, a heart between them. She drew a picture of a greenback. She drew a picture of her Mom's grave.

She looked at what she'd made. Visual gibberish full of wants and dreams. It looked as nonsensical as Jenna's old refrigerator exhibition.

"This is fucking stupid. God. I can't believe I'm actually doing this." She stood up and was about to trash the picture when she could hear Richard Stockton's voice in her head. "Like attracts like. Negative thinking draws negative reality."

She sat back down. "It's not stupid." She finished her drink. She stared at her board. He concentrated on it. She stared at it like she stared into Mary's wet eyes when that poor woman was crying over her dead son. Hannah stared at it long enough that the images were almost moving in her mind, like a collage of animations. The longer she stared, the less they seemed like drawings and the more real they looked. They looked less like fantasies and more like things that could be real. Things that should be real. Things that have no choice but to be real.

The sound of her phone buzzing on the table shook her out of her trance. It was Gretchen. She answered, "Hi."

"You gonna be there this time?"

"Where?"

"The hearing. You actually going to show this time? I don't want to tell Jenna you'll be there if you won't."

"What do you mean?"

"The hearing! The custody hearing? They had to reschedule because the judge was in the hospital with a burst appendix. Remember? I texted you about it."

"Hold on." Hannah looked through her text history and found it. "No. Way."

"Okay, fine, I'll just…"

"No, no! I'll be there! I was talking to Mom. I'll be there. How's Jenna? Can I talk to her?"

"She's at school."

"Oh. Okay. Well. How are you?"

"I gotta go."

"Okay."

They hung up. She looked at her text history. That text about the burst appendix wasn't there before. She hadn't missed the hearing while she was in jail.

"That's not possible." She looked at her vision board.

Her little girl ran across the county court's parking lot when she saw her mom and jumped into her arms and Hannah picked her up and they squeezed each other.

"Jenna! I missed you so much!"

Gretchen walked up and said, "Glad you could make it."

They walked into the courthouse together, wearing the best clothes they had, like they were still a real family going to church. In movies, courts look like nearly religious structures, places to worship the law, and to pray at the altar of order, and give thanks and sacrifice to the gods of civilization. This place wasn't that. The city built it in the 70s and looked more like a VFW. A miserable place with a ceiling just a few inches too short, with fissured, water-stained acoustic panels. The walls were wood paneling halfway up. The place barely had any windows and the neon ceiling lights put a sickening yellowish hue on everything, like the faint color of cigarette stains.

They had their hearing. The judge listened while they said their words. While her sister was speaking, Hannah took a moment to close her eyes and create her intention. She tried to bend the energy of the room. She visualized the way things should be. She spoke to the universe and told it that it was confused and needed to correct its mistake. She spoke to it firmly, but politely, like reality was a waitress who brought the wrong meal, as though Hannah expected the universe would gladly apologize and make things right again.

The topic of the DUI never came up. The judge awarded Hannah some scheduled time with Jenna. She was so emotional she could barely contain herself. Gretchen half smiled, a little bit glad to see her sister win one. Hannah and Gretchen and Jenna met in the hall and worked out the details of when Hannah and Jenna could be together. Jenna was all smiles and asked her mom about things they could do together.

She cried when they parted ways. Hannah always cried when they parted. But this time it was a happy cry.

When Hannah got back to her mom's home, there was a package on the porch from PathMinder. She brought it in with her. Her Mom was asleep on the couch again and didn't notice, as usual. She brought the box into the kitchen and opened it up. It was full of packages of nutritional supplements and some literature about how it unlocked the mind to maximize brain potential. DVDs. Magnets to balance spiritual energy. Cushioned shoe inserts. The whole thing was like a gift bag. A glossy pamphlet thanking her for joining the PathMinder affiliate program, full of smiling, successful people.

The next morning, Hannah got a call from her boss, bright and early. That stuck-up old bitch Nancy had quit and Hannah was getting a share of her hours. They were bumping her hours from 15 a week to 30 and needed her that day. Hannah accepted, hung up, and walked into the living room to tell her mom she needed a ride to work. She was still on the couch. She hadn't moved under the smokey afghan. Not at all. Not since yesterday. Hannah said her name a few times and shook her. Her mouth was a little slack, a black pit behind her stained, yellow teeth, her lips textured like dried apricots. Her eyes were just slightly open, and the air was drying them out.

She knelt beside her mom. She remembered some of the good times. She felt a crushing sensation in her chest, a suffocating guilt, like the judgment of God would reach inside her with ghostly hands and strangle her heart. She'd murdered her mother with her Shoshone poster. Hannah thought about the good times and cried a little. Then she remembered that the good times were just the brief interruptions between the bad times. The good times were when her mom was in a good mood with a new boyfriend, until he pointed his eyes at Hannah and Gretchen, and mom got jealous. The good times were when Mom got Hannah ice cream to help Hannah forget that Mom forced her to eat a cigarette as punishment for ruining a pair of sweatpants with her first period. Then Hannah cried more.

She called the police. When they knocked and she answered the door, there was another package on the porch. She picked it up and invited the police in. They asked a few questions, an ambulance arrived, and they took her mother away.

She took her mom's car and drove to work and wasn't a minute late. She didn't tell anyone that her mom had died. It wasn't until halfway through her shift that she remembered to call Gretchen to tell her.

When she got home, her mother wasn't gone. That cigarette smoke smell haunted the place vengefully.

In the morning, Hannah pushed the smoke-stinking couch across the living room. She rallied every muscle with every quarter-foot push, until it was out the door, off the porch, and on the front lawn. Then she rolled it to the curb. She took every hideous porcelain tchotchke, every cross-stitched piece of art, and she trashed them all. She left all the doors and windows open to air the place out.

Gretchen arrived with Jenna. Mother and daughter had a big hug. It wasn't a visit, really. Gretchen just promised that she would handle the funeral and that the coroner called. The cause of death was a stroke. Jenna grabbed onto Hannah when it was time for her and her aunt to go, and cried. Hannah reminded her daughter that they would see each other again over the weekend.

While her sister was organizing the funeral and all the legal stuff, Hannah spent all of her free time absorbing the lessons available online at PathMinder. She watched every internet video published with tips and tricks about manifesting, and common ways that people mess it up. She joined social media groups and found people talking about their great successes and how it changed their lives. She added her own story to the feeds. She threw herself into it like a convert, more faithful than the ones born into it. And every person she could talk into going to a meeting gave a credit towards the next course. She hustled every person she could think of to talk them into going to the first seminar. She made calls. She reached out to old friends and acquaintances online. Many of them already knew what she was talking about because Laney had already contacted them. She even told people at work. She felt Laney's energy for the first time in her life.

Hardly anyone came to the funeral service besides the sisters and Jenna. There were a couple of old ladies that Mom used to work with in the cafeteria at the elementary school that she still played bridge with once in a while. The pastor said some forgettable words about Bonnie VanLier, a woman he'd never met. It was hot that day. Dressing in black, conservative clothes made everyone eager to get it over with. The park was silent besides the words of the pastor and the waves of highway traffic that passed by. They kept the ceremony short. The old lunch ladies didn't stick around. The sisters and the little girl went to a chain diner across the street from the funeral home.

Jenna busied herself with crayons on the placemat while the grownups talked. Hannah said, "Hey, I just got into this new course and it's really great."

"You going to school? That's great! Over at Dyersburg?"

"No, not there. It's not really school, exactly. It's more like an educational course."

"Okay, like a correspondence thing or online or...?"

"It's a, uh, personal development technology."

"I don't understand. What's it called?"

"PathMinder."

"I don't think I've heard of that." Grethen took out her phone and looked into it. While she was looking at the top hits on the search results, Hannah continued. "It's really helped me out. Really given me a bigger perspective on stuff. Like, I'm seeing real changes now. Things are turning around for me. I got more hours at work, I'm feeling better, my injury from cheerleading isn't hurting so bad..."

Gretchen looked up from her phone. "Is this like Scientology?"

"No! No, it's nothing like Scientology! It's PathMinder."

"Some of these websites say it's a cult."

"It's not! Oh my God! That's so wrong. Don't believe everything you read online. PathMinder is trying to help people and these fucking idiots on the internet are so judgemental and cynical. PathMinder is not a cult."

"Okay. They're not a cult. I'm glad you're getting something out of it. But maybe you should think about going to actual school, I don't know..."

"I don't need school. Listen, this thing is so much better than school. I mean, in a way, it is school. I'm learning a lot with their program. Anyway, I thought maybe you would be interested in going to a meeting sometime."

"Yeah, I don't know."

"Hey, remember when you were all about that beauty box thing that came in the mail every four months, and you wouldn't shut up about how great it was? You remember?"

"Yeah."

"Well, this is like that."

"No, it's not."

"No, like I mean, I didn't think it would be cool, but you kept on about it and I tried it and you were right, okay? So this is like that. It's great. It doesn't cost anything if you just try it."

"Okay. Maybe."

"They have one in Memphis this weekend."

"I don't know."

"Just fucking go. It's no big deal. If you hate it, just leave and have a nice time in Memphis. It's no big deal. And it doesn't cost you anything."

"What about Jenna?"

"Jenna can stay with me."

"I don't know."

"I'm her fucking mother, okay? I won't drink anything. I can stay at your house if you like, okay? You can fucking call me every hour if you want, and if I don't answer, you can call the cops or whatever. Hey Jenna?"

Jenna stopped drawing and looked up at her mother.

"You want to have a slumber party with mommy this weekend?"

She smiled at the two women with big eyes that had seen a lot of disappointment in a short few years but never stopped hoping.

Gretchen looked at her niece and said, "Yeah. Okay. One day. Fine. I wouldn't mind a night to myself, to be honest."

"You deserve it, right? You been handling all of Mom's shit after she died. Just take a night off. Go to the meeting. No big deal."

That Saturday morning, Hannah came over to Gretchen's upper-crusty suburban home. Gretchen gave her a bunch of instructions like she was talking to a babysitter, not the girl's mother, then promised Jenna she'd be back tomorrow. Hannah reminded her to tell them that Hannah had sent her.

All day, the girls watched movies together. Hannah rented a few on Gretchen's account: *Footloose*, *Dirty Dancing*, *Grease*. Hannah ordered pizza from a place that also delivered alcohol. She got some white wine, which she told herself didn't really count as drinking. She kept checking her email every fifteen minutes while the girls snuggled under a blanket, ate popcorn and pizza, and Hannah dried a bottle. Every hour or two, she sent her sister a photo of them hanging out as evidence that Gretchen's niece was safe, always careful to not get the wine in the frame. It wasn't until late that night, when Jenna had fallen asleep on the couch with her head in her mother's lap, that Hannah got a notification. She followed the email. Her PathMinder account had been credited with another point, bringing her up to a $400 discount to her next course. She slept great that night and didn't even notice the text from her sister that said, "It's not for me."

In the morning, Gretchen got home. Hannah had already disappeared all evidence of drinking. Gretchen looked pretty content that Hannah hadn't accidentally burned the place down. When Hannah brought up seeing Jenna again, Gretchen seemed more comfortable with the idea. Hannah hugged her girl and went to work in her mom's car, a suspended license in her purse.

On her break, Hannah bought her ticket. She reached out to Alexis to see if she was going, too, but the number was disconnected.

The next day, Hannah drove her mom's car to a hotel in St. Louis with an attached convention area. A few dozen PathMinders were already getting to know each other in the lobby. Hannah checked in at a table where they gave her a name tag and a schedule.

"What about my room?"

"You'll have to talk to the desk about that."

She went to the desk and asked about her room.

"Uh, no ma'am, the ticket for the meeting does not include a room. I'm sorry. We have some available if you like."

"What's the cheapest you got?"

"Uh, we have a... single queen for $280 a night, and that includes..."

"No, thanks."

She called a motel four miles away that cost 70 a night and got a room. She looked at the schedule. She had enough time for a couple drinks and a couple pills before the first event.

The second meeting was a lot like the first, but more so. The speaker was even better. He was more polished, but better at looking like he wasn't. The crowd was bigger and there was even more energy in the room.

After the lecture series ended at 10:30, she drove to her shitty motel. The man at the counter didn't have her name registered and no amount of evidence of her reservation or yelling and cussing would change the fact that the place was full. She spent the night sleeping in her car in the parking lot of a tool & die shop. She fell asleep trying not to overthink what she did wrong, how she manifested this.

The second day, at the nice hotel, speakers filled every available minute. All of them were very energetic, very enthusiastic. They had testimonials. They explained why so many fail is that of their bad attitude, their negative manifesting. They weaved a theology where PathMinder was always right, and if it ever fails its customers, it's because the customer failed themselves.

They did exercises. In one, they chose a person at random and put them in a chair and surrounded them by other people in a circle. Her name was Lilian. The exercise leader called this exercise, *first-impressions*. The exercise leader instructed the circle to give their first impressions of Lilian—whom none of them had met before today—and to only say negative things. People were hesitant at first, but with some coaxing, they began. And after a few insults, the mob got into the spirit of things.

They said things that weren't meant to be hurtful, which is why they were especially cruel.

"You look like you aren't a very confident person. You could work on your posture."

"Your lipstick doesn't match your outfit."

"I can smell your perfume from here.

When they ran out of things to say, the exercise leader encouraged them to keep going. The first-impressions became more and more inventive and wicked.

"You look exhausted. Like you have a lot of kids."

"You dress like you've stopped trying."

"Your bra doesn't fit you very well." Hannah said it without thinking. The woman in the middle reminded her of herself when Hannah was a teenager and the difficulty Hannah'd had finding a bra that fit right.

"You remind me of my best friend. She married the wrong man way too late in life and is afraid of leaving him. You remind me of that."

"You need to floss more. I'm a dental hygienist. I notice that stuff."

"You look scared. I bet you're scared a lot."

"You seem like you need to get laid more. You have that stiffness like someone who doesn't get good sex."

Lilian cried. A lot. The energy of the room turned immediately. Some felt a terrible guilt and others smiled at the success of their words. The leader stood up and said, "Everyone, come in together and give Lilian a great big hug. The crowd stood up in their chairs and the circle collapsed around Lilian and hugged her. Many of the crowd started crying too.

"We love you. We accept you." The leader started a chant, and the others repeated it. "We love you. We accept you. We love you. We accept you."

The leader broke up the group and got everyone to sit down again.

"All of us are terrified of being judged by others. It's natural. It's one of our greatest fears. We spend so much time worrying about what other people think of us, we can drive ourselves crazy. Lilian has just learned what people really think when they see her. We've given Lilian a gift. She doesn't have to worry anymore. She knows. And she survived it. The judgment of others didn't defeat her. They are just first impressions. They don't define her. They can't destroy her. And despite all of those first-impressions, we all love Lilian and accept Lilian."

The group nodded and clapped.

"Thank you, Lilian. And please thank the group for the gift

they've given you."

"Thank you, everyone." Lilian was smiling and wiping away the tears.

On her way home from the meeting, Hannah rattled the last pill bottle, and it made the sound of six. She swung by the pharmacy to pick up her mom's last prescription. The credit card machine declined her card. She tried again twice. She checked her account on her phone. She had a negative account balance, charges paid to PathMinder. She called PathMinder and was on hold for 10 minutes before she got into her car, put the phone on speaker, and drove home. When she was walking up to the door, the call automatically hung up on her.

"What the fuck?"

She called again, and they put her on hold. She went upstairs to her room and looked at her dream board again. She was right the first time. It looked like shit. But she didn't let that fact distract her. She taped the poster to the back of the bedroom door. She stood and stared at it. She gave her complete attention to it. Individually looking at each image, what it represented, what it would mean if she had it, she clearly imagined it like she was watching a movie. And she slowly started integrating them together. She imagined what money would give her and Jenna back in her life for good. She stared at it until the fantasy seemed more real than the reality she was living. Then the phone hung up on her again.

She called her credit card company and asked about the activity and started cussing loudly when they told her PathMinder charges had overdrafted her account. She told them to stop all payments. She called Laney.

"Hello?"

"Hey, Laney!"

"Hi, Hannah!"

"I am getting all these boxes from PathMinder and getting charged for them. What's that about?"

"Did you sign up for the membership program?"

"Yes?"

"And the partner program?"

"Yes.

"Well, that's why."

"Why what?"

"If you didn't want it, why did you sign up?"

"Want what? What is this program? I only signed up because I wanted to watch the videos on the website and get a discount on the next course."

"That's the membership."

"That's what I got, and it's $40 a month!"

"Yeah, but you also became a partner. Only partners get the discount for referrals. That's 40 plus additional fees."

"Fees? Meaning all that shit they've been sending me?"

"That's material to help you engage potential students as a new freelance partner with PathMinder."

"What? I don't want it. Any of it. I'm not interested in doing recruitment for PathMinder."

"Well, l okay, that's your prerogative. But the discount pays for itself in the long run—"

"Fuck the discount, Laney! They're charging me out the ass for this! The discount's for a few hundred bucks, but it's already cost 600 plus almost a thousand in fucking overdraft fees!"

"If you can get 10 referrals a month, it's totally worth it."

"10? I can't do 10! And these fuckers won't even pick up the phone so I can cancel."

"Oh, I wouldn't do that."

"Why the fuck not?"

"Partnering commits you to a 2-year contract. They'll send the bill to collections." Laney pulled the phone away from her ear when she heard Hannah screaming.

"I get a discount for getting other people to go to classes. What kind of discount did you get when I started the partner thing?"

"I get 2 points every month."

"Points? What the fuck are points?"

Laney started describing the elaborate and arcane points redemption system and Hannah hung up on her.

The next morning, Hannah shook her pill bottle, and it made the sound of one. She had less than a day before she started hurting. She heard a knock on the door, went downstairs in her pajamas, and answered it. It was Gretchen.

"You don't call first?"

"I did call. Like four times. Did you just wake up?"

"Come on in."

There was no couch anymore, just a strange open space where it used to be, so the sisters went into the dining room and had a seat at the long wooden table. Hannah grabbed a green energy drink from the fridge and cracked the tab as she sat.

Hannah asked, "Where's Jenna? Why didn't you bring her?"

"She has a swim lesson today, so I thought I'd get away for a minute to talk to you in private."

"Okay. What's up?"

"Listen, Hannah, we have a little bit of a thing." Gretchen corrected herself. "No. It's not a little thing. We have a thing."

"Okay. What's that mean?"

"So, Mom made me the executrix of the estate."

"Right."

"So, um, there's no estate. Mom owed a lot of money. Like, a lot."

"What's that mean no estate?"

"Before we get anything, Mom has to settle up with the people she owes."

"What's she owe?"

"Like… everything."

"I mean, we already knew Mom wasn't rich. No big surprise there."

"No, Hannah, I don't think you get what I'm saying here," she sighed loudly. "They're gonna take the house."

"No. No. That's not right. Mom owned the house free and clear."

"Mom was running up credit cards like crazy. And, apparently, she hasn't paid her property taxes in like 3 years. It's so much money, Hannah. Between what she owes, you and me are looking at getting maybe a couple thousand dollars after the house is sold and we pay back her creditors."

"What are you fucking saying, Gretchen? What the fuck are you saying?"

"I'm sorry, but I… either, we sell the house or the state and creditors are going to take it."

"That fucking bitch. Fuck!" Hannah screamed fuck several times. Her sister knew her well enough to let her get it out of her system without interrupting. Hannah continued. "I know

I've fucked up a bunch and everything, but Mom takes the cake. I can't believe her!"

Grethen nodded.

"How long do I have?"

"It could be a while. Maybe a couple months. These things take time."

"What the fuck am I gonna do?"

"I guess you'll have to get an apartment or something."

"I can't afford a fucking apartment right now."

"Well, you're an adult. You'll figure something else out."

"Can I stay with you?"

"That's... I don't think that'll work."

"Why not?"

"I just... I don't think that's a good idea."

"Just temporarily! I can be with Jenna when you're at work or doing errands and shit."

"Moving in with mom was just temporary, too. Listen. You have the house for a little while longer. You have time to figure out..."

"Is this... is this because of Jenna?"

"What? What's she have to do with anything?"

"I think you know what."

"I don't, Hannah. What are you implying?"

Hannah forced a knowing laugh. "You fucking asshole."

"Asshole? Oh my God, what? What?"

"You did this, right?"

"Did fucking what, Hannah? What are you accusing me of?"

"Executrix? Yeah. I see. You worked this out yourself, didn't you? Make me fucking homeless so you can keep Jenna, right?"

"What the actual fuck, Hannah? How can you say that?"

"Just because you can't have kids, you think you can come and take your niece from me, is that it?"

"Oh my God, Hannah. Oh my God! I cannot believe you right now."

"Don't even try that innocent shit with me, okay? I know that worked on Mom, that worked on Peter, but I've known you too damn long to fall for that shit. Executrix. Mom set you up to set me up. If I'm homeless, there's no fucking way I'll get custody. You fucking bitch."

"Hannah, you need to stop this right now, because you are saying a bunch of shit that you can't take back easily."

"I ain't taking back shit!" she slammed on the table and startled her sister. "You fucking married rich and forgot where you came from. Looking down on me, all the while jealous that I could have a baby, but you couldn't. Fuck you."

A couple polite tears spilled out of Gretchen's eyes. "You think I wouldn't give all the money I have to bring Peter back? Don't you? I watched the love of my life die of pancreatic cancer. Fuck money!"

"Easy for you to say while you got it."

Gretchen said the next part quietly. She chose her words and spoke slowly. "No, Hannah. No. The state gave me Jenna because you are a drunk. I didn't take her from you. I took responsibility for Jenna because of you. I'm her auntie. She needs a mom, but I can't be her mom. But you can't either, apparently. I love her. She's my niece. She's family."

"Yeah fucking right."

"Listen to me, Hannah. Listen to me really carefully right now. I did not take Jenna from you. You got legless fucking drunk and forgot to pick her up from school. She tried walking home in the freezing cold weather until a cop saw her and picked her up. I didn't do that to you. You did that to Jenna. I'm the reason you can see her at all, okay? She's with me and you can see her anytime you want. It wouldn't be like that if she was in foster care. How don't you see that? I want you to have her back, but you're too... fucked up. You know that a stable home is better for her until you can..."

Hannah ended the conversation by grabbing a dirty dish and throwing it against a wall and screaming. Gretchen got up and left in a hurry.

After Gretchen left, Hannah looked up Laney online. Laney put every second of her day on the internet. Every passing thought, every meal, every moment she stood in front of something expensive, every smile, every vacation. Two minutes ago, she posted herself at her parent's country club.

Hannah drove out to the perfect green lawns and Tudor-style homes, to the club with an annual membership higher than most people's yearly take. She parked and walked in through the wood and glass double doors into the country club and walked to the desk and said, "Hi, Laney Birch invited me."

The pointy-faced man said, "I'll just call her and let her know you've arrived." He picked up the phone, and it rang for a while.

"I think she might be in the steam room or something. She said I should just come in."

"She's supposed to let us know in advance..."

Hannah looked at his nametag. "Some people just think they're too good for the rules. That's Laney, all right. I mean, she's like my best friend, but she's one of those people that think that money means they can just do anything they want. Am I right, Ted?" Hannah gave a big smile.

Ted tried to not smile, but the tiniest bit appeared in the corner of his mouth before his professionalism ironed it back out. He gave her a lanyard with a card that said GUEST.

"Thanks, Ted. You're the man."

She texted Laney.

Hannah: *I'm here. Where r u?*

Laney: *Here where?*

Hannah: *Here here*

Laney: *I'm downstairs in the changing room*

Hannah found an elevator, took it down, and walked past a bar where two retired men were drinking, past a rec room where older women were doing yoga, past a laundry room, and then into the ladies' changing room. The place reminded her of high school, with lockers and benches, but this one had private showers.

"Laney? You in here?"

"Yeah, I'll be out in a second." Laney sniffed.

Hannah followed the sound of her voice to a bathroom stall and looked under and saw a pair of furry boots inside.

"You alright?"

Laney sniffed, "Yup. I'm fine. Everything's fine."

"Open up."

"I'll be out in a second."

"Open the door, Laney."

She did. She was sitting on the pot with her pants on. Her mascara was running, and she was blowing her nose into a huge wad of toilet paper.

"What the fuck happened to you?"

"Just. Life." Laney laugh-cried at that moment when the

ridiculousness of human drama and pain makes itself clear in the brief moments of clarity. "I'm not in town because I love this place. I got stuff going on."

"No. Seriously. Laney. What. The fuck?"

Laney came out and took a seat on the bench. Hannah stayed standing.

Laney explained. "My husband, Nicolas, he's been seeing someone else. I didn't want to see it. I knew it was happening. I knew it. I told my therapist I knew it. But I didn't want to know it. Fuck. I'm such an idiot. And we can't keep living the way we have. Nicolas makes good money but, I don't know, we are living paycheck to paycheck still. I'm in the 1% and somehow I'm living nigger-rich."

"The fuck did you just say?"

Laney kept talking. She didn't even hear the question, "My kids all fucking hate my guts. I don't know why. I do everything for them. I just. I can't get a grip, you know? And my yoga pants business just isn't going anywhere. I'm sitting on $12,000 of yoga pants. The market is just so saturated right now. It's impossible."

"Laney, you told me this PathMinder shit works!"

"It does! It does!" Hannah watched the programming kick in as Laney repeated a slogan, "It works if you work it."

"No, Laney! It doesn't fucking work! Your life sucks! My life still sucks! You got me into this horseshit just to save yourself a few bucks!"

"No, Hannah, no! The ambassador program discount is nice, but I did it because I want other people to enjoy the power it's given me!" She looked up at Hannah with sobbing-red eyes and a runny nose. "I'm just full of so much negative thinking, probably from my childhood and my relationship with my dad. I still have a lot of work to do, to cleanse myself of those engrams..."

"Laney, you stupid fucking bitch! These people are fucking using you! They used both of us. They got you to use me, so they could use you! It's so fucked up. I cannot believe you are fucking defending those people."

Laney stood up and pointed a manicured finger at Hannah. "Hey! I gave you an opportunity, okay? I let you in so that you could be as successful as I am! And now you're acting so above it, just like in high school, too cool for everyone else. Too cool to learn anything. Too cool to graduate. I don't know why I thought I could help some stuck-up white trash..."

She didn't finish her sentence because Hannah slapped the thought right out of her head. Laney looked up at Hannah's stone-faced, hard eyes and started crying again. Hannah saw Laney's purse and picked it up and reached in.

"What are you doing?"

"I'm getting back my money. This shit is your fault!" She started digging around in there, and Laney grabbed the purse and pulled on it. They went back and forth and the thing tore in half and spilled the contents all over the floor. Laney screamed about the brand of it and the price tag that comes with the name. Hannah walked out of the dressing room.

When she made it to the lobby, Laney caught up and was crying and yelled, "That woman attacked me in the dressing room and tried to rob me!" and pointed at Hannah.

Hannah stopped and looked at her, and she cowered. Two security guys approached Hannah. She put up her hands, and she said, "I'm leaving. I'm leaving. Don't put your hands on me. Do not put your fucking hands on me! I'm leaving." They put their hands on her. They were a lot bigger than her, but she gave them a fight like they'd never seen at a country club. She screamed and thrashed and kicked them, meaner than a cat grabbed by its tummy fur. She scratched and bit and spit and made them regret taking this fucking job. They tossed her into the parking lot.

"I was on my way out to the parking lot already, you dumb shits! Fuck!"

She got into her car and screamed at the steering wheel while the security guards watched with folded arms. She drove away on squealing tires. When she got far away, she parked on the side of the road and screamed some more. Only then she realized she'd grabbed a handful of things from Laney's purse and taken them. A tampon, a pack of gum, and a laminated card. A ticket to the PathMinder National Convention.

Hannah sold her mom's car with a forged signature, backdated to before her mom died, and bought a plane ticket to Orlando.

In the terminal, she sat at the bar, and when she shook her pill bottle, it made the sound of zero. She felt the tug. She tried to hold it off by chewing three pieces of nicotine gum. She had some drinks at the bar before the woman at the kiosk announced they were boarding the plane.

The ride was an hour and a half and she was dope sick before the wheels left the runway. The mild ambient hum shredded her nerves like bad car brakes. She had the itch, that gravity in your center, a hunger without a mouth. Her skin felt hot and her core felt cold. She was sure she would be crushed, stuffed between a very large man whose ass fat spilled into her seat and a teenage girl who reminded her of Gretchen when she was that age, filling that flying, metal tube like it was a toothpaste bottle. The emergency hatch called out to her, and promised Hannah a 30,000 feet drop to peace and quiet. She sweat a lot. She gripped the back of the seat in front of her with white knuckles. She took long, slow breaths through her nose. She cried a couple times and the people next to her pretended not to notice. The first two times the flight attendant asked her if she was alright, Hannah was polite and said she was fine. The third time, Hannah called her a bitch and told her to mind her fucking business. After that, the flight attendant honored her wishes. She threw up in the tiny bathroom. It was the longest plane ride she'd ever been on.

After her plane landed, she breezed past the people pulling down their bags and filling the aisle, and when it got too congested, she climbed over seats and people like the cabin was on fire. When she was off it, she headed straight for the Florida-themed terminal bar. After ordering and drinking four whiskey sours in record time, she locked herself in a private family bathroom and laid on the floor and let it happen. She took off her shirt because she felt too hot. She wadded it and stuffed it in her own mouth to muffle her yells. A gravity inside her center, like she could collapse inside her hunger for pills. A star finally surrendering to time, collapsing into an infinity of nothingness.

She must've fallen asleep because she woke up to someone knocking loudly. Then the door opened and a TSA woman let himself in, helped Hannah get up, and escorted her out of the airport. The worst of it was over.

She got a cab and made one quick stop at a pawnshop to pick up something special before she went to the convention center. The guy took one look at her and almost refused to sell. But she smoothed herself out and talked him into it.

She took another cab to the convention center. Right away, she didn't fit in. She looked sloppy. She'd made it through detox and her hair was wet and dirty and her eyes were dark. Her skin felt dried out and wet at the same time. The place was absolutely packed with women with big smiles, and big sparkling eyes, and the place was noisy with chatter. The sound of it, the brightness of the lights, was all excruciating. The crowd was packing in tightly behind the barrier of long tables where women with mom haircuts, tousled short layers in the back, the deep side part, and streaky highlights that made no attempt to look natural. They were checking IDs and giving out name tags on lanyards.

Hannah was stuck in the smile-riot for 40 minutes before she made it to the table.

"Hi there! So glad you could make it to the 2015 PathMinder National Convention! Can I get your name, please?"

Hannah said, "Laney Birch."

She checked the record on her laptop. "So happy to have you here, Laney! It looks like you are a member of the ambassador program and you opted in for the platinum-package! Now, all our platinum members have a prepaid hotel room and food card, which you can use just by letting the cashier scan your 2D barcode there..."

"Hannah? Is that you?"

Hannah looked around by reflex. She saw a big, muscular pink bald man. Richard Stockton. The guy from her first free session. He saw her see him. He was the tallest person in the room and he waved at her. She tapped a woman behind her on the arm. "Hey, I think that guy's trying to get your attention." She looked back at the woman she'd just lied to about her name.

The woman continued, "Um, well, yes, so as a platinum member, you also have access to the VIP room where some of the higher level participants will be..."

Richard was still calling her name over the noise.

"Thanks," she took her lanyard, put it on, and walked in.

Just behind her, she heard him still trying to get her attention. "Okay, well, I'll see you inside, I guess!"

The whole thing was a Spring Break party weekend for single moms. The bars were always packed, people drinking strawberry margaritas and chocolate martinis. Hannah was the soberest person in the building, which was a new experience for her. She looked at the schedule on the glossy trifold they'd handed her. There were dance parties, prize giveaways, and seminars telling every business owner why the power of positive thinking is the only skill a person needs. Her brain was free of this trick and once she saw it for what it is, she heard their words for what they really were. She saw the thirsty faces of women who hadn't yet seen these people for the frauds they were. The ladies happily slurped mojitos and PathMinder fiction about how anything wrong in your life is always your fault, never PathMinder's fault. The pamphlet made it clear that the biggest and most important event, one which every person here was sure to attend, was the talk by Nathan Davenport himself.

Her platinum pass came with a room this time. Nicer than anything she'd seen since her prom night. She had nothing but a backpack. She took a shower and went for a meal because her pass also included meals and drinks. When she was cleaned up, she went downstairs to the hotel restaurant. She ordered crab because she was in Florida and Laney was paying, followed by several beers.

"Hey, Hannah!"

She looked up from her meal. Fucking Richard. The big, pink, smiling man walked up and invited himself to sit with her.

"Hi, Dick."

"I thought I saw you! I was calling out, but you didn't see me, I guess."

"I'd like to eat alone."

"Oh, that's fine. I thought I'd just swing by and say hello. So… hello!" He laughed to himself awkwardly. "Glad to see you stuck with it. All the way to the National Convention! Wow! Can you believe it? We're really here!"

Hannah nodded and finished her beer, then waved for the waiter to bring another. Richard continued. "Is that a platinum executive pass?" He pointed to her lanyard.

"Yeah. I guess."

"Wow! Those cost a pretty penny! You really have taken on the PathMinder way, huh? Have you been to the VIP room yet?"

"Nope."

"Wow. I don't even know what I'd say if I met Nathan Davenport in the VIP room!"

"Wait. What?"

"I said I don't know what I'd say if I met Nathan Davenport."

"In the VIP room?"

"Yeah, silly! That's the best part of the Platinum Executive package! It's like a backstage pass at a rock concert!"

Hannah stood up just as her beer arrived. She chugged the whole thing, while Richard watched in silence and his perma-smile withered. She wiped her mouth. "Thanks, Dick."

She walked out of the restaurant while the pink man meekly reminded her, "I prefer Richard, actually."

She looked around for any place that had velvet ropes and security. Wherever she flashed her badge, security let her in. She had access to the whole place. She could walk around freely into the hidden halls between rooms, into the green rooms. Anywhere the staff could go, so could she. After walking through the maze of halls and asking around, she found the VIP room. A bunch of PathMinder honchos were there, but not Davenport. On the 80-inch screen TV in the VIP room, a crowd was gathering in the main event area. The women and men in suits in the VIP area finished filling their small plates from the buffet and sat on the deep and lush couches to watch.

"What's this?"

"It's the lecture by Nathan. Have a seat and a snack and watch."

"Where is this happening, exactly? In the building?"

A uniformed staffer volunteered to escort her. She followed the young man to a backstage area, just behind the curtain and main stage. She could hear someone on stage already, warming up the audience for Nathan Davenport's big entrance. She reached inside her purse and felt the 1911 she had sweet talked from the pawnshop.

It looked just like she imagined the backstage of a movie studio looked. A bunch of people working hard, walking around in a hurry, too busy to notice or care about Hannah. She asked someone where the stage entrance was. They pointed her in a direction and followed it.

She froze when she saw him. She saw the man himself. Even now he seemed like a vision of a person in video imagery, not a real- corporeal, mortal person. A woman was dabbing his face of any perspiration and he took a big sip of some bottled water. He walked out into the blinding light to a roaring applause. Unlike most actors, he looked even better in real life.

The intro speaker said his name, and the crowd roared, whistling, clapping, saying his name. He walked like a man running for president. Hands up, waving, smiling, gliding towards center stage, the crowd going absolutely crazy for him. He simply said, "Welcome!" and the crowd behaved like girls at a Beatles show.

Hannah had stage fright. It was a strange thing to be feeling at a time like this. She was drunker than she thought. It was the six beers or the nerves or both, but she vomited onto the backstage floor. People yelled out in surprise and jumped back to avoid any splatter. She spit and wiped her mouth. She breathed deeply a few times and then marched out onto the stage. A woman with a tight ponytail and a headset told her not to, and Hannah pushed her out of the way when she tried to block her.

Davenport noticed her when she was only just a few feet from the center of the stage. He stumbled on his speech and looked at Hannah and gave the audience a reassuring smile, then asked Hannah, "Uh. Is everything alright?"

"No." Hannah stood on the stage. The audience was nearly invisible under the scorching stage lights that made her squint. She could only see the vaguest shadows of an audience.

Davenport gave a practiced laugh, a technique he learned to hide his own discomfort so that the audience wouldn't see it. "Uh. What is the problem?"

Hannah addressed the room. "This man is a scam artist!"

Security was quick and moved in to grab Hannah, but Davenport stopped them. "No, no! She's fine. She's fine." He addressed the audience and said, "PathMinder sure has its critics!" and he laughed. The audience laughed, too. The security backed away into the shadows of the stage edge, but ready to move if Hannah gave them a reason. Davenport nodded and closed his eyes and used his hand to say silently everything would be fine.

"Come on up here."

Hannah came closer.

"PathMinder has its critics, but we are not afraid to confront our critics," he said to the room. "What's your name?"

"Hannah. VanLier."

He extended a hand to shake and said, "Nice to meet you, Hannah. I'm Nathan Davenport."

"I know. I took your courses. And you're full of shit. You're a fucking snake oil salesman."

Someone in the crowd yelled, "Speak up!"

Hannah yelled, "I said he's a fucking snake oil salesman!" Without a microphone, she had to shout to be heard. She yelled everything she had to say after that.

Davenport laughed. "Well, this is an awkward introduction." The audience laughed, too.

"It's not funny! Why are you all laughing? He didn't even say anything funny!"

"Hannah, if you did the program, then you know that the program only works..." and he pointed to the crowd who said back in one voice, "...if you do the work!" Davenport clapped and the audience clapped with him.

Hannah yelled, "I did the work! I did everything you said! I got kicked out of my home. I'm fucking homeless now. My mom is dead! I can't even see my daughter anymore! And I'm not getting her back because I listened to you!"

Davenport gave exaggerated sympathetic eyebrows, like a stage actor, big expressions so that the audience could see it. He nodded with a considered look, a fist under his chin. The false concern and thoughtfulness was maddening.

She looked back at the crowd. "I want you all to see this! I want everyone who is watching the stream at home to see this! This man is a liar! He's a false prophet!"

Davenport interrupted, "I am not a prophet, Hannah. I am just a man trying to help others with the techniques and skills that I learned in Tibet and on Wallstreet."

"God, I cannot believe I bought your bullshit! I am such a fucking idiot for listening to you! And so is everyone watching this! You're all idiots, just like me!"

The blurry silhouettes in the bright stage lights booed her.

"Hannah. You are projecting a lot of negativity. Everyone in the audience can see that." The audience clapped and whooped.

"And that negativity is where your problems come from. Like attracts like. We know this from quantum physics. Negative feelings attract negative outcomes."

"That's not real! That's some stupid voodoo shit you tell people so when your bullshit program doesn't work, you can tell them that any bad feelings it causes them are really their own fault. God! It's just like my mom always fucking telling me I made her hit me! Fuck!"

"I sense that there is a great deal of trauma in your past..."

"No, asshole! You don't sense it! I just said it! I literally just said I have trauma in my past!"

"...and until you deal with your past trauma, you won't be ready for the advanced courses. Have you read my bestselling book, *Yesterday Strangles Today*? I feel there is a lot you could gain from it. You don't need to be a victim of your own past. You can release the hurt of the past and allow the positive vibrations to manifest a better future. Hannah, I want to thank you for coming here today. I think it was a great opportunity for the audience to see what negativity and self-hatred can do to a person who hasn't interrogated their own decision to be born. Ladies and gentlemen, please, could you all give a hand to Hannah for being brave enough to come out here?" The crowd applauded and whistled for her.

Davenport nodded to the security. They took a step forward, and when Hannah saw them, she drew a gun from her purse. A chrome plated 1911 with an image of Elvis Presley on the grip, the only pistol they had at the pawnshop. She pointed it at the corporate cult leader. Loud sounds of "Oh my God!" and "She's got a gun!" came from the blurs of the crowd behind the lights.

"Do not fucking move. Nobody. Move."

The security drew their guns. Hannah put Davenport between herself and security. The producer was screaming for somebody, anybody, to cut the livestream.

Davenport said, "Hannah. We can work something out, okay? What do you want? I can give you some free courses if that's what you need, okay?"

"I want my daughter back! Can you give me that?"

"In my book, *The Quantum Power of Family*..."

"Jesus fucking Christ. You can't turn it off, can you? You can't even stop with a fucking gun to your head."

Davenport kept trying to sell her his book. She screamed and thumbed the hammer. She turned him around so he could see her. She put the gun in his mouth to shut him up and then she pulled the trigger. *Click.* It was close enough to his mic that it got picked up and transmitted through the speakers and onto the stream.

The security pounced on her, tackled her and disarmed her, while two others grabbed Davenport and rushed him off the stage.

The audience was in a state of panic until someone in the audience yelled out, "He manifested it! He stopped the gun by manifesting it!"

Someone else yelled, "The law of attraction protected him!"

Another yelled, "It's the power of intention!"

The audience stood and cheered and clapped and chanted, "PathMinder! PathMinder! PathMinder!" The thick-armed men pinned Hannah on her stomach. She was zip-tied, while a security man's shin pushed her face down, forcing her to watch Davenport return to the stage to face his flock, his arms open and welcoming like a painting of Jesus. They cheered for Davenport and the miracle that Hannah created for him.

The Elvis

The first time I was served this drink was at a card game in Vegas back in '04. Mine tasted weird because a woman from Indiana spiked my drink with ketamine and robbed me. Long story short, I ended up marrying her, so this drink has a special place in my heart.

Time: 3 days to get the sherry infused. Once that's done, less than a minute to mix.

Ingredients

- ½ a banana, sliced
- A bottle of sherry
- Peanut Butter Whiskey. Yes, it's a real thing
- Normal Whiskey. I like Jim Beam for this
- Bitters
- Bacon salt

Gear

- A glass
- A jar
- Something to strain with

Prepping

1. Put the banana and sherry in a jar and let them infuse for 72 hours
2. Strain out banana slices and throw them away

Mixing

3. Rim a glass with bacon salt
4. 1 part regular whiskey
5. 2 parts peanut butter whiskey
6. 3 parts banana sherry

Serve with

- A deck of playing cards
- Poker chips
- The music of *Frank Sinatra*
- $10,000 of the Cornbread Mafia's money that you need to clean

CHAPTER 1: I GOTTA KNOW

Bakersfield, CA

10/8/77

6:31:54

Oakley opened his eyes, but he couldn't see anything. Wherever he was, it was near-perfect dark. He could tell he was in a stuffed recliner, the kind his dad sat in. He reasoned he must be looking at a roof or the sky, because he was leaning all the way back, legs up on the extended leg rest. He tried to lean up, but couldn't. He tried moving his arms but couldn't. His head hurt. His lip hurt and he could taste metal. And his right hand hurt.

"Fucking assholes," he griped. "Very funny, guys. Hey! Cut this tape off me!"

No one answered. It was so quiet he could hear the tiniest whistle in his nose and the sound of tape stretching every time he breathed. Where was he? No wind. No bugs. Was he inside? Then the sound of a refrigerator clicked on, and gently buzzed. He was indoors.

He flexed his legs and abs but couldn't move. His hand felt around for the wooden lever on the right side. He pulled it and the contraption folded him up so he was sitting upright.

The room was about as black as a place can be except for the sign that sat on a small chair in front of him. It was a Lite Brite, glowing like Christmas. The lights spelled out, "Press pedal when awake." He could just barely see the shapes of a few other things in the room, the faintest outlines visible in the children's breakfast cereal colored light. A desk to his left. Maybe a workbench, and the buzzing refrigerator to his right.

He looked down and saw a pedal with a cable that trailed off to somewhere in the blackness past the sign.

He yelled a lot of questions out into the darkness. The same questions you'd ask, like, "Hello? Is anybody here? What's going on?"

The only thing that answered his questions was the Lite Brite sign, which reliably gave the same answer no matter what question he asked.

He put a foot on the pedal, then hesitated before applying any pressure. "What are the odds anything good will happen if I press it?" he asked himself without speaking.

He pressed it. Nothing happened. He pressed it again just to make sure. Then he pressed it repeatedly, furious at it for not answering any of his questions. He kicked it and heard it skid away into the darkness. Then just silence.

Oakley heard creaks and thumps of footsteps coming down old and aching wooden stairs ahead of him. He couldn't see anything, but when the sound stopped, he knew someone was in there with him.

"Hello?"

The darkness sent the pedal back, skidding across the cement floor until it stopped by his foot.

"Who's there?"

A light came on with the tug of a chain. Oakley closed his eyes from the blinding strength of it. He let himself look slowly as his eyes adjusted. A lightbulb, hanging from a chain from the ceiling, maybe 6 feet in front of him, just above the Lite Brite.

"Oh fuck. Oh, fuck." The sounds came out of him when he saw the man, or rather when he didn't see him. Every inch of him was covered. A gray hooded sweatshirt, drawstring pulled tight around the face. Sweatpants. Gloves; the latex kind that doctors wear. Tennis shoes. On his face, a wrinkly, paper maché mask, with a pair of tiny black holes that hid some eyes. The thing had an image of a face pasted on it, torn from the cover of a magazine, wrinkled and poorly pasted on, like something a child would make as a gift for their parents. In his hand, a plastic grocery bag from Fazio's. Oakley wondered what was in the bag. Then he hoped he'd never have to know.

He got a better look at the room with the light on. A work table against the wall with a mechanical ammo press on it. Next to it was recording equipment: a pair of cassette tape decks for dubbing and a machine for mixing. A pair of speakers on opposite sides of the room.

There was the refrigerator. The walls were covered with soundproofing foam pyramids, like a vertical field of dragon's teeth. Just behind the man with the paper maché face was a heavy, red velvet curtain, like he was standing on a stage performing.

"This isn't funny," Oakley said, hoping he was wrong, and that this was all going to be very funny.

The masked man walked up to the table with the cassette deck and pressed play with a latex-gloved finger. Click.

"Do you know Russian roulette?" The paper maché man didn't speak with his mouth. That's what the tapes were for. He spoke through the speakers from two directions. When the sentence was done, he pressed the stop button. Click. The speech was all sampled from different recordings, like an audio ransom note chopped out of letters from different newspapers. The voice, tone, accent, and recording quality changed several times in every sentence. It sounded like a drunk minah bird.

Oakley nodded. "What?"

The paper maché man carefully rewound the cassette and pressed play again. Click. "Do you know Russian roulette?" Click.

"Um... yeah. I've heard of that."

Click. "Do you know Latvian roulette?" Click. The same recording samples from the previous statement with one word replaced.

Oakley shook his head.

Click. "Latvian roulette is Russian roulette but with a semiautomatic." Click.

"That's just a guaranteed dead person. That doesn't even make sense."

Click. "I guess the joke is that Latvians never win." Click.

"I don't know shit about Latvia or why I'm tied to this chair."

Click. "I came up with a way to do Russian roulette with a semiautomatic, but it isn't Latvian roulette. It isn't always a death sentence." Click.

Oakley swallowed hard. He detected something in the background of the recordings. Laughter? Some portions sounded vaguely familiar, but they changed so quickly he couldn't pin it down.

The man unplugged the Lite Brite and removed it from the chair. He sat down and placed the plastic grocery bag in his lap. He put a hand in and took out a Colt 1911. Oakley struggled against his restraints.

The paper maché man reached back into the bag and produced an unopened box of .45 ammunition. He held it up so Oakley could see. He opened the box and took out one round.

Oakley fought the tape with everything he had. "This isn't funny! Let me go!"

The paper maché man sat at a workbench and placed the round on its primer, business end facing up. He reached into an old coffee tin already on the table and took out brass casings, one at a time, and set them all in a row next to the fresh round. Seven empty casings. He knocked the hopper on the press with his knuckle. It had some kind of powder in it, but it wasn't gunpowder. It looked more like sand. The paper maché man carefully placed each round in and pressed a fresh new bullet into every casing. When he was done, he walked back up to Oakley so he could see. Seven rounds, weighted with something other than gunpowder, but he hadn't changed the spent primers. He walked over to the fridge and picked up a bright orange plastic jack-lantern pail that was on top, the kind that kids go trick-or-treating with. He held it to Oakley's face so he could be sure it was empty. Then he dropped the dummy rounds into the pail, one at a time, so Oakley could count them. Plunk. Plunk. Plunk. Plunk. Plunk. Plunk. Plunk. Then he picked up the one hot round and showed it to Oakley so he could see. He dropped it into the pail with the seven dummy rounds. Plunk.

The paper maché man held the pail up by the handle and he gently bounced it, shuffling all the rounds together, just a few inches from Oakley's face.

Click. "Do you think this is shuffled enough?" Click.

Oakley didn't say anything. He just swallowed hard. "Listen, man. I don't know what you want from me."

The paper maché man rewound the recording, making a squeaky garbled sound. He carefully monitored the display showing the exact time in the tape, then stopped it, and played it again. Click. "Do you think this is shuffled enough?" Click.

Hearing the same sample twice in a row helped. Oakley could

hear that the background noise in a couple of samples was an audience laughing. Definitely.

"Not really, no."

Maché Face bounced the pail a bit more. Oakley could hear the tumble of them rattling and clinking together. The man put the plastic handle up to Oakley's mouth. Oakley looked at the wrinkled, crevassed face, into the tiny empty eyes. Oakley opened his mouth a little and Maché Face put it in. Oakley bit down.

Click. "Cut the deck." Click.

"How?" Oakley asked through his teeth.

The man shook his head a little back and forth like he was saying no. Oakley imitates the motion with the pail in his teeth, like a dog on a chew toy, and he could feel the rattle sound of the cartridges tumbling around.

The man took the pail back from Oakley's mouth. He sat back down and put the gun, a magazine, and the pail into his lap. He removed the empty magazine from the gun and reached into the pail, and fed one round directly into the chamber through the breach. The rest he fed into the magazine one at a time. Oakley looked carefully to see if he could tell the difference, but they all looked the same from where he was sitting.

Once he'd loaded the gun with 7+1 rounds, the man stood up and walked to the tape player, and once again consulted his list of times. He wound the tape, and pressed play. Click. "You have a 1 in 8 chance with this gun, which is better odds than a six-shooter." Click.

That one voice again. Oakley knew he knew it from somewhere.

"It's not Russian Roulette. It's not Latvian Roulette. So what's this called?" asked Oakley.

The man checked a sheet of paper on the desk, moving his

pointing finger like he was looking for something. When he found it, he started fast-forwarding his cassette quickly, then slowly, until he found the right time.

Click. "I think I invented it, so I get to pick a name. I call this Polish roulette." Click.

Steve Martin. One of the voices was definitely Steve Martin from *Let's Get Small*.

The maché-faced man pointed the gun at Oakley and Oakley winced to his side reflexively and looked away like he didn't want to make eye contact with the barrel. That's when he realized the chair was on a painter's tarp laid down underneath him.

"You gonna tell me why I'm here or what?" Oakley asked.

The tape wound backward, then stopped. Click. "Tell me why you're here, and I'll let you go. What did you do to deserve this?" Click.

Oakley knew that voice, too. Those corny guys that his mom liked. What were they called? The Smothers Brothers. *At the Purple Onion*. Mache took all his samples from comedy records.

"You brought me here!"

The tape wound then clicked. "You have between 1 and 8 chances to guess why you are here. What did you do to deserve this?"

"Man, I don't fucking know!" said Oakley, and then he heard a click of the pistol's hammer slap and he yelled, "Fuck! Fuck! Fuck you, man, fuck you! Stop it, fucking stop it!"

The tape clicked and played, "That was not the right answer. You now have between one and seven more chances to guess why you are here."

The man racked the gun and ejected the bad round.

"I didn't do shit, man! Why the fuck are you doing this?"

The tape rewound then, click. "That's the question you need to answer. Why am I doing this?" Click.

The man found another answer on his notes, wound forward, then pressed play. Click. "I am setting a clock. You will have one hour between every try. If you need something or you are ready to take a guess early, press on the pedal." Click.

The man set the clock and placed it on the chair alongside the gun. He reached up and pulled the chain on the light and everything vanished into the darkness. The only thing was the glow-in-the-dark face of the clock ticking down one hour, and the silhouette of the gun laying in front of it.

Oakley was alone again. He spent the first thirty minutes pulling, twisting, and fighting the duct tape. He figured if he could stretch it just enough, he could wiggle his way out. That might've worked if it were duct tape. This was that twine tape that people use for sealing boxes, and it had no give. He didn't make any progress. He was just tired. The maniac left the gun right there in front of him, taunting him to come and take it.

His brain was moving too quickly, with too many thoughts going at once, all competing for his attention, pulling him in every direction at once. He interrupted them, just like he was organizing a room full of panicked people. He spoke to himself out loud and the mental noise got quieter, and listened to the one that was talking.

"Okay. This guy's pissed at me for something. Maybe he thinks I did something I didn't do."

He did math without numbers, a kind of survivalist pre-thought, a million years evolved risk assessment. He measured every bad thing he ever did against the likelihood that the masked man would be the person who wanted revenge for it; the heinousness of the act, multiplied by the likelihood this guy knew about it, multiplied by the chance that the person he wronged was enough of a psycho that they'd do this.

When the clock finished ticking down, it was just a few seconds later that Oakley heard the creak of the steps. He noticed something odd on the steps. He could hear a step, then a squeak as he put his weight on it, then another, lighter step, no squeak. Then again. The paper Maché man was putting one foot on the next stair down, then the other on the same step. He had trouble walking downstairs.

The light came on, blinding Oakley again. When his eyes adjusted, Maché Face was standing by the tape deck again. Click. "Tell me why you're here, and I'll let you go. What did you do to deserve this?" Click. Then he sat in his chair again, the gun in his lap.

Whatever it was, Oakley had to say the most likely first, because he didn't know how many chances he had left.

"I think this is about Lewis. Everyone knows about me and Lewis. How I took his future. A lot of people are still sore with me about that."

The Story About Lewis

Lewis Álvarez was already first-string QB on varsity his freshman year. They say he was being scouted by UCLA at fifteen.

You probably think you know the story of what happened between me and him. How I crippled the Humes High quarterback. How I cost him his college scholarship. How I ruined our chances at a championship. How I wrecked a kid's future when he was just 17.

I didn't know him. Not really. I knew his dad, though. George Alvarez owned The Sixer. You know that drive-thru liquor store up on Glanton? George was my boss. I woulda been... 23 at the time? I didn't know or care about high school football.

One Friday night, Lewis came into the drive-thru feeling high on a victory against Corona. The car was packed with kids. Lewis, a couple of other guys on the team, and a couple of girls. Lewis gave me a big order. Lots of beers. Lots of bottles. And he said his dad would cover it. At the time, I didn't know who his dad was or why he thought I was gonna sell him liquor. Lewis told me he was George's boy and that it was no big deal if I gave them booze. He said I must be new.

So I told him, "George didn't tell me about that. How about I call him?" I meant it, too. I reached for the phone to call.

Lewis didn't like that one bit. He got out of the car. The other boys followed, then the girls, too. They walked right in and Lewis told the others to help themselves to whatever they wanted. Five kids in there, snatching up bottles like a riot, taking as much as they could carry.

Maybe you can imagine my position. If this was anyone else, I'd be getting hands on with these little shits and calling the cops, right? But the owner's son? What am I supposed to do? I can't whup his ass. And I can't let him steal, either.

One boy popped the trunk, and they all started dropping the alcohol in. Must've been four cases of beer and as many fifths of liquor.

What do I do? What would you do? The kids started climbing back into the car, ready to take off, so I stood in front of it. The kids honked and cussed me out. The driver put it in reverse, but another customer had just pulled up behind. The kids were blocked in on both sides. The kids all got out, and they popped the trunk and started drinking the booze right there in front of me, under the awning of the drive-thru. They looked at me defiantly, like I was the asshole cop or teacher they were rebelling against. I never had a teenager look at me like that.

Lewis said something snotty, like, "That's cool. We'll party here." They passed a bottle of 151. Customers were lining up and yelling out their windows and honking.

Two of the kids were sitting on the hood. One leaning on the door. They were acting ridiculous. I couldn't just stand there all night. When I saw my chance, I walked up to take the keys out of the ignition. I almost got em, but Lewis stepped up to me. Maybe he thought I was stepping up to him. As soon as he was out front, puffing his chest out at me, crowding me, then his friends backed his play. One next to Lewis and one standing right behind me. Just how hyenas do it. The girls weren't any help. They laughed. They thought it was great.

Lewis started talking tough, which was easy when he had 3 deep sips of strong drink and three-to-one numbers. The more he talked, the more those two girls egged him on. If they hadn't been there, if Lewis hadn't felt the need to impress them, I don't know. His life coulda gone a lot different.

I moved towards the car. He pushed me. I pushed back. The guy behind me grabbed me, just like I knew he would. Slipped out of my jacket, though. We traded some punches. Customers in the cars behind them got out and tried breaking it up; a man in plaid and a cowboy hat, who had to be 70 years old, and another fat guy with a beard. It wasn't easy for them. These kids were liquored up athlete's.

Well, it seems Lewis's friend who was driving left that car in neutral. In the scuffle, Lewis fell to the ground. I was pushing one of the other guys up against the car door, and a girl was behind me, pushing on me, and the car rolled. Lewis had one foot under the tire and it rolled over it at the worst angle you can imagine. Think about exactly how you wouldn't want your ankle twisted. Yeah. It happened like that. I could hear the pop, even over all the scuffling and yelling.

When the kids saw what happened to Lewis, they stopped fighting me. They surrounded Lewis and got him back into the car. The girls were petting his hair and cussing me out. The boys made some tough guy promises before they drove him to a hospital. They never followed up with those.

From what I heard, Lewis was in the hospital for a while. He mostly recovered. But only mostly. He just never could perform like he used to. Couldn't run the same. Couldn't sidestep a tackle like he used to. He could play, but he needed a lot of time on the bench to recover from the hurting. The scholarship never happened.

I got fired. Wasn't a great job, anyway. But I liked George and didn't feel great that he blamed me for ruining his son's life. A lot of people in town blamed me. I was the adult in the situation. I should've known better. There were a lot of rumors. Probably spread by those kids. They changed up the story to make me sound a lot worse than I was, like I attacked those kids. Like I crushed his foot on purpose. I don't know. Maybe people believed them so easily because they wanted to. Lewis was a star and I was a dirtbag selling booze through car windows. Maybe people just believe the first version of a story that they hear and think anyone who tells them differently is a liar.

The cops arrested me, but those two other guys backed me up and told them how it was. Only they told the cops that I was the one who put the car into neutral. That's not how I remember it.

An event like that'll teach you who your friends really are. Not everyone really gets to test who their friends are. It's not always who you think. A good friend isn't a person you spent the most time with or had the most fun with. A good friend isn't someone who's been through the most shit with you or who knows they owe you for all you did for them. A good friend is a guy who doesn't give a fuck. A guy who will slap the nonsense out of someone's mouth. Hard-headed. The kind of guy who won't be moved. Who won't be lied to. That's a friend.

That's what I learned.

"I think he changes oil now, instead of throwing for the Chargers. I heard that when it rains, it aches so bad he calls off at work. I took that boy's destiny from him. I didn't even know him. I still wonder if I should've just let that kid take the booze and go."

The paper maché man nodded thoughtfully.

"Are you Lewis?" Oakley asked him.

The masked man raised the gun.

"No no no nononono," the word became like a stutter.

Click. He ejected the bad cartridge. It bounced and rolled under the fridge.

Oakley was panting, and his eyes were wild-looking. "Goddammit just tell me what I did! Why are you doing this?"

Maché Face played the tape. Click. "That was wrong. You now have between one and six more chances to guess why you are here." Click.

Maché Face left him in the near-perfect darkness and quiet. Just the green glow-in-the-dark clock ticking away one hour and the gun. Then some music upstairs. A gospel quartet, muffled through the ceiling.

Oakley started talking to himself again.

"To know what I did, I gotta know who the fuck this is. If I know that, it will be easy to figure it out. What do I know about this guy?"

He looked around the black room and mentally populated it

with the things he remembered being there when the light was on.

"He's a man. Pretty sure about that from the shape of him. He loves Jesus. Or gospel at least. Might be half deaf, he plays it so damn loud."

Oakley looked around the room, and even though he couldn't see much, he could easily remember what was there.

"Okay, okay. Work bench. This guy works with his hands. He has an ammo press. He's a gun guy. He shoots a lot. He shoots enough that it's worth it to have a press. Hunter or soldier? It's a little chilly. I'm in a basement. I think. He's upstairs. He has a basement. Or access to a basement. He soundproofed the walls. That means we are close enough to other people that he's worried someone would hear me yelling. I don't know if this is enough to muffle a gunshot, though…"

He looked at the recording equipment. "Or maybe he records down here, and he already has the soundproofing installed. Shit.

"He's a he. He works with his hands. Likes comedy records. Enjoys shooting. Maybe he records music. He fucking hates me. Smart enough to set this whole thing up. Who the fuck do I know like that?"

He dug around through the noise of his head, the constant suggestions from one portion of his brain, and all the reasons those suggestions were wrong from another. A loud argument, and in a room as perfectly dark as this one, they were the only thing he could hear. A few names came up, but none of them were perfect. They had a few of the traits, but not all of them. A lot of noise in his head until the music stopped. Oakley heard the creaking stairs again. He closed his eyes. When he heard the light click, he opened them slowly, so it wouldn't sting. The paper maché faced man went to his tape deck and pressed play.

Click. "What did you do to deserve this?" Click.

Oakley chose a name. Someone who liked comedy. He was in the Army, so probably knew how to shoot.

"I think... I think this is about Herman. Is it?"

Maché Face didn't say yes, but he didn't shoot Oakley, either. Oakley went on.

"I wasn't nice to him. In high school. I don't know if you're Herman or you're a friend of his or what. Am I right?"

Maché Face sat down and crossed his legs, ankle on a knee, and leaned back, hands and gun in his lap.

"Um. I don't know what else to say. I was hard on him."

Maché Face extended a hand, palm up, then put it back in his lap, gently encouraging Oakley to keep going.

"You want me to be more specific?"

Maché Face nodded.

The Story About Herman

Um. Herman was a kid in high school who... I don't know. He didn't do anything to me, exactly. He just had this way that made me... angry. In class, he'd raise his hand every five fucking minutes, you know? And when the teacher called on him, he just talked and talked and talked. He took over the classroom. And he sat in front. He made it like... class was just a private conversation between him and the teacher. I had trig with him. Mr. Ericsson was sick of it, too. You could see it. He'd try to get anyone else, fucking anyone, to participate, calling on random people, you know, just to snap their attention back to his lessons. But fucking Herman. Always with his hand up.

And he had this way about him. This kind of sneering. A fucking air or superiority. I bet in his mind, everyone thought they were better than him. He had fucked up posture and his nipples were always popping out through his shirt. I don't know what was with that. He needed a better shirt. Or better nipples. And he had a nasally voice. And a terrible fucking laugh. That was the worst because he loved telling jokes. You never wanted to see him have a good time because when he laughed, it was like fucking dental work. That fucking sound would rattle your whole skull. The worst sound I ever heard.

But, yeah. I think he thought that we thought we were better than him. But he had that all the way backward. He thought he was better than us. He was smart. But he wasn't some great fucking mind. All I ever heard him say was what he thought the teacher wanted to hear.

He was one of those kids who thought the teachers were his friends. When he graduated, it's not like the teachers would come and hang with the guy at the Palladium, play pinball, or pool with him. Nah. You know. Now that I think about it. Herman didn't want friends. Not really. I think he wanted to be close to the people in charge. He wanted to be friends with the teachers cus the teachers were in charge. He was a Boy Scout. I only know that cus he'd wear that goofy outfit to formal events like it was a damn service uniform. I think he was one of those junior cop kids, too. Those narcs in training. ROTC for the Sheriff's Department. He was weak, and he just sucked up to the people in charge, like being their friends would protect him. It didn't.

Whatever it is, I did to him... I don't know. What's the worst thing I ever did to him? It wasn't one thing. It was a few things. Nothing that big. Shoving him. Telling him to shut up when his laugh was too much. Dumping his books if I saw him looking at me sideways.

The worst thing, though? I guess... I know. One time, I pushed him into the girl's bathroom. I shut the door behind him and I held tight to the handle. He tried to get out. He was pulling with everything he had, but I had a good 50 pounds on him.

I could hear the girls inside yelling at him to get out and he kept trying, but I wouldn't let him. Then I let go, and he fell backward and fell on another girl. No one got hurt too bad. Herman hated me after that. Didn't really bother me, though, to be honest. Herman's hatred didn't mean anything to me.

I've thought about finding him and calling him. Telling him I'm sorry for being so mean, but, honestly? That guy was an asshole. I feel a little bad, yeah, but fuck. There were a lot of nerds at that school, but he's the only one who was enough of a prick that I'd actually slap the books out of his arms.

"I haven't really thought about that guy in a while. I heard he joined the Army and was playing French horn in the marching band or something. So? Am I right? Am I here for bullying Herman?"

Maché Face pointed the gun at him.

"No! Wait!"

Click.

"Goddamn! Fuck!" He could feel the blood pressure in his neck and face. His heart was beating so hard.

Maché Face stood up, ejected the bad cartridge, reset the clock, set the clock back down on the chair with the gun, then pulled the chain on the light. He vanished into the dark, just like every other thing except the glow of the clock and the silhouette of the gun in front of it.

Click. "That was wrong. You now have between one and five more chances to guess why you are here." Click.

Oakley could hear him go back up the creaky stairs to whatever was up there.

Oakley picked up where he left off. "A LiteBrite. And a Halloween candy bucket. He's got kids. Or younger siblings. That thing wasn't new. He's near kids. He could borrow it. He likes comedy. He likes comedy a lot. He has a fuckload of comedy records. He has to, to make those recordings…"

Then he wondered how he even got into that room.

"When did I get nabbed? And why's my memory totally fucked? Someone must've dosed me. At the party? There was a party. There definitely was a party. Was that freak at the party? Is anyone looking for me right now?"

He had vague recollections. He kind of remembered coming back and picking up Denise and the keg. Then they went together. Who was at the party? It was in that barn at Theo's parents' house. Shit. Who was there? He remembered pouring a cup and talking to some girl. With red hair. Did she have a cowboy hat? Shit.

"He doesn't want me to know who he is. Probably means he'll let me go if I guess right. But maybe he just doesn't want me to know because then I'll know the answer right away. I must know him. Okay. Guy likes comedy. Likes guns. Has high-end musical gear. Has kids, probably. Has access to a basement. Thinks I did something to him. That leaves… fucking who?"

He started making a list of anyone who could match that description. The more information he had, the harder it was. It narrowed down the options towards… who?

The clock ticked down. The steps on the stairs. The light clicking on. Oakley's eyes closed before they came on.

Click. "You have between 1 and 5 chances to guess why you are here. What did you do to deserve this?" Click.

Oakley thought out loud. He couldn't see the man's face,

but maybe he could see something in his posture, his body language. If he walked Maché Face through his thinking out loud. Maybe the guy would reveal something, give him some kind of clue, show Oakley if he was on the right track or the wrong track.

"You like guns, right? Me too. You shoot a lot. A hunter? You love comedy records. You have a house. In a neighborhood. Close to other people."

Maché Face froze up when Oakley started describing him.

"You have kids."

Maché Face's posture relaxed. That's a miss. No kids.

"I think I got this. I think this is cus I told on Uncle Paul and he went to jail. But… you're not Uncle Paul. He was a much bigger guy. But you got a lot in common with him. Really into comedy. Love hunting and fishing. I think you're Little Paul. I think you figured out I was the one who told on your dad and you're mad about that."

The paper maché head tilted a little.

Oakley asked, "Am I right? Are you my cousin Paul?"

Maché Face pointed at Oakley, then made his hand into a sock puppet without a sock, and his hand started yacking silently like Pac-Man.

"You want me to say more?"

Maché Face nodded and sat down.

The Story About Uncle Paul

Okay. I was staying the night with a friend. I was eleven. We had a fight about something; I don't even remember what, but I just got up and left and walked home. My mom always told me never to go through that park by Bessie Owens at night.

I thought she meant cus there were drug dealers or muggers. But that's not why.

I didn't listen to my mom. I cut through the park. It was dark as hell because people smashed the lights in that park so many times, the city just stopped fixing em. I couldn't hardly see a damn thing, so I walked slowly. Halfway into the park, I already regretted it. But once you're halfway in, there's no good reason to turn back.

I didn't think anyone else would even be there that late. I definitely didn't think I'd see Uncle Paul. It was fucking weird. He was just sitting on a bench in the dark. Kind of looking around. I wasn't sure at first. It couldn't be him, right? Why the hell would Uncle Paul be there that late? I didn't call out and say hi. That'd be weird if it wasn't him. I kept walking towards him and figured when I got close enough, if it really was Uncle Paul, then I'd say something.

Then this other guy came around some trees and sat right next to him. Seemed like they must be friends at first. I thought about what my mom said, about drug dealers. I heard Paul's voice and then I knew it was him. He had a really distinct voice, like Kermit the Frog with emphysema. I don't know how, but I could tell that they didn't know each other. They were meeting for the first time. They talked for a minute and then they went off into some denser wooded spot.

I didn't know what that was about, so I just kept walking. I got home and my mom was furious with me, saying I shouldn't have walked home by myself that late. She was right. I shouldn't've been in that park. She grilled me and got it out of me that I went through the park and that I saw Uncle Paul. She got even more upset. My mom made me swear to Jesus I wasn't making that up. I didn't know what was going on. It was true. I told her it was true. Mom called her sister, my Aunt Helen, Paul's wife.

Aunt Helen didn't take it so well. She was pretty fucking angry.

I don't know for sure that she's the one who told the cops about what Paul was up to... but, I mean, who else? I told, but I didn't even know what I was telling on. All I knew was that Uncle Paul was in the park with some guy. I was 10. I didn't know about that stuff.

The cops set up a sting in the park and caught him and another guy in the act. Paul did a couple years in state. Helen divorced him. He lost custody and visitation. He got out and I don't know whatever happened to him after that. My family never talks about him anymore.

Everyone liked Uncle Paul. He was fun, and he didn't need to drink any alcohol first. He was great to his kids and his nephews and nieces. After the thing in the park, people started suspecting he'd been, uh... interfering with Little Paul. But I don't believe it. Uncle Paul wasn't a molester. He was a faggot, but he wasn't a molester. There's a difference.

"Is that why I'm here?"

Maché Face stood up and just looked at Oakley for a little while. Oakley thought this must be it. He smiled a bit. Then Maché Face raised the gun.

"No, man! No! No!" Oakley bobbed and weaved his head, hoping he might dodge the shot. *Click.*

"Fuck! Fuck, man, goddamn it!" He yelled.

Maché Face ejected the bad round.

Click. "That was not the right answer. You now have between one and four more chances to guess why you are here." Click.

Darkness and silence and one more hour.

"What else? What else?" He thought about it more, but the same ideas kept coming to his mind on a loop, like every idea was certain it solved this puzzle and wouldn't hear any other idea. "What am I missing? Think. Think. Think."

"I'm coming at this wrong. How did I get here? I was at that party at Theo's." His memory was hazy. "How much did I drink?" He just had a handful of moments of memory. "I picked up the keg from the brewery. Brought it to Theo's barn. Shit. Who was there? I think there was a fight. Did I get into a fight? Shit. Was that even last night? Maybe I've been here longer than that. Shit. Was this psycho at the party? Who was even there? Did he grab me after the party? I might've gone to Fanny's after for late-night waffles. Someone at the truck stop nabbed me?"

He had a vague memory. Maybe just a dream. "Did I get in a limo? Why do I remember a limousine? There was a limo."

He saw the fresh scratch on the knuckles of his right hand. "Did I fight him?" Something glinted green. A piece of broken glass. "How did that happen?"

The clock ticked down. The steps on the stairs. The light clicking on. Oakley opened his eyes. He knew the routine by now.

Click. "You have between 1 and 4 chances to guess why you are here. What did you do to deserve this?" Click. He took his seat on the chair across from Oakley.

"This might be... it might be about the old lady. As mad as you are... I must've killed her."

The Story About The Old Lady

I was working at the carryout on Brundage, not long after I got fired from The Sixer. I was only there for a year before my friend Will got me the job at Leather & Lead. This old lady was a regular. One day, she bought her Fireball liquor and Kools, like she always did. I didn't notice until she was gone, but she left her check book I took it. I could've chased after her, but I had a line of customers. I figured she'd figure it out on her own and come back. I put it in my pocket. I don't know why. I forgot about it until after work. I was doing laundry and I found it and remembered I'd put it there. I knew it was wrong, but I passed some checks. Not a ton. I think $50 worth. I did it in places far away from Bakersfield, so no one would know me. I told them I was buying things for my grandmother and that she gave me her checkbook to use, and they always said how I was a good grandson.

I told myself it wasn't a lot of money. I told myself she's old, she's been saving. She's getting a social security check. She's probably collecting her husband's pension. She's good for it.

But I didn't really know that, for sure. That's what I told myself, though. I heard from a co-worker that she came back the next day asking if she'd left it. I wasn't there, but the girl working checked the lost-and-found box. It wasn't there, so she told her no. And I never saw that old lady again. She never came back for her Fireball or Kools. I don't know what happened, exactly. I burned the checkbook after. Didn't want anything coming back to me.

A year later, I found a carbon copy of a check I'd written, balled up in a pair of pants I hardly wore. I opened it up. I'd forgotten about the checkbook. And a lot of the stories I told myself about why it was okay didn't seem right anymore.

Her address was on the checks. I drove to her house. I don't know what I was gonna do. I think I just wanted to see her there and know for sure that $50 didn't ruin her life. But she wasn't living there anymore. A family was there now, with kids. I didn't ask them. I don't know. Maybe she just moved. Or maybe she couldn't pay for her medicine because I robbed her, and she died. I don't know. Maybe I just think too much of my own effect on other people, thinking I could control the entire course of someone's life with $50.

"So I wonder if I hurt that old lady by taking $50 and maybe, I don't know… maybe you're her son or grandson or someone."

Oakley noticed something for the first time. When he was talking, Maché Face favored the left side of his head, just slightly. Oakley's grandpa was deaf in one ear, and he did the same thing.

Maché Face raised the gun.

"Fuck no!" He squeezed his eyes shut tight. *Click.* He opened them. Bad round ejected.

Click. "That was not the right answer. You now have between one and three more chances to guess why you are here." Click.

Maché Face had one bad ear. Oakley didn't know anyone with a bad right ear. It could be anyone. It wasn't anyone he wronged. He was sure of that now. It had to be someone who cared about someone he'd wronged.

Oakley had one story left. The worst one. One he was sure nobody else knew about. But it was the only one he had left. The only possible thing that Oakley did that was so bad, someone would do all this to him. He didn't spend any of his hour thinking about who Maché Face was, how he got here, or what he wanted. There was only one possible answer. He thought about Olivia. He tried not to. He had a hard time breathing whenever he imagined her freckled face. He didn't want to talk about Olivia to anyone, ever. But there was no way anyone else could know.

He heard Maché Face come down the stairs, and then he turned on the lights.

Click. "You have between 1 and 3 chances to guess why you are here. What did you do to deserve this?" Click.

"I'm the reason for what happened to Olivia Hommel. And why Patty Hommel disappeared. And I'm the reason Nicolas Hommel is dead. I did that."

Maché Face sat on the chair, leaned back, crossed his legs so one ankle was on the other knee.

The Story About The Hommels

I was eighteen. Olivia was a sophomore. I remember when I was a senior, she liked me a lot. She had it bad for me. And if I'm being honest, I wasn't into her. She wasn't ugly .. she was just… not what I wanted. You know how there's good curly hair and bad curly hair? Some curly hair is pretty and sometimes it just looks… I don't know… not pretty. She had the second kind. Her teeth were kinda big. I'm not trying to be mean. I would never be mean to Olivia. I'm just saying I wasn't into her like she was into me.

First time I really noticed her was at basketball practices. She was sitting in the stands watching. She didn't even know anyone on the team. She came anyway. She always cheered, especially when I was the one who scored. It's just a scrimmage, not a real game. Why was this girl getting so excited like it was a division championship? I'd see her looking at me and then looking away when I saw her looking.

The cheer squad threw her mean looks. They said nasty things about her, just quiet enough that they could pretend they were saying it behind her back, but just loud enough that she could hear them talking about her. Olivia came anyway. Those girls didn't scare her off. She was always keeping eyes on me while we ran suicides and burpees. I'd be sweaty as hell and she'd be looking at me like... the point is, she liked me. That's all. She liked me a lot.

She wasn't going to come up to me, though. I knew she wouldn't. She was too shy for that. She thought I was so cool. Honestly, I never would've even seen her if she hadn't kept coming to those games. If she wasn't sitting in the stands, every game, every practice. Passing her in the halls, I wouldn't have noticed her. But she was always at basketball. Never skipped. Reliable and there.

One day I went and talked to her. I don't know why. I just wanted to know who this girl was. I walked up into the stands and I could see she was nervous. Her eyes looked around and she fussed with her curly hair. She was used to looking, not being looked at. I introduced myself. She smiled and stumbled at first. And we got to talking. And when I talked to her, it was so... easy. I sat down and we talked. I don't even remember what about. Just talking to me made her smile. She laughed at things I said, even when they weren't funny. She was interested in any story I'd tell, no matter how boring it was.

It wasn't an ego thing. I know you're thinking that, but it wasn't like that. It was just so... easy being with Olivia. To her, I couldn't do anything wrong. I couldn't say anything that could make her mad at me. She was... I don't know. Cozy. A big warm blanket. I guess she was like that. I could talk to her about anything. She was so in love with me that nothing I said bothered her. It never offended her or scared her. A golden retriever never loved a person like that. She didn't have many friends, and she had a lot of attention to give.

We hung out. I don't even remember how that started, but we started spending time together. Not at school, really, but people knew we knew each other. We'd say hi in the halls. We went out after school and on weekends. Not like dates.

Not exactly. Maybe for her it was, but I didn't feel that way. I should've just been straight with her, but I wasn't. I don't know. It would break her heart and ruin everything.

We'd go get pizza. We'd wander on the railroad tracks. I took her to the woods a couple times and taught her to shoot my .22, shooting soda cans. We'd climb onto the roof of her dad's station wagon, lay out on a blanket, and watch movies at the drive-in. She was just so happy to be with me, it was... contagious. I've had a few girlfriends, and they always had reasons to be mad or disappointed in me. But never Olivia.

I didn't try to fuck her. Again, I know that's what you're thinking. It wasn't like that. I said she was cozy. You wanna wrap yourself in a cozy blanket, but you don't fuck a blanket. But she tried. She started off with small little hints. Then they got more and more obvious. You know. Like I hurt my hamstring and she offered to massage it. She did a good job. It really helped, but I could see she was getting more out of it than I was. One time we were by that bridge, the one on Golden State, sipping some beers she'd stolen from her dad. And she pretended to be drunk and said all kinds of things. I told her she was just drunk. The next day she tried to play like she was so wasted she forgot. I didn't call her a liar. No reason to embarrass her.

I felt like as long as I didn't kiss her or touch her, then she wouldn't get it in her head that we were like a thing, like a boyfriend and girlfriend. But she kept getting more and more brazen. Like saying that if she had a boyfriend, she'd let him do anything to her. Saying things like she never sucked a dick, but she always wanted to try, and how she thought she'd be really good at it. Stuff like that. It was awkward.

But she whittled me down. I know it'll make me sound like an absolute shithead, but I felt like I owed it to her. I had some shit going on at home and... I felt like she'd been such a comfort for me that, like... I don't know, like I'd be a jerk for not giving back. Sounds awful to say it out loud, but that's how I felt. Things weren't great at home for me. And anytime I wanted to leave, Olivia was always there.

One weekend, her folks were out of town for a wedding in Modesto. Olivia didn't know the newlyweds, so she talked her parents into letting her stay in Bakersfield. Her folks didn't trust her to stay alone at the house, but they let her stay the night with a friend. She worked it out so her friend would pretend Olivia was staying with her family for the weekend. Oh. This was after I graduated, by the way. She was a junior.

I went over to her place. First time I'd ever been there. Nice place. Nicer than mine. She let me in through the back door and she was already in a silk nighty that she must've bought special for the occasion. She took me upstairs by the hand and into her room. We didn't turn on any lights. We didn't want any neighbors to know anyone was home. She'd already had some candles lit and a blanket hanging in front of the window to block the light. It was really... It was really sweet. I didn't deserve it. I didn't deserve all this attention and devotion from her. This was definitely a big deal for her, and it wasn't for me at all. But then it felt like I was doing something terrible to this girl. This was some seriously lovey Valentine's day stuff. She got the ball rolling, and the whole time I couldn't focus on what we were doing. I just kept arguing it over in my mind. Was it worse to do this or was it worse to not do this and just end it all?

Well, I never really had to choose. I still think about that question a lot, because I never even made the decision I could regret later. We heard the front door open downstairs. I was reaching for something blunt, like someone was breaking in. Then we heard their voices. It was her mom and dad. Olivia got up right away. She blew out the candles and opened the window. It was sticky, though. Too many layers of paint will do that. She had to fight it a little before she got it open, then she shooed me out the window. I went out and onto the awning just as we heard them coming upstairs.

She scrambled to get a coat on, quiet as she could, but she put on mine cus it was on the floor. I'd forgot it. I dropped from the overhang into their backyard. I remember it. The whole house was dark. I stood there, looking up at the window, in my mind saying, "C'mon, Olivia, c'mon." I was only out the window for ten seconds maybe, but it felt like a hundred. I looked up at the dark window, waiting to see her come and follow me out, to drop onto the lawn, and sneak off with me into the night together, so we could laugh about it later after the adrenaline had cooled down. I looked up at that black window and then there was a flash and a bang inside her room, like a 12-gauge lightning bolt. Then I heard her mom screaming. Fuck. The hairs on my arms are sticking up right now just talking about it. Fuck. This is hard. You know, I always wondered if I told someone if I'd feel better about it. Not like this, obviously. To a friend or something. But I don't feel better at all. Not at all.

I heard her mom scream. Then her father screamed, "Oh my God! Olivia!" Just like that over and over. Her mom kept yelling, "What did you do? What did you do?" Their minds were just in a loop like that. Like they couldn't even have another thought. "Oh my God! Olivia!" and "What did you do?"

I ran away. I didn't know what else to do. I ran away, and I stopped at that bridge we always sat at. She was supposed to be there with me. She was supposed to sit with me and we'd laugh about how her parents almost caught us. Her parents would spare me one more day from the terrible responsibility of being her first. We'd laugh and it would be a story we'd never get sick of telling.

I learned what happened later. The wedding was a good three-hour drive away and Olivia's folks were supposed to stay the night out there. They drove all the way out, but the hotel lost their reservation and everyone else was booked. They went to the wedding and the reception and just drove home after, so they didn't get home until late. When they got home and walked inside, they heard the noise upstairs from Olivia fighting with the window. Her dad thought there was a burglar and brought his gun with him upstairs. He kept it in the coat closet. I don't understand why he would do that. Hee went upstairs and into her room, and he saw my jacket on Olivia... he couldn't see well. It was dark. I don't know why the hell he didn't turn on any of the lights before he opened the door. Maybe he didn't want to alert the burglar that he was coming.

You already know the rest, though, don't you? That's why I'm here, right? Keep going? Okay...

Ambulance came. Police came. Olivia died, but she didn't die. Olivia barely has a face. She wasn't a beauty pageant kind of girl before, but her face had a... I don't know. The more you looked at her, the more you liked looking at her, you know? After her dad shot her, I couldn't look at her. God... I can't even think about that. Not like Olivia is even there anymore. The fucking brain damage. God. She's still walking. Talking, sometimes. Not words, just... sounds. Babble like a baby. Her eyes are open. She stares. But it ain't her. I don't know where my Olivia went, but that ain't her. My Olivia died.

I never even met her dad, Nicolas. I figured I would've, eventually. He never knew about me. No one did. I don't think it's a guess to say that Nicolas couldn't take it. He couldn't keep going after what he did to his girl. Their only child.

Olivia once told me about how she was a miracle baby. How when she died someday, in Heaven she'd get to meet her stillborn twin sister for the first time, and three other unborn siblings. She was Nicolas and Patty's miracle baby. That's why they were so protective. So strict. That protectiveness, that strictness, that's why she was so afraid of getting caught by them.

I lost my train of thought. Right. Olivia was still eating through a straw where her mouth ought to be. She's breathing, but her face and mind are gone. Him and Patty, Olivia's mom, just kept feeding and caring for this… mannequin. That living body that used to be their daughter. Nicolas couldn't do it anymore. He did to himself what he did to his daughter, but he did it right. Nic went chasing after Olivia to wherever she went. I hope he found her. I hope they figured it out, and she forgave him. I'd like to think that but…

And Patty. She was devastated when she found Nicolas; head opened up, laying exactly where he shot Olivia, with the same 12-gauge in his lap, and the room painted red. Shit. I can't even believe she didn't divorce him after what happened. I guess she didn't have anyone else. With Nicolas gone, too, she couldn't do it anymore either. She dropped Olivia off at some hospital somewhere upstate and then took off. I don't know where she went. No one does. Shit. Maybe she went chasing after her husband and daughter the same way they went.

"That's it. That's the whole story about how I destroyed the Hommel family. Worst thing I ever did. Nobody even knew about me and Olivia. When she was gone, nobody knew how it was for me. No one came up to me to help me feel better or give me warm regards. I was so fucking miserable and alone and there was only one person in the world I wanted to talk to. And it was Olivia. Honestly, saying it out loud here, I realize she was my best friend. I killed my best friend. The miracle baby."

Maché Face put both his feet on the floor. One of his knees was bouncing.

"So? What now?" asked Oakley.

Maché Face raised the gun and pointed it. This time Oakley didn't flinch or argue. *Click*. Oakley almost felt disappointed. The masked man ejected the cartridge.

Maché Face returned to the tape deck. Click. "That was not the right answer. You now have between one and two more chances to guess why you are here." Click.

The kidnapper left Oakley alone in the dark again, with one last hour to think it over.

That was all Oakley had left. He told Maché Face things he'd never told anyone, and none of it was what he wanted to hear. The psychopath was like a Soviet cop. Keep confessing forever, then get executed for it anyway.

Steps. Lights. Tape deck. Click. "What did you do to deserve this?" Click. Sit.

Oakley sighed. "I got one more. Just one more thing. I didn't say it yet because it wasn't such a big deal. But that's all I got. It's my last story. But there's no way it's what you want me to say. I might as well tell it. Why not? You're gonna shoot me anyhow."

The Story About Will

I cheated at cards at Will's bachelor party. I was drunk. It didn't matter. I lost my money anyhow. That's it. That's the story.

"Do it, you fucker."

Click. "That was not the right answer. You now have one more chance to guess why you are here." Click.

Maché Face raised the gun at Oakley. This time, Oakley started cussing him out, hurling every insult he could think of, promising to get out of the chair and beat the shit out of him. *Click.* Oakley kept making promises until Maché Face left.

He calmed down, huffing and puffing through his nose. Oakley tried to remember. He'd been to a party. He blacked out. Vague memories. He got into a fight. That's why he can taste metal. He had a cut in his mouth. How'd he get hit? He cut his hand. Not on a person, though. On glass. Did he punch a window? A weird car. A limo. He got into a limousine. Why?

He saw it again. The tiniest glint in the green glow of the clock. Glass. A little piece of glass in his hand. He pulled and slipped his arm out through his shirt, just like when he fought Lewis. Slipped in under the tape. He twisted and fought right at the end, yanking his shoulder, but finally got his arm into the shirt's torso. He did it again with his other arm. When his arms were close, he winced and pulled the glass out. It was bigger than he realized and it started bleeding again. He looked at the clock. 54 minutes to saw through his shirt with a tiny little fragment of glass, not much bigger than a dime.

The light clicked back on and the masked man was standing under the lightbulb. There was nobody in the chair, though. A ripped shirt and some blood. He looked behind him and there he was. Oakley, shirtless, with a rusty red hand pointing the gun at him from three feet away. Maché Face put his hands up slowly and faced him.

"There's one left. We both know what that means."

Maché Face nodded.

"It's real lucky for me I got out when I did because I don't have anything left to confess. You already know every bad thing I ever did."

Maché Face shook his head. He spoke with his own voice for the first time and said, "Not every bad thing."

"Take off the mask."

The man pulled back the hood from his sweatshirt. He reached under his chin and removed the mask and tossed it onto the floor. It was just some guy.

"Who the fuck are you?" Oakley's voice got high-pitched at the end, actually disappointed by what he saw.

"I don't expect you to remember me. You see new people every day. They come and go and you forget them as soon as they leave your shop. I thought maybe you'd remember Elvis, though."

"Elvis? Are you high right now?"

"You notice a lot. You're observant. But you didn't see Elvis, even though he's been here with us the whole time."

"God fucking damn it. I don't know why I thought there was going to be more to this. There's no damn mystery. There's no puzzle to solve. You're just fucking crazy."

The man reached for the small of his back. Oakley warned him, "Don't do that! Keep your hands where I can see them!"

He didn't listen. Oakley pulled the trigger. *Click.* Misfire.

The man laughed. The muscles in his forearm adjusted as he took a hold of something and began drawing his hand back. Oakley took the pistol by the barrel and used it as a hammer on the unmasked man's face. He struck the man between the nose and eye. He went limp and fell backwards. Oakley heard the back of the man's head bounce off the concrete floor.

Oakley stood over him. "What did I do? Huh? Tell me!"

The guy didn't tell him. His eyes were only partially open. He was breathing, but he wasn't moving. He wasn't blinking, either. His cheekbone was broken. The ocular maxilla cracked. His nose busted like a crushed beer can and blood bubbled up out of it when he breathed. The white of one of his eyes became black and red.

Oakley checked his pulse. He was alive. He patted him down

for any other weapons. Nothing. He found what the man was reaching for. A folded piece of newsprint. He picked it up and unfolded it. The ironic headline read, *Two Dead at Funeral Home*. February 14th, 1976.

The Story About Angelo

Theresa was still in her nightgown, no shoes to protect her feet from the motor oil and broken glass. Lennox Street was shiny from the rain that just ended. Her hair was a tangle like a bird's nest and her eyes looked into something too far and vast for sane people to see. She walked through the suburb with an antique lever-action Winchester resting in the crook of her arm like a baby. It was late and the decent people of the neighborhood were asleep.

She wandered up to the large Victorian two-story and up the front steps. She tried the door, but it was locked. She reached into the pockets of her light pink nightgown and produced a few .44-40 cartridges and fed them into her rifle before she smashed the window with the stock.

Angelo was a deeper sleeper and Linda had to shake him awake.

"What? What is it?" He asked groggily.

"Someone's downstairs!" she whisper-yelled.

"What?" his eyes opened wider.

"I heard the glass break downstairs."

"Wait. Shh." He sat up in bed. They were both quiet. They could just hear the creaking sound of footsteps downstairs."

Angelo got up and said, "Call the police." He went into the closet and started pulling things off the top shelf.

Theresa picked up the phone and called 911, and told the

operator the situation.

Angelo took out a pink wrapped present with a red bow. He stepped over the mess of objects he'd pulled down and set the box on the bed.

"This was supposed to be a Valentine's gift." He removed the lid and grabbed the Colt 1911 with the Elvis Presley grip. He loaded it and handed it to his wife. "If someone comes in here and it's not me, shoot them."

She put a hand over the receiver of the phone. "Wait, where are you going?"

"I'm gonna check it out."

"No! Don't! Just stay in here with me!"

Angelo didn't listen to his wife. He took the 20-gauge out of the closet and checked if it was loaded. He walked out of their bedroom, and peeked over the banister. He looked down over the balcony into the entryway. There was glass on the floor. Some droplets of blood from the glass led into the kitchen. He crept down the stairs, gun pointed forward, rounded the landing, and down the short walk towards the kitchen. His eyes darted up and down from the blood droplets to ahead of him.

He found the intruder in the kitchen.

"Hey!"

Theresa looked at Angelo. She had the look of a drug addict in a desperate moment. Not the first one to come creeping into their home looking for chemicals.

"We don't have any formaldehyde, okay? Is that what you're looking for? You may as well move on."

"Where's my mom?"

"I... I don't know. I don't know your mom."

"Sarah McKenna."

"She's downstairs. Are you related to her?"

"Why are you keeping her prisoner?"

"I'm not keeping your mother prisoner, lady. Your mother passed away. Do you understand that? You need to put the gun down, now, okay? I don't know if you're on drugs or something..."

Theresa shot from the hip and nailed him in the gut. His every muscle clenched, including his trigger finger. The scattershot removed a bit of her ear. He hit the ground. She shot again and shattered the floor tiles by Angelo's head. He tried firing his second and final shell, but his arm was going numb and wasn't working. Theresa tried walking over him. He grabbed her by the ankle. She pointed the gun at his head. He grabbed the barrel and pointed it away. She fired. That ear started ringing and it never, ever stopped. She pulled the gun away. He was dizzy, unbalanced, and about to vomit from his inner ear getting trashed. He heard his wife scream upstairs with his good ear. She'd heard the shots.

He was holding himself together, worried how deep the shot went in, fighting through the pain every time he inhaled, and terrified that his one working hand was the only thing keeping his insides inside. His legs didn't want to move. He watched Theresa head back down the hall. "Mom? Is that you? I'm coming to rescue you!"

Theresa went upstairs. Angelo tried to yell after her. "She's coming upstairs! She's got a rifle!" but it came out as a raspy squeak. Without his abdomen, his voice had no power.

A few moments later, he heard two shots. One used to breach the lock to the bedroom and one to shoot Linda. Angelo screamed but it came out as a pathetic wheeze.

The papers said the cops shot Theresa when they arrived. Angelo had serious injuries. A limp. A bad ear. His missus didn't make it.

Oakley put the paper in his pocket. He removed the magazine from the gun and ejected the cartridge. He looked at it. The brass had a dimple from being fired already. It was one of the dummy rounds.

"What the…?"

He crawled around on the floor, looking for the other casings. He found six more of them. All dummy rounds. Where was the live one? He remembered something. He peeked under the fridge. He couldn't see it. He got up, unplugged the machine, and shimmied it away from the wall. There it was. He crouched and picked it up. No dimple. The other rounds all had dimples. This was the live round. This round was the one Angelo pointed at him on his second guess. Oakley should be dead.

He looked at the gun again. A 1911 with Elvis on the grip. His eyebrows scrunched.

"I know this gun. I know this gun! Fuck. This… that's why he laid the gun down right in front of me. The whole time, it was right in front of me."

He sat at the workbench and quickly disassembled it, looking over every part with an experienced eye. The problem was easy to find. The firing pin was gummed up with something. A glue or epoxy. The gun don't fire. He put it back together and stuffed it into his pants.

He felt around on the curtains until he found the gap and he pulled them apart. It looked like a surgical theater. A metal table, like a bed. Some small side tables on wheels with metal trays. Some machines with hoses for pumping fluid. Tile floor with a drain. The metal bed had a drain on it, too. This wasn't a surgical theater. It was an embalming room.

He found the stairs and walked up to them and opened

the white-painted door. The sunlight hit hard, pouring in through large windows. It was daytime. For some reason, that surprised him. He adjusted his eyes. He was in the kitchen. He looked down and saw where the crazy woman had deafened Angelo with her Winchester. A year later, Angelo still hadn't fixed it.

He walked through a door on a swinging hinge. It was an old Victorian home with a large front entranceway, with a wood and glass door. To the right, a large room full of folding chairs and a casket on the far side, walls covered with heavy drapes, and several large flower arrangements on tables. A record player was close by, with the sleeve showing *The Songfellows*. He walked past the viewing room towards the front door. Next to the exit was an end table with a small shrine. A cabinet with a plaster figurine of Elvis. A rosary. A framed photo of a woman. He looked closely. The one in the article. Linda. And a lit 7-day black prayer candle, with the Virgin Mary, surrounded by roses... only she was a skeleton. A jar filled with a lemonade-colored liquid with something in it that looked like a small prune. He almost picked it up until he realized what it was. He recoiled.

He walked out the double-doors, into the sunshine. A suburb. The smell of fresh cut grass and the sound of yard sprinklers. He wasn't thinking about how he looked. A bloody hand, a pistol, and no shirt He went down the porch steps that led to the corner of the sidewalk. On the corner of Lennox and Orchard. Oakley turned around. The number on the door said 2282. The sign outside said *Keyes Family Funeral Services*. There was a hearse in the parking lot with a busted window.

"It wasn't a limo. I was in a hearse."

He went back inside, called the police, and said, "Guy here is hurt bad. He needs an ambulance. Come pick him up. 2282 Lennox." Then he hung up. He took a shirt from a closet upstairs, bandaged his hand with another shirt, and walked out to the bus stop down the block.

Oakley got off the city bus and walked into the shop under the big sign that read, Leather and Lead.

The showroom had walls of pegboard and hooks, holding rifles of all eras, like a Natural History Museum of the evolution of weapons. Glass cases full of pistols. Clothing racks with holsters. The place was soaking in Wild West aesthetics, with cow skulls, a wooden Indian statue, and a mural of a California cowboy on a horse, just like on the covers of those cheap novels.

No customers. Will looked up from his inventory clipboard. "Hey, Oak. You're not scheduled to work today, are you?"

"No. Where's Eddie?"

"Office."

"What happened to your hand?"

Oakley ignored the question and walked through a door with an *employees only* sign. He breezed through the storage area, past a work table and several racks of shelves with ammunition boxes. He stopped. He looked at the boxes. He picked up a case of .45 and kept walking. He found the office and the door was open. Eddie was behind a desk, filling out paperwork, and didn't notice Oakley until he knocked on the jamb.

"Hey, Oak. You're not scheduled for today."

"Yeah, I know."

"Where'd you get the shiner?"

"From a fight. Listen. I need to look at some sales records."

"What for?"

"There was a gun I sold about a year ago. You remember the 1911 with Elvis on it?"

"Yeah. Sure I do. What do you need the record for?"

"I need to know who bought it."

"You know, Oak. You keep answering my questions, but you're not answering the actual meat of the question."

"I don't know what that means, Eddie."

"Why are you here on your day off with a black eye, asking about year old sales records?"

"I think the guy we sold it to just tried to kill me."

"What? Are you fucking with me right now?"

"Lemme see those records."

"If someone tried to kill you, talk to the cops about it. There's no sense coming here and…"

"If I tell the cops, they'll be the ones digging through your receipts instead of me. They'll copy everything. Every sale. Every customer. Every dollar. And who knows? Maybe we end up in the paper."

Eddie opened up a deep sliding file drawer under his desk. He plucked his glasses off the top of his head, fitted them into his nose, and leaned over and started fingering through the tabs of the manilla folders. He found the one labeled Feb 76. He pulled it out and started flipping through them, saying over to himself. "1911… 1911… 1911… Colt. Nope," He tried January. He pulled out a sheet and laid it on the desk.

"Purchased January 30th. Colt 1911 with the Elvis Presley grip. Yeah. I didn't make this sale."

"I know. I did."

"Angelo…"

"Keyes. He live at 2282 Lennox?"

Eddie searched the sheet with an index finger. "Uh... yes. 2282 Lennox street. Yeah. Oak, what the fuck is this about?"

Oakley reached behind him and held up the Elvis gun.

"Oak, you're scaring me, man. Why do you have that? What's going on?"

Oakley set the ammo box on the desk, opened it, and took out a live round. He held it up so Eddie could see it. Then he fed it to the gun and leveled the iron sights onto Eddie. His boss's hand reflexively went to pull the pistol appendix-carried under his fat gut. But he stopped halfway, realizing he was dead to rights.

Eddie said it slowly, like he was talking to a crazy person or someone who didn't speak English very well. "The fuck you think you're doing, Oak? Huh?"

"Why am I pointing a gun at you right now?"

"I have... no... fucking idea."

"You got one chance to guess right, so make it a good one. What did you do to deserve this?"

"Oak. I don't know why you are acting crazy like this, man. I am your friend, okay? Put. The gun. Down."

Click.

Eddie drew his Walther. Oakley tossed the 1911 onto Eddie's desk with a loud clunk. Eddie was sweaty and his nostrils were flaring. "I don't know what the fuck is happening with you, Oak, but..."

"The gun's busted, Eddie! It doesn't fire! You didn't check it before I sold it!"

"That's bullshit, Oakley. I check every gun. You know that."

"Not this one. Angelo Keyes' wife, Linda, died because she tried to defend herself with a damaged piece they bought here! Angelo found me somehow, looking for payback. Locked me up in his basement and made me play his own version of Russian roulette."

Eddie's hands were shaking, while two competing streams of adrenaline took over his body: anger and shame. He finally lowered the gun and set it down next to the 1911. He got pinker and pinker. He put one of his hands over his mouth. He looked down with REM eyes. He was shaking even more.

"Why didn't you check this gun, Eddie? You always check used items before you buy them. Why not this one?"

"What did. How? He… I… I don't… I guess I forgot. I don't know. No. I did check. I always check. Didn't I?"

"What's going on?" asked Will.

Oakley turned around and Will was standing right there, looking concerned, looking back and forth between Oakley and Eddie. Oakley took Angelo's news cutout from his pocket and handed it to Will. "That's us. We did that." Will looked it over.

Eddie held it up close and skimmed the article. "I fucked up. I must've forgot. It was really busy. Lots of business. I don't know how I forgot."

"You always check the guns," said Will.

"That's right. And he should've checked it himself. It's not all my responsibility!"

"Maybe something happened to it after we sold it?" suggested Will.

Oakley shook his head. "No. No way. California's two week waiting period. I remember. He came in to get his wife a gun for home defense. He said crime in his neighborhood was getting out of control. He said Ronald Reagan cut money for the crazy houses and they started letting them out. There were a lot of break-ins. It was just stupid luck he came here that day, because his wife loved Elvis and we had the 1911 here. Like it was meant to be. I remember the waiting period because I told him he was just under the wire. If he bought it that day, it would be ready for him on the 13th. The day he was cleared to pick it up, he called the shop and said he was swamped at work. I told him I'd stay after closing so he could get here. I wanted him to have it for Valentine's Day. I don't know. It was sweet. I wanted his wife to have it. It was over a year ago and I didn't remember what he looked like. But... He picked it up after dark. Maybe eight. He was really grateful. He even brought his own heart-shaped box to put it in and tied it right in front of me. Then he left. No way anyone messed with it. He went right home as far as I know. I doubt he even had a chance to look at it."

Will skimmed the article. "Saturday morning. 13th would've been a Friday," noted Will. "Bad luck."

"February 14th, 1911. That was the day Colt patented the 1911," noted Eddie. "Valentine's Day."

Oakley looked back at the two men. "What are you two trying to say? Huh?"

"It's just... weird is all," said Will. Eddie nodded.

"This was just some kind of astrology thing? The stars were in conjunction? When did you two get so damn superstitious, huh?"

Will shrugged. Eddie scratched his chin.

Oakley continued, "This gun has a curse on it? Hm? It's no one's fault? It's just fate?"

The other men didn't say anything.

Oakley yelled, "It's not cursed! Curses aren't fucking real! You did this, Eddie! Not the stars! Not some voodoo bullshit! You! That's it! That's the whole damn thing!"

"Just seems weird that the one time I forget... if I even did forget... it's just weird."

"Fuck you guys." Oakley took the pistol and swiped Eddie's keys off his desk.

"What do you think you are doing?"

"If this thing has a curse, I'm taking your car and throwing this gun into Lake Isabella."

Oakley left. That was the last time the men at Leather and Lead ever saw Oakley. Eddie filed a missing person's report and a stolen car report and never heard back. They reached out to his parents. They were distraught. But they didn't know anything.

A week later, the cops called. They found Eddie's car abandoned on the side of the road off 160, about an hour from Vegas. It was in perfect condition. Even had an oil change. The odometer had about 800 new miles on it.

No clues after that. Oakley and Elvis vanished like smoke.

It was in '85 that Eddie bumped into an old acquaintance at a gun show in Reno; a man from Utah with some impressive collector's items he wanted to show off. When Eddie saw it, his heart stopped. There he was. Elvis Presley on the grip of a Colt 1911, shiny and chrome. The damn thing found its way right back to Eddie for a third time. Prettier than the last time he saw it. All dressed up and just reaching out to hold his hand.

Eddie told the man from Utah a story. A story about a cursed gun. About Valentine's day. About a married couple and a crazy woman and a young man named Oakley who vanished. The collector thought Eddie was trying to trick him into lowering the price. He knew it wasn't a trick when Eddie told him you couldn't pay him a million dollars to take that gun home.

Eddie didn't leave, though. He stayed at the booth and stopped anyone who looked at the gun. He told them it was evil. He told them not to buy it. The collector from Itah got physical. Security came and they hauled Eddie out. He didn't leave easy.

He yelled the whole way, warning everyone else who could hear. Every eye in that place was on the madman raving about a cursed Elvis gun.

Trail Mix

I've never seen anyone use meat in trail mix before. We're changing the world.

You can just buy all this stuff at the store and throw it into a bag before you go out into the woods. Or if you wanna be the cool guy who makes all their own shit, I'll show you how to dehydrate your bananas and jerk your pig ribbons.

If you head out into the woods to evade law enforcement or some moonshiners you ripped off, I recommend you don't include bacon, as it will only encourage the bloodhounds.

Time: Anywhere between 30 seconds to 12 hours, depending on how difficult you want it to be.

Ingredients

- Bananas (or banana chips)
- Peanuts
- Thick-cut Bacon (or bacon jerky)

Gear for pig ribbons

- An oven
- An oven-safe wire rack
- A pan

Gear for banana chips

- A dehydrator

What you do to make banana chips

1. Own a dehydrator
2. Chop up your bananas into disks. A quarter inch is good. Remove the peel first. Do I even need to say that?
3. Dehydrate them at 135°F until they're done. It's gonna take a while. 6 hours minimum. Maybe 12, depending on your climate

What you do to make bacon jerky

1. Preheat your oven to 200°F
2. Lay the bacon on a rack. The rack needs to be on a pan so that the drippings don't get all over your oven
3. If you're going to try any of the variations from down below, now would be the time to do that*
4. Let that bake for 2-3 hours. It depends on your oven, altitude, humidity, and whatever else. Just check on it after 2 hours and use your best judgment
5. Take the bacon out. Use some towels to remove the extra liquid fat. If you're adding flavors, now would be a good time to re-apply them. Then put it back in
6. Bake for another 2-3 hours. I don't know. Just stop when it's done
7. Pour out all the pig butter from the catch tray into a mason jar. Save that stuff

Serve with

- A canteen of clean water
- The music of *Stan Rogers*
- Something with a 18"+ barrel, chambered in .30-06 or 6.5 Creedmoor to fend off hungry critters like bobcats and manitous

*Variations

Bacon is salt, fat, and smoke. Those three things go with damn near anything. If you want to make your pig ribbons even sexier, you can brush on some extra flavors before you dehydrate it.

- A 1:2 mixture of honey and rooster sauce (aka sriracha)
- Maple syrup
- BBQ sauce

Or you could dip the bacon into melted chocolate and freeze it. That'll get melty on a hot day, though, so think it through.

CHAPTER 7: A LITTLE LESS CONVERSATION

Austin, TX

6/28/2018

19:00:01

Luca woke up to the Zen chime of a metal bar, a high-pitched ding followed by a soft low hum that hung in the air, produced by a machine manufactured in a country where Zen Buddhism is outlawed. An artificial sunrise warmed the room with an electric glow. When Luca closed his eyes, it wasn't dark enough. He could feel subtle vibrations in the floor and the vague sound of bass. Someone was having a loud party. Outside, some birds were chirping. He pulled off the sheets and sat up on the $3,000 mattress that their marketing department claimed was designed by NASA engineers. He rubbed his eyes and looked at his room while trying to remember which day of the week it was, and he yawned. The room was white and there were no decorations or furnishings besides the mattress on the floor and the cardboard box that once housed a computer case and now served as a nightstand. He pressed the button on the Zen wake-up chime and a button on the machine that sprayed warm orange and yellow glow on the room to simulate a sunrise and play sounds of birds. He got up and peeked between the blinds of his window and saw the sun just setting behind the trees and the concrete wall that did its best to muffle the highway next to his condo complex, just on the other side of the parking lot.

He went into his living room, which was also nearly empty except for a high end PC and monitor on a desk, an expensive desk chair marketed to professional gamers, a 72-inch TV mounted to a wall, and a foldable lawn chair like the kind you see people pack and sit at Fourth of July fireworks and camping trips, and an impressive surround sound system with a volume that never went higher than eight because any louder would bother the neighbors.

"Hey, Ilsa."

A machine in the kitchen, shaped like a hockey puck, responded with a beep and a green light.

"Play some lofi."

The machine said, "Playing Cycles by Philanthrope X Kupla."

The machine that pretended to be a woman obliged him by playing a deep, slow beat with a synthetic piano, with enough energy to keep him from falling back asleep but mellow enough to never excite him or let him feel much besides calm.

He went into the kitchen separated from the living room by a bar and he looked into his fridge. He removed yogurt and poured it into a bowl with a handful of mixed fruit and some almond and granola. He started an electric kettle and when it was hot, he poured it over a yerba mate tea bag in the single coffee mug in the condo labeled PermaSoft with a logo of the letter P with a forced perspective S wrapping around it to suggest the imagery of a protective moat. He began going through his breakfast buffet of pill bottles, one by one. He swallowed vitamin B complex, Men's multivitamin, a nootropic melange, kratom, mushroom complex, CBD, Lexapro, Ativan, and omega-3.

He ate his breakfast, then brushed his teeth with an electric toothbrush and then took a shower with a peppermint castile oil. When he was dry and toweled, he put on jeans and a t-shirt with the logo of some cartoon from the 90s. He checked the time. He put on a coat marketed to hikers, outdoorsmen, and rappers, and left his place and locked up behind him. The party was louder in the hall and got more so as he walked past 302, which had a piece of yellow paper taped to the door giving notice that the inhabitant was being evicted by the condo co-op. He walked down the outside stairs between the two halves of the condo complex and found his way to his Miata and when he was inside, his phone connected to the car's computer and he said, "Ilsa. Play more lofi," and she did.

He drove onto the highway, after the traffic of day workers had passed, and few people still were on it. It was an easy drive guided by the hypnotic passing of street lamps and the brightly lit digitized road signs that drew your eyes away from the road and towards products to buy. Most people had already gone home to their families or to the bars or whatever normal people do. He pulled aside just one time to let a convoy of screeching police cars and ambulances and firetrucks pass him.

He got off a highway exit that didn't exist four years ago: PermaSoft road, built explicitly as a bargain between the city and the company as a condition of them moving to a state where Silicon Valley investors could escape California taxes.

It was called a campus, but it looked like a Taj Mahal made of iPhone material. A glass monument to Boolean algebra. Fountains, a small bridge over a koi pond, perfectly manicured gardens with angularly cut bushes, flawless geometry that looked like they were conceived in the mind of an Apple product engineer; sleek, simple, functional, clean, shiny. No character or personality; a blank slate you can imagine whatever you like into. The sun was almost down and the electric lights were on, revealing every walking path.

Luca found a parking spot and nodded to some people he

recognized who were also coming in for work that day. He spotted a guy he knew from the third floor, sitting on a bench in front of the black, sparkling pond. His eyes stared into the water without a muscle moving except occasionally to raise a glass bottle of something golden brown to his lips with his white-knuckled fist.

Luca entered through the array of always-clean half-dozen sliding glass doors into the wide open entrance way designed by Dutch aesthetics experts to impress everyone who came in; merchants, potential employees, investors, press, politicians. A grand hotel minus features and color. The centerpiece of the thing was an enormous oak tree planted just behind the security desk and it reached up three stories, captured under the A-framed glass ceiling like a greenhouse. During orientation, they told Luca they imported it from an important Louisiana battlefield from the War of 1812.

The security guy nodded at Luca and Luca waved the lanyard badge around his neck in front of a metal pillar that beeped and an indicator glowed green, and he walked through. He took a silver elevator to the third floor. When he stepped out, he walked down the hallway into what might be called a complex of cubicles, but reimagined by people trying to solve the negative connotations that the word cubicle had earned in the 1980s. These were glass, see-through, and decorated so that each employee could express their unique individual personality and interests in the confines on a 3x3 foot space, just so long as it was in accordance with HR policies and the sensibilities of the most sensitive employee within the company.

He found his desk, which he kept as empty as his condo, and took his seat and entered the password into his terminal.

"Good morning."

Luca turned around to see Chelsea standing there, smiling, holding a big cup of something caffeinated purchased from the in-house barista kiosk on level 1.

"Citation needed."

Chelsea laughed a little, even though it wasn't funny, and she said kindly, "You're always so grumpy in the morning."

Luca looked out the wall of glass at the darkness, the only light from the cars and lamps in the parking lot and the path from the lot to the building. Chelsea looked at what he looked at and said, "You know what I mean," and she took a sip from her drink.

"Yeah," said Luca, because he didn't know what else to say.

"I'll see you at the 9pm Morning Meeting?"

"Yeah."

"Cool," and she left.

Luca spent about twenty minutes parsing through which of his emails were the 95% that could be ignored and which were the 5% that mattered. At 9:00pm people got up and headed towards the conference room and he did too. They funneled into another glass room, where he found a seat with 12 other people. Sanjay fired up the projector for his presentation, then went right into it.

"We've got a few things to go over." He flipped to a digital slide of slang terms, "I've posted all these slides on Slack so you can look at them as you need to. These words are all terms used by people with radical political views. Really popular with the alt-right, white supremacists, militia, that type of thing."

Dragan added, "We've gotten updates from Reynolds about these terms which relate to child pornography."

Someone new that Luca didn't really know yet raised a hand.

"Yeah," Sanjay pointed to him.

"I'm sorry. Who is Reynolds?"

Dragan explained, "He's the guy from the FBI task force that works with us on this stuff."

"Oh. I didn't know we were getting stuff from the FBI."

Chelsea chimed in, "We give them information, too. We share."

The new guy nodded.

Sanjay went on, "Speaking of which, now might be a good time to bring up the problems we've had with the whitelisting system..."

He continued his chat on bugs in the listing system, pedophile code words, crypto-anti-government neologisms, a new non-profit partner called SurfSafe, and Islamic radicalization talking points. Hyun raised his hand a lot and asked a lot of questions. Chelsea took notes on her laptop. Luca zoned out. His mind utterly cleared. He vanished into a perfect silence inside himself. Every meeting was the same meeting with the same bullet points that were summarized in an email that Sanjay put out an hour before the meeting started. Even as his brain was doing it, Luca remembered: the brain takes what it already knows and discards it if it doesn't believe that anything new or useful is being added. Luca pondered for a moment how much of his life was automatically designated to be overwritten by the OS installed by evolution's own bloody QA process. His brain routinely deleted most of his life's moments after they happened, just like everyone else. He wondered if it was a curse or a gift.

Luca realized the meeting was over when people started standing up. He went back to his terminal and started his work. He signed in and began his first report of the day. A social media post calling for the castration of people with an IQ one standard deviation below the mean. That was a good start to what Luca saw that day. Most people on the internet are posting pictures of their new baby, a meal they ate, their dog at the beach, or the other inane posts that gather thumb-ups out of a sense of politeness. But there are all the things that probably never make it in front of good people. The things they don't want PermaSoft to let them see. Things people share with each other that ordinary people don't want to know about. Luca once tried to explain to his grandmother what he did for a living and she changed the subject when Luca described how Hezbollah was selling martyr trading card NFTs in the marketplace to finance bombings in Israel.

A few bland and predictable racist comments. A few empty threats to kill politicians. That was most of what he dealt with. Then Luca watched a video of a policeman, tied up, gagged and in the backseat of his own police car, eyes busted bloody, nose half collapsed, one of his fingers twisted into an angle fingers don't normally do. He said things Luca couldn't understand, but it was all the things you'd assume a person would say as the young cartel men in cowboy hats and Halloween masks welded the doors of his car shut. When they were done, men poured gasoline over the top of it and set it on fire. The camera captured the whole event and it would take 8 minutes before the screaming finally stopped. Luca flagged the video for deletion. Reason for flag: violence. He clicked the checkbox to forward it to law enforcement.

He watched a video of a naked woman on all fours inside a dog crate, while a man outside of it fucked her mouth. She was crying loudly enough you could barely hear the tinny sound of the man's pelvis slamming into the crate. Luca flagged the video as inappropriate material. Reason for flag: sexually explicit content. He did not click to hand it to the police. The video had a watermark for a website for porn simulating violent rape. He'd seen this couple plenty of times before. He moved on.

He saw two beheading videos from Mexico. It was a loud night for Latin America before his lunch break. Sanjay once told him that the cartels started making their own beheading videos after they saw the attention that the ISIS videos were getting. Cartels were avid consumers and plagiarists of the worst things people do to each other. He flagged one video because the Oaxaca Cartel had published it to their public social media page. He let an identical video stay because it was being shared by a whitelisted cable television network. The system was supposed to sort whitelisted users automatically. Sanjay said something about that at the meeting. Another dashcam video from Venezuela, driving under a highway overpass where two local judges hung from their necks, bloated and discolored under the hot sun as the gasses in their insides cooked and tried to escape them. Flagged.

One video of a lecture by an imam of the religious edicts that permitted wife beating. Luca flagged for endorsing violence against a protected class and also for hate speech because it was posted by a self-proclaimed UK patriot group.

A video of a young girl, maybe twelve years old. She was crying and clutching onto her mother who was also crying, as her new 40-something husband pulled his child bride violently from her family in an Afghani village, taking her somewhere where he would forcefully introduce to an adulthood that she wasn't ready for. Luca paused and looked over the policy on it to see if it violated any guidelines. Unsure of it, he forwarded it to a channel on Slack to discuss how to handle it. He continued onto the next post and the next and the next and between them checked in on the discussion to see how the staff wanted to handle it.

He spent a lot of time adjudicating whether individual users had a right to say the word *nigga*. He checked the personal info, name, and photos, to determine if they were allowed to use that kind of language. Most of them could.

A video of some preteens in Serbia, filming themselves shooting Combloc surplus rifles at bottles. Lots of pictures of people posing with guns got flagged. Sometimes a father and son posing with a dead buck. Sometimes a son without a father posing with a stack of stolen money. Flagged for promoting violence.

Certain words had scores attached to them, a mathematical formula that calculated the likelihood of a violation, based on proximity to each other. Then the algorithm compared that to a general word score in the user's post history. Saying *tree* is fine. Saying *liberty* is fine. Saying *watered* is fine. But if you say those things enough times, especially in the same post, the robot flagged it and put it in front of Luca and the other people on the 3rd floor.

This was Luca's day, every day. He was the psychic sanitation department for the internet, disappearing things that might make ordinary people upset. He vanished videos of crimes imagined in horror films and conducted by a rare few. He removed posts of photographs of guns and knives and even swords and tagging other users. More than once, he'd seen arguments escalate between two people badly enough that he forwarded them to law enforcement. One time, he learned the next day that the combatants had found each other and made good on their promises that most belligerents on the internet never do.

Most of it was nothing, though. The things that got in front of him were usually the junk from the automated robots, the digital sweepers that clean off posts with keywords and posts with flags from white-flagged users against gray-flagged users and black-flagged users. The algorithm removed them without understanding them, an idiot machine god at the center of the digital universe, weeding the imagination of the world. An invisible information dietician counting your calories.

The woman in the next cubicle broke Luca's concentration when she started sobbing. Naomi again. Someone came to her and put a hand on her shoulder and she stood up quickly and said, "I can't. Okay? I just can't! I'm sorry!" and she rushed off to the ladies' room. Another woman followed her in and Naomi's crying was still barely audible over the soothing sounds of her friend's comforting words.

A few people walked up to her desk to see what she saw and Luca watched the new guy's eyes go damp and Hyun just said, "Fuck." Penelope put both her hands over her mouth and walked away. Sanjay came up and saw it for himself and his lip curled. He typed something quickly and handled it. When he saw Luca not reacting at all, he approached him in his cubicle.

"Listen, uh, I've been meaning to mention it to you. Trisha said you haven't been by in a while." Sanjay was careful to speak quietly enough that others wouldn't hear him.

"Yeah."

"Trisha's here to help. I think it would be a good idea if people here take advantage of that fact."

"I'm good. Thanks." Luca tried to discern the look on Sanjay's face. He wasn't sure, but it looked like concern.

Sanjay leaned in and said in a quieter tone, "This stuff gets to everyone after a while. Everyone. That's the job. It's nothing to be embarrassed about."

"I'm not embarrassed. I'm fine."

"I can't make you go to see Trisha. I think everyone should, though. Once in a while. I was going over the numbers and you haven't seen her in six weeks. You know what the average time between visits for everyone else is?"

"I don't know."

"Guess."

"Three weeks?"

"One week. Most people see her once a week. I think you should go. Today."

Luca sighed, "If you want me to."

"I do. I want you to," then Sanjay returned to his normal speaking voice and gave Luca back his space and said, "Good talk, bud. Appreciate what you do around here," and he walked off.

Luca opened up the scheduling system to find a time to get in with Trisha. He marked his name in for after the 1am lunch, which was coming up soon.

Everyone handled it differently. Naomi cried. Hyun cracked jokes. Brian was too dumb to even understand. Chelsea intellectualized it like an anthropologist. Dragan drank. Sanjay managed. Luca created a big black hole inside him with a Lagrange point exactly where his human feelings started; a dense empty nothing that swallowed up all the misery he looked at every day.

Luca ate his lunch on the first floor, where the in-house restaurant made a quinoa salad, a vegan lasagna, and a fruit medley. The meal was calibrated by nutritionists employed by Corporate to maximize the energy and focus of employees and minimize sick days and insurance premiums. The meal wasn't bad today. Chelsea invited herself to sit with him and tried to make small talk, and Luca couldn't discourage her with his short answers. She asked him about his private conversation with Sanjay.

"He wants me to go see Trisha."

"Will you?"

"Maybe."

"I always feel better after I talk to her."

Luca changed topics abruptly. "Remember that diversity meeting we had a few weeks ago?"

"Yeah. Sure." Chelsea shifted uncomfortably in her chair.

"The woman said—I forgot her name—she said that trauma

victims often forget the traumatic event to protect themselves psychologically."

"Yeah..."

"I looked into that. I was curious. It's pertinent to our work, in a way. I wanted to learn more about it."

"Uh huh..."

"It's not true. The opposite is true. When people suffer from traumatic experiences, they remember it vividly. They remember strange details. Little things we don't remember ordinarily. The brain automatically treats this information as important because our survival might depend on absorbing that information and using it again in the future to avoid another similar trauma. It makes sense. I found an article where a woman could identify her rapist by his smell. She never even saw him. They actually had a smell lineup. Crazy, right? I guess smell is a strong trigger for memories."

Chelsea didn't say anything. She looked around a bit to check if anyone else was listening in.

Luca took a sip of his wheatgrass smoothie then said, "Something about what that lady said bothered me because, well... okay, think about this. Imagine that rape victim..."

She made an awkward fake smile and laughed. "Okay, I don't know if this is an appropriate lunch conversation..."

"If what that diversity trainer told us was true, that would mean a rape victim's brain gets wiped or distorted from it."

"Luca. C'mon."

"No, really. If getting raped zero-fills a woman's hard drive, their testimony in court wouldn't be worth anything. If that lady was right, cops should be skeptical of anyone coming in with a rape accusation. They should believe someone raped her, but they shouldn't believe any of the details that would help them catch the rapist."

Chelsea was keeping close attention to whoever might be in earshot in the cafeteria.

Luca continued. "That diversity trainer was full of shit. Trauma gets locked in. You think the victims we see every day just forget all that stuff that happened to them? No way. The brain doesn't protect itself by forgetting. That's not what brains are for. The brain protects itself by remembering. Remembering trauma is useful. We forget everything else."

When she was sure no one was nearby, she said, "Yeah. Luca, I guess... that makes sense."

"What did we have for lunch five days ago?"

"Um... I don't remember. I think... we had... tilapia? That was a... Saturday, right?"

"I don't know. What did we have for lunch on the Friday before?"

"Uh..." she looked up into her own memory and smiled, "Vegan beef stroganoff."

"See, I thought you would remember that one."

She chuckled. "Why?"

"Because it was terrible."

Chelsea laughed, "It was! It was so bad!"

"Yeah. Memorable. Bad is memorable."

"I see. Yeah. Our brains made a sticky note to avoid repeating a mistake in the future, like eating vegan beef stroganoff."

Luca nodded. "But let me ask you something else."

"Okay, shoot." She leaned over the table on her elbows, hands cupping her chin.

"How many cellphone videos have you watched this week of high school fights?"

"Um... I don't know. I guess... probably, like, twenty?"

"I don't remember either. Isn't that weird? We remember the stroganoff, but not teenagers beating the crap out of each other."

"Well, following your theory, it isn't weird at all. The fights are an ordinary daily experience for us that are forgettable. They are common. And they don't actually affect us directly, unlike the stroganoff. We don't remember good-enough tilapia. And, I'll add, those high school fights are traumatic for someone else, not us."

Luca nodded.

She cocked her head sideways. "Yeah. It is funny that vegan stroganoff is more traumatic and memorable than violence. I guess after you've seen enough of those fights, it just doesn't hit as hard anymore."

"Exactly. I was thinking about that because of those prostitution ads for trafficked girls from Vietnam. Remember those?"

She nodded. "The ones that looked like K-pop music videos? Yes. They were so creepy. I wish I could forget those…"

"I just wonder if the first time those girls were raped, if that experience is locked into their brain forever. A perfect recall of every detail. But maybe the 20th rape they don't remember it at all. After enough times, maybe even that became routine and forgettable. The first rape was stroganoff, but then all the others were tilapia."

Chelsea stopped smiling. She was quiet for a moment. "I think… I think this is a good conversation to have with Trisha. When was the last time you talked to her?"

After lunch, he went back up to the third floor, towards Trisha's office and passed by Naomi. Her eyes were pink and puffy, but she was calm and didn't look up at her co-workers. Luca silently reminded himself to say "team members" not co-workers in front of others.

Luca knocked on the door. A small sign said NO CELLPHONES.

"Enter."

Luca walked into the small room. Trisha's desk was small and against the wall, and she turned around in her office chair to face the big, soft armchair on the opposite wall. It was the only room that wasn't white and glass. There was a small wooden coffee table between the chairs with a box of tissues and a stress ball with a PermaSoft logo on it. The room was sponge-painted in warm earth tones and the lights were a tad dimmer. The walls were lined with shelves with books on psychology, some legitimate, some pop. A wax diffuser burned and released a smell of something like cinnamon. The room was just a tad warmer than anywhere else in the building.

Luca settled in the chair. Trisha put her hands in her lap and gave a warm but sad smile and said, "It's good to see you, Luca. I don't see you here very often. What can I help you with today?"

"Sanjay asked me to come in."

"Ah. So you didn't come in of your own volition?"

"I guess not."

"I don't believe that I can help a person who doesn't want any help. But how about you stick around for a half hour, give yourself a little break from your regular stuff, and hang with me? How's that sound?"

"That's fine I guess."

"Everything in here is confidential, so if you just sit there, Sanjay won't know. Sound good?"

"Sure."

She was quiet after that. She just sat and looked at him.

Ordinarily, he would look at his phone, but Trisha's no phone rule was non-negotiable. She was still looking at him. He finally asked, "What?"

"Nothing. It's just going to be an awfully boring half hour if we just sit here in silence."

"True."

"So how about we make some small talk? Nothing job related if you don't want to. Just something to do for the next little while."

"I guess."

"So how's it going, Luca?"

"It's fine."

"Would you say it's more fine or less fine than usual? Or the same amount of fine?"

"Same amount."

"Do you think your amount of fine is more fine or less fine or the same amount as others?"

"I don't know. More fine than some. Less fine than others."

"When you talk to your parents, does it drive them crazy when they ask you how you are and you just say fine?"

Luca laughed a little. "Yeah. It does."

"That's because they want to know how you are. How you really are."

"I don't want them worrying. They want to know I'm okay when we talk on the phone, so I tell them I'm okay."

"And you actually are okay?"

"Most days I'm okay. You know. You have good days and bad days, but mostly you have days that are fine. Same as anyone."

Trisha nodded and said, "Most people here on the third floor aren't fine. You know that, right?"

"Yeah. I know that."

"The job is tough. It gets to people. They take it home with them. We have a lot of turnover here. The average employee makes it less than a year before they quit or request a transfer. Not too many stay as long as you have."

"Yeah. I know that."

"But you. You're fine. I'm asking you—not as a therapist—as a scientist. I just want to understand. How is it you're fine? How do you stay fine?"

"I don't know."

"Maybe you could teach me something, hm? Maybe you have some methods to cope better than others. Maybe you have some experience that other people don't. I'd really just like to understand."

He thought about the benzodiazepines and the strict diet and the soothing music and the countless over-the-counter products he tried at least once, and the black hole inside him that ate anguish before it could find him. He lied and repeated, "I really don't know."

"Hm. Well, you tough it out better than most, it looks like."

He made sharp eye contact and said, "You don't believe me."

"Honestly, Luca? I don't know if I do. Some people hide their pain and anxiety inside. They compartmentalize their emotions and imagine them outside themselves. It's often easier to put our feelings into a place where we don't have to confront them."

"Yes."

"That's what you do?"

"Yes. That's what I do."

"It's not healthy to hide from your own feelings. You deal with them. It's just like if you have physical pain. You can try to ignore it, but eventually it will get bad enough that you will have to see a doctor. The longer you wait, the harder it will be to treat."

Luca shook his head.

"You disagree?"

"Yes, I compartmentalize my feelings. No, it's not unhealthy. It's what people should do. You shrinks act like it's a bad thing to keep your thoughts and feelings to yourself. I'm not like Naomi, who explodes her feelings all over the room. She can't control it. She lets it out. Does it help her? Does making all that shit public help her? I don't see how, since she's back here twice a week to do it again."

"We're here to talk about you, not Naomi."

"Feelings aren't like a blister you need to lance. Emotions can't be purged. And honestly, doing it loudly and visibly for everyone else is just rude. If you ask me, that shit makes it worse. Way worse. Crying isn't your head cleaning itself from pain. You want to know what I do every day without confiding in the on-staff therapist making 130K a year to watch people cry? Here's how. Take out that pad and write this down. I know you like to write shit down, so why not do it when I'm telling you what you want to know. Human feelings are just physiology. Feelings are chemicals. Feelings are drugs. A biochemical process that you experience. They make us see things incorrectly. They make us imagine bullshit. When you're feeling, you can't process information correctly. Starvation does that. Being horny does that. Anger, physical pain, everything. All of it is the same. We just see our own feelings reflected back at us and most people think those feelings are real. They aren't real. They aren't even in your mind, really. They're in your body. When you get angry, you can feel your pulse increase, you can feel your blood pressure going up, you can see that tiny tremor in you like when you lift a weight that's too heavy and you're about to drop it. When you're sad, you feel it like a pit in your chest, a cold inside you with its veiny little lead fingers crawling around, and it's so damn heavy it drags you down. People need to get out of their own fucking heads. Stop thinking with their feelings and start feeling their feelings. Feeling them in their body because that's where feelings really live. Feel it like you feel an itch or you feel the temperature or a stubbed toe. If you put your feelings in your body where they belong, you realize feelings are just the flu. They're a thing your body goes through and eventually you get over it and you're fine. If the feelings are in your mind, you can't get away from them. People get over the flu. They get hangovers. I get over my feelings the same way."

Trisha took a moment to think about what Luca said. "It's not healthy to keep your feelings bottled up."

"Alright. Good chat," and Luca got up and left before Trisha could think of any words to convince him to stay.

Luca went back to his terminal, took a seat, logged himself into the machine, and began the rest of his day of hideous things. The night shift was always the worst. The worst things seemed to get posted at night as though the people who posted them believed that the darkness would conceal their actions from others. The eyes are everywhere. Nothing escapes the AI Azathoth, dancing to a MIDI flute at the center of the cyber universe.

The weakest stuff had no effect on him. People doing drugs, people getting in fights, people doing sex acts with cellphone videos. These things couldn't touch him at all. He saw a video of three men beating up a woman in a fast-food parking lot, laughing. No explanation for why it was happening. He saw social media posts awkwardly implying that they might start shooting up their high school. He saw a video of someone kicking a skinny horse they'd chained up. The animal was too psychically defeated to even think of running away.

Mostly it was petty, benign personal grievances, like ex-wives making outrageous claims getting flagged by ex-husbands. Middle school teachers openly telling their feed about how much they despise their students. It was like the world's Catholic confession booth, but there were no requests for forgiveness and none were ever given.

The day Luca walked out on Trisha was a special day. It was the day that Luca saw the worst thing he'd ever seen in his life. He'd seen just about every ugly thing you can imagine and plenty of things you can't imagine. Things he once believed were rare, he learned were commonplace. About once a week, he'd see something that actually bothered him. This thing, though? This wasn't like that. This was different.

That night at about 2:03am Luca saw a video posted in a private chat. There were two kids, maybe seven or eight years old. A boy and a girl. They were sitting on a bed in a room with flaking white paint and tanning discoloration. It looked like a basement dressed up to look as childish as possible, with bedsheets, blankets, and pillows from well-known IPs. Posters of popular children's shows on the wall, toys on the floor, a Raggedy Anne doll, and a plush elephant just to be as on-the-nose as possible. It wasn't stuff for the kids. It was stuff for the people watching the kids. From behind the camera, there was the voice of someone using that lightened, soft voice that adults often use when talking to kids. Someone off-camera gave the two children instructions they didn't understand, and they asked a lot of questions like "why?" The director gave them answers adults give when they don't want to explain. There was a point when the director instructed the kids to undress each other and they complied. That's when Luca stopped the video. The cursor on his mouse darted to the portion to report the video to the police, but when the white arrow got there, he didn't press the button. Luca stared into the video-grainy faces of the kids. He didn't delete the account or the video.

He felt that big black hole inside him grow until that's all there was; an unsatisfiable, hungry vacuum that wanted to swallow up time itself.

He looked around and when he was sure no one was hovering behind him to make small talk and kibitz his work. Something was off with the video. He looked closely. At first, he thought someone had edited it. It looked grainy, fuzzy, like it was on VHS. A few digital artifacts, minor corruptions. There was something strange with the little girl's hair. It had a look to it. An aesthetic. It looked like the producers made it shitty on purpose. They wanted it to look even more ugly than it was.

Luca minimized the window. He leaned back into his chair and crossed his arms, and thought for a minute. He stood up and looked around the office. He saw Sanjay's desk in a cubicle just like everyone else, a technique to create the illusion of a flattened hierarchy of equity. Directly behind his spot was Brian. Luca picked up his phone and made a call.

"Yes. Hi. This is Sanjay Bajaj from the 3rd floor. Yeah. Hi. I'm having some trouble signing on. Can you reset my password? Thanks so much." He hung up. Luca put the worst thing he'd even seen on hold and continued processing flags. He kept an eye out, constantly looking towards Sanjay's desk. His boss finally came back from a meeting on the 2nd floor and sat down at his desk. Luca opened his video conferencing software and called Brian.

"Uh, hi?"

"Hey, Brian."

Luca saw Brian look up over his cubicle and then sit back down. "You're like 50 feet from me, man. You could just walk up to talk if you wanted to."

On the webcam video, Luca could see Sanjay behind Brian

trying to login in but having trouble. Luca said, "I'm having some weird technical issue here."

"Okay. Call IT."

"Could you just do me a favor, real quick?"

"Uh. Sure. I guess."

"Could you just hold up your webcam?"

"What, like pick it up?"

"Yeah."

"Like this?"

"Yeah, but higher."

"Okay, like this?"

"Higher. And point it downwards."

"Like this?"

"Yeah, but all the way up."

"Like this?"

Luca began recording the call. The camera was high enough that he could see over Brian, over Sanjay's shoulder, as his boss was entering his new password. "Perfect."

"Okay... so... how long do I need to hold this for? My arm's getting tired."

"I got it. Thanks for your help, Brian."

Brian put his webcam back on top of his monitor. "What's the issue?"

"Gotta go." Then Luca hung up.

Luca watched the recording of the video. Of the 11 characters in Sanjay's password, he was sure of six, pretty sure of two, and not sure about three. He wrote it down and deleted the web video.

He had to get back to work and at the end of his shift, he had one item still pending. The worst thing he'd ever seen. He cleared it. He lifted the suspension. No deletion. No ban. No police notification. The system automatically reinstated the user and issued an email apology.

On his way out at 5am, Luca snagged one of the company laptops that they reformatted every time an employee quit, which was often. He left without saying goodbye to anyone. He passed someone else in the lobby who was upset and being consoled by another team member at the fountain. The clean design, the enormous tree, and the soft sound of new age music had no effect.

Luca drove to a chain diner and connected to the Wi-Fi in the parking lot. After a few tries, he got into PermaSoft's system using some guesswork and deduction to use Sanjay's account and admin privileges. He looked into the personal account of the man who shared that video. The account was mostly blank of any personal info, not even an avatar image, but the algorithm sees things we don't see. It can find commonalities between the two profiles. It can see where they are, what passwords they use, when they sign in and out, and it develops shadow profiles. With Sanjay's API and broad suite of tools, Luca could see these secret things. He looked at the fake account and made notes of the times it signed in and signed out. He filtered out millions of other accounts by logins and logouts, looking for a pattern. He found one. The accounts were never signed in at the same time. He saw both accounts used the same password. He saw they signed in from the same IP. The algorithm is stupid, but it sees things.

Forrest Perry. His real account with his real face. Ironically, the account that his friends and family saw was his fake account. It was the manufactured person who hid who he really was. He didn't look like what people assume a pedophile looks like. He looked... normal. He was fit. He posted every place he'd worked in his adult life. He had pictures of him with a dog. Pictures of him with a girlfriend. A picture of him on vacation. Pictures of breakfast. No politics. No drama. Normal, healthy stuff. Nothing suspicious. Open as a book. Nothing to hide. Luca saw the groups Forrest was in. He played in a baseball beer league. He listened to psychedelic rock from the 60s. He spent Christmas with his parents and two older sisters.

He hadn't updated with his current job over the last two years. Strange.

Luca copied all the information down. He found alternative nicknames and found the same nick used on different platforms, and he pieced it together so Luca knew where he was on seven different social media platforms. He found Forrest's little club, too. The video had been passed between several people, all tied together through a group page made by Perry, and it had more users than you'd believe if I told you.

Luca headed home as the sun was coming up and the rest of the world started waking up and starting their days in cozy ignorance about the things Luca had scrubbed. He got home and ate a snack, but only barely. He went into his bedroom and closed the blackout curtains to hide the sun and he lay in bed but he couldn't sleep. He took a pill, and it made him dizzy and his mind got weird in a half-conscious dream-like state where he wasn't quite awake or asleep. His conscious mind and unconscious mind had the rare occasion to meet each other face to face, one of those odd moments when you wake up from a powerfully realistic dream and you aren't quite yet aware that it wasn't real. He thought about Forrest Perry and his mind conjured the image of him as a child's book villain. A creature in a well that calls the name of children and lures them to peek down into the damp, cold black pit so he can pull them in and eat them with teeth big like a horse's, and glowing eyes like a raccoon's when you point a flashlight at them.

He didn't sleep.

When his alarm beeped, he picked up his phone and called work and said he was sick, which wasn't entirely a lie. He hung up before Sanjay could finish saying, "Feel better." He went into his living room and got onto his stolen laptop, and connected to the password unprotected Wi-Fi of the old lady who lived next door. He looked into one of Perry's accounts. An online gun market. Perry'd been using it for a while and when he wasn't filming children, he also had a side business. He bought busted old guns, refurbished them, and sold them on the private market. Just like flipping houses. Perry had one for sale for $2,300.

Luca drove to the worst neighborhood he knew about and bought a prepaid debit card and a cellphone. He walked into a small coffee shop, walked into the single-person bathroom, locked the door, connected to the Wi-Fi, and started working. He did some research. He ordered some things using a prepaid card with a fake name and had them sent to his condo, the newly empty apartment 302. He paid extra to expedite next-day shipping.

Luca sent a private message from a burner account with a fake name he created from a random name generator he found online.

John Burrows: *I'm interested in the pistol*

Forrest Perry: *Cool. I accept all the common payment apps. Just send me the address of your LGS*

John Burrows: *I was hoping to see it in person. You're an FFL right?*

Forrest Perry: *I move around a lot. Right now I'm near Glen Rose.*

John Burrows: *I'm in Abilene.*

Forrest Perry: *That's pretty far. We can meet up halfway somewhere. I'll also need to see a CCW.*

John Burrows: *I'm going to be heading into your part of town on the 4th anyway on business so I can just swing by while I'm already there.*

Forrest Perry: *Great! What time works for you?*

Luca searched for any fireworks in the area. One show scheduled to start at 7:30 pm just 2 miles away.

John Burrows: *I can make it there around 7:30*

Forrest Perry: *awesome, see you then.*

Perry sent Luca an address. It wasn't the one Luca found during his investigation. He looked it up. It wasn't even a home. It was an RV lot in a state park.

Luca went to work the next day and the day after, but was distracted thinking about Wednesday. Before he left on work two days before, he mentioned in passing that he wouldn't be in for a few days and Sanjay didn't object.

When he got back to his condo, he saw a pile of packages accumulating at the doorstep of 302. The yellow eviction notice was gone except for a little tear of paper and a piece of invisible tape. He looked both ways to make sure no one was looking and picked up the packages and walked towards his apartment.

"Hey."

Luca looked behind him.

The door to 302 was open and filled with a woman squeezed into sweatpants and a t-shirt that once fit but didn't anymore. "What's all that?"

"What's what?"

"Those packages you just plucked off my doorstep. What's all that?"

"None of your business." Luca turned around and took one step before she stopped him.

She spoke louder than she needed to. "Oh, I think it is. Looks like you're stealing from me."

"I'm not stealing!"

"Drugs? Is that drugs?" she said even louder.

He whisper-yelled "It's not drugs!" and he walked back to be closer to her so the woman would stop speaking so loudly. He showed her the label, James Davis. "See? These aren't yours."

"You ain't James Davis, neither." He could smell the beer on her.

"You don't know my name."

"It ain't James. You ain't no fucking millionaire cartoon cat man." She laughed, "Why didn't you have it sent to your own place using your real name, huh?"

"I'm not having this conversation with you in the hallway."

"Then come inside and have it."

Luca looked around again to see if anyone else saw them, then took his packages inside. The place was emptied out. No furniture. Lots of red cups, plenty of empty beer cans, many with cigarette ashes on the rim. A few pizza boxes with a few hard slices, sitting on the gross carpet. Indentations in the carpet where the furniture used to be. She walked into the living room and sat on the floor. Luca just stood there.

"Those packages gotta be getting heavy."

Luca sat down and set the packages down.

"You sent that here cus you thought this place was empty, right? So what you got there, James? Hm?" She lit a cigarette.

"None of your business."

"It is if you want me to keep my mouth shut. Open it up. I want to see. Come on. Is it lasagna?" She thought she was funny.

He didn't do anything.

"James, I'm just curious. Show me what you got. I won't say shit to nobody."

He opened up the packages. She leaned forward with eager eyes, like a kid on Christmas morning. A case of .45 ACP 230gr JHP ammunition. A burner phone. A prepaid phone card. A magazine for a 1911. A fake mustache. Aviator sunglasses. A Baltimore Orioles t-shirt. A VFW baseball cap. Track pants. Disinfecting wipes. A backpack. A GPS jammer that fit into a car's aux power outlet.

She puffed out a big cloud. "Damn, son. You don't look like the bad boy type. What're you planning with all of this?"

"None of your —"

She flicked her cigarette at him and it bounced off his bicep and shot sparks. "What the fuck!"

She retrieved her cigarette from where it was burning the carpet and she took a drag and stared at him.

"I'm going... I'm using... I'm..."

"Mm hm?"

He met her eyes and said, "I'm going to kill a pedophile."

She smiled. She didn't even look surprised. "He rape one of yours?"

"No. I don't have kids."

"He rape you?"

"No. I don't know him personally."

She rested a hand on her chin and looked James Davis over. "Good. I'm glad you're gonna kill him." She nodded. "I'm glad. I won't tell. Scout's honor. You ever kill a pedophile before?"

"No. This is my first."

"Your first. Hm. When you say it that way, makes me think he won't be your last."

Luca began gathering his things.

She asked, "Wanna fuck? I had a hot date planned for this party last night, but he left early. You're cute, though."

"Um. No. Thank you."

"You gay?"

"No."

"Oh, so I'm not pretty enough for you?"

"It's not that," he lied.

"I'm too old?"

"No. I just. Don't feel like it."

She dropped her cigarette into a beer cup and it sizzled. She shook her head. "You fucking lying piece of shit faggot. Think you're too good for this? Huh? You'd fuck me if I had a dick, right? You wanna suck my cock, huh? You like big fucking dicks? You couldn't handle a real woman like me, anyway. You wanna fuck a skinny bitch built like a 10-year-old boy? Huh? You want some little girl cuz you can't handle a real woman. You just a little boy with a little faggot dick. That why you wanna kill a pedo, huh? Cus they rape little boys? Pedos wanna suck little faggot baby dick, like you got. They wanna fuck little boys and that's what you are, a little fag boy with a tiny faggot baby dick. Yeah. You look twelve years old, you baby-faced faggot. You never had a woman, probably. Probably a fucking virgin incel. Probably never even been with a woman. Probably like those little skinny girls who look like little faggot middle school boys, like you. Fucking kill pedos? Kill yourself, you baby dick loving pedo faggot." She threw her cup at him, but she missed her mark, and sprayed a trail of ashy black flat beer.

Luca stood up. She lunged for him and started trying to unbuckle his pants. He pushed her off. She tried again, and he shoved her harder the second time. She started crying. Luca left as quickly as he could. He was sure to lock the door of his home as soon as he was inside.

In the morning, Luca did his regular routine before leaving the condo. He left his phone at home so that if anyone were to check after the fact, the GPS record would say he was home. He ran a little script he'd written on his computer which automatically made a video call to a fake burner account that he also owned, timed to happen around the time he would see Forrest Perry, and for the program to auto-delete itself after hanging up.

He was very careful to sneak past 302 to get to his car. Luca drove out to Glen Rose, almost three hours from Austin, and took an exit onto a strip where everything was fast food and nothing about the town was special, corpo-homogenized, like lots of towns in America. It had no identity, just rows after rows of familiar brands that always told you you were in America but never where in America you were.

He took the road into an RV park. There were scale statues of dinosaurs along the road. Luca drove slowly, carefully looking around for the RV the seller described. The place was already mostly full. Kids were running around. Grills cooking. Parents scolding. Beer cans cracking. American flags waving. When Luca saw the camper, he drove a little further and parked. He walked through the park. There were no cameras. No security booths. The place was mostly lawn and firepits and trees. A lot of dog lovers. He walked past Forrest Perry's place. None of the RVs had surveillance cameras on them. People didn't worry about break-ins when they brought their homes with them everywhere they went. Unhitched from the back of the RV was a trailer with a WaveRunner. There was a dog bowl outside. Parked in a little grassy pocket surrounded by trees, pretty far back into the woods, relatively isolated. The living situation looked semi-permanent. There were clay-potted plants around the outside like a mobile garden, a sizeable stack of firewood, and a grill and picnic table under the shade of a pullout canopy.

Luca got back in his car and wrote notes with pen and paper, because none of it could ever touch an internet connected device like a phone. He looked up Airbnb locations nearby that had immediate availability. He found one just a mile and a half away and used his GPS to get there. A nice little house on a dirt road. No cameras and no one home.

He drove out to the home, pulled into the driveway, and killed the engine. He reviewed his notes before he put the seat back and fell asleep in his car.

The next morning, the actual sun woke him up for the first time in a year. He put on his fake mustache and the clothes with designs meant to misdirect witnesses. Luca ran through the plan in his mind over and over again. He said what he would say. He did the movements he would use.

He went back to the park around 7:30 and the sun was still out. The park was busier than the day before. There were a lot of cars parked along the curb and Luca could see the colorful strings of chili-shaped lights hanging across one of the RVs, and across to a few pop-up gazebos, wrapped around the edges. There was smoke from grills and the popping of fireworks in defiance of city ordinance. American flags everywhere; on RVs, trucks, shirts, face-painted on kids, paper plates, and napkins.

He knocked on the door of the RV. The door opened. The owner in the Van Halen t-shirt asked, "John, right?"

"Hi. You're Forrest."

Perry extended a hand, and they shook.

The inside looked bigger than he thought, and the place kind of reminded him of his own. Minimalistic. Spartan. Functional. They heard the cracks of the fireworks show beginning. Luca noticed a photo on the fridge. Perry with three girls, maybe six, eight, and ten years old.

Forrest saw him looking. "My nieces."

Luca nodded.

"Great kids. So cute at that age." Forrest stood next to Luca and looked at the picture. Luca looked at Forrest, who was smiling fondly at a memory of them. "Do you have any kids?"

Luca swallowed hard and stuck a hand in his pocket and felt the loaded magazine he brought. "No."

"I love kids. They're the best."

Luca could've strangled him right there, but he decided to stick with the plan. He knew the plan.

Forrest walked to the small table and two wall-attached chair-booths. On the table was a bottle of tequila, a cutting board, a couple limes, a knife for cutting them, a salt shaker, two shot glasses, and a shoebox.

"Anyway, lemme show you what I got here." Forrest opened up a shoe box and handed it to Luca. Chrome-plated, with an image of Elvis on the grip.

Forrest put his hands on his hips. "So, uh, are you an Elvis fan?"

There was a loud bang outside from a firework. Luca flinched. "No. Not really."

Luca removed it from the box and looked it over. It was in mint condition. "Where did you get this from? If you don't mind my asking?"

"I got it at an estate sale in Pennsylvania. I thought it would be a great gift for my stepdad, but he passed away that same weekend. It didn't really feel right to sell it, you know? It wasn't like it was ever really my stepdad's, but it felt like it was his. I just know he would've loved it. I feel like I've—I don't know—moved on since then. Like I can finally let it go. I never even shot it."

Another loud bang outside from a firework. Luca flinched even harder. He didn't realize his nerves were so amped up.

"You alright?"

"Yes. I'm fine."

"It's just fireworks."

"I know. I said I'm fine."

"I used to get that when I would shoot. I would go to the range and I'd hear that first crack and my adrenaline would just go, like, BLAOW. It'd make me jump every time. Took me a while to mellow before I could get my hand tremor under control and get good groupings."

"Okay."

"My stepdad taught me to shoot. I guess selling the gun just got me thinking about him again. He always said adrenaline is just a drug. I remember that. You are on drugs when your adrenaline is up. You just gotta stop being a lightweight and get that feeling out of your head. It's just like what your body does when you drink too much coffee. It's your body that's amped up, not your mind. Something to think about when you finally take this out to the range."

Luca didn't want to hear this guy talk about himself like he was an actual human being. Luca interrupted. "You got a cat or something?"

"Uh, no. I have a dog. Why?"

"Oh, nevermind. Looks like there's a squirrel or something in here." Luca pointed past Forrest to the other side of the camper.

"What?" Forrest turned around to look. Luca reached into his pocket and retrieved the magazine. His heart was pumping, and he had a tremor from the adrenaline. He slid the magazine in and pointed the gun at Forrest's back, holding it using a teacup grip.

Forrest turned around to ask what Luca saw. Only then, Luca remembered to rack the slide. He used his support hand, but the magazine wasn't locked in and it fell out and bounced onto the floor towards Forrest. There was a still moment between them. No one did anything. It was a second at most, but time slowed down.

Forrest went for the mag. Luca dove for it, too. Forrest had both hands on it and Luca had one on the mag and one on the gun. Forrest yanked it from his grip, bottom first. As it slipped through his hand, one round popped out and landed on the floor. Luca grabbed it and sat back, trying to lock the slide open. Forrest threw the mag behind him and jumped onto Luca.

Forrest struggled to take the gun from the stranger in his home. Luca tried to get the round into the chamber through the breach while Forrest grabbed his wrists, but Luca got it in. Forrest had him mounted and held Luca's wrist of his gun-hand and punched Luca in the face with the other. He did a good job on Luca's face. Luca bent his wrist to point it at Forrest's head. Forrest grabbed the barrel. Luca released the slide lock, but it didn't move while Forrest's hand was on it.

Forrest stopped punching and put both hands on the gun. He had all the leverage and pulled it away so hard he fell onto his back, banging the table and knocking the knife onto the carpet right between Luca's legs. Forrest sat up and pointed the gun at Luca from the ground, but he didn't fire. Luca looked at the gun. Then at the knife on the floor in between them. Then the gun.

"You tried to kill me for this gun? For $2,300?"

"No. I don't care about the gun."

"Why then?"

Luca wanted to say a lot of things to the pedo. He wanted to say so much. But all he said is, "For your nieces."

"What?"

Luca grabbed the knife lunged at Forrest. The seller pulled the trigger, but nothing happened. It would've been a perfect kill shot through the sternum and right into the heart and trachea. Luca's knife went into the pedo. His hands scrambled to push Luca's face. Luca stabbed again and again until he was too tired to keep going, perforating his lungs, holes to let blood go in, and more holes to let air go out. When Forrest's arms went weak and his eyes looked far away, Luca got off him. But it took Forrest two more minutes to stop making noises. Luca sat and waited with him and two minutes sitting with a man dying was the slowest time he'd ever felt. By the time he was done, Forrest's blood on Luca was crusting.

When Luca stood up, his hand pressed on the carpet, the blood saturated it and welled up from the pressure. He looked over his good deed, still trying to catch his breath. When his breath was under control, he took the gun and put it back into the shoe box. He locked the door.

He walked into Forrest's bedroom and found some clothes. They were too big, but at least they didn't have blood all over them. He stripped down and took a quick shower. He thought it over. It went badly, but not too badly. He didn't even need the cover of the fireworks to hide the gunshot. Where was the dog, though?

He heard the voice of a woman outside, "Come on, Scatter!" Then he heard someone try to open the side door.

"Forrest? It's me! Open up."

"Fuck," Luca said under his breath.

He heard her knocking on the window of the bathroom. "Are you taking a shower? Come on, open up." The dog could smell what she couldn't see and was barking like crazy, slamming into the door.

He poked his head out of the tiny shower and could see her through the thin, white curtains in the window. She couldn't see Luca with the sunlight on her side. She looked familiar. The girlfriend. He'd seen her from Forrest's social accounts.

"I didn't bring my keys, and I gotta pee! Come on!" The dog's nose smelled several liters of murder in the carpet and was in a frenzy. "Damn, Scatter! Chill out! What is wrong with you?"

Luca didn't move. He waited. And waited. Eventually, she got the dog to relax, but he whined a weak protest. Then he didn't hear her at all. He peeked out the curtains and saw she was heading towards the row of blue and white porta johns about a hundred yards away. He jumped out of the shower and into some sweatpants he found. The dog was still outside the RV and started barking again. No way he could just walk out. He tossed the vehicle, looking for the keys. He found them in Forrest's pocket. He got into the driver's seat and turned on the ignition. Luca pulled out of the spot in the dirt lot, tearing down the canopy over the picnic table. He could hear the dog chasing and barking. The barking only stopped once Luca was out of the park and on the main road.

He was doing 55 on 205 when he heard honking behind him. He looked in the rearview mirror. A pickup with roof rack lights was honking and flashing their lights, driving really close. Luca was afraid to stop. Maybe they knew what happened and were trying to make a citizen's arrest. He looked for an escape. He made a turn and followed the road past farmhouses and fields. The other car kept honking and flashing and followed him. There was a red light. Luca stopped. He kept his eyes on his mirrors. The truck was right behind him. Their doors opened and two guys climbed out, one wearing mossy oak and the other a wife-beater. They started approaching from either side. One pulled out a knife and disappeared behind the RV and the other was closing in on the driver's side door. The RV had barely any acceleration, and when Luca gunned it through the red light, he almost got t-boned by a boomer driving a Slingshot. He dipped into a turn on a dirt road nearly invisible behind a crop of trees. He didn't see the truck following him anymore. He drove a few more miles. He didn't know where he was going yet. He didn't plan on escaping in an RV. Or the misfire. Or the dog. Or the girlfriend.

Luca pulled down the first road he saw and took it a quarter mile before he pulled over. He heard a buzzing sound. He looked around the red-spattered room and found Forrest's phone on the floor, along with everything else that was on the table. The phone was lit up. 18 attempted calls from Amanda. Several text messages. He picked up the phone. New model. He held it up in front of Forrest's face. Nothing happened. He used his fingers to hold his eyes open and tried again. The phone unlocked.

She was freaking out. He texted her.

Forrest: *It's not working out.*

Amanda sent back a lot of hateful words. The two sentences caught his attention, though.

Amanda: *Scatter is MY DOG. Bring him back NOW.*

Amanda: *And I want my bike back asshole.*

He got out of the RV and looked at the back. There were a pair of mountain bikes hanging from a rack. He took one off. Then he noticed a leather strap tied to the hitch, cut on the loose end. He crouched and examined it. Scatter's leash. Amanda must have tied him to the RV before she went to the porta john. And the guys with the knife cut it when they saw poor Scatter being dragged across asphalt by the neck for a half mile.

"Sorry, Scatter." He crouched and held the leash. "I'm sorry."

He looked around. Not a damn thing, but trees and scrub. He didn't even know how many miles he'd driven. He went inside and looked at what he had to work with. He opened the fridge and found a bunch of water bottles. He grabbed a pot and found some olive oil and poured all of it in. He set it onto a portable gas stove. He went into the bedroom. He found a sock, put the water bottle into it, and looked around for somewhere to hang it. A doorknob. He tied it there and set up the oil pot and burner underneath it and turned it on. He took some sandals and a shirt and put those on before leaving.

He got on the bike and rode back towards his car. It wasn't a half hour before the oil got hot enough to catch fire, burn through the sock, drop the water bottle into the pot, melt the plastic, and start a major oil fire inside the RV, torching most of the evidence that Luca was ever there.

Luca rode his bike back to his car. He ditched the bike and took a long drive home. A long drive like that is plenty of time to imagine everything that could lead back to him. Every possible error. But he felt safe. He got home at about 2am, set his keys on the kitchen counter, and checked his computer. His fake video call program worked just fine. He flopped into bed and fell asleep immediately. For the first time in a year, he went to sleep without Ambien, Trazodone, or melatonin. He slept the deepest sleep he could remember. He woke up to his alarm. He got out of bed, feeling refreshed and rested. Then he realized that the sweatpants he was wearing were Amanda's, with big pink text on the ass that read QUEEN BEE.

He did his regular morning routine. He listened to some music on his way to work. He walked in and said hello to Chelsea and Sanjay. Took a seat at his desk. He checked the news to see if there was anything about what had happened the night before. He searched for any mention of a knifing or an RV fire in Somervell County. One local story, but no details, and no followup article the next day.

The next night he slept great again. He came to work feeling good. Nothing in the news. The day after, the same. Then he didn't bother looking anymore.

It was almost a week later, Luca came to work and Sanjay and some other employees were laughing until the moment Luca walked in. They quieted down when they saw him. Chelsea found him as soon as he came in and told him the news. "Did you hear?"

"Hear what?"

"About the murdered guy in Glen Rose the other day?"

"Um. Maybe. I don't know."

"He was stabbed to death and his camper was set on fire. Someone said they saw the guy dragging his own dog behind him."

"Damn."

"Yeah."

"So... why are you telling me?"

"Oh! Because he worked for SurfSafe."

"Okay?"

"SurfSafe!"

Luca shook his head slowly.

"They're that nonprofit that baits pedophiles and then gives the info to the cops."

Hyun and some other guys invited themselves into the conversation. "Hey, Luca."

"Hi."

The guys were all smiling and trying not to.

"So, how you doing, buddy?" They were holding back their snickering.

"I'm fine."

"Hey, uh, have you ever seen the movie The Mighty Ducks?"

"Uh, I don't think so. That's a kids' movie, right?"

"Oh man. You would love that movie. And *Home Alone*, too, probably." The guys all started laughing uncontrollably. Chelsea looked away and made a fist and put it over her mouth.

"I don't get it. What's funny about that?"

"Show him, show him," said Hyun.

Brian held up his cellphone to a news article with a police sketch.

"Who's that?"

"It's you, man!" said Brian.

"What are you talking about? That doesn't look like me." He swallowed and his heart started beating hard enough he had a fleeting suspicion the others would hear it.

"Bro, it looks a lot like you! Come on! But with a pedo 'stache."

"Who is that?"

Sanjay invited himself into the conversation from out of nowhere. "That's the man the cops think killed the guy from SurfSafe. They're an affiliate of PermaSoft. We went over this during the morning meeting earlier this week, remember? They use AI-generated deepfakes of kids to bait child abusers. This ring any bells? They register all their accounts with us to get whitelisted. Any flags against their accounts are supposed to be automatically removed, but we had a few get by the filtering process and we had to update the account. Seriously, Luca, I don't know why we have meetings if you aren't going to pay attention. Anyway, the police think this guy in the police sketch is a pedophile, and he found the SurfSafe dude and murdered him."

Hyun added, "And the police sketch looks a lot like you."

"It does, man! Come on! You have to admit it," said Brian. The guys were dying laughing. Chelsea told them to stop, it wasn't funny, but they ignored her.

"Bro, we're just busting your balls!" said Hyun. "It's just fucking funny, is all. Seriously, you should make that your profile picture on your socials."

Brain laughed, "Oh shit, you have to! That'd be so funny!"

Sanjay said, "SurfSafe has been sending around emails warning everyone involved with them, including us. They worry that maybe this guy is targeting people doing that kind of work."

The article ended with, *Police are asking anyone at the park that day to check any photos or videos taken that day; they may have images of the killer in the background.*

Luca looked at the drawing of himself on Brian's phone. Now Luca was an alleged pedophile who murdered a good man trying to stop him. On a longer look, it did kind of look like Luca.

It boiled up in him. A lot of stuff that was supposed to die with Forrest. He could feel it coming a few seconds before, like vomit. Luca lost his composure. He couldn't turn it off like he used to. Not this time. Luca started crying. Not his face. Just his eyes. Silent and still.

"Oh, shit." said Brian. All the guys stopped laughing.

"Luca, man, we were just kidding, man. We know it's not you. We weren't trying to—"

Chelsea yelled at them, "You guys are such fucking assholes!"

"Come on, man. We know it's not you. You gotta admit the pedo kind of looks like you, though, right?"

"I quit."

"What?"

Luca turned around, walked to his desk, grabbed his things, and headed towards the elevator. He waited in front of the doors for the elevator to arrive. Chelsea approached him and was about to say something when the door opened and two police detectives walked out, plain clothed with shiny copper badges hanging from chains on their necks. Luca got in the elevator. The doors began to close. Then a hand interrupted, and they opened again. The cops were looking at him. "Are you Luca Amante?"

"Yes?"

"Step out here, please."

He did.

"I'm detective Heller from Somervell County Sheriff's Department. This is detective Robins with Park and Wildlife. We'd just like to ask you a few questions, if you have a moment."

Chelsea couldn't move or speak.

The detectives followed Luca into a conference room in the center of the work area with glass walls, a modern workplace panopticon. The whole office was pretending not to be looking. Luca dropped the blinds before the three of them sat together at the long conference table. The police asked all the questions he expected them to ask.

"Where were you on the night of July 4th?"

"At home. Sick." He'd told Sanjay the day before.

"Do you have anyone who can corroborate that?"

"Yes." He talked with a friend on video chat.

"Who?"

"I know her handle. I don't know her real name." He told them the name of the straw account he used. Even if they couldn't reach the person, there would be a log that the conversation existed.

"Do you know a man named John Burrows?"

"I don't think so. The name doesn't ring a bell."

"Have you ever been to Glen Rose?"

"Maybe. Where is that, exactly?"

The questions went on like that for a while. He was expecting more from them. Something connecting him to the murder. But they went in circles, asking similar questions using different words. Luca finally asked, "I'm sorry, but I don't understand why you are here. Why are you asking me all these questions?"

"We're investigating a murder case."

"Okay, but still. I don't understand why you're talking to me. Like, who was even killed?"

"A man named Forrest Perry. He worked for a nonprofit that tracked pedophiles and forwarded their info to the police."

"Yeah, my co-workers were just telling me about that. But what does that have to do with me?"

"We received an anonymous tip that you could be involved."

"What tip?"

Detective Heller checked her notes. "The tipster told us you were planning on murdering a man and that you, quote, *like sucking little faggot baby dicks,* unquote."

Frozen Nana Nugs

As a man who runs a demolition derby sportsbook, I spend a lot of time at county fairs. My first love will always be funnel cakes and meth, but frozen bananas are a crowd pleaser.

Time: 20-30 mins to assemble, and then a couple hours to freeze

Ingredients

- 4 Bananas
- 3 oz Peanut Butter
- 4 pieces of Bacon (or more if you're really into bacon)
- 6 oz Chocolate
- 1/4 tsp Vanilla extract
- Some water

Gear

- Popsicle sticks
- A freezer
- Parchment paper

How to make it

1. Mix up the vanilla and peanut butter with 1 ⅓ Tbsp of water
2. Cook up the bacon. Save the fat. Get it good and crispy. When it's cool, break it up into little bacon bits
3. Melt the chocolate in a saucepan. Go low and slow. Don't burn it
4. Undress the bananas and chip them into discs, about an inch thick
5. Arrange the nanner discs on the parchment paper
6. Smear the vanilla peanut butter on them
7. Sprinkle the bacon on top of the sticky peanut butter
8. Pour some chocolate over the top
9. Put the tray in the freezer for a couple hours

Serve with

- Carnival games
- Beer in a plastic cup
- The music of *Connie Francis*

Variations

- Swap the peanut butter for a hazelnut spread from a well-known Italian brand
- Make em like popsicles by cutting the nanas in half, lengthwise, and run a stick through em

CHAPTER +1:
HEARTBREAK HOTEL

Henderson, NC

4/20/1996

09:22:44

The phone rang. The high-pitched, tinny sound slapped Michael out of his sleep. He reached blindly to the side table and took it off the receiver and put it to his ear. He could hear how groggy he was from the sound of his own voice. "Yeah." His eyes just started adjusting to the room lit by flickery television light.

"Wake up. We got something for you."

"Hm. Gimme a minute." He hung up.

The TV was playing the hotel channel on a 30 minute loop, touting the hotel's accommodations, written by a marketing team at corporate who had never been to this hotel. Michael turned on the bedside lamp. He sat up in the queen-sized bed, planted his feet on the crunchy carpet, and stretched. The room was listed as non-smoking, but you wouldn't know from the smell of it. Michael shuffled into the bathroom and turned on the shower. It sputtered and struggled to spit out some red rusty water for a moment before the clear water came out. He let that run a bit. It always took a minute for the warm water to come out. He brushed his teeth until he could feel the steam, then took his shower using a bottle of hand soap, and rinsed his mouth in a tub where the grout was the color of dental tartar.

He dried off with a beach towel he owned, and walked to the dresser, always careful not to step on the red-brown stain on the carpet. He got dressed. Everything spotless and new: hoodie by Ecko, snapback by Hilfiger, jeans by FUBU, and kicks by Jordan. He stuffed his pocket with some cash and his room key.

He sat on the edge of the bed and looked at the phone number written on a scratch pad with the header labeled *Grandview*. He dialed the number and let himself fall back onto the bed. Someone answered the phone.

"Hi, I'm calling for Delmar. Delmar Bryce. This is Michael." The woman on the phone put him on hold, and the smooth jazz waiting music started. He looked up at the acoustic ceiling panels. The big brown ring was now 1/8th inch larger than where he marked it with a black sharpie two days ago.

Finally she came back. "I'm sorry, he's sleeping right now. I can forward you to his private voicemail if you like, and he can listen to it when he wakes up."

"Yeah. Sure." The phone clicked. A recorded voice prompted him to leave a message. Beep. "Hey, Del, it's me. I'm just calling to see how you doin. Lady said you asleep. Hey, you know that shitty music they play? When you on hold? I thought it's supposed to mellow you, but it makes me angry. You know? It's annoyin. I think maybe they play that music cus they want you mad so you hang up, cus they don't want people callin. Anyway, I'll call again later, I guess. Feel better. One."

He stepped out into the hall. There was a weird smell like burnt tires and fry grease. He knew from looking at the books that the place was half-full of guests, but it looked abandoned.

A guy was pacing back and forth in front of a room door, wearing nothing but sweatpants. He saw Michael and started staggering his way. Michael turned his back and headed towards the stairs in the opposite direction.

"Hey, kid. Hey. Hey," the guy said from behind him.

Michael stopped, turned around and said, "Don't never speak to me." He locked in eye contact so the guy knew he wasn't playing around.

"I was just…"

"Say one more thing, junkie. Say one more thing to me."

"Naw, I…"

Michael raised a fist and took a couple of steps towards the hotel guest. The skinny man cowered, stumbled backward, and fell on his ass. He stayed quiet then. Michael continued his walk to the stairwell, took it down to the door to the main floor, just and past the laundry room. A little girl sat on the dryer, eating chicken nuggets. Michael found the conference room and looked inside. Empty. He walked to the front desk, where Tiana was leaning over the counter.

"Good morning, sweety."

"Hi, Tiana. Jeff said he needed me. He around?"

"They outside."

Michael walked out through the dirty glass doors to the parking lot. The pavement and sky matched colors and promised rain. There wasn't a sign for the hotel anymore, but locals knew it was The Grandview. The place was just a block from the freeway overpass, close enough to hear the constant Doppler ocean wave sounds, like a beach resort with a concrete-diesel tide. The small hardware store next door had just one car in the parking lot. The waffle joint across the street still had yellow tape around it and signs taped to the door telling the owner and customers that it was unlawful to sell food at this establishment. A lawyer had also posted flyers looking for any potential clients for lawsuits against the corporate HQ. In front of it, the 11-year-old lookout, Tyson, was sitting in a folding beach chair, listening to his portable radio playing Buju Banton's gravelly voice. He saw Michael and waved. Michael waved back.

A 40-something hooker named Jolly came up to Michael. He tried to stuff some money into the kid's hand and said, "Here's what I owe you. From that thing."

Michael pushed him off. He looked around in all directions, then told him, "Not outside, dummy. Talk to Tiana." Jolly put the money back into his purse and gracefully walked in heels across the cracked and potholed parking lot and went inside.

Michael saw Kish and Jeff leaning against Kish's new LX SUV. He walked their way, passing by a wandering man who moved like a space alien doing a poor imitation of what it thinks a human is: stumbling, jittering, making sounds like talking, but they weren't words.

"Took so damn long?" asked Kish, freckled and curly red-haired, dressed in a flawless baby blue sweat suit. Michael once heard Kish tell a girl that he was a chocolate gingerbread cookie. Jeff was the opposite: dark-skinned with the physique of a beach ball, wearing gold on his neck and fingers.

Michael asked, "What's up?"

Kish asked, "Things been good here? Any problems?"

"Nah. It's good."

"No problems then?"

"Yeah. There's problems. But then I fix em."

"Good man. Good man. You been doin good here at the hotel. Better than the last guy, and he was almost twice your age. Tiana tells me you don't take shit from the customers. That's important. Me and Jeff have been talking. We think that you're due for a promotion." Jeff nodded along.

Michael tried to hide a smile and said, "Alright."

Jeff heaved his fat body into the driver's seat, Kish rode shotgun, and Michael sat in the back. The motor turned. The music came on loud as fuck.

You niggaz talk shit, then abandon ship

Niggaz talk shit, then they abandon ship

They pulled out of The Grandview. The couple regulars in the lot knew better than to be in front of Kish's ride. They moved out of the way like they'd be rundown if they didn't. The drizzle started and the car's wipers slapped at it. No one said a damn thing the whole ride. Michael looked out the window. They drove past the little tent village under the freeway overpass, the narco-nomads who moved to wherever the weather was good and the drivers were generous. They drove past the flea market that was the local clearing house for fencing stolen property. They drove past the gas station that had been robbed so many times, they didn't allow customers inside anymore.

They got onto the parallel service road. The trees and grass covered everything that humans hadn't yet gotten around to civilizing with cement and strip malls. You could just barely see the houses behind the foliage. This area had that quiet country poverty. Not the kind that begs you for change or ODs in your driveway. Out here, the poor vanish into the wilderness. It's not like that city poverty, garish and proud in the high-towered projects you see in places like Chicago; that soul-crushingly bland, brutalist aesthetic, obelisks raised in worship of human error. In the country, the poor did their duty. They suffered quietly behind curtains of trees and distance of acreage.

Jeff made a few turns before pulling onto a blacktop parking for businesses that had almost all vacated this place. Buildings with particle-board windows beneath the names of small shops that weren't there anymore. Jeff parked by a vacant shop that used to be Geller's Barbershop. Michael pushed his hands deep into his hoodie pockets. His knee was bouncing. The car was too quiet, even with the music playing through the car speakers.

Kish turned down the music and said, "You ever handled one of these before?" He held up a shiny chrome 1911.

"Yeah," said Michael.

Kish turned around and looked directly at Michael. "Sometimes youngbloods lie when they get asked that."

"I ain't lying," said Michael.

"I ain't sayin you is. All I'm saying is a lot of young guys do. When they get asked the first time, they say they've handled a heater before. But they ain't. They wanna seem like they badass. Like they hard. Like they seen some shit. But there's no reason to pretend. Everyone's got a first time, even me and Jeff."

"I ain't pretendin," said Michael.

"I ain't sayin you is. I'm just sayin a lot of youngbloods do. How old're you?"

"Thirteen." Michael raised his chin a bit like he was daring anyone to call him a kid.

"That's a good age. That's a good age. You remember bein thirteen, Jeff?"

"Yeah," said the driver.

"Your big brother was about thirteen, too, when he got his first promotion."

Jeff nodded. "That boy was ruthless."

"Is," Michael corrected.

Kish said, "I'm not saying you do or don't know how to handle a heater, Mike. But I'm gonna show you anyhow."

"I don't need you to show me."

"I'm gonna show you anyhow. Then you gonna show me you know what I shown you. And we ain't gonna say shit about if you already knew or not."

"I don't need you to show me."

Kish performed every action as he described it to the boy. "Clip goes in here. Make sure it faces the right way. There's a front and a back, so put it in the right way like this. Just cus the clip's in the gun don't mean the bullets are. It won't fire just cus you put the clip in. You gonna cock it. All the way back. Not halfway back. Not mostly back. All the way back. See? Now there's a bullet in the gun. See this thing here? That's the hammer. It's locked back now, so this gun is ready to pop. After the first shot, you don't need to cock it again. Got it?"

"Yeah."

Kish removed the magazine, cleared the chamber, and put the round back into the magazine. He handed it to Michael and said, "Show me you got it."

"I got it."

"Show me you got it."

"I said I got it."

"You stuck in here with me and Jeff until you show me you fuckin got it."

Michael took the gun and did all the things Kish said.

"Okay. You got it, soldier. Seven plus one slugs."

"What's plus one mean?" asked Michael.

"Seven in the mag, plus one in the chamber."

"Who's this?" He pointed to the image of a white man dancing with a microphone on the grip plates.

"That's Elvis."

Michael didn't say anything.

"You don't know who Elvis is?" Kish smiled.

Michael didn't say anything.

Jeff laughed from the driver's seat without turning around.

Kish said, "This kid don't know who Elvis is."

Michael looked out the window, hiding his embarrassment behind a scowl without knowing why he should be.

Jeff said, "Nigga, he made Christmas music."

Michael said, "Well, I don't know no Christmas music, aight?"

"How the fuck you don't?"

"Cus, I was raised Jehovah's Witness."

"What's that?"

"They Christians who don't celebrate Christmas."

"I never heard of that," said Jeff.

"Well, I never heard of Elvis, so we even."

Kish got them back on topic. "This dude you gotta deal with. He's gonna roll up in front of that quarter car wash right there. He thinks you're here to give him a sample of some molly. But that's not what you're here for."

"Aight."

"He don't know I set this up. So keep my name out your mouth."

"Why?"

"So he don't know it was me."

"Yeah, but I'm 'bout to kill him. So who cares if he knows it was you?"

"Cus, sometimes things don't work out. Maybe you don't kill

him. Maybe you just wound him."

"I'm not gonna just wound him."

"But sometimes you might."

"I'm not, though."

"Alright, my man," said Kish, "You keep an eye out for cameras. Just do what you gotta do."

"What'd the guy do?"

"Don't matter."

"What'd he do though?"

Kish took a second to think about what to say. "You ain't gonna murder him. You like a delivery man, here to bring him the suicide he ordered when he made the choices he made."

"What were the choices, though?"

Jeff interceded. "He put his dick somewhere wasn't his to put it. You understand?"

Michael didn't, but he nodded like he did.

"And after, what're you gonna do?"

"I'mma throw it in the river."

"You ain't gonna keep it. You ain't gonna show it off to anyone. You ain't gonna fucking take a picture of yourself with it."

"No."

"What're you gonna do with it after?"

"I'mma throw it in the river."

Kish reached out and gently slapped down on the brim of Michael's cap. "Alright. You got this." He gave a smile like the little league coach putting a kid up to the plate.

Michael didn't smile back. He wore his wish-a-nigga-would face. A face that said that there's nothing you could do to hurt this boy worse than what he's already been through. Eyes perfectly relaxed, unfeeling. Mouth without a twitch of a smile or a frown. The samurai death trance of a child soldier.

Michael stuffed the pistol into the pocket of his hoodie. He got out of the car onto the street and into the drizzle. The SUV drove off. Michael took a couple of steps and leaned against the rolling metal overhead door, blocking a storefront underneath the awning with the name of an electronics store that had been closed for two years. He stuffed his hands in his hoodie pockets to keep them warm and he fondled the gun.

This area used to be one of those small shopping areas that sprout up near suburbs. Now it was mostly empty. The neighborhood had more concrete than grass. Short buildings with iron bars in their windows and neon signs that half worked. Grass poked up through the cracks, sidewalks bulged as tree roots grew beneath them, like the earth was slowly grinding the pavement back into dust. Barbed-wire fences blocked off lots empty of cars or purpose. Big wooden poles carried electrical lines along the road, right in front of the paint-peeled homes who didn't have money to pay for it.

Michael waited and waited under the narrow lip of vinyl, keeping him almost dry, listening to the pitter patter of the rain above him, watching the occasional car to splash by. He was getting impatient. He spotted a brick store fifty yards across the flat top. Michael's mouth was dry. He hustled through the rain, his sneakers slapping and splashing in the tiny pools that formed in the dips of the pavement. He walked inside and the radio was playing some old warbly song. He got a bottle of something with sugar and bubbles and paid the guy through the lazy-Susan in the bulletproof wall of plexiglass. He eyed some stacks of homemade CDs sold by local artists, cover art printed at Kinkos, and a few bootlegged VHS: On top of the stack were *Con Air* and *The Wiz*.

When Michael walked back out, a car was out by the electronics shop. A very new SUV, not a scratch or a dent in it, with tinted windows and loud music rattling the frame.

Michael hustled back across the empty lot and up to the driver's side window. It rolled down a bit, and some skunk smoke crawled out of the small gap. Michael gestured with his head towards a vacant grocery store with spray painted particle board windows. "Over there."

"Nah, just climb in."

He heard the rear door on his side unlatch. Michael hesitated. He looked back at the store. Then looked around for any surveillance cameras.

The driver repeated himself with different words, "Get in."

Michael did as he was told. He climbed in. It was foggy with white endo smoke. He sat on the leather seat interior next to a guy in all white, who was passing a smoke to his driver up front. Michael closed the door. The guy looked at Michael. His eyes were so light they were past amber, almost khaki. They looked wrong, like he had some other guy's eyes in his head.

"What you got?" He pointed his khaki eyes back towards the front and he settled deeper into his seat.

Michael swallowed hard. His hand was wet, either from sweat or rain. He gripped the gun hard. He could feel his heart beating through his whole body. He took a sip of his drink, but it didn't help. He reminded himself he was just the delivery man. This guy ordered what Michael was holding.

Michael tried pulling the gun out, but the beaver tail snagged on the inside of his pocket. The man didn't seem to notice. He calmly let the smoke crawl out of his nose. After a few tries, Michael got the Elvis gun out and pointed it at the man's face. His finger pulled the trigger. *Click.* The khaki eyes went back on Michael. They got big, but not from fear.

Michael pulled again. Nothing. He tried to rack the slide to eject the cartridge. The man drew a Glock from the belt at his crotch and put two into Michael. It was so loud. Michael melted into the door. The man reached across and opened the door and pushed him out into the wet parking lot. Michael heard the crunch of the tire driving over his leg as the car sped off. It was a moment later that he felt it. Parts inside him hurt that he'd never felt before.

His ears were ringing, and he fought for breath like the time his brother dunked his head under water at the community pool when they were kids. He'd lost consciousness and almost died that time, too.

Michael woke up to pain and a bright white room. His vision was blurry. A hand was caressing the top of his head.

"Michael. Michael."

"Ms. Carter?"

His eyes took time to focus and he could see his foster moms. Then his double-vision corrected.

"You're lucky, kiddo. It was really close."

The next few days all bled together. Michael slept a lot, foggy from the morphine drip, and sometimes when he woke up it was night and sometimes it was day. Sometimes he pretended to sleep so he didn't have to give vague answers to questions asked by doctors, nurses, and police. He didn't tell them anything they didn't need to know. They all told him what Ms. Carter said: He was lucky.

The doctor told him that his lower intestine had been trashed by a hollow point that split when it hit a rib. The other one caught mostly muscle but fucked up a nerve, and that's why Michael's left arm felt pins and needles sometimes. His ankle had been bent wrong when the car ran over it and the tendon had nearly snapped. Some bones had been rearranged. They told him all that, then they told him he was lucky.

He had two more surgeries. One for his foot. They saved that, mostly, but he'd never walk right ever again. His guts didn't all make it. They installed a shit-bag onto his side. They told him it might be there for the rest of his life, just like that tingle in his arm.

The second week, Ms. Carter came in, red-eyed from crying, and she told Michael the bad news about his brother. Michael wouldn't cry. Not even for Delmar. Ms. Carter told him over and over that she was so sorry for his loss. He wouldn't move one facial muscle in honor of Delmar. That scared Ms. Carter more than the gunshot wounds.

The third week, the docs finally let Ms. Carter wheel Michael out to her car. It was a struggle getting into her ride. She bungee roped her half-open trunk to hold his wheelchair and Michael wondered if Delmar was the lucky one. She drove them back to the place she called his home. It wasn't the nicest part of town, but not the worst, either.

They parked in the driveway. Ms. Carter had built him a ramp up the front porch. She took him to his new makeshift bedroom, the reading room with hanging sheets tacked to the entryways on both sides.

She said, "I know you can't make it up and down the stairs yet. So this area is yours until you get back on your feet."

The three other foster boys living there didn't say much to Michael. He'd been with Ms. Carter longer than any of them, but this was his first time meeting them since he'd been staying at Grandview for the last couple of months. They came and went. Temporary stays, bounced between homes, too old to hope for adoption.

Michael hadn't settled in yet when the police came by and wanted to talk one more time. Ms. Carter told the other boys to stay upstairs, and the two detectives and Ms. Carter sat in the living room, them on couches, Michael in his wheelchair.

The detective asked a few questions, and Michael kept his mouth shut. The cop showed him a printed picture of a young man. "We think this is the guy."

Michael refused to look.

One said, "Do you know him? Do you know Marquis Fowler?"

Michael peeked for a second. Khaki eyes. Then he looked away again, hoping the cops wouldn't catch any glimpse of his curiosity. They saw it, though.

"That's him, isn't it. You're not in any trouble, Michael. We just want to get the guy who did this to you."

"Nope. Never seen him in my life."

The detectives gave each other a quick glance. Michael could see they didn't believe him.

"Listen, Michael. This guy, Fowler, he sent someone to the hospital that same day. He waited outside in his car in the parking lot while one of his flunkies came in looking for you. Security made him leave. Do you understand what I'm saying? These guys aren't done with you yet. He's probably still out there looking for you."

They showed him another picture. A still from hospital surveillance. Dark-skinned man, built like a beach ball, and all blinged out. "I don't know why cus I never seen him before in my life."

The detectives encouraged him to snitch a couple more times before they let Michael leave the room so they could speak privately with Ms. Carter. When the police finally left, Michael's foster mother called him back.

"Michael!"

Michael wheeled out of his curtain door and stopped halfway in and out.

"What?"

"I cannot for the life of me understand why you would protect a person who did what he did. Why?"

"I ain't protecting nobody."

"You know who did this and you're not gonna tell the police? You heard what the man said. They followed you to the hospital. What if that Marquis comes 'round here trying to finish the job? Huh? With the other boys and me in the house! You think about that?"

Michael avoided eye contact and shrugged. "That's not gonna happen."

"How do you know that, hm?"

"I just know."

"I don't know what to do with you, boy. You're too damn smart to be acting this dumb."

Michael rolled his eyes.

"Hey! Michael! You don't roll your eyes at me! You don't like me speaking to you like a child, you don't act like one, you got that? Those other boys you've been hanging with, I don't know their names, but I know exactly who they are. I been around a lot of years, Michael. Nothing surprises me anymore. It's the same story over and over. I see you. You're just living a syndicated rerun of a show that's been on since I was your age. Hey! Look at me when I'm talking to you!"

Michael looked at Ms. Carter.

"They talk to you like a grownup, right? They give you grownup responsibilities. Don't look away! I know. I can see it. You are not the first. You know what every boy wants? Hm? More than anything?"

Michael shrugged.

"What every boy wants is to be a man. Especially boys who

came up the way you and Delmar did. Boys are vulnerable. Boys can't do anything on their own. Kids have to rely on the grown-ups to take care of them. If the grown-ups can't or won't don't do it—like it was for you and your brother—then they gotta become the grown-ups or they gotta find some older boys to be the grown-ups in their life. A grown man can make their own choices. But you aren't a grown-up, Michael!"

Michael shifted in his wheelchair.

"They just usin you to do their dirt. Don't you get that? They usin you! You want to be a man? Then you gotta grow the hell up and be a man! Do what's right, not what's easy! You ain't a bad kid, Michael. I met enough of em to know the difference. You want to be bad cus bad seems strong. It's not. Bad isn't strong."

"What if it's the other way?"

Ms. Carter put her hands on her hips. "What's that mean?"

"No one ever thinks they got the bad kid. They always think it's someone else's bad kid influencing their good kid. What if I am the bad kid?"

"I don't believe that, Michael. I don't. And I been trying to show you that you shouldn't neither."

"Was Delmar the bad kid then?"

Ms. Carter sighed and looked down. She wanted to say anything but the truth. Ms. Carter could be a lot of things but she wasn't a liar. That was something Michael always liked about her. When other people would've lied, she just stopped talking. So she said, "Listen. You know I don't believe in speaking poorly of the dead."

Michael broke eye contact.

Ms. Carter said, "You only get to be lucky so many times. But you can choose to be smart every time. You understand?" She saw he was actually considering what she said, which was a rare and precious thing. "I want you here, Michael. But I need to know that whatever is happening out there won't come back here to the house and bring problems for the other boys. You have a home here, but you don't have a right to bring your problems onto other people. Do you understand me?"

The first week back at Ms. Carter's, Michael barely left his room. He barely ate because he was disgusted knowing that it would come out into the bag in his side. He'd kissed a girl once, but he was sure it would never happen again with this thing attached to him. Most of all, he missed his brother. He cried sometimes, but he never let anyone see it or hear it. No one could see him being weak. Not once. Not for one second.

For all its flaws, the foster care system gives good healthcare. Michael had appointments. He always had appointments. Lots of specialists and tests. Most of his appointments were with a physical therapist, a huge bodybuilder named Phil, thick-necked and definitely juicing. Phil was a strong man, a man who looked dangerous, but he was patient and calm. Whenever Michael tried to puss out, the PT wouldn't let him. They met four days a week. Michael's legs were skinny and his knees were knobby for lack of using them for just a few weeks. Phil started him in a pool, walking in low gravity. When Michael had that down, Phil worked him up to walking in regular gravity while holding onto bars. Then he had Michael doing stretches and lightweight training.

Three weeks in, Michael lay on his back on the leg press at the hospital gym and Phil wasn't happy with him. "I can see you aren't even trying."

"I just can't today."

"Who told you that?"

"No one told me that."

"Then how do you know you can't?"

"I can feel it."

"Oh, so you told you that?"

"I guess."

"And what the fuck do you know, huh?"

"What?" Michael looked at him. Respectable people like teachers and doctors didn't use cuss words.

"I got a degree in this. I went to college. You aren't even in high school."

"So? I know my body."

"I know human bodies even better. You can do this."

"This is just me now."

"See? That? That attitude right there? That's what got you fucking shot, little man."

Michael's eyes glazed over. The moment an adult used the word "attitude" his brain simply filtered out the rest. Phil knew that look immediately and snapped his fingers in Michael's face and said, "Hey, I'm talking to you!"

"Man... just..."

"Just what?"

"Leave me alone, already. Damn! Why you sweatin me? The fuck you care if I walk or don't, huh? Why you acting like you my dad, nigga? You get paid whether or not I get helped, so how bout back the fuck up off me?"

Phil put his hands on his hips and said, "You think you got a weak body, but you got a weak mind."

"Hey, fuck you, nigga! Fuck you! You know who I am? You know who I roll with?"

"That right there," Phil pointed at him, "That's what I mean. Anger. Anger is a sign of weakness."

Michael tried to get up to fight this man, but his guts screamed at him to shut up and stay down. He lay back on that weight bench and looked at the ceiling and huffed and puffed, but couldn't do anything about it.

"Anger is powerlessness. That's all it is. When you strong, when you have control over your own life, you don't need anger anymore. You're here to get strong. When you do, you won't need that anger anymore. But your body won't get strong while your brain is weak. So we gotta work on that first. You look like you wanna hit me. You wanna hit me, little man?"

"Fuck yeah I do."

"Tell you what, Michael. I'll cut a deal with you. If we can get you to a point where you can sit up on your own without a railing or someone helping, if we get you out of that wheelchair and get you walking, I'll let you punch me."

"Shut up, man." He kept his eyes locked on the ceiling.

"I go to church every Sunday and I'll swear to Jesus right now. I will let you punch me and I won't do a damn thing back. But you gotta get the fuck up and walk up to me on your own to do it."

Michael's eyes fixed on Phil's with a new flavor of hatred. He didn't want to do what the man wanted. He could hurt the man, but only if he did what the man wanted. But what he wanted was to make Michael strong enough that Michael could hurt him. He looked up at the ceiling. He quietly tried untangling that paradox. "Can I hit you in the face?"

"Yeah."

"How 'bout the balls?"

Phil laughed, "*Hell* no. Professional boxing rules. Above the belt."

Michael laughed, too. "Drop that weight by 5 pounds and I'll try it again."

326

Phil smiled and removed the plates. Michael couldn't put that much weight up the first time he tried, but it was the first time he actually tried.

Michael came out of his bedsheet-walled space that night when he heard one of the other boys crying. The others were bullying him. They took the TV remote away from the littlest one, Jaylon. Michael watched and seethed, not because the boys were being nasty to the little one. Michael knew that he'd be even more helpless if those boys ever started messing with him. Just knowing that those boys existed, cruel boys who could torment Michael, raised his temperature. It's not enough that they leave Jaylon or Michael alone. Michael needed to destroy the very possibility that they could hurt him.

For Michael, every day he spent in that wheelchair was a day he narrowly avoided victimization. He needed to be on his feet again. He wouldn't let anyone fuck with him like those boys fuck with Jaylon. For the first time in a long time, he listened to what the grownups told him. He pushed himself hard. He followed instructions. He listened to what the orthopedic specialist told him. He didn't listen to the gastroenterologist, but only because he couldn't understand her accent. Most of all, Michael listened to what Phil told him.

The next day at PT, the first thing Phil said to Michael was, "Are you strong enough to hit me yet?"

Michael answered, "Maybe. But if I only get one punch, I'm gonna be strong as fuck before I throw it."

They said those same words to each other every visit for six weeks. Michael was for real the first week. Soon it became more like an inside joke. Then a tradition. Then a mantra, a deeper meaning contained within the words, passed from the master to the disciple in their practice. *You only get one punch, so you better be strong as fuck before you throw it.*

Ms. Carter had been pushing him to heal since the first day he got back, but when Michael started recovering, when he refused his wheelchair, Ms. Carter asked him to slow down, to take it easy. Michael wouldn't slow down. He wouldn't take it easy. He demanded she take down the sheets that walled the space he used as a temporary bedroom. He demanded to sleep upstairs in a proper bedroom. The stairs were a fight, but he won that fight every time. When Phil wasn't in the room, he could imagine what Phil would say if he were. He could sense Phil's judgment: a man who didn't hate him for being weak— the only man Michael'd ever met who didn't hate him for being weak—but who wouldn't tolerate Michael remaining weak, either.

Michael learned to walk again, barely. He still needed help Sometimes. Ms. Carter bought him a cane. The other kids joked it made him look like a pimp. It didn't bother Michael. When they could see it didn't, the other boys didn't fuck with him. Sometimes his ear would ring or his arm would feel pins and needles for no reason.

On his last day at PT, when he was strong enough that he could continue training without Phil's help, his trainer asked him, "Are you strong enough to hit me yet?"

But Michael broke their tradition. He violated the edicts of the mantra. Instead he said, "Nah. Anger is a sign of weakness. I'mma wait till you 80 and I'll come to your old folks' home and punch you then." Phil smiled warmly and nodded at that, with a kind of pride in the kid that Michael had never seen before, not even from Delmar or Kish.

"Not in the balls, though," Phil reminded his patient.

Michael's doctor visits were less frequent, his PT was over, and he was mostly just doing what he needed to do to stay well and get strong. Late one night, Michael couldn't sleep. He often had trouble sleeping. Sometimes because of the pain. Sometimes thinking about what happened the day he got shot. Certain details he kept thinking about, like a song stuck in his head. Things that didn't seem right.

He snuck downstairs, picking the spots on the steps on the stairs that didn't creak. He found the wall phone and punched in some numbers.

Someone answered, "Yeah?"

"Yo, Tyson."

"Michael?"

"Yeah."

"I heard what happened. How're you doin?"

"I'm fine. I want to ask somethin."

"Yeah. Yeah. What's up?"

"Who is Marquis Fowler?"

Michael snuck out of Ms. Carter's place, same as he'd done plenty of times. He had to walk four blocks to meet up with Tyson in a 24/7 laundromat parking lot. Took twice as long as it used to and it hurt the whole way.

"Damn," was the first thing Tyson said when he saw the cane.

"Yeah."

"I like the cane, though."

"Tell me about this nigga Marquis."

"He's from the neighborhood. I never met him but I heard he parties a lot. He's always got girls around. People say he makes dirty movies."

"Where's he live?"

"Why you wanna fuck with him again for?"

"I just wanna talk to him."

"That's stupid."

Michael turned to walk away.

"Hold up, Michael. Stop. Stop."

Michael stopped but he didn't turn to face Tyson.

"He has big house parties every weekend. On Fernwood. I don't know where exactly. 400 block, I think."

"Thanks, Tyson," Michael started walking away.

"Michael. Don't do something crazy."

Michael walked for an hour and every step hurt more than the one before. He walked into a neighborhood where half the houses had no lights on inside, where the yellow humming street lamps were out of order for entire blocks. He walked past young men sitting on porches, passing bottles and smokes, and eyeing him the whole way. He walked past a man on a bicycle with a potbelly and no shirt or teeth, who asked him for money. He walked past a fat woman thirty years older than Michael and she lifted her skirt to show that she wasn't wearing anything underneath.

He heard the party before he saw it. He followed the throbbing bass to where the sidewalks and streets were crowded with cars bumping music, and young men wearing colors, and young women wearing as little as possible. Eyes were all over him as he limped through the block party, up to the house and up the porch steps. A guy with bloodshot eyes stopped Michael at the door.

"You lost, little nigga?" He gestured at a neon pink dipped Glock shoved down the front of his pants

"I'm here to see Marquis."

"Run along, now." Bloodshot waved him away like he was sweeping Michael with a hand broom. He looked around to other people on the porch to see if they thought it was funny.

"I owe him something. You wanna stop me, then you can tell him you're the one who kept him from a payday."

"Show me."

"Show you what?"

"The money, nigga! Show me you got money!" Other people started paying attention. Michael looked around at the eyes on him, coming from all directions. His arm started feeling numb and his ear started ringing again. He grabbed his crotch. "My money's right here. I'll let you suck it for a hundred."

A couple of girls started laughing. Bloodshot stepped up to him. They locked eye contact. Bloodshot was a head taller and a decade older than Michael. One girl called out, "Shit, tough guy! You gonna beat up on a kid?" Her friend backed her up. "Leave him alone."

Bloodshot motioned with his head to someone past Michael. Before he could look, arms grabbed from behind. Michael struggled until Bloodshot punched him in the gut. It hurt like a son of bitch. It was all healed up, but still tender. Michael folded and stopped squirming. Bloodshot patted him down and found some keys and 14 dollars. He lifted the shirt and pointed at the medical implant. "The fuck is this?"

"My colostomy bag."

"What's that?"

"It's where my shit goes."

"You don't shit out ya ass?"

"Not anymore."

"Fucking disgusting." He let Michael's shirt drop. "You ain't got no fucking money," he said as he stuffed Michael's bills into his gym shorts.

Bloodshot walked into the house and the guy behind Michael brought him in with. The living room was glowing pink and teal from neon lights on opposite sides of the room. The guy pushed Michael from behind to follow Bloodshot through the dancing women and men. Some were doing more than just dancing. A kid not much older than Michael watched it all through a shouldered Panasonic VHS video recorder. When he saw Michael being pushed around, he pointed his lens at him and followed them into the kitchen.

A topless woman was at the stove, smoking a cigarette and stirring up a pot of macaroni and cheese. A khaki-eyed man was leaning over the kitchen counter, vacuuming a line of something. He whipped his head back and snorted down the aspirin-flavored snot.

Bloodshot said, "Marquis. This kid say he owes you some money."

"I didn't say I owe him money."

Marquis looked at the kid. His eyes looked even stranger under the blacklight. He smiled and pointed, "You." Michael was about to speak when Marquis interrupted, "You stupid fuck." He started laughing, a big grin with some metal teeth. He did another line with the other nostril.

Michael said, "I want to talk to you."

Marquis sucked it down and then clapped a few times to get everyone's attention before he addressed the room. "This is the kid. This is the little man tried to shoot me a couple months ago in my car!" He looked at Michael, "The fucking balls on you!"

Michael felt that pink Glock on his temple. The woman with the tits plated the food and pushed it in front of Marquis.

Marquis said, "Take this kid to the pool and air him out."

Bloodshot and the other guy grabbed Michael's arms. Michael finally saw the man behind him. It was the driver of the SUV at the meeting.

Michael asked, "Don't you wanna know who greenlit you?"

"Shit. I already know," said Marquis.

They dragged him out the back door. Michael fought the whole way. He made them work for it, but he didn't have a chance. They dragged him off the back porch and into the backyard, just as crowded with people as the front. They took him through a wooden gate into another yard, and threw him into an empty, concrete swimming pool. Michael used his hand to get himself back on his feet and felt a spent brass on the ground. There were a lot of them. Michael looked up to see the silhouette of Driver, the kid with the video camera, and Bloodshot, who was pointing his pink gun at Michael's face. Marquis and his plate of macaroni and cheese arrived a moment later.

"I kinda like this kid, so make it easy," said Marquis. He took a bite of his dinner.

Michael said, "It was Kish."

Marquis pushed down Bloodshot's shooting arm. "Say what?"

"Kish greenlit you. But I think, really, he greenlit me. I'm not a hundred on that. Not yet."

"It was Sicko who set up that meeting."

"I don't know Sicko."

"Bullshit."

"I'm with Kish. He sent me."

Marquis shrugged. "I guess I owe Sicko's mama an apology." The other guys laughed at that. "Cus why Kish do that?"

"Something about a girl wasn't yours."

He spit some mac and cheese, trying to hold his laughter. "Fuck. That nigga still mad I put his girl in a movie? Too funny. Too funny."

"I need something from you."

"You asking for favors now?" Bloodshot looked pissed, but Driver smiled.

"I need that gun back. The one with the dancing white man on it. I dropped it in your car."

All of them laughed. Marquis said, "This kid's balls. I swear. If I had ten of this little nigga, I'd be running Raleigh."

Bloodshot asked, "You really think we gonna give you a fucking gun?"

"After you hear what I gotta say, I think you're gonna give me two guns. Including that one you pointin at me right now."

Michael limped into the Grandview, leaning on his cane, a backpack on his shoulders. He breezed past Tiana. She said something nice, and he said "thanks" without slowing down or looking at her. He walked through the door into the conference room. Kish and Jeff were sitting at the long table with paper spread out and covered with grilled shrimp from *Colonel Tom's.*

Kish smiled brightly when he saw Michael. He stood up and met him and gave him a hug. Michael didn't hug back.

Kish said, "Fuckin unkillable, this kid!"

"Bulletproof Mike!" said Jeff.

"Bulletproof Mike! How you feelin, Mike?"

Michael said, "Bad."

The two men laughed.

Kish invited Michael to sit down with them at the table and said, "It's good to see you walking. Mostly walking."

Michael took off his backpack and set it in his lap as he sat down. He unzipped it and took out two guns: The Elvis gun and Bloodshot's neon pink piece.

"What's all that?" asked Jeff.

"I got your gun back. And I got the gun from the guy who took it." He set them down in the center of the table, halfway between him and Kish, the 1911 closer to Kish, the Glock closer to Michael.

"Jesus, little man. Are you shittin me right now? Well fuckin done."

"Kid's got balls," said Jeff.

"I told you. I told you. This kid has some fuckin balls, right? Kid. I'm sorry I didn't make it to the hospital to visit."

Michael said, "Don't sweat it."

"You're like a kid brother to me. I'd have gone if I could, but the cops are all over when shit like that happens." He sat back in his seat at the head of the table.

Michael said, "I want to tell you about what happened."

"Drinks first."

Jeff poured the kid some rum and soda into a large paper cup. Michael took a sip. "The guy must've known something was up. He shot me before I could draw on him."

Kish's eyes got wide, exaggerating surprise. "Really! Huh. So, uh, you never even fired that gun we gave you?"

"Naw."

Jeff said, "Well, shit."

Kish agreed. "Shit," and he nodded his head.

Jeff asked, "So how'd you get that gun back, little man?"

"I went to his house and visited him."

"You fuckin what?"

"I went to Marquis Fowler's house."

Kish asked, "Hold up. You went to the Ghetto Bunny Ranch? You just walked up to the house of the nigga you tried to murder?"

"Yeah. And I talked to him."

"Oh, you talked?" asked Jeff, who clearly thought this was bullshit.

Michael continued, "Yeah. I asked for the gun back."

"He just gave you the gun back?" asked Kish. "Just like that?"

Michael scowled. "How about you two stop repeatin shit I say as a question, huh?"

Kish looked at Jeff. "Yo, is Bulletproof Mike gettin snippy with me?"

"I got the gun back from him on the condition that I would kill y'all."

The two men laughed until they saw Michael wasn't laughing with them.

Michael continued, "So, yeah. I'm here to kill y'all. I never killed no one before, but Marquis said he'd gimme a G for each of you."

"You bein fuckin serious right now?" asked Jeff.

Michael slapped the table, and some of the shrimp bounced.

"Yeah, nigga! How many fucking times you gonna ask me a question after I already told you the fucking answer?"

Michael reached across the table towards the two pistols. Kish snapped out faster, reaching past the 1911, and grabbed Bloodshot's pink gat and pointed it at Michael. Michael took the Elvis gun and pointed it back. Kish grew a big grin on his freckled face. Jeff was smiling, too.

"Somethin funny?" Michael asked.

Kish said, "Yeah. Yeah. Kinda."

"You gonna shoot me or not?"

"How about you first?"

Jeff laughed with his whole fat body jiggling right until Michael pointed the Elvis gun at him and pulled the trigger. The bang was deafening in the small room. The round hit Jeff just below his nose, shattering his upper jaw and throwing teeth across the room. The bullet skimmed off his spine and blew apart several muscles that keep your head from falling forward. A lot of what was Jeff's head ended up on the wall behind him. The force of the shot pushed him backwards, his chair tilted, and stopped with Jeff's fat body at 45 degrees against the wall.

Kish and Michael didn't know that Jeff was still alive. He was completely paralyzed, fully conscious, terrified, unable to cry for help, unable to save himself from drowning in his own blood simply by tilting his head a few degrees to the side. Jeff was as alone as a person can be. He could hear everything and say nothing.

Kish pulled his trigger. *Click.*

Michael pointed his gun back at Kish.

"What the fuck...?"

"The Elvis gun was closer to you, but you grabbed the Glock."

"What?"

"When I was at Marquis's place, we opened up the Elvis gun and looked inside. Someone glued the firing pin. Marquis's guy knows a lot about guns and he showed me before he fixed it. Then he removed the firing pin from his Glock so it don't work. I brought them here to see if you knew the Elvis gun didn't work. You grabbed the Glock. That means you knew my gun didn't work when you sent me to kill Marquis. I was the one supposed to get shot, not him. And Marquis thought the meet was with one of Sicko's boys, so they beefin now."

Michael took some napkins off the table. He ripped off small pieces, wadded them up, and put them in his ears. "I should've known when you said not to mention your name. Seemed sketchy at the time."

"This was, what, a test?" He looked nervously at the hole in Jeff's face.

Michael pointed his gun under the table and fired. Kish fell onto the floor and grabbed himself just above the pubis.

Michael had to raise his voice loud enough that Kish could hear him over his own shrieking and the ringing in their ears. "What did I just say, nigga? Huh? I said, stop asking questions after I already told you! You tried to kill me. That was you at the hospital, not Marquis! Why though? I been loyal! What'd I ever do to you?"

"Delmar!" Urine thinned the blood coming out of his bladder that Michael had just perforated. The mixture was spreading on the carpet he was rolling around on. He tried in vain to hold it all in with his hands on his crotch.

"What's it got to do with my brother?"

"He snitched. We couldn't get to him after he ran, but we warned him we could get to you. He didn't hear it."

"My brother didn't snitch! And he didn't run!"

"Yeah, he fuckin did! He got out in three weeks on a fuckin aggravated battery charge! With a sheet like he got? Of course he fuckin snitched! We told him! We told him if he ever gave us up, it would fall on you. He understood that. If he ran, you'd get it. He ran anyway. He gave you up to save his self."

"Naw. He didn't get released. He went to hospice. Delmar was feelin like shit his first week inside. He saw the doctor. They told Delmar he had pancreatic cancer. Delmar's lawyer talked the judge into letting Delmar go die somewhere nice upstate. He passed while I was unconscious, in surgery in the hospital. Cus of what you did, I didn't get to see him or talk to him before he went."

That was the moment Jeff finally lost consciousness.

"Aw. Fuck. Fuck! I messed up, Michael. You right. You right. You got every right to be angry…"

"Do I look angry to you?"

He didn't. Not at all. There was no anger in Michael as he raised the Elvis gun again. Kish raised up a hand to defend himself. Michael shot Kish again. It passed through Kish's defensive hand and his thumb became disconnected from the bone, but not from the muscle and skin. The round came out the other side, close enough to his face he could feel the air move.

"Stop! Fucking kill me or stop!"

"I'm trying to, but I've never shot a gun before. It's harder than I thought."

"Come up closer, then!"

Michael did. Kish still had more strength in him than Michael realized. He grabbed Michael's cane with his good hand and pulled the boy and the gun down onto the floor with him. Kish grabbed the gun by the top. Michael fired, but the webbing on Kish's hand caught the hammer before it could strike the firing pin. He got up and pushed Michael over and climbed onto him. They both fought for the gun, wrists twisting, till the thing was nearly upside down, and their hands were a tangled mess. Kish was stronger, but he was missing a thumb and was bleeding from a hole an inch above his dick. He managed to re-cock the hammer and pushed the barrel back towards Michael's head. His blood was all over both of them. With his wounded hand, Kish forced a finger into the trigger guard and pushed on the trigger like a button. Nothing happened because no one was palming the grip safety.

Michael held on. He didn't get a better position. He didn't let Kish try to, either. He held him there and let the bleeding do its job. Kish's strength drizzled out of him, a little less life in him with every heart pump. Michael could feel Kish getting weaker and weaker until he barely had the strength to keep his eyes open. Kish went limp. Michael pushed him off without resistance, flopping like a salmon filet.

Michael emptied out the two brown paper bags the shrimp came in. He took them with when he left the conference room and walked up to the reception desk. No one was there. "Tiana?"

Tiana peeked out from the office where she was hiding and muffled her mouth with her hands when she said, "Oh my god!" when she saw Michael was covered in Kish. He took out a piece of paper from his pocket, reached over and took the phone, and dialed the number. Tiana was afraid to move.

"Hey, yeah. We good," He hung up. He walked around the desk and into the back office.

Tiana backed up against the wall.

"Naw, Tiana. Relax. Relax."

She didn't relax.

"Tiana. Hey. Kish and Jeff tried to kill me. Okay? I'm not gonna hurt you."

She nodded and Michael could see she believed him.

"Open this up for me." He pointed at the floor safe.

Tiana knelt by the safe and spun the lock and cracked it open. Michael took a few stacks of wrinkled, rubber-banded money and shoved them into his backpack. He handed a couple of stacks to Tiana. She took it.

"What's the money for?"

"What they call it when you pay someone to quit they job?"

"Severance?"

"Yeah. This is severance."

"What's that mean? I don't work here no more?"

"Grandview is a movie studio now."

"What?"

"New management. They gonna come clean up the office."

"I don't understand, Michael."

"You got a car, right?"

"Yeah."

"I gotta change my clothes, but after, can you gimme a ride?" He put the money into the paper bags.

Michael put on an extra set of clean clothes from his room. He left the bloody ones in the conference room. Tiana followed him out to the parking lot. The regular guests that usually haunted it were all gone. The ones in their rooms kept to themselves. Gunshots have that effect. Everyone was gone except for Tyson. The little man was still across the street, faithfully at his post. Michael waved him over. The kid looked both ways, then jogged across the street. Michael gave him a couple of stacks.

"Everything okay?"

"Yeah. Yeah. Here. This is severance." He gave him one of the greasy paper bags.

He peeked in and said, "Thanks, Mike. So it went okay with Marquis?"

"You said, *don't do something crazy*. I figure it's only crazy if it don't work."

He got into the passenger seat of Tiana's 2-door Toyota compact, and she sat in the driver's seat. Michael gave her directions back to Ms. Carter's place. She drove. She was shaky. She snuck glances at Michael, who was perfectly calm. That didn't relax her one bit.

Ms. Carter saw him before he even got out of the car. She was waiting on the porch with her fists on her hips. As soon as the car door was open, she yelled, "You cannot just come in and out anytime you like, Michael! Sneaking off in the middle of the night like that? Mm mm. I am not doing this with you anymore. I filed a missing child report, and you can be the one to call the police and explain where you were last night."

Michael took some strained steps up the porch. "Okay, Ms. Carter. This time, I'mma be honest with you." He sat on the porch swing.

Anger vanished from Ms. Carter. She sat next to him. "Go on."

"I listened to what you said. It's not right that I bring down my problems on you. You right. I had to go fix it. I talked it out with the guy. We worked it out."

"Michael, are you being for real right now?"

"You said it. It's better to think things through. You can't just rush into things. I have to think about my future. Like you said, I gotta be smart cus I can't be lucky every day. I can't just follow dudes who tell me I'm a man. They just use people. I get that now. Naw. I have to be a man. When others see that, when they see me bein a man, they will treat me like man."

"What… what happened last night, Michael? Where were you?"

"You been nicer to me than anyone. But I was still angry cus I felt like you treated me like a kid. That's not right. I shouldn't be mad at the nicest person I know. You were the only one who came to the hospital. The only one. I was acting like a kid and so you treated me like one. I get that now. But I'm done with all that."

Ms. Carter had never heard Michael say anything like that before. Not even close. She had a little pang of faith she hardly ever felt anymore. Whatever part of the brain that processes hope had withered under the churn of disappointing decades of boys passing through her home, tossing away the chance she offered them. "You are serious. You listened, huh?"

He nodded.

She hugged him tight and forced back some tears. "So you coming home? For good?"

"Naw. I have a new living situation. Much better than before."

Ms. Carter let him go. "Wait, what? Hun, you going back out there? But you just said…"

"I'm bein a man. Men don't live with they mom…" He reached into his bag and took out a few stacks of banded money and set it down between him and her. "Men take care of they mom." He stood up.

"What is this? Where did this come from? I don't want this! I'm not taking this money, Michael!"

Michael walked down the stairs back to Tiana's car, got in, and told his chauffeur, "Okay. Back to the hotel." He looked at her CD book and flipped through a few pages before he found *The Infamous* by Mobb Deep. He put it on the stereo and jumped to track 15.

Chicken And Waffles (And Bacon)

Good for breakfast. Good for lunch. Good for dinner. Good for that extra dinner at 3 AM.

The best cure for a hangover is huevos rancheros. But the second best cure is chicken and waffles.

Time: I don't know. A while. It's a lot of work. You gotta have this mostly prepped and ready to go before it's time to eat.

Banana Waffles
Ingredients for waffles

- 1 ¼ C flour
- ¾ C sugar
- 1 tsp baking powder
- ½ tsp baking soda
- 1 or 2 mashed up bananas. Like 1 C is good.
- ½ C sour cream or Greek yogurt
- 2 large eggs
- 1/4 teaspoon fine salt
- Some pam or oil for the waffle iron
- Optional but recommended: ½ tsp cinnamon, nutmeg, and/or vanilla extract

Gear for the waffles

- A waffle iron

Making the waffles

1. Get the waffle iron going to like 200°
2. Mix all that stuff up
3. Spray some pam in the iron
4. Pour the batter into the waffle iron. You own a waffle iron, don't you? You should know how to do this already
5. Remove the waffles when they're done

Chicken
Ingredients for the Marinade

- Chicken breasts. Or thighs. I like thighs, but you do you. As much as you want to eat. This recipe covers about 6 breasts or equivalent
- 1 ½ buttermilk
- 1 Tbsp salt and pepper (white or black, whatever)
- 1 Tbsp garlic powder
- 2 Tbsp pickle juice (not mandatory but it's good)
- 2 Tbsp hot sauce (also not mandatory, also good). I like Claude's BBQ from Missouri
- I changed my mind. Pickle juice and hot sauce are absolutely mandatory

Ingredients for the dredge and fry

- 1 ½ C flour
- 2 tsp garlic powder
- 2 tsp paprika
- 2 tsp cayenne
- Some salt and pepper
- Oil. I like avocado oil or lars. Whatever you use, it's gotta have a decently high smoke point. That means don't use olive oil, you fucking maniac
- 3 eggs

Gear for the chicken

- A deep pan for frying (or a fryer if you got one)
- spatula
- A few bowls for breading it
- Wire rack

Making the chicken

1. Add all those marinade ingredients into a big plastic bag with the chicken. Shake it up. Squeeze out any extra air. Put it in the fridge and let it marinade

overnight

2. The next day, when you're ready to cook these up, set up two bowls for the dredge. In one bowl, add the eggs and beat 'em up. In the other bowl, add the flour and seasoning

3. Put a piece of chicken into the seasoned flour. Roll it around and get it covered. Let it chill for a half minute to make sure it sticks. Then dunk it into the egg bowl. Get it good and covered. Then back into the flour. Then set it on a rack and let all that stuff solidify. Takes about 10 minutes. Don't rush it. Repeat for all the pieces of chicken

4. Add oil to the frying pan and get it heated up on medium. Make it deep enough you can at least half cover the meat

5. Fry them chickies up. Flip em when it's looking brown and crispy. They're done they they are very firm. If they are still floppy, they aren't done.

6. Pull em out and let em dry and cool on the rack

7. If you're not 100% sure, there's no shame in cutting into them to make extra sure they're done. Don't eat pink chicken. Shit, I've been known to microwave em for 30-60 seconds just to cover my ass

Peanut Syrup
Gear for the syrup

- Stove and pan

Ingredients for the syrup

- ¾ of a stick of butter
- ½ C half-n-half
- ¼ C maple syrup
- ¾ C sugar (brown or white, it don't matter)
- 1/2 C peanut butter (crunchy or creamy, it don't matter)
- A tsp drops of vanilla or cinnamon or something else that

346

sounds good

Making the syrup

1. Throw all that stuff into a medium or large saucepan, except the peanut butter
2. Heat it on medium heat. Stir it all up till it's melty and mixed.
3. Once that's good and done, add the peanut butter. Keep stirring. Let it get to boiling. Crank the heat if you have to
4. The second it's boiling, kill the heat. Let it simmer for a minute. Then it's good to serve

Assembly

You can make it into a sandwich or just stack it all in a heap on a plate. Or fold that waffle like a taco and do it that way.

Serve with

- Frank's Red Hot sauce
- Cigarettes
- Cream Soda
- The music of *Danny Brown*

Variations

- Make it German by subbing fried chicken for a breaded and fried veal/pork schnitzel
- If you don't have a waffle maker, you can substitute waffles for pancakes. Same thing, different shape
- Lazy mode: Use frozen chicken strips and waffles from the grocery store
- You know that little floppy bit on the end of a chicken breast? That's the tender. You can use just chicken tenders and make 'em chicken fingers

CHAPTER 0 (AGAIN): DON'T LEAVE ME NOW

That's it for now.

If you're the type that notices the tiny details, you might be feeling bothered by a couple. Maybe you're the type that gets a poison ivy brain when things don't add up. You might be the type to ask, *If Michael Bryce fixed the Elvis gun in 1996, how come it was busted again in 2005 when Larry the junkie had it?* Or you might be thinkin, *How's it that Juan swapped the plates in 1988, but the plates were already on it when Donny Lao had them?*

Well, maybe that's cus the gun's got a few more stories that you ain't heard yet. Come back later. If I'm in the mood, I'll tell you a few more yarns about the Elvis gun. If you've been a good boy or girl, the story won't be about you.

APPENDIX

Some people call em Easter eggs, or deep references. Whatever you call em, there are 22 in this book. My early draft readers didn't notice even one, so I figure the odds are pretty good that you didn't either. My missus thought it was a shame to include em if no one would ever see em. I agree.

Don't read this bit until you've finished the book.

Chapter 0: Devil in Disguise

- The title of every chapter is also the title of an Elvis song
- Elvis's favorite food was a fried peanut butter, banana, and bacon sandwich. All the recipes in this book include those three ingredients. Some might say I'm cheating in Chapter 5, using pork belly instead of bacon. Pork belly *is* bacon. Don't listen to Canadian lies

Chapter 4: My Way

- Officer White pretends to impersonate a cop. One of Elvis's hobbies was impersonating police, going as far as using a flashing light on his car, pulling over motorists, and issuing them warnings for speeding
- Elvis earned his 7th-degree black belt in Chitō-ryū Karate. Officer Jacob Black mispronounces it as "Cheeto Rye You"
- White's Army unit, the 32nd Cavalry, was formerly part of the 1st Battalion, 32nd Armor, which was Elvis's unit

when he was drafted into the Army from 1958-60

Chapter 3: Lonesome Cowboy

- Most of the items in the museum are based on actual Elvis relics, including the TV with a bullet hole in it
- The museum address is 1835 (1/8/35), Elvis's birthday

Chapter 5: In the Ghetto

- Wolf's phone password is 0816, Elvis's death day (08/16/77)
- D was caught with several drugs in his car: Pentobarbital (aka yellow jackets aka Mexican yellows), Diazepam (aka Valium), and Codeine (aka lean, when mixed with cough syrup). According to Elvis's autopsy, all three were present in his system when he died

Chapter 2: Ku'uipo

- The Big E was the nickname for the USS Enterprise, one of the few aircraft carriers built before WWII that survived that war. The Big E is also the name of an annual ETA competition. ETA means "Elvis Tribute Artist," aka Elvis impersonator
- Bradley Manu's red 1960 MG MGA sports car—purchased with supplemental income from his drug smuggling side hustle—was Elvis's car in the film Blue Hawaii

Chapter 6: If I Can Dream

- Laney's phone number is the number to reach the Graceland Mansion

- Hannah's pendant has an image of Saint Ailbe of Emly, also known as Saint Elvis
- Before being successful in music, Elvis drove a delivery truck for Crown Electric in Memphis

Chapter 1: I Gotta Know

- Like Olivia, Elvis had a stillborn twin: Jesse Garon Presley
- Before fame and fortune, Elvis auditioned to sing with a gospel group, *The Songfellows*. Oakley saw a copy when he was leaving the funeral home. Elvis didn't get the job

Chapter 7: A Little Less Conversation

- Luca's fake name is John Burrows, which happens to be the fake name that Elvis used to book into hotels
- Elvis also owned a pet named Scatter; his Scatter was a chimp, not a dog
- There are many people who believe that Elvis faked his own death. According to one theory, he secretly appears as an extra in the 1990 film, *Home Alone*, which Lucas coworkers mention as they tease him.

Chapter +1: Heartbreak Hotel

- *Con Air* and *The Wiz* star Nicolas Cage and Michael Jackson, respectively. Both men were briefly married to Priscilla Presley, Elvis's daughter
- The barbershop shares the last name as Larry Geller, the man responsible for Elvis's hair
- The shrimp comes from *Colonel Tom's*, a restaurant that shares the name of Elvis's huckster manager: Colonel Tom Parker

ABOUT THE AUTHOR

Yankee Grawlix

 Yankee has received several awards for his writing from The Cincinnati Department of Corrections parole board and was honored with a Narcocorrido Fellowship from the Juárez Cartel.

He received his undergraduate degree in Civic Arboreal Phlebotomy from St. Heemeyer University and his masters in Confabulatory Communications from GZU. He got his HAM radio license from this dude named Kevin.

Yankee is no longer welcome in Canada, Belarus, Malaysia, and Azerbaijan. Any rumors about unlawful distribution of prosthetics are slander. Investigations by the ATF, DEA, and Senate Intelligence Committee proved fruitless.

He lives with his wives and daughters on a well-secured compound in an undisclosed location somewhere in America. When he isn't writing, Yankee is a volunteer firestarter, plays in an outlaw country / nasheed band, reads fortunes at the local farmer's market, and freebases.

He is a monster and must be stopped at all costs.

Made in United States
North Haven, CT
30 November 2022

27587843R00202